American Rebirth

1865–1893

4 Stories in 1

Print ISBN 978-1-61626-672-1

eBook Editions:
Adobe Digital Edition (.epub) 978-1-60742-754-4
Kindle and MobiPocket Edition (.prc) 978-1-60742-755-1

All scripture quotations are taken from the King James Version of the Bible.

This book is a work of fiction. Names, characters, places, and incidents are either products of the author's imagination or used fictitiously. Any similarity to actual people, organizations, and/or events is purely coincidental.

Cover design: Thinkpen Design Inc., www.thinkpendesign.com

Published by Barbour Publishing, Inc., P.O. Box 719, Uhrichsville, Ohio 44683, www.barbourbooks.com

Our mission is to publish and distribute inspirational products offering exceptional value and biblical encouragement to the masses.

Printed in the United States of America.
Bethany Press International, Bloomington, MN 55438; January 2012; D10003111

Elise the Actress

Norma Jean Lutz

A Note to Readers

While the Brannon and Harvey families are fictional, the situations they faced in Cincinnati during the Civil War are very real. Famous people as well as ordinary soldiers and civilians wrote diaries, letters, and memoirs that give us a great deal of information about life during the four-year war. Food was often in short supply, and widows and their children had to depend on help from others to survive.

In northern states like Ohio, feelings against the "Rebels," as Southern soldiers were called, ran high. Like Milt Finney, some people in the North had sons who chose to fight for the South. They faced prejudice every day.

By the end of the war, people in both the North and South were bitter about the suffering they had experienced. Most historians believe that President Lincoln had the best chance of bringing forgiveness between the North and the South when peace was declared. Because of his assassination, we will never know if the hard times people in the South experienced after the war could have been avoided.

Contents

Chapter 1

New Year's Eve

Music and laughter floated throughout the expanse of the large Brannon house. The guests who'd come for the New Year's Eve celebration were dancing and singing and visiting. If Elise Brannon stood still and closed her eyes, she could almost forget for a moment that a war existed. The War between the States was now going into its fourth long year.

But at this moment, she had no time to close her eyes because there was too much to do. Elise and her friend Verly Boyd were in the kitchen just off the ballroom. Berdeen O'Banion, their Irish maid and nanny, expected both Elise and Verly to help take the large serving trays full of food and pass them among the guests.

Handing a tray to Verly, Elise said, "Can you handle this one? It's pretty heavy."

Verly's blue eyes shone as she smiled. "I can handle it just fine."

Elise picked up another tray and said, "Forward, march. I'm right behind you."

"Careful you'll be, lassies," Berdeen said as she held open the door that led from the large kitchen into a pass-through and out into the formal ballroom.

Before the war, Mama would have hired extra help for such an occasion, but Elise didn't mind helping at all. In fact, she rather enjoyed it.

As she moved among the crowd, she heard her papa saying, "I never thought I'd live to see the day—Congress finally allowing the contrabands to fight in their own war for freedom."

"And good soldiers they've made, I hear," another man put in.

To which Elise's papa retorted, "I've been trying to tell people that for many years. Now they can see it for themselves—clear as day."

Elise knew that contraband referred to the freed slaves. Ever since President Lincoln had issued the Emancipation Proclamation a year ago, freed slaves had been longing to don uniforms and join the fighting. At last it had happened. Elise's papa, attorney Jack Brannon, had long been a fighter for the abolition of slavery. Elise was overjoyed that his dreams were at last coming true.

As Elise moved through the little knots of people gathered in the vast ballroom, she also heard men discussing President Lincoln's speech at the battleground in Gettysburg last November. Others discussed the ineptness of Union generals. Conversation of the women covered men who were off in battle and the work being done at various hospitals to aid the war wounded.

Verly's papa had died in the first fighting at Bull Run, and now her brother, Alexander, was off fighting, as well. She and her mother had been forced to sell their home and move into Aunt Ella's boardinghouse. Mrs. Boyd supplemented their meager income by taking in sewing. All these troubles had made Verly understandably sad.

Through the crowd, Elise could see her friend smiling shyly as she offered her tray of sandwiches to the guests. At least the festivities had managed to cheer Verly and keep her smiling.

After her tray of meat and cheese was emptied, Elise went over to Verly. "It's time to gather our troupe and go to the playroom," she said.

"Oh, good!" Verly's eyes lit up. "This'll be such fun!"

After taking their trays back to the kitchen, Elise said, "We're going to the playroom now, Berdeen. Will you come and help?"

"Aye, lassie. I mun put the fresh teakettle back on the stove, and I'll be with ye."

"Verly, you go gather the others. Berdeen and I'll go up the back way. We'll meet you upstairs."

Verly gave a little giggle. "Meet you upstairs."

A few moments later, Elise entered the playroom, where her brothers and the other children of attending guests were gathered. From the table, she picked up Mama's little portable writing desk.

"Make a straight line," she said, making checks on the paper lying atop the wooden frame she was holding. "Let's have the oldest at this end, down to the youngest." She watched as they scrambled a moment to line up, some having to ask the age of the others.

"But I don't want to be on the very end," protested Elise's eight-year-old brother, Peter. "I always have to be on the tail end."

"It doesn't mean anything bad, Peter," Elise said in a gentle tone. "It simply serves to make our presentation more organized." She took him by the arm and guided him to the end of the line.

"I don't mind being on the end," Verly said. "I'll trade places."

"Hurrah for Verly," Peter said. "Let's trade."

But Elise shook her head. "It's important that one person be the organizer, Peter. Stay where you're placed."

Peter groaned, and Verly reached out to pat his arm in sympathy.

Just then Berdeen, who was keeping watch in the hallway, stuck her head in the door. "Be ye nigh ready?"

Berdeen had promised she would help get the adults seated and quiet just before Elise and her troupe were ready to come downstairs to perform their recitations.

"A few more minutes, Berdeen," Elise said.

Elise hoped that the humorous recitations she'd chosen would brighten the evening for everyone. The other youngsters were agreeable. Earlier in the evening, they'd all been given scripts and poems to present, and each had had a chance to practice. Now the room fairly bristled with excitement. Even Elise's older brother, Samuel, had acquiesced to her leadership—which was a surprise. At eleven, a full year older than Elise, Samuel could be pretty bossy at times. But as he said, this program was all her idea. Because Samuel followed, the other two older boys, Cleve and Adam Scott, did the same. The Kilgour sisters were also cooperative. With a little luck, Elise's plan would come off smooth as silk.

"Let's run through the order of presentations one more time," she said, making little checks on her list as she did so. Once she was satisfied that each one knew his or her place and lines, she said to Samuel, "Tell Berdeen we're ready."

Samuel strode to the door, opened it, and gave Berdeen a wave.

"Stay at the balcony rail and watch," she told Samuel, "then let us know when they're ready."

It took a few minutes for Berdeen to quiet the revelers and get them all into the parlor and seated. When it was time, Elise led her troupe to the balcony. At her signal, the first half of the line went down one of the curving twin staircases while the last half took the other. They converged at the bottom, fell back into line, and marched into the parlor, where the gathered guests applauded their entrance.

Reading from her written notes, Elise introduced her troupe and then announced the first presentation. "Each member of our troupe will recite a verse from a humorous poem titled, 'Our Minister's Sermon.' "

Sandy-haired Cleve Scott stepped forward. He was a bit nervous at having to go first, but as the oldest of their little conclave, he wanted to set a good example. Clearing his throat, he gave the opening lines.

Elise smiled as twitters and chuckles swept over the crowd. Next it was Adam's turn with the second verse:

I tell you our minister's prime; he is—
But I couldn't quite determine,
When I heard him givin' it right and left,
Just who was hit by his sermon.
Of course, there couldn't be no mistake
When he talked about long-winded prayin'
For Peters and Johnson, they sot and scowled
At ev'ry word he wuz sayin'.

Following Adam, Samuel took his turn speaking clear and full as though he were already a professional attorney like his papa. Amelia and Madeline Kilgour took the next two verses.

Elise scanned the crowd and saw the smiles on the faces. Her heart raced. There was Aunt Ella, whose husband, Dr. George Harvey, was off tending wounded soldiers at the front lines. Beside her sat her elder daughter, Melissa Baird, whose husband, Jeremiah, was also in the war. Alicia and Alan, the Harveys' fifteen-year-old twins, were too old to be a part of this troupe, but they were both laughing aloud at the skit.

It was fairly possible that at this time next year Alan might be in the heat of battle, as well. Elise knew he was torn between staying home to care for his mother and sisters or answering his call to duty.

Elise's papa was smiling, as were his business associates. Mama was standing in the doorway beside Berdeen, and Mama's beautiful dark eyes were crinkling with laughter. How thankful Mama was that Papa was past the age of serving in the war—how thankful they all were.

Now Verly stepped forward. Though her voice was rather soft, she managed to recite the sixth verse without a mistake. When she was done, the laughter in the room had grown a bit more boisterous. Peter, loving the sound of it, launched into his part:

Just then the minister sez, sez he,
"And now I've come to the fellers
Who've lost this shower by usin' their friends
As a sort of moral umbrellers.
Go home!" sez he, "and find your faults
Instead of huntin' your brother's.
Go home," sez he, "and wear the coats
You're trying to fit on others!"

Elise had to wait a moment for the laughter to subside before she finished with the final verse:

My wife she nudged, and Brown he winked,
And there wuz lots of smilin',
And lots of lookin' at our pew—
It sot my blood a-bilin'.
Sez I to myself, "Our minister
Is gettin' a little bitter,
I'll tell him when the meetin's out
That I ain't that kind of a critter."

At Elise's hand motion, her cast made their bows and curtsies to the sound of rousing applause. Then the Kilgour sisters went to the piano and played a duet while the others sang about a fly on the head of a bald-headed man.

Following the song, which also caused a good deal of guffaws and snickers, each performer gave a short recitation, beginning with Peter. Elise stood back near the piano with her notes as each of the troupe members performed.

The grand finale was to be a recitation titled “How We Hunted a Mouse,” which dramatically told of a husband rushing to the aid of his wife, who was frightened by a mouse. He was rewarded for his efforts by having the mouse crawl up the leg of his trousers. It was Elise’s favorite recitation, and she’d liked to have presented it herself, but she deferred the honor to her older brother.

She had laboriously copied it from the recitation book and made it large so it would be easy for Samuel to read. He’d run through it earlier in the playroom and had put all the other children in stitches.

Now she introduced her brother to the crowd. He’d asked her if he could announce his selection himself, and she’d agreed. Samuel stepped forward, and everyone grew quiet. “Our Flag,” he said solemnly, “an essay by A. L. Stone.”

From behind the piano, Elise tried in vain to get his attention, shaking her head and waving, but he ignored her. Samuel was taking matters into his own hands, after all.

“Ringed about with flame and smoke of rebel batteries,” he began, “one solitary flag went down, torn and scathed, on the blackened and battered walls of Sumter.”

Inwardly, Elise groaned. The last thing she wanted was for the war to be brought into this happy moment. The whole point of the entertainment was to help the guests forget the war for a little while. Samuel continued:

“Then the slumberous fire burst forth and blazed up from

the hearts of the people. The painted symbol of the national life, under which our populations of city and country had walked to and fro with tranquil footstep, stirring its peaceful folds with no shouts of chivalrous and romantic deference, had been torn down and trodden under the feet of traitors."

The Union officers in the room who were in uniform stood to their feet. Samuel held his head high and continued the reading that he'd memorized many months ago.

"It was torn down from a single flagstaff, and as the tidings of that outrage swept, ringing and thrilling through the land, ten thousand banners were run up on every hilltop and in every vale, on church towers and armed fortress and peaceful private homes, till the heavens over us looked down upon more stars than they kept in their own nightly vault. . . ."

Now the rest of the guests were standing. Some held their hands over their hearts in a proud salute. Samuel's eyes were shining.

"And then the cry went forth, 'Rally 'round the flag, boys!' and every instrument of martial music took up the strain and church bells pealed it forth, and church choirs sang it. . . ."

Elise looked at Mama. Her fair cheeks were wet with tears as were Aunt Ella's and Cousin Melissa's. The men were solemn and grim-faced. That Samuel—why did she agree to let him take the final act?

"And the voices gathered into a mighty chorus that swept over the New England hills and across the breadth of midland

prairies and dashed its waves over the summits of the mountains and down these western slopes till they met and mingled with the waves of the Pacific—the full unison echoing here through all our streets and homes, 'Rally 'round the flag, boys! Rally once again!' "

When he was finished, Samuel bowed his head. It was quiet for a moment, then the entire room erupted into cheers and shouts. "Rally 'round the flag," some guests called out. "Let this year bring the end to the war!" others cried. "Hurrah for the Union!"

Verly evidently noticed Elise's downcast expression. She came over and put her arm around Elise's shoulder. Ever since Verly and her mother had moved into Aunt Ella's boardinghouse, Verly and Elise had become close friends. Now she seemed to sense how Elise was feeling. "Everyone thinks you planned the program to end like this," she said. "You look like a heroine."

Elise just shook her head. "Oh, Verly, I wanted everyone to laugh and be happy. Laughter is the best medicine. Why can't people forget the terrible war, even if it's only for one evening?"

Chapter 2

Sledding

Though Elise was upset with Samuel, it was too nice a party to let a little thing ruin it. Mama had planned to send Peter to bed after the recitations. After all, before Elise turned ten, she was made to go to bed before midnight. But Peter begged so hard that Mama relented.

At the stroke of midnight, Papa partially opened the windows so they could hear the church bells sounding across the city from their vantage point in Walnut Hills. The guests were still somber from Samuel's dramatic reading as they lifted cups of eggnog and punch in toasts to the year of 1864. The long, costly war put a damper on looking forward to a new year. Everyone said it would only be more of the same. Elise wasn't sure she could bear another year of the news of so much killing, so much pain, so much sorrow.

She stared at one of the opened windows as silvery snowflakes came blowing inside. She knew her uncle George was on the battleground in the cold somewhere in Tennessee. And Melissa's husband, Jeremiah, was out in the winter cold somewhere in Virginia. Verly, who was standing close beside her, was quiet. She was no doubt thinking of her slain father and her absent brother.

Papa came to the center of the room and asked that everyone be quiet for a moment. Pastor Terrence Thomas and his wife, Hope, were among the guests, and Papa asked the pastor to pray. As the guests bowed their heads, Pastor Thomas prayed for an end to the war and violence, for the Union to be preserved, and for family members to be kept safe.

Elise allowed herself a peek at her handsome father as he bowed in prayer. She was terribly proud of him. He was a good and fair attorney and had helped many people by giving his services away. Elise had asked Papa many times why God would allow such a terrible war. He spoke often of the unimaginable atrocities of slavery. "Perhaps," he told her once, "we are suffering God's wrath and judgment for those despicable sins."

Before the war, Elise's papa and another Cincinnati lawyer, Salmon Chase, defended runaway slaves who had no money to defend themselves. Papa still kept in close touch with Mr. Chase, who was now the secretary of the treasury in Washington, D.C. Papa knew many people in high places of government. Even though Elise was proud of her father, she couldn't help wishing he had a little more time for her. He was a terribly busy man.

As the prayer continued, Elise heard a little sniff beside her and realized Verly was fighting back her tears. She reached out and took her friend's hand. Verly looked over at Elise and managed a weak smile.

Elise was glad she could be Verly's friend. The Boyds had lost so much since the war began. In spite of Mrs. Boyd's talents as an excellent seamstress, it was a struggle for the two of them. Due to the war, there was so little cloth to be had and so few people were purchasing new clothes. Much of her work was patching, hemming, and altering.

As soon as Pastor Thomas said "amen," someone muttered,

"Close those windows; I'm freezing." A ripple of laughter moved through the room, dispelling the solemn mood.

Elise guided Verly closer to the heating stove. "Can you come over tomorrow to play?"

"Mama needs my help in the morning. I may be able to come later."

Elise couldn't imagine having to work during Christmas vacation from school. She was relieved there were no studies to tend to. "When you come, we'll have Berdeen serve us tea up in the playroom. I'll have the dolls ready for a tea party."

Verly's face lit up. "That sounds like such fun. I hope I can come."

The menfolk were pulling on their cloaks and going outside to bring their carriages up to the front portico. There the ladies were able to embark without getting in too much of the deep snow. In spite of having boots, no one liked to get their long skirts wet.

Presently Cousin Alan drove up in the Harvey buggy, and Verly boarded it along with her mother and the Harvey family. Elise waved as her friend departed. Elise hoped the bright evening had helped Verly during this trying time.

Snow continued to fall during the night, and by morning the view outside Elise's upstairs window was of a vast white blanket as far as the eye could see. Down the tree-studded hillside, every bare limb appeared to be coated in creamy white icing, and every house was topped with a dollop of whipped cream. In spite of the chill in the air, she slipped out from beneath the heavy feather comforter, grabbed her wrapper, and stole across the cold floor to the window for a better view.

Just then, Peter came running into her room without even knocking. He was at her side in a flash, fairly exploding with excitement. "Look how deep, Elise. Just look how deep it is. This is the most snow we've had all winter. And on a day with no school!"

"It's beautiful, isn't it?"

"Do you suppose Samuel would go sledding?"

"I suppose you might ask," Elise said.

"You go ask with me."

"You saw last night how well Samuel listens to me," she said, still thinking about how her older brother had changed the closing recitation. "But let's get dressed and eat breakfast. Then we'll see what the day holds."

Elise wanted to remind Peter that *she* could easily go sledding with him, but she knew he put great stock in being included in Samuel's comings and goings. Samuel spent much time talking with Papa about legal matters, war matters, and whatever other matters he felt Papa might want to talk about. Often he worked at the law office doing odd jobs as a clerk and messenger. It was a rare day when Peter could actually play with his older brother.

"Bet I can beat you down to breakfast," Peter said.

"Of course you can, silly." Elise lifted a lock of her long black hair. "You don't have all this to brush and braid."

"Well, I bet I can beat you in a snowball fight."

"That wager I'll accept."

Satisfied, her little brother went bouncing back out of her room. As she turned back to the window, she saw Chancy Wilmot ride up to the Brannon stable on his spotted pony.

At age sixteen, Chancy was old enough to be off fighting, but because he'd had a lame ankle since birth, he was rejected. Papa then hired him to help with the horses. Chancy was quiet and kept to himself, and Papa was pleased at how well he could handle the foals—he was an excellent trainer. Even though they had fewer horses than Elise could ever remember, still there was too much for Papa to do, even with Samuel's help.

Elise hurried to pull on her day dress and to plait her hair in two long braids. When she arrived in the dining room, Berdeen was already bringing platters of ham and eggs out from the kitchen. Peter was at the table and made a funny face at her. Papa and Samuel were discussing war matters, and Mama listened quietly as she always did.

Midway through breakfast, Elise turned to Peter and said, "Are we still going to go sledding together after we eat?" She gave a secret wink as she said it.

Peter caught on quickly. "We're going sledding, all right. Down the east ridge, and we'll have a swell time."

Samuel spoke up then. "Hey, isn't anyone inviting me to go along?"

Elise smiled at Peter. Her little ploy had worked. To Samuel, she said, "I didn't think you needed an invitation. We assumed you'd want to come, too."

Peter jumped up from his place. "I'll go on out and get the sled down and wax the runners."

"Not so fast," Mama protested. "You've not eaten much breakfast."

But Papa said, "Oh, Louisa, can't you see how excited he is? Let him go. He'll be starved by ten o'clock."

"Thank you, Papa." And Peter was gone.

When Elise finished eating, she pulled on her rubber boots over her leather button-up ankle boots and took her fitted coat from the front hall tree. A flowing cloak would never do for sled riding. When she was bundled up, Samuel was still talking to Papa. She'd heard Samuel say many times that he would someday be a great politician like Lincoln. "Great politicians have the power to change the world," he would tell her.

Elise, however, didn't feel her older brother was cut out to be a politician. But she held her peace. After all, what did girls know about such things? And that's just what Samuel would tell her if she broached the subject.

On her way out, she stopped in the kitchen to ask Berdeen for a carrot to feed her horse.

"I declare, Elise, you be spoiling that horse of yours more with each passing day."

"He's worth a lot more than a carrot or two," Elise replied. She loved her horse with a passion. When the war started and Papa learned of the desperate need for good breeding stock, he sold off much of his fine herd in order to help the cause. Elise had been only seven at the time. She recalled crying herself to sleep, thinking Papa might sell her horse while she slept. She told the agonizing fear to no one.

Of course Papa never sold Dusty Smoke, but it made her more protective of the horse. Although Chancy did a fine job, she still checked on Dusty every day. Sometimes twice a day. With the carrot Berdeen gave her and an apple to boot, she headed out the back door.

The brilliant sunshine on the white snow was almost blinding as she walked across the porch and down the steps into the deep snow. Immediately, there was the feeling of cold on her ankles in spite of her long wool stockings. She carefully tried to step in the tracks that Peter had made. It made the going somewhat easier.

The stable was cozy warm with the wonderful sounds and smells of horses—one of Elise's favorite places in the whole world.

"Morning, Chancy."

The shy boy mumbled a reply but didn't stop his work of mucking out the stalls. Peter was sitting on the floor, waxing the runners of their big sled with a piece of beeswax.

"We're gonna fly down that hill," he said as Elise approached. The excitement fairly bubbled in his voice. "Do you think Samuel will take me down once?"

"I'm sure he will," Elise assured him. She hurried past him to go to Dusty's stall. "Dusty," she called out. "Good morning, Dusty. I've brought you something."

Dusty swung her head about at the sound of Elise's voice. The silvery-gray mare wasn't a large horse. Papa's love for the Arabians showed in all the Brannon line. The breed was distinguished by the long, finely arched neck and high-set tail, which went like a flag at the least move—and Dusty had the best of those attributes.

Elise reached out and offered Dusty the carrot, feeling her horse's soft breath caress her hand. The carrot was gone in a moment, and Dusty lifted her head over the stall, snuffling about for more. Elise laughed. "What makes you think there's more?" she teased.

Just then Samuel was beside her. "You have that horse as pampered as a house pet."

Elise extended the apple on the flat of her hand. "I could only wish she *were* a house pet. Think she'd do well in the playroom?"

Samuel grinned. "Only if it didn't give Berdeen a case of dyspepsia." He stepped over to the next stall, where his horse, Vardan, was stabled. The roan gelding stood taller than Dusty and was more boisterous. Mama always said his heart was full of run.

"Come on, you two," Peter called anxiously. "Let's get to the hill before the whole neighborhood arrives."

"He's right," Samuel said. He reached out to grab Elise's arm and pulled her along. "Come on, sis. Let's go!"

Elise could only giggle as she ran to keep up. "Bye, Dusty," she called out. "I'll be back after a while!"

They put Peter on the sled, and Elise and Samuel pulled the sled up the road to where the ridge offered a clear slope with few trees and no houses. It was the favorite sledding area in the neighborhood, and already there were a few sledders shouting as they zoomed down the hill.

The first few times, all three Brannon children loaded on their sled, with the two boys sandwiching Elise between them. She wasn't sure if they wanted to protect her or whether Peter purposely enjoyed falling off the back into the deep powdery snow. Samuel held the rope and worked the steering mechanisms. She held on to Samuel's sides, clutching handfuls of his thick coat, and buried her face into his back. They sailed down so fast that it sucked her breath out of her lungs. She tried not to squeal, but she couldn't help it.

They laughed and giggled as they pulled the sled back up the hill. Peter begged to go alone, but Samuel kept saying he'd better not. "You're not old enough to handle such a big sled all by yourself," Samuel said.

As a consolation, Samuel set Peter in front of him, and the two went down with Peter steering. But that only made him more determined to go alone. "I can do it," he insisted. "I bet you were going down alone when you were eight. You didn't have any older brother to help."

"No, I didn't," Samuel agreed, "but Cousin Alan kept a close watch over me."

But in the end, Peter's begging won over Samuel's soft heart. Samuel looked at Elise and raised his brows. Elise shrugged in response. She figured Samuel had gone down the hill alone when he was much younger than eight, but she kept quiet, feeling it should be his decision.

"Oh, all right. One time," Samuel said. "But be very careful, and remember to steer clear of those trees at the bottom."

But Peter wasn't listening. "Hurrah," he shouted. "I'll fly faster all by myself!" He turned the sled to aim it down the hill just right. Then he settled himself on it, bracing his feet on the steering bars. "Give me a push, Samuel. A big old push."

Samuel did as Peter asked, giving a shove that sent his younger brother careening down the hillside. Peter was doing fine, squealing with delight as he went. Suddenly, from out of nowhere, another sled carrying three bigger boys came flying down beside him. Elise's breath caught as she saw them. They should have waited.

"Look out, Peter!" Samuel called out. But it was too late. The presence of the other sled frightened and confused Peter, causing him to veer sharply away. With a great crash, he hit a small tree and tumbled into the snow.

Elise and Samuel went running down the hill, calling their brother's name as they ran.

Chapter 3

Letters to Soldiers

Samuel reached him first. "Peter, are you all right?"

Peter tried to sit up and gave a groan. "It's my ankle."

"Don't move," Samuel instructed. "Lie still so I can look."

Elise saw Peter's face wince with pain. "Those big kids should know better," she scolded.

"They have as much right to the hill as we do," Samuel told her. "Peter, old boy, you should have kept going straight. They weren't going to hit you."

"It scared me when I saw them," he said. "Ouch!" He reached down to hold his ankle. "It hurts bad."

Elise helped Samuel to set the sled aright, then they carefully lifted Peter up on it. Samuel pulled up Peter's trouser leg and eased down the woolen stocking. "It's swelling already," he said. Samuel sat down in the snow and pulled off his own shoe and stocking. Then he filled his stocking with snow. He packed the icy woolen stocking about Peter's ankle.

Peter grimaced, but he didn't complain.

"There," Samuel said, pulling his shoe back on over his bare foot. "That'll help to keep the swelling down till we get you home."

"We can't pull him up the hill," Elise said.

Just then the older boys came running back up the hill. "I told Jay not to take it down at that moment," one of them said.

"We're sorry," said another. "Is he hurt bad?"

"His ankle," Samuel answered.

"We'll help you get him back up," said the one named Jay. Each of the four older boys took a corner of the long sled and lifted it like a stretcher. That put a smile on Peter's face, in spite of his pain. Elise followed behind, pulling the other boys' empty sled.

The boys were impressed that Samuel knew to make a cold pack out of his sock, but it didn't surprise Elise. She'd seen him work with horses in the same gentle manner that he was using with Peter. It seemed to be second nature to him. Other horse owners—friends of Papa's—often called on Samuel when their horses were ailing or hurt. They nicknamed him *the young horse doctor*.

The boys offered to help Samuel and Elise take Peter home, but Samuel said they could easily pull him on the roadway. He thanked the boys as though it hadn't been their fault at all. "It was nice of them to come back and help," he said as they pulled the sled homeward.

Elise just wished they'd been more careful in the first place, but she said nothing. Peter insisted over and over that he would have done fine if the big boys hadn't come by. Samuel kindly agreed with him.

Peter's sprain turned an ugly purple, but his older brother's quick thinking prevented much swelling. By the time Verly came over that afternoon, Peter was hobbling about with the aid of a crutch that Mama had retrieved from the attic.

He played soldiers in the corner of the playroom while Verly and Elise set up the table for tea.

"You're a good sport to go sledding with your brothers," Verly said to Elise as they arranged the dolls on the extra chairs.

"It's great fun," Elise replied. "It fairly takes your breath away."

"Doesn't it frighten you—speeding so fast?"

Elise set out the doll cups and saucers on the table. "Not frightening exactly. More like a delicious excitement." But she could see her quiet friend wasn't too convinced.

"Alexander, being nine years older than me, treated me more like a little doll than a sister." Verly picked up the china doll and smoothed its silken dress. "We didn't play much together."

"Elise and I play together a lot," Peter said from his side of the room, "and now I can beat her in checkers all the time."

Elise smiled. "He does, too."

"It must be fun to have someone to play with." Verly glanced about the room. "And in such a nice playroom."

Elise felt bad that Verly and her mother had been forced to sell their home. The room they rented at Aunt Ella's was smaller than the Brannon playroom.

"But you have us," Peter put in.

Elise was pleased at Peter's thoughtfulness, but she knew it wasn't the same. To Verly, she added, "We do want you to come whenever you can. It's fun to have another girl around. Peter doesn't much like to play dolls."

The door opened then, and Berdeen came in with the tea cart. "Teatime it is, for a bonny lad and two bonny lassies," she said in her lilting brogue. "Shall we set up on the doll table?"

"Oh yes, let's," Verly answered. "That is, if it's all right."

"Of course it's all right," Elise assured her.

Peter had shot down all his soldiers and was setting them up again in neat rows. "I'm having mine right here on the floor. The general can't leave his troops."

"If it warn't for ye hurt fut, I'd never let you get away with such a thing," Berdeen said.

"It's not my foot, it's my ankle," Peter corrected her. "I'm pretending I got hurt in the war."

"Peter," Elise scolded, "that's a terrible thing to play." Turning to Verly, she said, "How I wish the war were over and done with."

"Dearie me, I do, as well," Berdeen said, transferring the tray from the cart to the small table. "Sure and it's been a dreadful long and drawn-out affair."

"If there'd been no war, I'd still be living in our own house with my own room and back at my old school," Verly said softly. "And Papa would still be alive."

"Do forgive me, wee lassie," Berdeen said, all flustered. "I dinna intend to make you think of sad things."

"Please, don't apologize," Verly insisted. "I think of it all the time anyway."

"I would, too, if I were you," Elise agreed gently. "I know I would."

"Where is your dear brother, lassie?" Berdeen asked.

"The letter we received just before Christmas was from Chattanooga, Tennessee, where he serves with General Rosecrans. It was written back in September."

Berdeen's face grew pale. They'd all heard of the terrible fighting in and around Chattanooga all during the autumn.

"I have an idea," Elise said, wanting to break the spell of gloom that had come into the room. "After teatime, let's write letters. You write to Alexander, and I'll write to Uncle George."

Verly's face brightened. "That's a fine plan."

"I'll run down and ask Mama for stationery and envelopes," Elise offered.

"No need for you to bother when I'll be tripping down myself," Berdeen said. "I'll fetch the writing things to you when I come back for the tea cart."

"Thank you, Berdeen," Elise said.

The girls had a grand time pretending they were grown ladies, serving tea and cakes to one another and the dolls. Peter, of course, pretended he was doling out army rations to his soldiers. Looking up from his games, Peter said, "In Uncle George's letters, he says the army food is awful."

"Alexander tells us the same thing," Verly agreed as she sipped tea from a dainty cup.

"That's why Mama helps Aunt Ella and Cousin Melissa at the Soldiers' Aid Society," Elise said. "They pack crates of good things to eat and send them by train to the battlegrounds. Mama told us they sometimes pack jars of fruit and jams in cornmeal. The cornmeal keeps the jars from breaking, and then the soldiers can cook gruel or pone with the cornmeal. Isn't that a clever idea?"

"My mama would help at the society, too, but she has to work to pay our rent." Verly's voice was sad again. "Some nights she sits up sewing long after I'm asleep. I wish she didn't have to work so hard."

"I wish so, too," Elise agreed. "Have another cake?"

Taking the little cake, Verly said, "I'm going to study very hard, and when I'm old enough, I'll hire out as a schoolteacher and help Mama with the money I earn."

Elise had never thought about having to earn money. What a terrible thing to have to be concerned with when Verly wasn't even eleven.

Just then, Berdeen returned to take the tea tray. In her hand were the sheets of stationery and envelopes. Once the tea things were cleared away, the girls spread their work out on the table.

The room was quiet except for the scratching of their pens as they wrote letters to the men who were so far away fighting a terrible war. Elise glanced over at Peter. He'd fallen asleep on the floor with his head resting on his arm. She smiled and went back to her letter.

After a few moments, Verly looked over at Elise's letter. "Whatever are you doing?" she said. "You're messing up your pretty letter with those silly drawings."

"I like to draw silly things in my letters to Uncle George. I do the same thing for my cousin Jeremiah."

"Why?"

Elise looked at her friend. "Because I think they need something to laugh about."

"But war is a serious thing. The men are doing a great service for their country."

"All the more reason for them to laugh. I don't just draw silly pictures. I put in a few riddles, as well."

"You put riddles in your letters?" The serious Verly was incredulous.

"Sure. I ask the riddle, and when Uncle George writes back, he lets me know if he can figure out the answer. Sometimes he asks the other soldiers if they know the answers."

"Tell me one of the riddles," Verly said, her chin in her hand.

"All right. Can you tell me what belongs to yourself and yet is used by everybody else more than yourself?"

"Something that belongs to me but everybody else uses? I haven't any idea. What is it?"

Elise giggled. "It's your name."

Verly gave a little chuckle. "That's good. Of course. My name. I like your riddle."

Elise told a couple more riddles, which also made Verly laugh. "See what I mean?" Elise said. "They make you want to laugh. And the Bible says that "a merry heart doeth good like a medicine." Don't you think Alexander would like some of that good medicine?"

"Do you mind if I borrow one of your riddles in my letter?"

"Not at all," Elise told her. As she watched Verly add the riddle to the letter, Elise thought that perhaps Verly needed cheering almost as much as her older brother who was out on the battlefield.

Chapter 4

The Traitor!

The streets of downtown Cincinnati were floating in dirty slush. Elise hated that the lovely, pristine snow turned into such a dreadfully sloppy mess. She could feel water soaking the hem of her long skirts as she hurried to keep up with Berdeen. Even Peter on his bad ankle could move through the slush faster than Elise in her hoop skirts.

In the month since Peter's accident, his ankle had healed slowly. When school resumed after the holidays, he was still on a crutch, which made the other boys want to play with the crutch, as well. Now at the close of February, he still had a bit of a limp.

Berdeen was doing the Saturday marketing and needed their help to carry purchases as she bustled about from store to store. Her exasperation knew no end as she discovered one item after another was unavailable because of the war.

"No coffee, no sugar, precious little tea," she muttered to herself as they plunged through another puddle to cross busy Fourth Street. "I can find nary a bolt of good-quality cotton fabric in the entire city. A disgrace, that's what it is. An everlasting disgrace."

Peter looked over at Elise and grinned. Berdeen went through this speech every time they went marketing. Elise couldn't help but feel sorry for Berdeen. She tried her best to keep house and cook for an active family of five, and it wasn't easy with so many shortages. Only that morning Mama had said, "What I wouldn't give for a good cup of strong coffee." But there was none to be had.

Elise's warm woolen cloak was wrapped snugly about her, and her hood covered her head, but still she felt the icy wind piercing the cloth. She'd be quite relieved to get home and get out of her wet things. Her arms ached from carrying the purchases. Then she remembered what she'd heard about ladies in the South, some of whom were selling their lovely, expensive frocks to buy food. Here in Cincinnati, they still had money and still had their clothes. She knew she should be grateful.

"This here'll be our last place," Berdeen announced over her shoulder. She turned into Walker's Grocery at the far end of Fourth Street. After the shopping was finished, they would go to Papa's office, and Samuel would drive them home in the carriage.

The aromas of pickled herring, soda crackers, apples, and pickles met her as Elise walked past the open barrels in front of the counter. Mr. Walker turned from where he was stocking shelves to hail them with a hearty greeting. "Good day to you, Miss O'Banion. And to you, too, Elise and Peter. Looks like the snow is finally beginning to melt. Won't be long till spring now."

"Not long a'tall," Berdeen agreed. "If'n a body doesn't drown in the street first, I'll be glad to see the springtime come."

Elise and Peter gave polite greetings, as well. Then Berdeen walked back to the butcher counter and ordered a slab of bacon to be sliced. The friendly butcher, Mr. Stefano, laughed and joked with Berdeen as he pulled the slab from the case and threw it on the chopping board to make slices with his large knife.

Elise, not too terribly interested in bacon, joined Peter at the candy counter. As she did, she noticed a man walk into the grocer's. There was something about his expression that held Elise's attention and touched her heart deeply. Sadness etched his face. In this awful time of war, many people had faced terrible losses. It must be so with this man.

Elise waited to hear Mr. Walker sing out his greeting. Instead, he glanced at the man and returned to stocking the shelves. She could hardly believe her eyes. Why would he do such a thing? The man was not old, but his wide shoulders beneath a worn cloak drooped with a weight too heavy to bear. He came a bit farther into the store, as though testing ice on the river. Except for Berdeen's chattering in the back, all was quiet. Peter gazed at the candy, picking out his choices. Tin cans clinked as Mr. Walker fastened his attention on the shelves and kept his back to the customer.

The man had removed his hat, and his eyes scanned the store. Before Elise could think to look away, their eyes met and locked. His hazel eyes were not angry or bitter; rather they were filled with profound sadness. He seemed to give a deep sigh. Then he replaced his hat and walked slowly out the door.

It had all happened in a matter of a few moments, but it seemed like an eternity. She turned back to the candy case.

"The selection is getting smaller all the time," Peter muttered, not unlike Berdeen. "Before this old war is over, there might not be any candy at all."

The packages of bacon and salt pork were wrapped in brown butcher paper. Berdeen placed them on the front counter, and Mr. Walker wrote up the ticket and put it with the Brannon account.

"Thank you kindly for your business, Miss O'Banion," he said.

"What about the candy, Berdeen?" Peter insisted. "We get candy, don't we?"

Berdeen gave a little snort. "Candy you be a-wantin'. Rotted teeth is what you'll be a-gettin'."

"But Mama said—"

"The missus spoils you terrible bad, but there's nary a thing I can do about it." She gave a wave of her hand. "Pick what poison you'll have today."

Peter grinned at Elise. Berdeen always went on about not wanting to be responsible for their teeth falling out. But Elise knew they didn't eat that much candy. To begin with, Mama wouldn't allow it. Secondly, there just wasn't that much extra money for luxuries these days.

When they were out on the sidewalk once again, Elise asked, "Who was that man who came in to shop, Berdeen?"

"What man?"

"Didn't you see him? He came inside and waited a moment, but Mr. Walker wouldn't speak to him, so he left."

"Ah, you've heard of him, lassie. That would be Mr. Milton Finney. His son went off fighting for the South, and nary a soul in the city will have a thing to do with him."

"But that's not right. *He* didn't join the Rebels."

"I know how you must see it, darlin', but feelings are hot and not given to reason in wartime. People look at him and wonder if his son has shot one of their sons. It's wretched, but that's how it is."

Elise slowed her pace as she thought about such a horrible thing. Then she had to hurry through the puddles to catch up again. "Where does he live?" Elise wanted to know.

"Are you meanin' to tell me you never laid eyes on the man riding by your own house?"

Elise shook her head. Both her bedroom and the playroom were situated at the back of the house. She certainly didn't see all the traffic that went by.

"I never did. He lives by us? In Walnut Hills?"

"Farther into the woods, in a small cabin. Moved up there a few months ago."

"By himself?"

"Naturally, by himself. Now pray tell who would want to live with a traitor?"

"But he's not a traitor—his son is."

"Dinna matter. I tell ye again, lassie, there's no reason in wartime."

"I think I've seen him." Peter spoke up. "Does he ride a speckled gray horse, and he rides sort of bent over in the saddle?"

"That's him," Berdeen said. "See there? Your brother's seen the man."

"But I didn't know he was a traitor."

"Peter!" Elise said. "He's *not* a traitor."

"But Berdeen just said—"

"She was just saying what people *think* of the man, not what he truly is."

"Aye, laddie. Elise is right. None of us may ever know what or who he truly is."

The sign on Papa's office door read BRANNON LAW FIRM. Samuel had often said to Elise that he dreamed of the day when that sign would be changed to BRANNON & BRANNON LAW FIRM when he entered the profession, too. Papa's friend Salmon Chase had often told Papa how relieved he would be when the war was over and his duties in serving on Lincoln's cabinet in Washington, D.C., were finished so he could come home again.

Samuel was out running an errand, so they had to wait a few minutes, but none of them minded. They warmed their feet by the stove in the reception area and relished a few moments of rest. Papa was in with a client, so he wasn't even able to say a proper hello to them. Frank, Papa's clerk, offered them cups of tangy hot cider, which helped to warm their insides.

Presently, Samuel came breezing in the door. "Hello, all," he said, touching his hat. Under his arm were packets of documents, which he laid on Frank's desk. He'd been to the courthouse delivering and fetching needed papers for Papa's work.

"Peter, come help me get Aveline hitched to the carriage, and I'll get you home." He surveyed the three of them for a moment. "You look a little peaked."

"It's cold, the streets are full of slush, I can't find proper supplies, and we're footsore," Berdeen said. "I wager that'd serve to make a body appear a bit peaked all right."

Samuel smiled. "Your coach'll be ready in a jiffy."

"I'd be most obliged," she answered.

On the way home, Elise couldn't stop thinking about Milton Finney. If no one would wait on him, how could he ever purchase food? How could he live so closed off from the rest of the world? *It must be terribly lonely,* Elise thought.

Peter fumbled about in Berdeen's shopping bag and pulled out the bag of candy. Then he offered everyone a piece. Elise sucked on a peppermint stick and wondered where Mr. Finney's cabin was located. Perhaps Samuel knew. But then she thought better of asking him. Or anyone else for that matter. Berdeen was right about there being no reason in this long war. People were full of hate and suspicion. She'd just take a ride after the spring thaw. Walnut Hills wasn't that big. She'd find the cabin on her own.

At the Brannon house, Samuel pulled the carriage close to the back kitchen entrance so they could all help Berdeen with the parcels and baskets. As they were putting things away, Mama came into the kitchen.

"Ah, how good it is to see my children being such kind helpers to Berdeen."

"Aye, ma'am. They're hearty troopers, the lot of them."

Mama's hands were behind her back. "I have a little surprise for such good workers," she said.

Peter ran to her. "A surprise for all of us?" He tugged at her arm. "What is it?"

"Guess which hand," she said. Peter tapped one, but she shook her head. Then he tapped the other, and she pulled out a handful of tickets. "We're going to the National Theater this evening."

"Hurrah!" Peter cried out. "A night at the theater!"

Samuel wasn't quite as excited, but Elise was thrilled. How she loved the large, old theater that was the pride of Cincinnati. Papa, who'd seen the famous Drury in London, said the National far surpassed the Drury. Some old-timers fondly called Cincinnati's theater "Old Drury."

Looking at Elise, Mama added, "I've a bit more to add to the surprise. There are two extra tickets. Do you think Mrs. Boyd and Verly would want to accompany us?"

Elise felt like squealing. "Oh, Mama, they never get to go anywhere special. Not like the theater. It'll be such a treat for them both. Thank you for thinking of them."

"I'll be going back to town now," Samuel said. "Should I stop by to let them know?"

"Yes, Samuel," Mama said, "please do. Tell them we'll fetch them at half past eight."

Elise could hardly believe this delightful news. What a bright spot this would be for Verly and her mama. How she wished she could relay the message herself.

Since Elise knew Verly would be self-conscious about her lack of fancy dresses, Elise opted not to wear her best pink silk. Instead she chose a church dress of navy poplin with white lace trim. Still a nice dress, it was not nearly as fancy as the silk.

When she came down the stairs, Mama looked at her, studied the dress a moment, then smiled. She understood. Elise released a little sigh of relief.

If Verly was worried about her clothes, it was a short-lived worry. The two girls sat together in Papa's large carriage, laughing and talking as they drove from Walnut Hills into the city. When they stopped in front of the grand building on Sycamore Street, Verly's eyes grew wide. "I've been by here many times, but I've never been inside."

"You've never been to a play?" Elise asked.

Verly shook her head. "Only little skits and dramas at school."

Papa and Samuel assisted each of them as they stepped down from the carriage and went up the stairs and into the vast lobby. Verly gazed about at the marble floors, the gold-leaf ceilings, and heavy glistening chandeliers full of glowing candles.

"Papa was never interested in such things as the theater," Verly whispered to Elise. Then she paused. "But I'm not criticizing him," she added quickly.

"Of course not," Elise assured her. "Different people like different things. I'm so glad Mama and Papa love the theater, because I do, too!"

After Papa had taken care of the team and the carriage, he joined them, and they all went upstairs to their special balcony seats. Verly touched the velvet seats and smiled at Elise. "I'm so pleased you invited us."

"It was Mama. She's the one who thought of it."

The drama was powerful and moving. Elise considered it to be a perfect remedy for forgetting about the war for a few short hours. During intermission, as they stood about in the crowded, lavish lobby, Elise said to Verly, "Isn't it amazing how the lively drama on the stage can help people forget their troubles?"

Verly nodded. "You're right. This is the happiest night I've had in a long, long time. It's certainly helped me to forget about my troubles."

Elise thought about that for a moment. "Verly, let's you and I write a play together. Perhaps we could use it to cheer sad people."

Verly's face brightened. "Write a play? Together? Why, that's a splendid plan."

"Come, girls," Mama said, shooing them back in. "The second act is about to begin."

"We can begin it next week," Elise whispered as the lights went low and the curtain rose.

Chapter 5

Cabin in the Woods

Mrs. Boyd couldn't stop thanking the Brannons for their thoughtfulness in including her and Verly in the festive evening. As Papa and Samuel escorted the Boyds from the carriage to the front steps of the Harvey Boardinghouse, Elise felt all warm and happy inside. Bringing joy to other people, she decided, was about the best feeling in the world.

She and Verly now had a secret because they'd promised each other that they wouldn't tell a soul about their play until they were ready to begin casting. The next morning at church, they made funny faces at one another across the aisle. Verly and her mama always sat in the Harvey pew. Aunt Ella, Melissa, and the twins treated them more like family than boarders.

Elise was sure that must ease Mrs. Boyd's burden somewhat. But life was still difficult for the widow. Elise hoped they would soon receive a letter from Alexander so their hearts would rest easy once again. Elise couldn't imagine how awful it would be to have Samuel gone and not know where he was or even if he was alive.

This Sunday, Aunt Ella's elder son, Charles, sat with the family. Charles's work with the Little Miami Railroad kept him away from the city a good deal of the time. Trains were constantly moving supplies and troops and bringing the wounded home. Elise knew Charles's life was in danger in his locomotive just as much as the soldiers fighting out on the battlefields. He told many stories of being shot at and having railroad bridges blown up.

His bride-to-be, Alison Horstman, sat primly by his side. Their wedding was set for spring—that is, if Charles could get a day or so of leave. Alison's father, Ted Horstman, was an executive for the Little Miami, and it was he who introduced the tall, handsome, quick-thinking Charles to his youngest daughter.

Elise looked at Alison, who was as pretty as her name. How fortunate she was to be getting a husband during these times. Elise had heard Cousin Alicia say that by the time she was ready to be married, all the young men would have been killed in battle.

After services, the cold gray of the day prevented churchgoers from doing much visiting in the churchyard. Everyone wanted to get home and get warm. But Elise and Verly captured a few minutes to talk.

"I've been so full of ideas for a play," Verly said, "that I could barely sleep last night."

"That's good. We'll need lots of ideas."

"Have you ever written a play before?"

Elise shook her head. "Never. But I've read plenty of them. It can't be too hard. And we'll want to create enough parts so several of our friends can help us put it on."

"Let's begin tomorrow at recess." Verly looked up at the sky. "Looks like it'll be an indoor day."

"And remember, we want to keep it a secret."

Verly smiled. "That'll be the most fun part."

During recess for the next couple weeks, Elise sat with Verly as they penned scene after scene. Their story was about an Ohio backwoods farmer, his wife, and several children and their funny escapades on the farm.

"They'll talk funny," Elise said, "like the Squirrel Hunters who came to Cincinnati during the siege." Though she'd been only eight at the time, she remembered helping to serve food to the hundreds of backwoodsmen who rushed to defend the city when Rebels threatened attack.

"A good idea," Verly agreed. "They'll say things like, 'I was sartain them peaches was spiled.' "

Elise laughed. "You're good at that. Do some more."

"How about this: 'The dogs follered the coons right close, but we brung no meat home cuz the crick was up.' "

Elise put her hand over her mouth to stifle the giggles. "Do you think you can teach that to our actors?"

Verly thought a minute, then shrugged. "I don't see why not. It's pretty easy once you get the hang of it."

"I heard the Squirrel Hunters, too, but I never picked up on the way they talked like you did."

Verly smiled shyly at the praise.

When Verly first came to Walnut Hills Elementary School, she'd kept mostly to herself. The loss of her home and her father had broken her heart. Now here she was laughing and becoming excited about their play. Elise's plan to cheer up sad people through her play was working even before the play was presented. Miss Earles seemed pleased as well to see Verly so interested in something.

Whenever Miss Earles took her long rod and pulled down the map of the United States, Verly's face would go white. She'd told Elise one day that her papa was buried near a town in Virginia. Her mama grieved that they couldn't even visit Papa's grave.

The map of the war was changing. The Union now held the

entire Mississippi River, cutting off the Confederate states from Texas and from their supply bases on the river. Even though many of the students had lost brothers, cousins, fathers, and uncles in the war, Miss Earles felt it should be discussed and that they be kept informed of what was happening.

On a separate map on the far wall, she had the children write on tiny slips of paper the names of their soldier-relatives. These were then pinned to the map in the place where that person was fighting. The map was getting quite full of strips of paper. Each morning after Miss Earles read from the Bible, they prayed for the names on their map.

"You are living in a time of history that is changing our entire nation," Miss Earles told them one day. "It's vital that you learn from it as much as you can."

Elise wasn't so sure she agreed. Though she wanted to pray for Uncle George and Cousin Jeremiah, she wished she could ignore the terrible war altogether!

Spring was ushered in by downpours of cold rain. Every day, Elise thought about Mr. Finney, the man she'd seen in the grocer's in February. She wanted so much to go find his cabin, but she knew Mama wouldn't let her go riding alone when the weather was so nasty.

Most afternoons after school, Elise and Peter helped Chancy walk the horses. One of the mares—Mama's favorite, Allegro—was getting ready to foal, and they were all excited about the new arrival. Mama always said there was nothing like the sight of a foal in the paddock to make the heart glad.

In another week or so, Chancy would turn the horses outside every day, but Papa never liked his best horses to be out until the weather was warmer.

One afternoon when Elise and Peter arrived home from school, the sun was shining and there was a tinge of warmth in the air. This was the day she planned to locate Mr. Finney's cabin, but she knew it wouldn't be easy to slip away from Peter.

After changing from their school clothes and grabbing apples for the horses, they raced one another out to the stable. In her apron pocket, Elise carried a note for the man accused of being a traitor, but she wasn't sure what she was going to do with it.

Chancy was walking Allegro in the paddock. His plaid blanket coat was slung over one of the fence posts, and his long-sleeved red woolen underwear showed beneath his worn shirt. The too-large trousers, looking like hand-me-downs, were held up by plain gray suspenders. Chancy was gentle with Allegro, and it made Elise thankful that he was caring for their horses.

Elise climbed up on the paddock fence to watch for a moment. In her hand, she held her broad-brimmed straw hat by its ribbons. Berdeen had reminded her to be sure to wear her hat, but the warm sunshine felt delicious on her head, and Elise didn't want to block that warmth with her hat.

"When do you think she'll foal?" Elise called out to Chancy.

"Looks to be soon, Miss Elise. This week maybe."

"I can't wait," Peter said, climbing up beside her. "I'm old enough now—I can help train it."

"That would please Papa," Elise told him, turning to go inside. She went to Dusty's stall and fed her the apple, which the horse ate greedily. "You look like you're ready to stretch your legs," Elise whispered into the long, twitching ear. After giving the horse a good brushing, she took her into a paddock and walked her for a while. Peter did the same with his horse, Aleron.

As casually as she could, Elise said, "I believe I'll saddle up and take a short ride."

"Good idea," Peter said. And as Elise expected, he added, "I'll do the same and join you."

"Aleron will appreciate the exercise, I'm sure," she said, "but Peter, would you please ride somewhere other than where I do?"

The disappointed look on her little brother's face made Elise wince. "Why?" he asked.

"I need to be alone," she explained lamely. "I have some things that need pondering."

"Does your pondering have to do with all those papers you and Verly have been writing? You've sure been secretive about it."

Elise thought a moment. "In a way it does, yes." She led Dusty toward the back stable doors. "And Peter, I want you to know our secret writing is going to include you."

Peter's face brightened. "You don't say. Truly?"

"It'll be a few weeks yet, but you'll be included."

That seemed to appease him, and he continued walking Aleron around the paddock. Elise hurried inside, saddled Dusty Smoke, tied on her hat, and mounted up. She hadn't lied to Peter because some way, somehow, she fully intended to invite poor Mr. Finney to come to see their play.

As she rode down the lane to the road, she realized she wasn't sure how she would find Mr. Finney's cabin. But even if she never found it, she was happy to be out riding and enjoying the first signs of spring. The area past their house was largely undeveloped and featured thick stands of trees, each of which was beginning to sport tiny green buds. The road followed the trails that had been here since the first fur trappers came down the Ohio River.

A lively cottontail bunny hopped out in front of Dusty, causing her to stop suddenly and shy sideways, but Elise easily maintained control. She'd been riding for almost as long as she could remember. Even Papa said she was a good horsewoman. "You take after your mama when it comes to horses," he'd said so often.

Before the war, Mama spent almost every waking hour in the stables, working with her favorite mounts. Now she seldom got out to the stables. She was much too weary after working long hours as a volunteer with Soldiers' Aid and at the military hospital. The war had changed everyone and everything.

Elise spied the cabin after she'd been riding for about three-quarters of an hour. It wasn't tucked back into the woods as she thought it might be. It sat only a few feet from the road. The simple planked-over log cabin looked like a relic from the past. There was no smoke coming from the chimney, and there was no gray speckled horse about. She pulled Dusty to a stop and sat for a moment, thinking. From her apron pocket beneath her cloak, she brought out her note. It read:

I don't agree with those who say you're a traitor. I'm sorry they say those things and sorry that you've been treated badly.

A friend,
Elise

Urging Dusty forward, she slowly rode closer to the cabin. A tin washtub hung from a nail on the side wall, and the scrub board hung beside it. A cast-off wagon wheel lay beside the rickety front stoop. It appeared that repairs of the stoop were in progress. Fresh-cut lumber lay in a neat stack.

The front dooryard was mostly mud created by the heavy spring rains. Near the back door was a pile of split logs and kindling. The ax was embedded in a hickory stump where the kindling could easily be split.

"Whoa, Dusty," Elise said softly. All of a sudden, her heart beat wildly. What if the man was here but hiding? What if he was angry and had a gun?

Then she laughed to herself. “Crazy imagination. The man I saw in Walker’s wasn’t an angry man but a hurt man.”

Between the house and the road was a sprawling hickory tree that had a couple rusty nails driven into the trunk. Possibly it had been put there to hang clothesline rope. With the note in her hand, Elise slid off Dusty and hit the ground. Keeping the reins tightly in her hand, she stepped up to the tree. She pressed the note over one of the nails, making a little tear that slipped over the nail head. Stepping back, she looked at it hanging there.

Satisfied, she remounted Dusty and rode home.

CHAPTER 6

A Spring Wedding

A week or so after Elise visited the cabin in the woods, the bells from churches and fire stations began ringing across the city. Silently, she prayed that it was good news. Papa and Samuel came home from town that evening with the news that General Grant had been named general-in-chief of the entire Union army by President Lincoln.

"It's about time," Papa said. He'd long been saying that the president needed to get rid of some of the generals who were only seeking their own glory on the battlefields. Many times Elise had heard Papa say, "We need a military leader who wants the war to be over—period."

This appointment seemed to please Papa very much. A few days later, a letter arrived from Uncle George and echoed Papa's sentiments. After the family finished their evening meal, Mama read the letter to them. Uncle George relayed how pleased the soldiers in and around Memphis were. The letter read:

To a man, we are cheering our new leader, General Grant. The men seem to have been infused with new hope at the announcement.

In February, our troops moved south to meet Sherman in Meridian in hopes of making a grand destructive swath through the South. But our troops met an angry Nathan Bedford Forrest, who had brought fresh troops from out west. That Rebel fights like a maniac. We were told even after Forrest's own younger brother died in the fighting, it didn't slow him for a moment.

Our men said they saw Forrest have two horses shot from beneath him, but he grabbed saber and sword and continued to battle on foot. Men will blindly follow a leader of that sort.

We all know that the South cannot hold out much longer. Their supplies and money are dwindling to a trickle. In spite of that, you have never seen such bold, daring, fearless fighters. They are all spunk and grit. It grieves me that their gallantry is all for naught. There's no way they can win. It's only a matter of time. And yet so many more lives must be lost in the process.

"I wish I could go fight," Peter said when the letter was finished.

"Peter," Elise told him, "don't say such things. You'll worry Mama half-sick."

Mama reached over and patted Elise's hand. "He just means he wants to help," she said.

Elise shook her head. "How could anyone *want* to go into those places of killing and dying?"

"Our teacher says it's a cause worth fighting for," Peter replied, puffing his chest out just a bit as he said it.

"Don't you want the slaves to be free, Elise?" This question came from Samuel, who had a serious look on his face.

"Of course I do. And they are now. So why can't the fighting be over?"

Papa said, "If we had that answer, we'd stop the war this minute. The truth is, those Rebels—whom we thought could be put down in a few days—have more fight in them than we ever gave them credit for."

Berdeen came in just then to refill Mama's and Papa's cups of tea and to gather the dirty plates.

"It's me own brother who sed the very same words to me when the bloomin' Rebels first fired on Sumter," she said. "He said 'twould be a long, long war. Ernan was a-knowing more'n all them high-faluting generals put together."

Unlike servants in other homes, Berdeen was free to speak her peace in the Brannon household. Papa never raised an eyebrow at her. She was like part of their family.

"Papa," Samuel spoke up, "may I tell what Secretary Chase said in his letter to you?"

"You may."

"Secretary Chase said too many of the Union officers under-estimated the South and therefore didn't start out fighting to win. If they had, the war would have been over by now."

"Hanging onto what might have been," Mama said quietly, "will never change today."

"No," Elise said, "but it sure ought to teach somebody not to let this happen again."

"I doubt it ever will, Elise," Papa said. "I doubt it ever will."

The time Elise and Verly had to spend on play writing lessened as warm, sunny April made its appearance. Mrs. Boyd's orders for sewing increased. She got some piecework contracts from one of the city clothiers that sewed uniforms for the Union soldiers. Even though Aunt Ella let Mrs. Boyd borrow the treadle sewing machine, there was a great deal to do. Verly, of course, had to help. She and Elise promised each other that they would work on the play only when they were together.

Now that the dogwoods were in bloom and the trees were greening, Elise was on Dusty as much as possible, taking long rides. Every once in a while, she would leave another note on the hickory tree at Mr. Finney's house. She included funny stick drawings and a riddle or two. Since she could not expect him to reply, she penned the answer to the riddle at the bottom of the page.

"What's the difference between a sewing machine and a kiss?" she wrote in her note. Then at the very bottom, she wrote in smaller script: "One sews seams nice, and the other seems so nice." The riddle made her smile. She could only hope it did the same for Mr. Finney and that her thoughts toward him were making his life a little easier.

On occasion when shopping with Berdeen, she would see Mr. Finney about town. She always looked at him and smiled, but he looked away and never acknowledged her. Seeing his sadness made her pray even harder for the war to be over soon.

Saturday, April 23—the day of Charles and Alison's wedding—dawned cloudy. However, by the time the Brannons were in the carriage on the way to the Harvey home, the clouds began to break up and the sun was peeping through.

Verly and Elise had talked about the wedding all week at school. They could hardly wait. It would be such fun to have a festive occasion. Elise was to be among the attendants, and Verly had been asked to serve refreshments.

Verly was at the front door when they arrived. Grabbing Elise's arm, she pulled her aside. "You'll never guess what. Mama has given me this entire day off. She said I've worked so hard, she promises we'll not pick up a piece of sewing until Monday morning."

"What good news! That'll make this day even more special for you." That thought gave Elise an idea. "Say! Why not ask your mama if you can come home with us and spend the night? We'll have time to finish the play!"

Verly's eyes brightened. "Let's ask right now. Mama's upstairs helping with Alison's dress."

Elise followed as Verly led through the crowded parlor to the stairs and up to the room where Alison was getting ready. As she went, Verly said, "I've helped a little bit with Alison's dress. It's lovely, Elise. She told me it belonged to her mother, who died when she was just a little girl. But Alison's mother was so tall that we had to alter the dress a great deal."

"I know she appreciates all your help."

"She does. She's thanked all of us. Your aunt Ella is more like a mother to her than a mother-in-law."

"That sounds like Aunt Ella. Full of love."

The two girls slipped into the crowded room. What a joy it was to see everyone smiling and laughing as they helped Alison adjust her gauzy veil. Verly caught her mother's attention and motioned her to the door.

"Hello, Elise," Mrs. Boyd said. "When did you arrive?"

"We just got here."

"Is the parlor full yet?"

"Full to overflowing," Elise assured her. "What fine work you did on Alison's dress. It fits her perfectly."

"Your aunt Ella did most of the work, and of course Verly helped, as well." Mrs. Boyd put her arm about Verly's shoulder. "Verly's my strong right hand. I don't know what I'd do without her help."

"Mama," Verly said, "since you've given me this day off, may I spend it at Elise's house? And stay the night, as well?" she added.

"Of course you may. That would make a nice time off for you."

The two girls looked at one another and smiled. What fun they'd have on this beautiful spring weekend.

Soon the music started, and it was time to line up and march down the stairway into the parlor. Verly and Mrs. Boyd went down to find a place to sit among the other guests.

As Elise walked carefully down the stairs with a bouquet of fresh-cut flowers in her hand, she felt older somehow as a member of the wedding party. It was an honor to have been asked by Alison and Charles.

After the ceremony and after refreshments had been served to the guests, Alison changed into a tailored blue-worsted traveling dress, and the couple left in Mr. Horstman's carriage.

The railroad executive, who'd become rather wealthy as a result of the war, had presented the couple with train tickets to Columbus, where they would stay the weekend until Charles would have to report back to work.

Elise and Verly stood on the front porch with the other guests waving good-bye to the happy couple. Wistfully, Verly said to Elise, "I wonder if I will ever see Alexander's wedding day."

"Have you received a letter yet?"

Verly shook her head. "Nothing. And it's so frightening. I've heard that many of our soldiers are captured and put in prison camps."

"Verly, you can't let yourself dwell on the worst."

"I know, but I can't help it."

Elise put her arm about her friend. "I wish I could help somehow."

Verly smiled—a weak smile, but a smile nonetheless. "You *have* helped me, Elise. Just by being my good friend."

Chapter 7

The Play

Elise and Verly worked on their play all Saturday evening. The play, which they'd titled, "A Pig in a Poke," was filled with funny lines. By Sunday afternoon, the playroom was littered with sheets of paper where they'd copied the pages over and over again.

They discussed whom they would ask to take which parts and when they might schedule the play. Looking at the calendar, Elise suddenly had a great idea. "My birthday!" she said.

"What about your birthday?"

"It's in May. May 21. I'll tell Mama I don't want a party. Instead, we'll invite people to come to our play."

"You'd rather give a play than have a birthday party?"

"I sure would! Come, Verly," Elise said as she headed out of the playroom, "let's tell Mama our plan. It's time for the secret to be told."

Mama was pleased with their plan. They explained how they wanted to present it outdoors on a Saturday evening and ask as many people as possible.

"Samuel can help set up boards on crates to make your benches," Mama suggested.

"And we'll use blankets on the clothesline for our curtains," Verly said.

"You should hear Verly talk like a backwoodsman," Elise told Mama. "She's going to teach our troupe how to do it. It'll keep everyone laughing." Elise could hardly believe how well her plan was developing.

Chancy came running to the house late one afternoon. "Mrs. Brannon, come quickly. It's time! Allegro is having her foal."

Mama and Elise hurried out to the stable. As they did, the church bells began to toll. As usual, Elise felt knots forming in her midsection. While the bells sounded out news, one never knew if it meant good news or bad. Mama paused for a moment and looked at Elise with concern in her eyes, then hurried on her way to the stable.

Though Mama had worked with many mares during foaling time, she could see right off that Samuel was needed. Even Chancy deferred to Samuel's special ways with a horse in dire need.

"You ride into town," Mama said to Chancy, "and tell Samuel to come home quickly. If Mr. Brannon can't get away from his work, put Samuel on behind you and bring him back."

"Yes'm," Chancy said. And he was gone.

Meanwhile, Mama and Elise continued to work with Allegro, walking her back and forth and talking to her, rubbing her down and keeping her calm.

Elise saw the look of relief in Mama's dark eyes when she heard the carriage driving up the lane. When they saw Samuel and Papa enter the dim stable, Elise knew immediately that something was wrong. Mama did, too.

"What is it?" she asked.

"Another horrible massacre in Virginia," Papa said. "A place called the Wilderness. We can talk about it later."

Samuel was there, and that made all the difference. None of them could have explained what he did differently with horses than any of the rest of them, but no one denied he had a special way with the animals. Papa helped, too, of course. When Allegro finally lay down in her stall, Samuel and Papa got right to work. The foal was coming out all wrong and had to be gently turned. Before midnight, the little colt had slipped out onto the clean hay. Though she was weary, Allegro began licking and cleaning the long-legged chestnut foal. Suddenly, he stood on wobbly legs, falling a couple times before making his way to where he could find nourishment.

Elise marveled at the miracle of a birth and what hope it gave, in spite of the news of all the tragic deaths from the war.

After supper, Papa told of the news from the Wilderness campaign, where more than eighteen thousand men had lost their lives. "They were fighting in a heavily wooded area," Papa explained. He had three different newspapers spread before him where he'd read the different accounts. "The artillery and cannons caused the woods to catch fire. Sounds of the wounded screaming as they burned to death filled the night air," he read.

Mama gasped as he told the details. Peter had tears running down his cheeks. Samuel chewed his lip. Elise could take no more. She couldn't stand the thought of wounded men being burned with no one to help them. She ran from the table out the back door, across the porch, and stopped in the yard, where she promptly lost her supper. Soon Mama was by her side, gathering her in her arms and wiping her face with a cool, damp cloth.

"I'm sorry," Elise whispered.

"Don't be sorry, my darling. It makes all of us sick!"

Later as they prayed together, Peter had the idea to name their new colt Chancellor, after the town of Chancellorsville, which was close to the Wilderness and had also been the site of a brutal battle exactly a year earlier. They all agreed with Peter's choice. Then they grew quiet as Papa prayed.

The next few weeks flew by as the girls chose their actors and actresses and assigned play parts. Verly seemed happier than Elise had ever seen her. Cast members were asked to memorize lines before the first rehearsal. Even Chancy was asked to take a part. In spite of his shyness, he agreed to play the part of an old peddler who plays a trick on the family.

The rehearsals were great fun. Verly patiently taught the back-woods characters to mispronounce all their words. Their attempts at mimicking the Squirrel Hunters' speech prompted plenty of laughter. At times they laughed so hard, they could barely practice the lines.

Elise's twin cousins, Alan and Alicia, played the erstwhile parents, while Peter and the Kilgour sisters played the mischievous children. Samuel would be the parson who drops in at the most inopportune times.

Mama helped not only by serving refreshments at rehearsals, but also by penning the invitations. At one point she asked Elise, "What will be the price of admission? Should they pay something to see the show?"

Elise thought a minute. "Two things. One will be something for use at the military hospital, and the second is a riddle. Everyone must bring a riddle!"

Mama chuckled. "Just as I thought you'd say." And she went back to her work.

Costumes were another fun part. Everyone rummaged through trunks of clothes in their attics to find old castoffs that would do.

The yard was level between the house and the stables and paddocks. From there the land went up into the wooded hills behind the stable and sloped down over a ridge on the far side of the house and yard. The spot made a perfect stage.

Berdeen created a curtain with hooks that clipped over the clothesline so it would slide easily. Elise assigned Berdeen the job of stagehand to open and close the curtain at the right moments.

On the morning of the performance, Elise hardly had time to think of her own birthday. There was too much to do. Mrs. Boyd and Verly walked up from the boardinghouse early in the day to lend a hand. Refreshments would be served afterward, so plenty of help was needed in the kitchen.

As the guests arrived that evening, Mama and Papa took the "tickets." By the time everyone had arrived, there were baskets of items for the convalescing soldiers—everything from combs to stationery. And there were enough riddles to last Elise for a very long time.

Elise kept watch as guests came into the yard and took their seats. She was looking for one certain person. She'd left a note for Mr. Finney, inviting him to come and see the play. The note told where she lived and what time to come. But as she stood before her audience to announce the opening of the first act, he'd not arrived.

Elise sat on the front row with a script in her lap, ready to prompt any actors who forgot their lines. But she wasn't needed. Not only did her troupe remember their lines, but they hammed it up more than they ever had during rehearsals. Laughter rang out through the warm night air and filled the clearing. Even Mr. Horstman—who was usually very solemn—burst out with loud guffaws. The sounds of laughter made Elise happy all the way down to her toes!

As Berdeen closed the curtain after the last act, the people gave a standing ovation. Elise could hardly believe it. Then Papa came to the front and put his arm around Elise and made her stand. Putting his hand up to silence the crowd, he first of all thanked everyone for coming and helping to make Elise's play a success. Then he said, "Many of you don't know that this is Elise's birthday. Rather than have a party, she wanted to present this play for all of you."

Elise felt her face burning as the crowd began clapping. Papa again put his hand up. As he did, Berdeen and Mama came out the back door carrying a cake with candles on it.

"Three cheers for Elise," Samuel called out.

"Hip, hip, hooray!" the crowd yelled. "Hip, hip, hooray! Hip, hip, hooray!" Then they burst into singing, "For she's a jolly good fellow."

Elise blew out her eleven candles, after which Mama and Berdeen set up the refreshment table on the back porch, where guests could file by and load up their plates. And Elise was allowed to be the first one through the line!

As Elise took her plate back to a bench to sit down, Papa's cousin, Ruby Brannon, came over and sat down beside her. Elise had always admired Ruby, who had worked tirelessly at the hospital ever since the war began. Papa and Aunt Ella often told the story of how Ruby had fallen deeply in love as a young girl, but when her betrothed died in California, she threw herself into helping others through nursing. Ruby was short with rather plain features, but somehow she was very beautiful.

"Elise," Ruby said softly, "what a noble and generous thing you've done here tonight. I can't remember the last time I laughed so much."

"Thank you, Cousin Ruby." Elise couldn't avoid blushing a little at the kind words from this fine lady. "That's what I wanted," she added. "To give everyone a bit of God's medicine—laughter."

Ruby smiled gently. "Would you consider gathering up your troupe and presenting *A Pig in a Poke* on the hospital grounds for the soldiers? I believe there are many brave men who would gain great benefit from 'God's medicine' as you call it."

At first, Elise wasn't sure what to say. She'd never been to the hospital. Although Mama volunteered there often, Elise could never bring herself to view so much suffering. She truly didn't know how Ruby had done it all these years. "I'm not sure I could do it, Ruby," she said, shaking her head. "I got sick when Papa read a report about the Wilderness Campaign."

"The first thing that happens when you're among them," Ruby assured her, "is that you completely forget yourself. They are all so courageous. But you don't have to answer now. You think about it, talk to the others, and then let me know." Ruby stood to her feet. "I'll go through that refreshment line now before the food's all gone."

Elise studied Ruby's straight back and proud head held high as she strode across the grass. Suddenly, Elise realized how much her cousin had sacrificed, not to mention what the soldiers themselves had given up. How could she have possibly hesitated? She jumped up. "Ruby! Ruby!" she called out, running toward her.

Ruby stopped and whirled around, causing Elise to nearly stumble into her. "I know right now, Ruby. I don't have to think about it. I *do* want to put on the play for the soldiers at the hospital." Elise took a breath. "And I thank you so kindly for the invitation."

"I'll get word to the doctors in charge," Ruby told her, "and let you know a date."

School was out, and the welcome month of June warmed the countryside, bringing carefree summer days. Allegro and Chancellor were free to roam in the pasture just down the hill from the stable. Elise never tired of watching the frisky colt kick up his heels, flick his little whip of a tail, and run about. His antics made her laugh. He was already used to Elise's presence. When she went into the pasture and called Allegro, Chancellor came along right beside her. Elise could already tell he was going to be a good horse.

Now that Peter was nine, he worked at the office with Papa several days a week. While Samuel was given more responsible clerking duties, Peter now swept floors and ran errands. Elise might have been lonely had it not been for the upcoming play presentation. What time she wasn't helping Berdeen about the house, she was revising sections of the play. The thought still plagued her that she might get sick right in the middle of everything! How mortified she'd be if that happened. It took time for Ruby to clear all the red tape with those in official positions at the hospital. Finally they received word from Ruby. They were scheduled for a Sunday afternoon late in June. Now Elise was more nervous than ever.

They rehearsed with much more seriousness now. All the players seemed to sense how important their mission would be. They were more ready to listen to Elise's directions as they went through their lines.

Cousin Alan, along with Papa and Samuel, went to the hospital grounds the day before the performance to rig up a rope for the curtains between two trees. They also arranged plank seats in rows across the grass. Ruby told Elise that some of the men would be too weak to be brought outside.

"We plan to bring out as many as possible. Others will be brought near the windows." Ruby smiled as she added, "Be sure to have your players speak loud enough to be heard up on the third floor."

That made Elise more nervous than ever. Chancy's voice was pretty soft. The night before the presentation, she could hardly sleep. She thought of the note she'd left for Mr. Finney. He hadn't come to the first presentation, but perhaps he would come to this one.

The afternoon of the performance, when the Brannons drove up to the hospital in their carriage, Elise saw nurses and volunteers scurrying about like little ants, bringing beds, cots, and wheelchairs out onto the sloping lawn. Elise felt her stomach tighten in a knot.

Mama reached over and patted Elise's arm. "You'll be fine," she said.

And she was. Later she could hardly believe it, but as soon as she stepped down from the carriage and saw her troupe, she quickly went into action. She brought everyone together beneath a shade tree in the far corner of the lot and checked to see if they all knew their entrances and exits.

By the time she was in place to announce the beginning of the play, she hardly noticed the bandages, crutches, canes, and scores of empty sleeves and trouser legs.

As before, she sat in the front row with the script in her lap and marveled at the performers before her. Even Chancy surprised her as he nearly shouted his lines in order to be heard by all.

Then Elise heard the laughter. The delicious sound of laughter reverberated all across the shady lawn. For a moment, it made the pain and grief of war seem far away. Far away, indeed.

Chapter 8

Milton Finney

As the summer progressed, all the talk around town was of the upcoming presidential election. At the thought of thousands and thousands of men who'd given their lives, some folks were crying out for peace at any price, which was, as Papa put it, "a ploy to get Lincoln out of office." A ploy that Papa felt would be the downfall of the entire nation.

In mid–June, another massacre occurred at Cold Harbor, Virginia. Thousands of Union soldiers were mowed down within minutes of when the fighting began. It seemed the dying would never end.

That summer, Elise spent many hours riding Dusty Smoke, far from the thoughts, sounds, and news of war. Some afternoons, she filled a canteen with water and rode to the wooded hills outside of town. There she soaked up the peace and quiet and prayed.

She often asked Mama and Papa how God could allow so much pain, suffering, and dying, but no one had any answers for her. When she heard war news, God seemed very far away. But in the quiet, shady woods, He seemed very close.

She didn't ride to Mr. Finney's cabin as much these days. She'd given up hope of ever getting an answer from him. One day while in town, she'd seen people pointing at him and openly calling him a traitor. It was a terrible scene. She didn't blame him for not trusting anyone.

One afternoon a couple weeks after the news of Cold Harbor, Elise was looking through the stacks of riddles she'd received on her birthday. She took up a nib pen and copied two riddles onto a sheet of stationery. The first one read: "What is the best thing to make in a hurry?" The answer was: "Haste."

The next one was one of her favorites: "What is the difference between a politician running for office and a dog going into a kennel?" This being an election year, she felt it very fitting, for the answer was: "One lies to get in; the other gets in to lie."

Below the riddles, she wrote:

I wish you could have seen the production of the play my friend and I wrote. Everyone loved it. I hope these riddles make you smile.

Your friend,
Elise

Putting the paper in her apron pocket, Elise set out to saddle Dusty and ride up to the cabin. It was a perfect summer day with just a little breeze and a few wispy clouds scooting across the blue sky. She tied on her straw bonnet as she rode Dusty down the lane to the road and turned north.

Weeds and grass grew high along both sides of the narrow road. They were coated with layers of gray dust. The orchestra of insect sounds and chorus of bird songs kept her company along the way. Through the trees she heard rustling, and in a clearing she saw a doe with her twin fawns. Elise paused to watch till they bolted and fled. She made several stops in the shade to uncork the canteen and take a drink of cool water; and at the point where a small stream converged with the road, she let Dusty drink, as well.

Elise reined Dusty in at the hickory tree near the cabin and slipped out of the saddle to the ground. As she reached up to the nail to hang her note on it, she heard a noise. Stopping, she stood very still and listened. Perhaps it was an animal. A hurt animal. She pushed the paper onto the nail then listened again. It was a groan. Looking toward the house, she paused. Should she go closer? Her heart thudded in her chest, making her throat tight and dry.

Dusty's ears twitched and flipped back and forth. "You hear it, too, don't you, girl?" Elise whispered. "What do you think? Should we go have a look?"

The reins still in her hand, she moved cautiously from the hickory tree to the front stoop. Now it came louder. It was a groan. And it came from inside the house.

She tied Dusty's reins and hurried across the bare dooryard and up onto the stoop. "Mr. Finney? Mr. Finney? Are you all right? It's me, Elise Brannon."

There was another low groan. She pressed her ear to the wooden door. She tried the door, but the latch was fastened. Frustrated, she jumped off the stoop and ran to the window. Peering in, she could see Mr. Finney lying on the floor. She couldn't be sure if he was hurt or ill. Pushing at the window, she found it stuck fast. How could he have windows closed in the heat of the summer?

She rapped on the window. Then she saw him raise a hand. Cupping her hands over her eyes, she peered in. He was pointing to the back. The back door. It must be open. She raced around to the back, where the door was standing open. The tall man was lying on the floor with his leg all twisted.

"Oh, Mr. Finney!"

He gave a forced smile through gritted teeth. "Caught under my horse. He fell. Think it's broken."

"You need water?"

He nodded and grimaced again.

Elise looked about the cabin. The water bucket sat on a stand by the cupboards with a dipper in it. Taking the granite dipper, she filled a tin cup and brought it to him. Gently, she tried to help him lift his head to drink. It wasn't easy. She wouldn't make much of a nurse.

"I'll ride into town and get a doctor," she said.

With effort, he took another sip. "Won't do any good," he said with little emotion. "No one will come."

How stupid of her. She'd almost forgotten who this was. "When did it happen?"

"Shortly before you got here. Out back in the woods."

"You came all that way on a broken leg?"

"Didn't have much choice." The tone of his voice and the resolute look in his eye told Elise he'd come to terms with the way things were—that he was powerless to change it.

"My brother can set your leg," she said suddenly. "I'll bring the bucket over here beside you, and then I'll ride to town to fetch him."

At her words, she saw a flicker of light come into Mr. Finney's hazel eyes. It was gone in a flash. "He may not come when you tell him who it is."

"My brother's not like that." She stood and lifted the heavy bucket down from its stand and half-carried, half-dragged it over to him. Then she went to the cot at the far side of the room and pulled off the quilt. It was a pretty quilt. Not at all the kind of quilt she thought he would have.

On the wall by the bed was a large portrait of a beautiful lady. She was standing by an ornate fireplace. The lady was smiling, and there were flowers in her hair, but Elise had no time to look at more.

As gently as she could, she lay the quilt over Mr. Finney's bad leg then brought a pillow for his head. At least she knew to do that much.

Then she went to the cupboard and found a tin of crackers and brought it to him. "I'll be back before you know it," she promised. As she stepped toward the back door, he said softly, "Miss Brannon?"

"Yes, sir?"

"I'm much obliged."

Elise knew better than to run Dusty in the hot weather, but she alternated cantering and walking as she hurried out of Walnut Hills and all the way into town to Papa's office. As she rode, she tried to figure out what she would tell Samuel. Or Papa. How would she get Samuel to come back with her?

When she reached downtown, Papa was in his office with a client. Samuel was sitting at a desk in the outer office, his head bent over the papers. Peter wasn't there—probably out running errands, she figured. Frank and Samuel both looked up at her with surprised expressions as she came in. She'd almost forgotten she had her day dress on. Mama would faint if she ever found out that Elise had come into town dressed so shabbily.

"Elise," Samuel said, jumping to his feet. "What're you doing here?"

"I need you. I mean, we need you. Could you come?"

"It isn't Chancellor, is it?"

"No, no. Chancellor's just fine."

"What then?"

She glanced at Frank. "It's sort of private."

"I'll tell Papa I'm leaving."

"Couldn't Frank do that? We need to hurry."

With that, Samuel laid down his pen and came out from behind his desk. Grabbing his hat, he said to Frank, "Tell Papa I'm needed at home. Be back as soon as I can."

Out at the street, Samuel swung up onto Dusty Smoke then gave his sister a hand up behind him. As they rode quickly down Third Street, he said, "All right, out with it. What's going on?"

"It's Mr. Finney. He's hurt."

"Where is he?"

"In his cabin."

"Elise Brannon, what were you doing at the cabin of Milton Finney?"

"I was just riding by. But that doesn't matter. His horse fell on him, and his leg is broken. I told him you could set it."

"Did you now? What makes you think I could do a thing like that?"

"I know you can."

Pulling Dusty's reins to turn her about, he said, "We'd do best to fetch a doctor."

"No, Samuel. That'll only waste precious time. He said no one will come, and he must know. You've seen how they treat him around town. He can't help what his son went and did, but he's still suffering terribly."

Pausing for just a moment, Samuel urged Dusty forward. "I hope you know what you're doing."

Elise wasn't all that sure Samuel could set a man's leg. After all, Mr. Finney was a big man. But they had to try. When they got there, Mr. Finney had passed out from the pain. He lay so still, Elise at first wondered if he was alive.

Samuel knelt down beside the man. Pointing to the water and crackers, he asked, "Did you think of that?"

She nodded.

"And the blanket and pillow?"

She nodded again.

He seemed pleased. From his pocket, he pulled out his knife and slit the leg of the trousers so he could look at the break. As he did, Mr. Finney roused, and his eyes fluttered open.

"Now I understand why women faint," he murmured. "Can't feel much then."

Elise was surprised at his ability to joke at a time like this.

"Got any boards I can use as splints?" Samuel asked.

"Out by the woodshed."

Samuel went out the back door, and Elise could hear him rummaging about.

"Samuel's good with animals," she offered. "He just seems to have a touch about him."

Mr. Finney managed a smile. "Good with animals? That's pretty much in keeping with what folks in these parts think of me."

"You're not an animal!" Elise protested.

Samuel returned with two long, flat boards in his hands. "I'll need you to hold onto something," he told Mr. Finney.

The man nodded. "Help me scoot to the doorway. I can grab hold of the door frame."

Together, Samuel and Elise moved Mr. Finney the short distance to the door, but he couldn't help much. It took all their strength to do it. Then as Mr. Finney held to the door frame, Samuel took hold of the foot of the broken leg and prepared to pull it straight to set it.

"I'll do this as quickly as I can," Samuel told him.

Mr. Finney's face was white. Just the movement to the door had drained him. "Do what needs to be done," he said calmly.

Elise had full confidence in her brother, but even she was surprised at how he yanked the leg with one quick, precise movement. Mr. Finney promptly passed out again.

"That's a blessing," Samuel told her. "Find a sheet, Elise, and rip it into strips so I can tie these splints in place."

In the corner at the foot of the bed was a small chest. She opened it to find sheets and blankets stored there. A set of elegant hand-embroidered pillow sacks lay on top. She touched them gently to move them out of the way. She felt guilty rummaging through Mr. Finney's things. The sheets on top were nice, but the ones at the bottom appeared to be more worn. She drew one out and tore the strips as Samuel had instructed her.

The splints were in place and the leg was straight and rigid before Mr. Finney roused again. Looking at the leg, he said, "What a fine doctor you'll make one day."

"I plan to study law."

"Like your father," Mr. Finney said.

"Yes, but I'll take it further than a law office. I'll be in politics."

"Rough game, politics," the man said. To which Elise agreed heartily. She never had thought Samuel would make a good politician.

"Think you can hoist yourself up on a chair now?" Samuel asked Mr. Finney.

"Bring one here, and we'll see."

Elise brought a cane-bottom chair over to Mr. Finney, and she held it steady while Samuel helped him pull himself up on it. It was a chore, but they did it.

"Now," Samuel instructed, "you can use the chair rather like a crutch, and we'll help you over to the cot. You'll need to lie down and rest for a while. The floor's not the best place."

"Didn't have much choice when I first came in," he replied.

His remark made Elise smile.

By the time Elise and Samuel were ready to leave, Mr. Finney was lying comfortably on his cot with food and water nearby.

"I'll bring you some soup tomorrow, Mr. Finney," Elise told him.

"This 'Mr. Finney' thing is about to wear on me, girl. Call me

Milt. I'm much more accustomed to that name."

Elise looked at Samuel, and he nodded. "All right, Milt. I'll see you tomorrow."

"Before you go," he asked, "you got any new riddles?"

Elise really liked this man. She thought a moment and then said, "What's the difference between one yard and two yards?"

"I give up. What is the difference between one yard and two yards?"

"A fence."

At that, the pained man chuckled. "That's the best one yet," she heard him say as they went outside and mounted Dusty to ride back home.

CHAPTER 9

Suffering the Consequences

On the way home, Samuel and Elise discussed how they were going to tell their parents about Milt Finney. Samuel seemed to think Mama and Papa would be fair-minded about the matter, but Elise wasn't so sure. Feelings about Southern sympathizers were so strong in the city, and she didn't want her parents to stop her from going to see Milt again. He would need food for the next few days until he could hobble about on his own.

Thankfully, Samuel was right. Papa wasn't home until late, but they explained to Mama what had happened, and she commended them on their compassion.

"What do you think Papa will say?" Elise asked her.

"I'll talk to him first," Mama promised. And she did. Elise was allowed to take food to Milt the next day.

She stayed only a few minutes because he was still very weak. His eyes lit up as she set her basket on the table and began to bring out the goodies that Berdeen had packed inside.

Soup, muffins, fruit, boiled eggs, and even butter and marmalade for the muffins appeared. Watching Elise from his cot, Milt said, "Pretty well worth a busted leg to receive a banquet like this."

Elise wanted to ask how he could be so cheerful when he'd been treated so cruelly, but she refrained. Broaching the subject might be too painful for him. She set a chair near his bed to act as a little table then put his food there. He was able to prop up on one elbow and do a pretty fair job of polishing off most of it, though he spilled a little of the soup.

"Your ma's a good cook," he said as he finished a muffin in two bites.

"Mama doesn't cook much. Berdeen O'Banion, our housekeeper, does most of it."

"Please pay my kindest respects to Miss O'Banion. And to your parents for allowing you to extend this kind generosity."

"I will. I'll tell them." The imposing portrait on the wall above the cot kept pulling her attention. She couldn't stop looking at the painting—and Milt noticed.

"My wife," he said. "Beautiful, wasn't she?"

"So much more than beautiful. Elegant is closer."

"Yes, so she was, bless her soul. An elegant Southern belle. It's only by God's mercy that she was able to go to be with Him and not have to see our nation ripped apart."

Elise nodded. She rinsed out his soup bowl and straightened things up a bit. Then she put the towels back into the basket. "I must go now, but I'll be back tomorrow."

"Have another riddle for me?"

"Why, of course. What's the nearest thing to a cat looking out a window?"

Milt smiled and thought a moment. "A cat looking out a window? I give up. What?"

"Why, the window, of course." She gave a little giggle, and Milt laughed outright.

"That's a good one. How do you come up with so many riddles?"

"At the play we put on in May, I asked everyone to bring a riddle. That was the price of admission."

"Oh yes. I remember. That was written on my invitation, as well. By the way, thank you very much for inviting me."

"I wish you could have come."

"Oh, but I did. Sort of."

"Sort of?"

"I came through the woods behind your stables. I came as close as I could and heard most of it. I had a very difficult time not laughing out loud, in which case most of your guests would have chased me halfway back up the hill."

Elise knew that Milt was right. "I'm sorry you had to hide, but I'm so pleased you came." She put her basket over her arm and left then. Milt Finney was a very nice man, she concluded on her way home.

Elise never knew for sure how Verly found out about Milt. Eventually, she planned to tell Verly herself. She thought it might take time for Verly to adjust to the idea, but she never expected the reaction that actually came. Verly was nothing short of furious.

Elise had ridden over to the boardinghouse one hot summer afternoon to see if Verly could play. The minute Elise rode up, she knew something was different. Verly was sitting out on the covered porch with a lapful of sewing, but the usually bright greeting Elise had come to expect from her friend was missing.

Though Verly glanced up and saw Elise approaching, she acted as though she hadn't. Elise dismounted, tied Dusty to the hitching post, and walked slowly up the stairs. "Good afternoon, Verly. Can you play?"

"Even if I could, I wouldn't play with you."

"Is something wrong?"

Verly looked up, and the hate in her eyes matched what Mr. Finney saw every time he rode into town. “You should know if something is wrong,” she snapped. “You traitor!”

“I’m not a traitor, Verly. You have no right—”

“I have every right in the world. The son of the man you’re helping may be shooting my brother right as we speak.”

“Verly, that’s crazy talk. Milton Finney has no control over his grown son. Many people left Cincinnati to fight for the South, and many Southerners came to live in Cincinnati after the war started to side with the North.”

“For all you know,” Verly continued as though Elise hadn’t said a word, “that man may be secreting information to his son and spying on important troop movements.”

“There haven’t been any important troop movements in our city since the siege in ’62. All the troops are out on the battlefields.”

“That doesn’t matter,” Verly retorted. “There are still things he could spy about.”

“Verly, I came to see if you can play for a while. I didn’t come to argue.”

“Perhaps if you had a father who was killed by a stinking Reb and a brother who was out fighting them, you might understand. But since you don’t, you can live in some fantasy world, pretending like nothing is happening.” Verly jabbed her needle in and out, in and out as she talked. “But I know there’s a war on. Just living here and having to work hard every day reminds me of the truth. And I wouldn’t be caught dead playing with someone who fraternizes with the enemy!”

It was a good thing Elise was holding the porch railing, or she might have tumbled down. Her knees felt like jelly. “If that’s the way you feel, I guess I’ll leave.”

“Please do, and be quick about it.”

Elise mounted Dusty, giving the horse a gentle pat on the side as she did so. Sadly, she rode home.

As the long summer wore on, Elise spent more and more time at Milt's cabin. He was hobbling around a bit better each day. He referred to her and Samuel as two "angels of mercy," saying God sent them to him at exactly the moment he'd prayed.

He showed Elise daguerreotypes of his wife and son when their family was together and happy. "I tried my best to talk Simon out of siding with his ma's people," Milt told her one day. "But young men are so bullheaded. He was determined he would defend her honor by fighting with the Rebels. I'm not all that sure he even knew why they were fighting." He shook his head. "Maybe many of the young boys who die on the battlefields aren't sure why they're there."

"He's a very handsome boy," Elise said, studying the picture. The boy's face had all the gentle features of his mother's—the long straight nose, the generous smiling mouth. It was no wonder he felt he must go to her birthplace and defend her honor.

"He was a good boy. We had two other children who died in childbirth. Simon was all I had after Beth died. After he left, I didn't think things could get any worse. Then word got out that he'd joined the Confederacy, and I found out they very well could get worse. Much worse."

In their visits, Elise learned that Mr. Finney had had a shoemaker's shop downtown before the war, with many connections to the South. He was soon put out of business by angry people who labeled him a traitor. They boycotted his shop.

"I still have all my tools out there in the shed." He waved toward the back. "So if you ever need your shoes repaired, just let me know. I'll be pleased to do it for you for free."

"I'll tell Mama and Papa. I'm sure we have a few shoes you could work on. Especially Peter's. Mama says he wears his shoes out faster than she can purchase new ones."

Since Milt wasn't able to get out, Elise began bringing him a newspaper on each visit. He was so grateful. Even though he had no idea where Simon was—or if his son was still alive—he wanted to know all the war news.

When he read the news that George McClellan was the Democratic candidate for the presidency against Lincoln, Milt just shook his head. "He was inept as a general. What makes them think he'd be any better as a president?"

"His wife, Mary, was a friend of my aunt Ella's. That is, before they moved back east."

"Oh," Milt said, "beg your pardon. I didn't mean to speak poorly of friends of your family."

"That's all right," she assured him. "My papa's said the same thing about McClellan many times. 'A good organizer,' he'd say, 'but a poor fighter.' "

"That's about the size of it," Milt replied.

One day when she brought the paper, they read together about Admiral Farragut winning the Battle of Mobile Bay for the Union.

"That's just what Lincoln needs right now," Milt said. "This victory will help him win the candidacy."

"Do you think Mr. Lincoln will be reelected?" Elise asked. So many people whom she'd heard talking about it were divided in their thinking.

But Milt quickly said, "Yes, I do. Even those who are opposed to him know he's the only one who can bring us through this mess we're in!"

As August drew to a close, Elise dreaded the start of school. During the summer, she saw Verly only on Sundays at church. Verly was careful never to look across the aisle at Elise. She kept her eyes straight ahead, her face expressionless. If that was how she acted once a week, Elise couldn't imagine what she might be like once school started. But she found out soon enough.

When school began in September, Verly quickly told the other children in sixth grade that Elise had befriended a traitor. Some of them had heard of Milton Finney, though Elise was sure they didn't really know him—not like she knew him. The children avoided her, and at recess, no one would play with her.

As she sat in the classroom, Elise remembered when Verly first came to Walnut Hills—how she'd befriended the new girl and introduced her to the other students. She remembered how they'd sat together the previous spring and worked nearly every day on the play. How quickly everything had changed. The anger she felt made her want to lash out at Verly and hurt her somehow.

When Elise came home from the first day of school, Berdeen took one look at her and demanded to know what was wrong. Peter and Samuel had walked to town to help Papa after school, so she'd walked home all by herself.

"It's Verly," Elise said. "She's told everyone that I'm a Southern sympathizer because Mr. Finney is my friend." Suddenly, tears spilled down her cheeks. Tears that had been building up all day.

"There, there, wee lassie." Berdeen came close and wrapped her arms about Elise and held her close. "Your little friend is only speaking out of her own heart full of pain and anger. She canna get at a real Rebel to be angry at for killing her papa, so she's lashing out at the nearest thing she can find."

"But I'm her friend," Elise said between sobs. "I helped her make friends when she first came, and we even wrote the play together."

Berdeen nodded. "It's true, and you know it's true. But she canna see it just now. More's the pity, too, I say." Berdeen dried Elise's tears on her apron. "We'll set ourselves to praying, that's what we'll do. That the good Lord will take the scales off her eyes, and she'll see truth once again."

"But what can I do, Berdeen? She's turned everyone against me. No one wants to play with me."

"You dinna worry your pretty head about that, lassie. The others won't follow her lead for long. They know you too well."

"I hope you're right," Elise said, pulling out her hankie and blowing her nose. "I couldn't stand this for very long."

"Ah, and think for a moment how it is for Mr. Finney—every day and every night. You're tasting just a wee bit of his daily fare."

Elise knew Berdeen was right. "I've never suffered as much as he has. And you know something else, Berdeen?"

"What, luv?"

"I'm very sorry Verly's lost her daddy, but no matter what she says or does, I'll never be sorry I'm Milt's friend."

"That's my girl," Berdeen said, giving her a loving pat. "Do what you know is right and accept the consequences."

But Elise soon learned accepting the consequences was easier to talk about than to live out.

Chapter 10

Dr. Harvey Comes Home

"Mama, I want to quit school," Elise announced one evening in October. She'd come home from another terrible day at school and was surprised to find Mama at home. She'd come home early from helping at the hospital, and it provided the perfect moment for Elise to air her griefs.

"Girls don't need schooling," she went on. "I want to stay home and help you and Berdeen. I can study at home just as well as at school. And even better."

Mama's pretty brows rose, and her dark eyes showed surprise. "Whatever makes you say such a thing? You love school."

Mama had been helping Berdeen in the kitchen, and Berdeen chose this moment to say, "Nay, madam, our lassie *used* to love school. Not anymore!"

Mama pulled Elise to a chair and asked her to sit down as she listened to the story of what Verly was doing at school. Mama shook her head. "I'm sorry you've had to endure this, my little pet. I'll talk to Papa. Perhaps we can arrange something."

Mama glanced over at Berdeen. "The agonies of war," she said to her sadly. "I see them every day etched on the faces of the wounded men and boys. But the tendrils of it reach even into a schoolroom—miles from a battlefield."

"Yes'm. It's the gospel truth, it is!"

Papa was no stranger to persecution. Before the war, he'd been an avid abolitionist, aiding runaway slaves and defending them in court. He knew exactly what it was like to have people say cruel, unjust things. But Papa told Elise the answer wasn't in running away from the problem.

He told her about his experiences in school when he debated against slavery and how one student in particular constantly attacked him and tried to get the other students to do the same thing. "Continue to attend school," Papa said. "Continue to maintain your dignity, and the thing will work itself out."

They were difficult words to swallow. The days stretching out before Elise seemed endless. There was nothing to look forward to. Though the open insults at school gradually stopped, still no one played with her at recess, and no one wanted her for a reading or spelling partner during class. Elise couldn't remember ever feeling so alone. The only bright spots in her life were the interesting visits she had with Milt Finney.

Good news arrived in October—reports of General Philip Sheridan destroying the Shenandoah Valley in Virginia, which in effect cut off the food supply for the Confederate army.

"An army travels on its stomach," Milt told Elise. "No matter how experienced your troops, if you don't have food for them, they're useless. It looks as though the South will have no food." He shook his head; his hazel eyes saddened. "How wretched that it should come to this."

Milt Finney had been right about the Union victories working in President Lincoln's favor. In November, the president was reelected in spite of all the predictions to the contrary. Bells pealed out the joyous news, and people rejoiced in the streets of Cincinnati. Papa called his family together in his library that evening—Berdeen included—and they read scripture and praised God for the miracle.

"Only Abraham Lincoln can bind up the wounds that have so scarred this nation," Papa said to them. "We must be diligent to pray for him every day."

Milt Finney, who was now back on his feet and feeling fit, echoed Papa's remarks. When Elise next visited him, Milt told her that President Lincoln was "a man of love and compassion but full of godly wisdom." Elise knew in her heart that was true.

Since Verly and her mother, Gladys, were such good friends with Aunt Ella and her family, Verly was present at any events that included relatives and guests. Elise found herself dreading the upcoming holidays.

Then one evening only two days before Thanksgiving, Alan drove Aunt Ella over in a buggy to read them a letter from Uncle George. As soon as Aunt Ella entered the house, everyone could see that something was dreadfully wrong. "I've heard from George," she said after she'd taken a seat in one of the parlor chairs. "He's been wounded and is on his way home."

Stunned silence filled the room. Even though Uncle George was behind the lines working in the medical tents, and even though he had a white cloth tied about his arm, he hadn't been safe. Elise could tell her aunt wasn't sure whether to be sad about the injury or glad that her husband was coming home. Aunt Ella read them the letter Uncle George had written, telling how it had happened:

The musket balls were whizzing past us continually, and cannon fire was all about us with deafening explosions. I had to shut my mind to their existence. At last one came that I couldn't ignore. The one that took me down.

Aunt Ella looked up from reading the letter. "He says so little about how badly he was wounded, I have no idea what to expect."

"Where is he now?" Mama asked gently.

"The letter was posted from Washington, D.C. He's at a hospital there. He said they will be putting him on a train when he's able." She gave a shrug. "But I've no idea when that will be."

The years of being without her husband were beginning to tell on Aunt Ella. Though she was still gracious and lovely, there was a hint of weariness in her eyes and voice.

"I plan to be at the telegraph office each day until we hear details of his arrival," Alan told them.

Looking at her tall, rugged cousin, Elise wondered if Uncle George would even recognize his son.

"Has Melissa heard from Jeremiah recently?" Mama asked.

Aunt Ella nodded. "The letters are shorter. One can tell from the tone that he has suffered much. I believe all the soldiers are weary to their very souls of so much fighting."

"It won't be much longer now," Papa put in. "There's no way the South can continue to hold out."

"I hope you're right," Aunt Ella said as she rose to leave. "As soon as we receive word of George's arrival, I'll send Alan to let you know."

A cloud hung over their Thanksgiving celebration. Everyone's mind was on Uncle George's return. They even talked of postponing their celebration until he came, but Aunt Ella didn't think that was best. "He may be spending several days in the hospital when he arrives," she told them. No one knew what to expect.

Thanksgiving dinner was held at the Brannon home. It was the first gathering that included Charles's wife, Alison, the newest member of their family. Her cheery presence was a blessing for everyone. Elise asked Mama for permission to sit beside Alison at the dinner table. She wanted to stay as far away from Verly as possible. Alison's bright laughter made the day more bearable.

Shortly before Christmas, Dr. George Harvey, chief medical officer in the Union army, returned to Cincinnati. He was a changed man. The first time Elise saw him, she didn't think she could stand it. He was pale and gaunt. His eyes had a strange, faraway look in them. He'd taken a musket ball in his chest, which narrowly missed his heart. He was fortunate to be alive.

He was so ill that he was taken directly from the train to the hospital. Aunt Ella spent nearly every hour at his side. After spending years nursing the sick and wounded at the hospital, now she was tending her own husband.

Each time Elise went with Mama to visit Uncle George, she took a scrap of paper with her on which she'd penned one of her riddles. When no one was looking, she'd slip it beneath his pillow.

One day as they were leaving, Aunt Ella walked with them down the hall a short way. To Mama, she said, "His body is home, Louisa, but his heart is back with his men. He's suffering with guilt for having left them behind. Sometimes when I'm talking with him, it's as though he's not heard a word I said. In the night hours, he's still talking to his aides and calling for help for the wounded."

Mama patted Aunt Ella and said, "It's only been a few days. These things take time. He'll soon be his old self again."

"I pray so, Louisa," Aunt Ella replied. "I pray so."

The day before Christmas, Uncle George was allowed to go home. Aunt Ella told the Brannons she felt they would have their own small Christmas celebration alone. Guests and noise might be too much for the sick man.

Mama and Papa understood. Elise was almost relieved. Even though she loved her cousins, spending Christmas at home meant she wouldn't have to be around Verly and her cold stare.

But things weren't boding well for Uncle George. Though he was thankful to be home with his family, Aunt Ella said he just sat and stared into space. When his family attempted to engage him in conversation, he'd talk for a short time and then forget what he'd been discussing. The twins and Melissa were heartbroken. Aunt Ella was beside herself.

When Elise told Milt about it, he said, "War does funny things to people, Elise. Sometimes it can affect the mind."

She was sitting with him at his kitchen table. As usual, he had several newspapers spread out. He'd been doing a good deal of hunting since cold weather set in, so his larder was full once again. Nevertheless, Elise liked to take him special foods like Berdeen's delicious bread pudding all drizzled with maple syrup.

"But how can a person's mind be fixed?" she asked. "They can operate on the body, but what can be done about the mind?"

Milt shook his head. "Only God knows. We can pray for him. Perhaps in time, being surrounded by his loving family will take care of everything."

"Everyone thought he would return and jump right back into his practice. . . ."

"And take up where he left off?" Milt finished her sentence for her.

"Something like that."

"But that is to deny the horrors he lived with nearly every day for over two years. One cannot easily erase that, Elise. He's no doubt lost count of all the arms and legs he's sawed off and the young boys who've died in his arms."

Elise shivered at the mention of the amputations that she knew took place daily on the battlefields.

"Sorry," he said quickly. "I didn't mean to be quite so graphic."

But she knew Milt was right. They'd been foolish to think everything would be as before. As she rode home that day, she thought about it a great deal. Because of this war that had split their nation, nothing would ever be the same again.

New Year's Eve was even more solemn than the year before. It was as though war was a way of life for the country. January and February were interminably long for Elise. She spent hours in the stables with the horses. She and Chancy worked with Chancellor in the riding arena, getting him accustomed to a light halter. Chancy kept telling her that Chancellor was going to be one of their best horses.

On March 4, President Lincoln was inaugurated for his second term of office. The speech he gave was incredibly short. "Very similar," Papa said, "to the length of his address to the people at Gettysburg."

"A man of his wisdom takes fewer words to make his point," Mama added.

They were sitting together in Papa's library a few days following the inauguration. Papa shared with them the accounts from the newspapers as well as thoughts from letters he received from Secretary Chase. It was Secretary Chase who had held the Bible on which Mr. Lincoln placed his hand to take the oath.

"Salmon says in his letter that upon taking the oath, Mr. Lincoln leaned down and kissed the Bible," Papa told them. "If we know nothing else of our beloved leader, we know he reveres God's Word."

"I wish we could have been there," Samuel said.

"What did Mr. Lincoln say?" Elise wanted to know. "Tell us about his speech."

"The first of the speech points directly to the atrocities of slavery and how it was localized in the South," Papa said. Then he quoted from the president's speech: "'These slaves constituted a peculiar and powerful interest. All knew that this interest was somehow the cause of war.'"

Papa looked at them then. "Mr. Lincoln acknowledges that slavery was the fault of both the North and the South. That we have all suffered for the horrible atrocities of that institution." Papa then read the closing remarks: "'With malice toward none, with charity for all, with firmness in the right as God gives us to see the right, let us strive on to finish the work we are in, to bind up the nation's wounds, to care for him who shall have borne the battle and for his widow and his orphan, to do all which may achieve and cherish a just and lasting peace among ourselves and with all nations.' "

They were all quiet. Then Berdeen said, "It's like the music of a bubbling little brook. Such gentle, kind, and loving words."

"Sounds to me like he wants to forgive the South, Papa," Samuel said. "Is that what you think?"

Papa nodded. "That's exactly what I think. And we're all the better for it. When the war is over—whenever that blessed day may come—you can be assured that President Lincoln's forgiving spirit will allow us to bind up the wounds just as he said."

On a warm day in March, Elise saddled Dusty and went for a long ride out in the country. How she'd missed her long rides through the cold, lonely months of winter. If she had her way, life would be eternally spring with never a cold day.

Outside the city stood rolling hills full of dense forests. For the most part, she remained on the main roads. There'd been rumors of bands of army deserters in the area. Deserters were desperate men, often hungry, sometimes sick and wounded. They traveled in bands to help one another. If they were caught, they could face imprisonment or a firing squad for desertion.

But on this day, Elise nearly ran smack into one such band of men. She'd ridden to a small lake that she enjoyed visiting. As she approached the lake, she heard voices, and her throat burned from the acrid smoke of a campfire. Leaving Dusty tied to a bramble bush, Elise crept forward carefully through the thick underbrush. Peeking through the brush, she saw a camp across the lake.

A group of deserters had pitched their small tents in the clearing, and their voices carried clearly across the still water. Elise wondered how they were finding food at this time of year. There was no grain in the fields and no fruit on the trees. They had to be very hungry. And very cold.

The next afternoon, when no one was about, Elise filled a towsack with apples and sweet potatoes from Berdeen's root cellar. She slung the bag over Dusty's back and returned to the lake up in the hills. She wasn't quite sure how to leave the food so the men could find it and yet not discover her. Finally, she came up with the idea of hanging the towsack from a limb. Any soldier worth his salt would see it hanging there through the gray leafless trees.

The next day at school as Elise watched Verly across the room, she wondered what Verly's reaction would be if she knew Elise gave aid to deserters. She might be even angrier than when she'd learned Elise befriended Milt. Elise kept hoping through the passing months that Verly would have a change of heart. Her face was always sad. It made Elise think of her favorite verse of scripture: "A merry heart doeth good like a medicine, but a broken spirit drieth the bones."

A few of the girls were beginning to talk to Elise once again, and a couple of them asked her to play skip rope at recess. No one was aware of her ongoing friendship with Milt Finney. She didn't tell, and no one asked. It was as though nearly everyone had forgotten about it. One day Elise heard another girl say, "It's no fun to be with Verly Boyd because she never laughs or smiles."

Elise remembered how much the two of them had laughed together as they wrote their play and practiced it. How she would love to hear her old friend laugh that way once again.

Chapter 11

Caught by Deserters

Elise wasn't foolish enough to go near the camp of deserters very often. After all, these men were not only desperate, they were soldiers who knew how to keep an eagle eye out. She figured they wouldn't stay long in the area anyway. From what she'd learned from Milt, deserters had to keep on the move for fear of being captured. What a terrible life that must be.

One Saturday she was able to take a loaf of bread and a round of cheese from the pantry. Berdeen was out cultivating her kitchen garden, preparing it for the first plantings. That gave Elise the opportunity to take a few things from the pantry and carrots and turnips from the root cellar, as well.

Again she slung the towsack on her horse and rode out of town to the area where the men were camped. She found herself hoping the camp would be deserted and the men gone, but it wasn't to be. She smelled the fires before she even approached the clearing. This time, she left Dusty farther back so she could quietly move through the brush and hang the sack on the tree.

Suddenly, a voice behind her said, "That's as fur as you'll go, missy."

She gasped and turned about to see a lanky, bearded man pointing a musket right at her. She could feel her heart pounding in her throat, and her mouth went all dry.

"I'll be hornswoggled. Wait'll Duffy hears this," he said. "It's a little bit of a girl what's brung us vittles." He held the musket tight and reached out his hand. "Give me the sack."

Elise slung it toward him, and he picked it up. He waved the musket then. "Head on out thataway. I need to see what Duffy wants me to do with you. He said someone was trying to trap us and that we needed to get goin'."

"My horse—"

"I saw that horse. Purty thing. We'll lead him around with us."

After winding about through the thick brush and trees, they approached the camp. Duffy, she soon learned, was Sergeant Duffield, who acted as leader of the motley group.

"Looka here, Duffy," the man called out. "Here's what brung us them apples. Just a little girl."

Duffy was a lean, leathery young man with the look of premature age in the hardened lines of his face. "I knowed you was a fool, Gettler!" he spat. "You ain't even thinking. Shoulda left her be and come on back here. We coulda got outta here quick like afore she brings anyone."

Elise glanced around at the men who came up to see this intruder in their camp. Several were wounded, and none looked well. Just then she heard a loud groan coming from one of the tents.

"How's Boyd?" asked Gettler.

Another man squatting at the fire shook his head. "Not good."

Elise could hardly believe her ears. *Boyd. They said the name Boyd.* Could Alexander Boyd be lying ill in that tent? Struggling not to act surprised, she knew she had to do something. But what?

"Sergeant Duffield, my uncle is an army doctor," she said, forcing her voice to be calm. "He came home just before Christmas."

"Don't try no trickery, missy," the sergeant said, his voice cold and gruff. "We don't need nobody, and you ain't sending nobody. We got nothing to lose. We'd just as soon shoot anyone what comes after us."

"I know that," she said, "but you know army doctors are neutral. They have to be. He would understand. . ." She didn't know how to finish the sentence. Uncle George had spent years helping soldier boys just like these.

The man at the fire stood up. His leg was wrapped in bandages, and he limped as he walked. "Seems like she's truthful, Duffy. I say we let her bring a doc out here."

"Me, too," Gettler echoed. "We all need a doc bad."

"I don't!" The sergeant spat out the words.

"But the boy does." Gettler waved toward the tent.

"Whatta the rest of you say?" the sergeant asked.

They all agreed—all except the sergeant—that Elise should be allowed to go and bring back her uncle. Now Elise faced yet another dilemma. How would she ever persuade Uncle George to come?

Gettler brought Dusty up and steadied the horse as he gave Elise a hand up. She was touched by his mannerliness and thanked him kindly.

"Them apples you brung was right tasty. We shore want to thank you."

"I was pleased to do it," she replied. "I'll be back with the doctor soon as I can."

"She'll be back with the law," Duffy said. "Mark my word. No one cares about deserters."

"I do," she said simply.

As Elise rode back to town, she wondered what to do next. She'd promised to bring a doctor, and she would do her very best to keep her word to the men. Over and over she wondered if the boy lying in that tent might be Mrs. Boyd's son and Verly's brother. But there might be scores of soldier boys by the name of Boyd. They hadn't said his first name. She could only wait and see. One thing at a time.

When Elise rode up to the Harvey boardinghouse, Verly was outside. Seeing Elise approaching, Verly quickly went inside.

Tying Dusty to the hitching post, Elise tripped up the porch steps and knocked. Aunt Ella came to the door.

"Why, Elise. Welcome." She glanced outside as though looking to see whom her niece had come with. It had been many months since Elise had come over to visit alone. "What brings you out today?"

"Excuse me, Aunt Ella. Might I see Uncle George? I mean, would you mind if I visited with him? Just me?"

Aunt Ella smiled. "Why, Elise, I'd be pleased for you to visit with the doctor. He's always adored you so. When he first came back, he kept showing me the little riddles you tucked under his pillow. That was one of the few times I saw him smile."

Elise hadn't known. No one had told her. For all she knew, the riddles had been lost or tossed away.

"I'm glad they helped," she said.

"The doctor is around back in his office. He goes in there most every day, but I'm afraid it's wearing on him. He just sits in there and stares into space."

"Thank you, Aunt Ella." She turned to go back down the porch stairs.

"Bless you, Elise," Aunt Ella called after her.

Around back, Elise knocked gently on the office door. Through the window on the door, she could see Uncle George sitting at his desk. A book was open before him. "Uncle George? It's me, Elise."

"Come in," came the faint reply. "It's open."

She opened the door and went inside. She had many memories of coming in this office as a little girl with a stomachache or earache or some such ailment, and she always left feeling better.

Uncle George looked up from the book in front of him and managed a slight smile. "Welcome, my dear. Did you bring me a new riddle?"

Elise paused a moment and thought.

The doctor leaned back in his chair, and now his eyes appeared to have a little gleam in them. "Come now. Could you ever be without a riddle?"

"I have one. Just give me a minute. Oh yes, I have it. What is it that Adam never saw, never possessed, yet left to each of his children?"

Uncle George looked past her, gazing out the window by the door. Elise didn't know if he was going away in his mind as Aunt Ella said he did so often or if he was really thinking. Suddenly, he answered. "You've got me, Elise. I give up."

"Parents. Adam had no parents."

There was a little hint of a chuckle. "Parents." He shook his head. "I should have thought of that. Parents. Of course." He looked at her. "And to what do I owe the pleasure of this little visit?"

"I've been wondering, now that you're home, will I come to you if I have a stomachache?"

"Are you planning to have a stomachache?"

"No. But what if?"

"Not just yet, Elise. I can't seem to get my mind back onto stomachaches just yet. In fact, I can't seem to get the boys out there off my mind at all." He gave a wave of his hand, which Elise knew indicated the battlefields he'd left behind. "I feel I've deserted them. It's as though I hear them calling to me."

"What if there were soldiers here who needed your help?"

Uncle George shook his head. "You mean the hospital. No, Elise. Your aunt Ella's talked to me about that almost daily. But they have plenty of good doctors at the hospital. They don't need me there."

"I'm not talking about the hospital. I know where there's a group of soldiers. Some are hurt, one's sick real bad, and they have no one!"

Uncle George leaned forward, looking at her with new intensity. "Where, Elise? Where are these men?"

"About a half hour out of town north. In the hills. Deserters. I told them I'd bring a doctor. Would you come?"

"Can the buggy get through up there?"

Elise shook her head. "Not all the way. The underbrush is pretty thick. Horseback would be better."

Uncle George stood to his feet. "I don't have my bag ready."

"You can get it ready." She felt excitement building inside her. "It won't take you long. I'll saddle Sierra for you."

"I'll go tell your aunt."

Elise rested her hand on her uncle's arm. "I wish you wouldn't. I promised to keep their presence a secret."

He nodded. "They're desperate, I know. I'll just tell her that I decided to go for a ride in the country."

"Good."

Within a few moments, they were riding out of town, side by side. Elise was sure Aunt Ella saw Uncle George's bag fastened behind him—but that would only tend to encourage her heart. And her aunt was far too wise to intrude with needless questions!

As they rode along, Uncle George thanked Elise for her many letters while he was away. "I looked forward to every one," he told her. "Your jokes and riddles and drawings became a bright spot to me."

"I'm pleased to know I helped just a little."

"More than a little. Why, the boys started asking me if I'd heard from my niece with the riddles. They were all waiting for new riddles to arrive."

Elise thought about that. It had never occurred to her that her uncle might share her riddles. She tried to picture the men coming to ask about the riddles and the smiles on their faces as they shared them around the campfires. She liked the scene her mind created.

As they turned off the road onto the smaller trail, Elise said, "Don't be surprised if we're met with a loaded musket."

"Be assured, it won't be the first time," he said. Then he told her about the time they'd set up the camp hospital in an abandoned house. Rebels came in, pointed their guns at him, and demanded he treat one of their men.

"What did you do?"

"I told them I would have treated him whether they held a gun to me or not. I removed a musket ball from his leg, and they left."

"You helped a Rebel soldier?"

Uncle George nodded. "It wasn't the first time nor the last."

Elise wondered what Verly would have to say about that. Thinking of Verly made her suddenly remember. "Uncle George, there's a soldier up at that camp by the name of Boyd. I heard them say his name, and they said he was real sick. It could be Mrs. Boyd's son, Alexander. They haven't heard from him for a long time."

Uncle George was quiet again. Elise wondered if she'd lost him. Perhaps this was too much for him to handle right now. Perhaps she'd been too hasty to call on him.

After a moment, he said, "It's a good chance it's him. When a family doesn't hear from a soldier for a long time, he's either dead or deserted. The first of which means the family will usually receive an official notification letter. Even the ones who are hurt the worst can dictate letters to the nurses and volunteers."

His words made a shiver run up Elise's back.

As they came down to the edge of the lake, Gettler popped up from a bush. "Stop right there. Are ye armed?"

"I'm Dr. George Harvey," Uncle George called out, "chief medical officer for the Fifty-Fourth Ohio Volunteers."

Gettler came forward. He dropped all caution, lowered his musket, and reached out to shake Uncle George's hand. "Glad to meet you, Doc. I'm Private James Gettler. Leastwise I was a private. I ain't sure what I am now. Foller me. I'll take you around to camp."

Duffy wasn't quite as trusting as Gettler, but even he seemed relieved to have help arrive. As Uncle George dismounted, Gettler introduced him to Sergeant Duffield. Then Uncle George said, "I understand a boy here is ill."

Duffy waved toward one of the tents. "He's just a kid."

"Most of them are," Uncle George said. He untied his bag from Sierra and ducked as he entered the tent.

Gettler came over to Elise. "Shore don't know how to thank ye, little missy. That bread and cheese was mighty tasty."

"I'm pleased to help," she answered.

Just then, Uncle George came out from the tent. "Elise," he said, "could you come here?"

Elise knew she had no stomach for sickbeds or sick people in them. She hoped he wasn't expecting her help. When she came to his side, he said, "This *is* Alexander Boyd, Elise. He's inconsolable. He knows he's going to die, and he's begging to see his mother and sister."

Chapter 12

Sad Reunion

The reality of her uncle's words hit Elise hard. She knew how desperately Mrs. Boyd had waited for word of her son during the past months. And now here he was, only a few miles away from her, dying. Hot tears burned Elise's eyes. "What can we do?"

"Come and talk to him for a moment. Then we'll see about talking reason to these men."

Everything inside Elise wanted to run away. She forced herself to follow her uncle inside the small tent. On a pallet on the ground lay a handsome young man. The dark hair lying across his forehead made his face seem even paler than it was.

Uncle George motioned her to go to the boy. "Hello, Alexander," she said, kneeling down beside him. "I'm Elise Brannon. I'm friends with your mother and sister. They live in my aunt's boardinghouse." She motioned to Uncle George. "In Uncle George's house, actually."

Alexander managed a smile. "You wrote the play," he said with effort.

"Yes. Verly and I wrote a funny play and put it on."

"She wrote me about it." He coughed a little then. "I didn't want Mama to know I was here. Didn't want her to know I ran scared, but now I don't care. I'm gonna die anyhow. But I'd sure like to see her and little Verly." He reached out his hand and took hold of Elise's arm. "Bring them here, will you? Please?"

The look in his eyes broke her heart. "I'll get them both here. I promise."

His hand dropped. "Thank you," he whispered. "Thank you." Then he said weakly, "Tell Mama I'm real sorry."

When they were back outside the tent, Uncle George said, "Thank you, Elise. The boy needs something to help him hang on until they get here."

"But the sergeant won't let us bring anyone. What'll we do?"

"Leave that to me."

Elise watched as Uncle George talked to the men. He almost seemed like his old self again. Using his gentle persuasion and promising to stay with them through the night, he convinced them to let Elise go back to town to fetch Mrs. Boyd and Verly.

Duffy at first was dead set against it, but the others countered him. "We can skedaddle right out of here, soon as the wimmenfolk are gone," Gettler said. "I feel bad enough beings I'm a deserter. But I'd feel a might sight worse iffen I didn't let that boy see his own mama when she's so close."

Elise was relieved when they finally agreed, but she was greatly disturbed that she should be the one to bear the awful news. She had been so sure it would be Uncle George who would tell the Boyds about Alexander.

As Elise mounted Dusty, Uncle George said to her, "Tell Mrs. Boyd to rent a buggy at the livery stable and come as quickly as possible."

"A buggy can get through iffen she comes in thataway." Gettler pointed out away from the lake in a westerly direction. "When I hear you comin', I'll go up to the road to direct you."

Elise nodded. "I'll hurry."

As Elise turned her horse to head out, Duffy spoke up. "Don't think about double-crossing us, little girl. Or you'll be mighty sorry."

"I have no plan to," she assured him.

All the way back into town, Elise rehearsed how she would tell Mrs. Boyd the news, but she could think of no easy way to tell her. When Elise approached the house, Verly was on the front porch with sewing in her lap. As soon as she saw Elise, Verly got up to disappear into the house.

"Verly," Elise called out, riding Dusty right up to the porch, "don't go."

"I don't care to stay in the presence of the likes of you," she snapped.

"Verly, go get your mama, quickly. It's an emergency!"

"Well," Verly huffed, "what if she doesn't want to talk to you?"

Elise let out a deep sigh. As calmly as she could, she said, "It's time to put down your anger, Verly. This has to do with Alexander."

Verly's blue eyes narrowed. "Are you playing a trick on me?"

"It's no trick. Please hurry."

Verly dropped her sewing in the chair and ran inside. Soon Mrs. Boyd came out the front door, ashen-faced. "What is it, Elise? What about Alexander?"

"Dr. Harvey is with him right now. He's with a band of deserters. . . ."

Mrs. Boyd grabbed the porch post to steady herself. "No!"

"You're lying!" Verly said. "Alexander wouldn't."

"Verly, hush," her mother said sharply.

"Alexander's gravely ill. Dr. Harvey says you're to rent a buggy and come quickly. Quickly," she repeated. "The fastest way is for you to ride behind me to the livery."

"I'll get my cloak and bag."

"I'm coming, too," Verly said.

"We can come back and get you," Elise said.

When Mrs. Boyd came back out, Aunt Ella followed. "Your uncle is helping a band of deserters?" she asked Elise.

"That's right, Aunt Ella. But please keep it quiet. They're frightened, desperate men."

"Bless you, Elise," Aunt Ella told her. "You seem to be helping a number of people these days."

Mrs. Boyd wasn't accustomed to riding, but Elise brought Dusty close to the porch. With Aunt Ella's assistance, Mrs. Boyd was able to mount behind Elise.

"Ella," said Mrs. Boyd, "could you have food ready when we come back for Verly?"

"Of course. Come on, Verly." Aunt Ella put her arm around Verly as they went back inside.

In less than an hour, Mrs. Boyd was driving a buggy out of town, following Elise's lead on Dusty. Verly had said not a word. Elise's heart ached for the girl. What a terrible blow this must be for her.

Gettler was standing at the road when they came to the turnoff. He waved his musket for them to stop. "Sorry lady, but I gotta search your buggy."

"We've nothing but food for your men," Mrs. Boyd told him.

His eyes lit up. "I shorely thank you, ma'am, but Duffy still says I gotta look around."

"Please, can't you search it when we get there?" Mrs. Boyd fought back tears, her voice desperate.

Gettler softened. "Guess you ain't planning to harm nothin'." He stepped up to the buggy. "Allow me to drive you around, ma'am. Be faster that way." Mrs. Boyd scooted over, and Gettler jumped up and took the reins.

"I'll meet you at the camp," Elise called out. She turned Dusty off the road onto the trail, hoping against hope that Alexander was still alive.

Duffy saw her coming and reached for his musket. "Where's Gettler?"

"He offered to drive the buggy for Mrs. Boyd. They're coming around by the road." She slid down to the ground. "Is Alexander. . . ?"

"Barely alive. The boy seems to be hanging on in desperation. Your uncle's with him."

Another soldier, barely a boy, came up to her. "We thank you for bringing the doc up here," he said shyly. "My leg's a whole bunch better now that he's fixed it."

Elise smiled at him. "Dr. Harvey needed you boys almost as much as you needed him."

"Now how can that be true?"

"It just is, that's all."

Duffy stiffened as the crunching of the buggy wheels sounded in the distance. "I hope that fool Gettler searched that buggy," he muttered under his breath.

"Did you want him to inventory the food Mrs. Boyd brought with her?" Elise asked him.

Several of the men snickered, and Duffy said no more.

The moment the buggy pulled up and stopped, Verly and her mother stepped down. "Where is he?" Mrs. Boyd asked. "Where's my boy?"

"He's here," Elise said, pointing out the tent where Alexander lay ill. "Uncle George's with him now."

As she said the words, Uncle George appeared at the entrance. "He's been asking for you," he said to Mrs. Boyd. Stepping out of the way, he motioned for the mother and sister to go inside. Then he came to Elise's side and put his arm about her shoulder. "You got them here just in time."

Elise turned and buried her face against Uncle George and wept. He patted her gently in an effort to comfort her. "It's all right," he said. "Even after seeing so many thousands die, I still never grow used to it."

The other soldiers stood about awkwardly, as though they weren't quite sure what they should be doing. "Boyd was a good boy," Gettler said. "He wasn't too keen on cutting out when we did, but we talked him into it. Then he fell sick along the way. I been feeling sorta bad about the whole mess."

Gettler couldn't have been more than twenty-five or so, but he seemed older than the rest. He was squatting near the fire, staring into it. "Two other boys with us died along the way. It's a rough way to travel—running scared."

Uncle George looked down at Elise. "What do you say we take a look at what's packed in that buggy?"

Elise dried her eyes on her handkerchief and nodded in agreement. They brought out two hams, which made the soldier boys sit up and take notice. A towsack was filled with sweet potatoes, apples, and turnips, and a basket held a side of bacon and a dozen or so eggs.

"Iffen we'd had this fare earlier," one of the men said, "ol' Boyd there mightn't have fell sick."

"Fer sure," echoed another.

Suddenly, from the tent came a deep, wailing sob, and Elise knew. Young Alexander Boyd was dead.

"They'll need you now," Uncle George said to her.

"Me? What can I do?"

"You go in there and hug them and cry with them. That's what's needed at this moment."

Everything inside of Elise fought against it. The grief was too heavy. Too much.

Again, Uncle George's arm was around her shoulder. "Jokes and humorous plays are blessings, Elise, but then the time comes when we weep with those who weep. Just as Jesus bore our griefs, we reach out and help others to bear their grief."

Elise couldn't see that she would be of any use. But she forced herself to obey Uncle George. She made that long walk from the buggy to the tent. Verly and her mother were kneeling beside Alexander's still form, leaning on one another and weeping. Elise went over and put her arms around them. Then she wept.

Chapter 13

Alexander's Funeral

Shadows stretched long fingers across the clearing, and a cool breeze swept off the lake. Elise felt weariness deep into her bones. It had been an incredibly long day. They were sitting around the fire. The men had fried slices of ham in a skillet and baked the sweet potatoes in the hot coals. They offered tin plates of food to their guests. Elise managed to eat a little, but neither Mrs. Boyd nor Verly had any appetite.

At first, Mrs. Boyd insisted that she remain by Alexander's side through the night, but Uncle George advised against it. "The air will grow quite cold tonight," he told her. "There's nothing you can do for Alexander here. You must go into town and make arrangements. Ask Alan to assist you in hiring a buckboard to transport the coffin. I'll stay here at camp to make sure his body is safe. I'm used to this."

Uncle George glanced around at the men. "I have an idea the soldiers will break camp and move on now."

Duffy nodded. "We got no choice," he said. "We'll leave at daybreak."

"Let me drive the buggy back for you," Elise offered. "I can tie Dusty on behind."

"Thank you, Elise." Mrs. Boyd reached out to clasp Elise's hand. "You've done so much. If it hadn't been for you, Verly and I would never have been able to say good-bye to Alexander." She began to weep again. Verly remained ashen-faced and still.

When the Boyds and Elise were settled in the buggy, Gettler came up to Elise. "Can you find your way out?"

Elise nodded. "I know the way."

"Yer a right perky little thing. Hope someday I'll have a young'un just like you."

The kind words made her smile. "Thank you, Gettler. I'll be praying for your safety. For all of you."

"I'm much obliged."

Dusk was gathering as Elise drove the buggy away from the lake and onto the main road. Uncle George had lit the lanterns on the buggy, and the pale golden light shone down the road ahead. Elise made no attempts at conversation for fear of saying something wrong. Mrs. Boyd had gotten control of herself, but Verly continued to sniff and make whimpering sounds into her handkerchief.

They hadn't gone far when suddenly a horse came out of the underbrush onto the road. Elise pulled back on the reins. Then with relief she recognized Milt.

"Elise Brannon," he said. "What're you doing out and about at this time of night?" He shaded his eyes against the lantern glare. "And other ladies with you? What's your papa thinking of? Doesn't he know there're bands of deserters in the area?"

"Oh, Milt, we just came from a camp of deserters. This is Mrs. Gladys Boyd and her daughter, Verly. Mrs. Boyd's son was with the band."

"My boy was ill," Mrs. Boyd said, "but because of Elise here, we were able to be with him before his homecoming." She dabbed at her eyes with her hankie. "You must be Milton Finney. I've heard

Elise speak of you."

"That I am." Milt rode up next to the buggy. "And please accept my deepest consolation on the death of your son, ma'am. I hope you know that just because he was with deserters doesn't mean he was a coward. Many men both old and young have walked away from the fighting by the hundreds, not so much due to fear, but due to a weariness of all the killing."

"Thank you for saying so," Mrs. Boyd replied. "Your kind words are a blessing at a moment like this."

"I'll ride along with you for a ways," he said. "At least until you get to the edge of town."

"Thanks, Milt," Elise said. "That would make all of us feel better."

"Excuse me, ma'am, if I might be so forward, but have you plans for your son's coffin?"

The words brought a little sob from Mrs. Boyd, and she turned her head away. Elise rubbed her fingers together in a sign of money so only Milt could see and shook her head. She and Uncle George had already discussed Mrs. Boyd's dire financial situation, wondering how they could help her purchase a coffin for her son without offending her pride.

Milt caught Elise's meaning instantly. "Sorry if I caused you anguish, ma'am, but I'm a right fair carpenter, and I have plenty of lumber. I'd like to offer my services if you would allow me. Your son will have as fine a coffin as can be purchased and at no cost to you."

Mrs. Boyd looked over at Milt, and Elise could see a glint of hope in her eyes. "I'm not accustomed to receiving gifts from strangers," she said, "but it does sound like an answer to prayer."

"I'm not a stranger at all, but a friend of a friend." He made a little wave to Elise.

"Yes, yes," Mrs. Boyd answered. "So you are."

"I'll work through the night and have it done by midday tomorrow."

When they reached the edge of town, Milt tipped his hat. "This is where I'll leave you." To Elise, he said, "By the way, those boys up there at the camp, have they heard of Mr. Lincoln's amnesty plan for deserters?"

"Amnesty plan?" Mrs. Boyd repeated. "There's amnesty for the deserters?"

"Yes, ma'am, there is."

Mrs. Boyd looked at Elise. "Did you know?"

Elise shook her head. "Even Uncle George didn't know."

"All they have to do is report to the nearest recruiting office, and they'll be offered work camps till the end of the war. They need have no fear of prison." Milt turned his horse to leave. "I'll go back and tell them. Then I'll get to work on that coffin. See you tomorrow."

"See you, Milt," Elise called out. "And thank you."

As they rode down Montgomery Road toward Walnut Hills, Mrs. Boyd said, "If only the men had known, Alexander might still be alive."

"You can't know that," Elise said. "Papa always says no use speculating on the past unless you aim to learn from it."

"That's true," Mrs. Boyd agreed. "I should be very thankful. How many thousands of mothers have lost sons in this war and were never able to say good-bye. And so many of them were unable to provide even a coffin for their boys' bodies."

Elise didn't know what to say, so she kept quiet and concentrated on driving the buggy.

"What a gentle and caring man Mr. Finney is," Mrs. Boyd reflected. "And so free of malice. I can't believe he's the man I've heard so many terrible things about."

Elise could have said, "I told you so." Instead she said, "Your description of him is so true." She carefully didn't look at Verly.

Aunt Ella had gotten word to Mama and Papa of Elise's whereabouts. When Elise finally got home, both parents were relieved to see her. Berdeen had hot potato soup on the stove, and Elise downed two bowls. The family was gathered in the kitchen, sitting at the table with her, firing questions in volleys.

"Weren't you scared being with those deserters?" Peter wanted to know. She assured him she was not.

"How did you convince Dr. Harvey to accompany you?" Mama asked.

"And how did he act?" Papa put in. "Was he clear-headed? Your aunt Ella's been so concerned about him."

So Elise told them the story from the beginning, in as much detail as her tired body and mind would allow. When she came to the part about the amnesty, Papa said, "Many people were upset when the president put that plan into action."

"It's so like our forgiving president," Mama added. "Think of the young men it will help."

"But," put in Samuel, "think of the men roaming around the countryside, not knowing. They stay away from towns so as not to be caught, so they aren't aware they've been forgiven."

Elise nodded as she remembered Duffy, Gettler, and the others. They were in such a sad condition—cold, weary, footsore, and hungry. They would be overjoyed at Milt's news.

When she told of how Milt met them along the way, Mama smiled. "Sooner or later that man will receive his reinstatement to society. He's been treated so cruelly, and yet he's maintained his dignity."

"Mama, Papa," Elise said, "may he go with us to Alexander's

funeral? I mean ride right in our carriage? It would show folks that we believe in him." Elise's papa was respected in the city, and his vote of confidence might make a difference in how people treated Milt.

"You invite him, Elise," Papa said. "If he accepts, I will be proud to have him ride with us."

Gladys Boyd had become well known in the community during the years since her husband had marched off to war. Her excellent seamstress skills had put her in touch with a wide variety of people. In addition, her friendship with Ella Harvey had widened her circle of friends. Therefore, her son's funeral was attended by a large group of people.

To her credit, Mrs. Boyd never tried to hide the fact that Alexander was a deserter. She held her head high and managed to conduct herself with dignity. Close by her side, Verly was having a difficult time. From where Elise sat in the church, she could tell Verly was hurt. Surely she must feel more alone than ever.

Milt had accepted Papa's invitation, and he was sitting in the pew with them, right between Samuel and Papa. Even Peter took a liking to the big man.

Papa made sure Alexander Boyd received full military honors, with a volunteer militia company standing at attention outside the church. Papa said, "The boy might have died not knowing he was forgiven, but we know and will act accordingly."

Mrs. Boyd was deeply grateful and voiced her thanks many times to Papa, Uncle George, and Milt for all their help.

Following the funeral, the drums rolled and fifes played as the coffin was borne on a horse-drawn cart to the graveyard. The mourners followed on foot.

Mrs. Boyd and Verly wept as the coffin was lowered into the

freshly dug grave. A bugle sounded taps, and the melancholy notes floated on the early spring air and reminded each of them of the thousands of others who had died because of the long war.

When the burial service was over, people broke up into tight little knots in the grassy area, talking softly among themselves. Elise felt someone touch her arm. It was a red-eyed Verly.

"Oh, Elise, I was such a fool—blind and full of bitterness. I'm so sorry for the way I acted toward you. I called you a traitor when all the time my own brother was a deserter. Can you ever find it in your heart to forgive me?"

Elise flung her arms about her friend. Through her tears, she said, "I forgave you long ago, Verly. Just like with Mr. Lincoln's amnesty, sometimes it takes awhile for the news to catch up."

"I'm grateful to see you two becoming friends once again," Mama said with a smile.

"Look there," Peter said, pointing. "Mr. Finney is making a friend, too—it's Mrs. Boyd."

Elise looked to where Peter pointed. Sure enough, the two were talking together in the shade of a towering oak tree. In spite of her black widow's garments and her saddened countenance, Verly's mother looked quite attractive.

"They make a handsome couple," Papa said.

Verly smiled. "Right handsome," she agreed. "Right handsome."

Chapter 14

Verly's New Family

The boardinghouse sign had been taken down the very day Dr. Harvey arrived back in the city. But the sign that read GEORGE HARVEY, MEDICAL DOCTOR was still stored in the back of the family carriage house. The week after Uncle George helped the deserters in their camp, Aunt Ella told Mama that he went to the carriage house himself and retrieved his business sign.

He scrubbed the old sign, touched up the paint, and hung it on the hinges in the wrought-iron frame out front. Aunt Ella also told Mama that he seemed more like himself with every passing day. The patients who'd known and loved him in the years before the war slowly but surely began to come by the office again to see their doctor.

Melissa at long last received word of her husband, Jeremiah Baird. He was recovering in a hospital near Washington, D.C. He'd lost a leg, his letter said, but he was all right otherwise. His letter was cheery as he wrote:

They'll be fitting me with a cork leg here in a few days. That means if I ever tumble into the Ohio River, I'll float to safety and perhaps even carry a few folks along with me.

Later in the letter, he added:

My dearest Melissa, just think of the money we'll save on shoes and stockings, seeing as how I'll only need half as many.

The family was overjoyed not only that Jeremiah was alive, but that his sense of humor was intact. The entire Harvey household was in an uproar as they prepared for Jeremiah's homecoming.

School was fun again now that Elise and Verly played together every recess. The mood of all the students seemed to have changed for the better. Everyone was certain the end of the war had to be very near. The war map that Mrs. Myers followed closely now showed Sherman's march across the Carolinas.

Elise studied the map and wondered how the South could hold out much longer. So much of their food and ammunition supplies had been cut off. How could they be so desperate to continue fighting? Why should any more lives be lost?

Just as Miss Earles had done in fifth grade, Mrs. Myers had created a list of soldiers—friends and relatives of the students in the sixth-grade classroom. Each morning the students prayed for their safety and well-being, and they prayed for the long war to be over.

One day when Elise was visiting Milt, he said he had a favor to ask of her. From a shelf, he took down a nice bowler hat. Bringing it to the table where she was sitting, he handed it to her and said, "Might I ask you to take this to the hatter's to be steamed and shaped? It's been sitting for a number of years now, and it's in pretty bad shape."

Elise looked at her friend. "Many people saw you at Alexander's funeral, Milt. No one was unkind to you then. I think you should go to the hatter's yourself and see what happens."

He smiled and sat down at the table opposite her. "I had an idea you might say that." Raking his fingers through his dark, thick hair, he said, "That'll take some doing."

"You've come this far. By the way, what's the need of a spiffy hat anyway? Are you going calling?" she teased.

Milt's face colored a bit and he smiled. "I've thought on it. And *that* will take even more courage!"

"But you can do it." She folded up the newspapers they'd been reading together. "It's probably time to unlock your shop again, as well. I mean, you'll need an income if you're thinking of courting."

"Elise Brannon, you are the most candid child I've ever had the pleasure to meet."

"Is that a compliment?"

"Very much a compliment."

"Well?"

"Well, what?"

"When are you going to unlock the shop? How about today? We could pack up your tools and carry them down there today. I can help you clean up and straighten things."

Milt didn't take her bait right away. "It's not as easy as that, I'm afraid. Things have changed. During the war, factories turned out shoes for the soldiers by the hundreds, Elise. I'm not sure there'll be any market for custom-made shoes anymore. Everything is being manufactured these days."

"But people will always need their factory-made shoes repaired. And there'll always be the few who prefer your custom-made shoes." She paused. "The truth is, you'll never know unless you try."

"Well," he said, grinning, "I can't just sit up here all alone in this cabin, can I?"

"You could—but I don't think you really want to."

Milton Finney slapped both hands on the table, making Elise jump. "No, I don't. I don't want to sit here anymore. Come on, Elise, let's load up those tools."

All Milt needed to know was whether his old customers would return to him. Elise solicited all their friends and neighbors to take their shoes to his shop. Soon his business was moving forward once again. Only then did he come calling at the Harvey home to see Gladys Boyd.

Verly was all smiles as she told Elise about it at recess the next day. "He wore a fine suit and a trim bowler hat," she said excitedly. "He came riding up looking like a real gentleman."

"He *is* a real gentleman," Elise put in.

"Then he knocked at the door, and when Mrs. Harvey answered, he told her he'd come calling for Mrs. Boyd and could he speak to her in the parlor."

"And did your mama come down?"

"She did, but you should have seen her flying about our room, worrying about her hair, pinching her cheeks to pink them up a little, then changing quickly into a fresh dress. I wanted to laugh right out loud. She acted as though she were Alicia's age."

"Perhaps she felt that way, as well." The bell was ringing for recess to be over, but Elise hurriedly asked, "So what happened next?"

"What do you think? He's asked for Mama's hand in marriage!"

"Oh, Verly." Elise hugged her friend, and they squealed with delight until Mrs. Myers hushed them.

As they lined up in straight rows with the other students to go in, Verly turned around to Elise and whispered, "I'm going to be in the wedding. Mama's asked that I stand up with her!"

The Harveys insisted the wedding be held in their parlor. It was a small affair, but there was no lack of excitement. The joy of the day was made doubly so by the presence of Lieutenant Jeremiah Baird. Just as with Uncle George, Jeremiah had aged through the years of relentless battles. But his face was wreathed in a smile, and Elise heard him say how thankful he was to be safely home once again. Melissa sat close by his side and held his arm as though she never wanted to release him again.

The date was April 8. Elise felt it was a perfect time for a wedding, being so close to Easter. What promise and hope it represented. She hadn't been this happy for a very long time.

Milt had rented a small cottage. Though he had told his bride that she needn't continue her hard work as a seamstress, she informed all her customers she'd still be available to them. Elise knew Mrs. Boyd would continue to work for a time until Milt could make his way with the shoe shop.

Verly was to stay with the Brannons for a few days so the newly wedded couple could have time alone. That suited Elise and Verly just fine. In fact, it turned out to be perfect.

The girls were just leaving church when a messenger came flying down the street on his horse. "The telegraph lines have been singing all morning," he yelled out to them. Then he whooped and shouted, "The war is over! The war is over!" Sure enough, Lee had surrendered to Grant at Appomattox Courthouse, Virginia.

Suddenly everyone was crying, laughing, shouting, hugging, and whooping about. No one could stand still. No one could contain the infectious hilarity. Grown men had tears streaming down their faces as they smiled and laughed. Bells began their joyous pealing all across the city.

"Come quickly," Papa said. "Let's go downtown!"

They piled quickly into the carriage and joined the throng on Fifth Street. Elise had never seen such a spontaneous gathering. From out of nowhere, the Volunteer Militia appeared in uniform with their fifes, drums, and bugles. Bands were assembled. Music filled the air. Elise and Verly laughed and laughed as they watched people actually dancing in the streets. At the landing, cannons were shot and explosions filled the air. Soon after, echoes came from similar firings across the Ohio River at Newport Barracks and Covington. Rifles were fired into the air, and the fire bells and church bells never stopped ringing. Hour after hour, the celebration raged on at a fevered pitch.

At intervals, another message would come over the telegraph and send the crowds into another round of cheering and shouting. One such message said that following President Lincoln's remarks made from the balcony of the White House, he called for the navy band to play a rousing chorus of "Dixie."

"We fairly captured it yesterday," the president was reported as saying, "and the attorney general gave me his legal opinion that it is now our property."

As soon as that message was read, the bands on the streets of Cincinnati began to play "Dixie." This brought on yet another frenzy of jubilant cheering. Sometimes a person would just stop and say, "It's over. It's truly over." Hearing the words aloud helped to make it more real.

Several ministers of local churches gathered together and mounted the courthouse stairs. Waving the crowd to silence, they each offered up prayers of thanksgiving to God. One pastor reminded the crowd that the next Thursday would mark the fourth anniversary of the attack on Fort Sumter.

There was no school on Monday. The school superintendent said none of the children would be able to concentrate anyway. That gave Elise and Verly a full day for playing in the spring sunshine. Everything seemed so perfect. Almost storybook perfect.

They played with Chancellor in the grassy pasture and picnicked in the orchard. They had a tea party and read books. But mostly they just talked.

"Because of you," Verly said, "I have a new papa. And now I'll never have to work hour after hour again as I did for the past few years. You're a wonderful friend, Elise."

"And we'll be friends forever," Elise promised. "Come what may."

"Come what may," Verly agreed.

The cottage where the new Finney family settled was close to town, but Verly would finish out the school year at Walnut Hills Elementary.

"Papa says," Verly told her, "that by next school year, we may be living in Walnut Hills. Then we'll be neighbors once again."

Elise was sure Milt would do just as he promised.

The next Saturday morning, Elise was invited to go to Verly's new home and visit. Now Verly had her own neat little room. They hadn't a bed for her yet, but Verly cared not a whit. "I would sleep on a pallet on the floor forever if it meant having our own home again and having my new papa. He's so kind and good, Elise. And I've never seen Mama so happy." After Elise had seen the inside of the cottage, Verly pulled at her hand. "Come and see the little yard in back. The oak tree is a perfect place for a picnic."

And it was. There was enough room for Milt's horse to graze on the grassy areas and a shed for the horse, as well. The girls spread a blanket beneath the giant oak. Just as Verly's mother was bringing out their lunch, the bells began to ring. Elise looked at Verly. They were stunned. What could it be?

Milt came out the back door. He looked troubled.

"What, Papa?" Verly said, her voice sounding strange. "What is it?"

"I'll go find out." He slipped a bridle on the gray speckled horse and started to mount him bareback. As he did, a messenger came by on horseback with the news no one could believe: "Lincoln was assassinated!" he cried. "The president is dead!"

Chapter 15

The Giant Has Fallen

Elise felt as though someone had punched her square in the stomach. She sunk to the blanket beside Verly, and both girls burst into tears. "No, no," Elise cried. "It can't be! It just can't be."

Milt put his arms about Verly's mother as she buried her face in his great chest. Her weeping made a muffled sound.

"Let's walk down to the newspaper," Milt suggested, his own eyes tear-filled. "We'll get the story firsthand."

They found a somber group standing outside the newspaper office. Messengers from the telegraph office were running back and forth. Periodically, they received little snatches of news. After a time, the editor of the paper came outside with a dispatch in his hand.

"This is what we have so far," he said loud enough for all to hear. "President Lincoln and his wife attended a play last evening—Friday—at Ford's Theater in Washington, D.C. A young actor named John Wilkes Booth, who knew both the play and the theater well, entered into a box near the president's and shot him at close range. The president was taken to a nearby house, where he died this morning, April 15, 1865, at 7:22."

Murmurs rippled through the crowd as the reality of the news slowly sunk into their minds. Elise looked at the weeping people around her. Could it have been only last Sunday that these same people had been shouting and cheering? This just couldn't be. She felt numb, as though she were not really there. As though she were floating about in the midst of this sobbing, forlorn crowd. After all the long years of fighting and death—how could it have come to this?

Another announcement came then from the editor. "Major Robert Anderson and his party entered Fort Sumter last evening and raised the Union colors."

Robert Anderson was the same man who'd been in command of the fort when it had been taken four years earlier. Had that news come last week or even a day ago, it would have resulted in cheers and clamorous noise. Now it seemed almost trivial.

Elise whispered to Milt, "I—I think I'd best go on home."

"Yes, Elise. You need to be with your family."

As she turned around, Papa was there. And Mama and her brothers—all with reddened eyes and grim faces. Like all the others, they'd come to hear more concrete news. Papa put his arms about Elise and held her close so she could release her own tears.

Later, he purchased several newspapers and gathered his family together and they drove home. As they went, they watched dark clouds begin to form. The sunshine vanished.

Papa looked up at the sky. "The light's gone out," he said softly. "*Our* light has gone out."

The city was in mourning, the state was in mourning, the entire nation was in mourning. No one in all the land was not touched by the grim news. People felt as if they had lost a close relative or a dear, dear friend. Every house in Walnut Hills was hung with black crepe. Even houses in the poorer districts by the landing had little strips of black cloth fastened to the doorposts.

Elise felt at times as though she could not breathe, as though a vise were clamping down on her heart and soul. Sometimes she found herself weeping and was unable to stop. Each day Papa read to them from the papers. Gradually, the details of the carefully planned, premeditated murder were revealed.

"At least now," Papa said one evening, "Mr. Lincoln's harshest critics have been silenced. Only good will be said of him."

"And," Mama added, "at least now the weary man can have rest."

A letter arrived for Papa from Secretary Salmon Chase. It was Chase who had administered the oath of office to Vice President Andrew Johnson on Saturday morning after President Lincoln died. His letter told of the weeping crowds standing about in the cold rain all day Saturday. He wrote:

> *On Pennsylvania Avenue in front of the Executive Mansion were hundreds of people standing weeping in the gray rain. My heart broke for the colored folks who wailed and moaned as though from the very depth of their souls. They had called him "Father Abraham," and they loved him so dearly. Many of them are now wondering what will become of them now that their dear "father" is gone.*

President Lincoln's funeral was held in Washington, D.C., on the Wednesday after Easter. The newspapers reported that the procession was three miles long, that businesses were closed, and that everyone in the nation's capital gathered to mourn their loss.

One evening Papa read about the route that would be taken by the train carrying the president's body back to his home state of Illinois for burial. Papa looked at his family and said, "I would like the five of us to take the train to Springfield. I've wished many times that we'd gone to President Lincoln's inauguration in March so you could have witnessed that historic occasion. I don't want you to miss this one."

"It says here," Mama said, pointing at the paper, "that the train will be coming right through Columbus. That would be so much closer than going all the way to Illinois."

Papa nodded. "I know, Louisa. But the final destination is his home in Springfield. We'll say good-bye to him there."

"What will become of our nation now, Papa?" Samuel asked. Both Samuel and Peter had been so quiet since the news came. Elise knew each of them had been weeping in private.

"God's hand is upon us, Samuel. The same God in whom our president trusted—that same God will bring us through this wretched ordeal, as well. We can only trust in Him."

It rained day after day. Verly said that God was weeping, and Elise agreed with her. Daily, the newspapers described in vivid detail the hundreds of thousands of mourners who stood in long lines in pouring rain to view the president's body. The body lay in state first in Washington, then at New York's City Hall. Some people waited as long as five and six hours to pay their respects to their fallen leader. The numbers were the greatest, the newspapers reported, at night, when common laborers got off work at the shops and factories.

The scene was repeated at every stop. Papa commented, "How they do heap honor on a man who claimed none."

By reading the newspapers, the Brannons followed the progress of the funeral train westward through New York, to New Jersey and Pennsylvania, and then on toward Ohio. The train was covered with flags, bunting, and black crepe draping. One reporter said, "The outpouring of grief is more intense the farther west we travel."

Since railroad officials were clearing other trains from the tracks so that the funeral train could progress without delay, Papa said the family would have to leave for Springfield before the funeral train arrived in Ohio.

The morning of April 29, the five Brannons, dressed in their Sunday finest, boarded the earliest train out of the Cincinnati, Dayton, & Hamilton railroad station. At any other time, Elise would have been overjoyed to be going on such a trip. Illinois was two whole states away from Ohio. And the family hadn't taken any rides on the train since before the war started. This trip, however, would not be a holiday. It was a sad farewell.

Chapter 16

To Springfield

Peter, who was sitting between Mama and Papa, leaned his sleeping head against Mama's shoulder. The rhythmic rocking of the train had lulled him to sleep. Samuel and Elise sat side by side across from them. The ride seemed very long and tedious. Elise's hoops kept creeping up, and the stays in her new corset bit into her sides. She felt mussed and wrinkled. There'd not been a break in the clouds for ever so long. Though it was only a drizzle now, the dense cloud cover caused dusk to come early.

Samuel had been so quiet, it barely seemed like he was beside her at all. Elise knew he was grieving, but she also thought something else was on his mind, as though he was wrestling deeply with some problem.

"Mama," Elise said, "may Samuel and I walk through the car and stand at the end for a time? A little breath of fresh air would be so delightful."

Mama looked at Papa. "Do you think it would be all right?"

Papa nodded. "I see no harm."

Samuel seemed a little reluctant to move, but she gave him a shake. "Come on, Samuel. Let's stretch for a few minutes."

He got up and allowed her to lead the way down the aisle. She opened the door, and they stepped out onto the railed landing, where the brisk breeze cooled her face. Here the clattering of wheels against the tracks was noisier than inside. Samuel took off his hat, took hold of the railing, and leaned his head out as though to take a drink of the air rushing by.

"You've been so quiet," Elise said. "It's not like you to be so quiet. Is something wrong?"

He turned around and looked at her. He was so much taller now. His eyes were much like Mama's, but they were troubled. "No one's been talking much. Or hadn't you noticed?"

"I've noticed that no one feels like talking. But there's something more going on with you. More than the grieving for Mr. Lincoln."

"You seem pretty sure of yourself."

"Tell me I'm wrong."

He turned around so she couldn't see his face. "I have something I need to tell Papa. I don't know how to tell him." The words whipped around him.

"It wouldn't have to do with your plans for law school, would it?" she asked.

He whirled back around. "Elise Brannon! What are you, some kind of mind reader?"

She smiled. "Who has to be a mind reader? Why don't you tell me what's going on in that head of yours."

"Papa's counting on me, Elise. He's been counting on me for a very long time. But now I'm going to have to disappoint him."

"How could you ever be a disappointment to Papa, Samuel?"

"I'm not going to law school. I'm going to medical school. I'm going into medicine."

"When did you finally realize the truth?"

He studied her. "Are trying to tell me you've known?"

She nodded. "Politics is so rough and tumble, and you're so sensitive. I've always known you had a special touch."

"I guess I've known it, too. Especially after setting Milt Finney's broken leg all by myself."

"Is that what helped you make up your mind?"

"That and talking with Uncle George. He's offered to mentor me."

Elise was surprised. "You mean you've talked with Uncle George but not with Papa?"

"I don't know how to tell him."

"Perhaps he's like me," Elise said.

"And how's that?"

"He's just sitting back, wondering when you are going to discover the truth."

"I don't think it'll be that easy."

"When we get to the hotel in Springfield, you take him aside and tell him you want to talk with him alone. Then just tell him. The sooner he knows, the more he can help you."

Samuel considered her words. "Very well." He brightened and stood up a little straighter. "Very well, I will. I'll just tell him right out."

"That's the way Papa would want it."

When their train made a short stop in Indianapolis late that night, the conductor spread the news that John Wilkes Booth was dead. Shot to death by his captors.

Papa shook his head. "I can't ever remember being glad of a man's death before. I believe this is about the closest I've ever come."

Mama gently patted his arm. "Don't fault yourself, Jack. No one can be expected to feel any differently," she said.

Elise wondered how a man could be so heartless and cruel as

to kill a kind and gentle man like President Lincoln. Life was so terribly unfair.

By the time they reached Springfield late the next day, Elise felt stiff and sore from sitting for so many long hours. A carriage at the station took them the short distance to the downtown hotel. Intermittent drizzle still dripped from the sodden skies.

Springfield was much smaller than Cincinnati, and Elise thought it not nearly as pretty. As at home, nearly every building was draped with black crepe. Evergreen arches had been created along the route where the funeral procession would pass. A large sign read WITH MALICE TOWARD NONE; WITH CHARITY FOR ALL, quoting from the president's inaugural speech. Elise saw men wearing black armbands. Everyone was quiet and subdued.

After they were settled in their hotel room, Papa took them to eat in the hotel dining room. The hotel was crowded with guests, and the dining room was full, as well. Yet the atmosphere was quiet, almost like church.

The young man who came out from the kitchen to take their order asked, "Come to see the president?"

"Yes, we did," Papa answered. "All the way from Cincinnati."

The boy seemed impressed. "Cincinnati, the Queen City of the West. Well, welcome to President Lincoln's home."

Peter said, "My papa is a lawyer like Salmon Chase was before he became secretary of the treasury. We saw the president before he became president."

Again the waiter seemed duly impressed, and Peter appeared proud to have had the opportunity to brag a little. "Want to read the evening news while you're waiting?" The waiter handed them a Springfield newspaper, and Papa thanked him. "You've probably already heard that they killed Booth."

Papa nodded. "We heard it last evening in Indianapolis."

"Good enough for him, I say. I guess he thought he was going to be a hero in the South. Thought he was doing them some sort of favor."

"The South needed President Lincoln desperately," Papa said. "He was the best friend they had in Washington."

"Mr. Lincoln was a forgiving man," Elise put in. "His plan was to forgive all those who started the war and those who fought against us."

The boy nodded. "Now we'll never know, will we? We'll never know how Mr. Lincoln would have put his plans for forgiveness into action. It's a crying shame, that's what it is. A crying shame." The boy turned and went back to the kitchen.

Papa read to them from the paper. It told about vast numbers of people who filed by the coffin in Ohio and Indiana and how hundreds had stood out in fields in the rural areas to see the train pass by. At night, the train passed hundreds of torches and blazing bonfires lit in tribute to President Lincoln. Men stood bareheaded in the cold rain to pay their respects.

"It says here," Papa told them, "that at journey's end, the coffin will have traveled seventeen hundred miles and will have been seen by more than seven million people."

"It's like nothing I've ever heard of before," Mama said, keeping her voice low. "The people loved him so."

Papa explained that the coffin bearing the president was in Chicago at that very moment and would arrive in Springfield the next morning. "Then it will be our turn to pay our respects," he told them.

That evening before they retired, Samuel asked Papa if he could speak to him alone. Papa said, "Of course, Samuel," just as Elise knew he would.

The two stepped out of the room, and Mama looked at Elise.

The voices sounded low and soft out in the hallway.

"What's that about?" Mama asked.

"I believe you'll know shortly." Elise stepped behind the strung-up curtain and changed out of her travel clothes into her soft flannel nightgown. How good it would feel to be in a bed instead of sleeping upright in the railroad car seat.

There was a small cot for Elise, and the boys were to sleep on the floor. She crawled between the bedding and fought to stay awake until Samuel and Papa came back into the room.

When she heard the knob turning, her drooping eyelids flickered open.

"Louisa," Papa said, "Samuel has an interesting bit of news to share with us."

"Oh?" Mama was brushing out her long, black hair, having unfastened her chignon.

"Can I know the news, too?" Peter asked.

"You sure can," Papa said. He sat down on the bed, pulled off his boots, and gave a sigh. "Go ahead, Samuel."

Samuel's face reddened a bit. "I'm not going to law school."

Mama gave a little gasp and almost dropped her hairbrush. "Not going to law school? But that's what you've always said you wanted. To work with your papa and then go into politics."

"I guess I wanted that because all along I thought Papa wanted it."

"But I wanted it for him because that's what I thought he wanted," Papa added. "Now isn't that a fine howdy-do?"

Mama gave a little laugh. "So pray tell us, Samuel. What are your plans?"

"Can't you guess, Mama?" Elise asked from her cot.

"I can," Peter said. "I know how well he took care of me when I hurt my ankle sledding."

"And how he set Mr. Finney's leg," Elise added.

"And how lovingly he's worked with every horse we've ever had," Papa said.

"I've always said he has that touch." Elise felt herself sinking into a gentle sleep. "Now we'll have two doctors in the family."

"I can't think of a better mentor for you than your uncle George," Papa said.

The last thing Elise remembered was seeing Mama and Papa with their arms about Samuel, telling him how proud they were of him and how happy they were for him. Then she fell asleep.

Chapter 17

Good-bye, Mr. Lincoln

"Will it ever stop raining?" Peter asked when he first awoke.

"Will God ever stop weeping?" Mama said.

As each member of the family rose, washed, and dressed, the rain slashed heavily against the windows. A quick breakfast was taken in the hotel restaurant, after which they walked together through the rain to the train station. The train was originally scheduled to arrive at six thirty, but the station manager told the waiting crowd that the funeral train had met with delays along the way and was running late.

As the Brannons waited, the crowd continued to swell until they felt pressed from all sides. But it wasn't a boisterous crowd. As in the restaurant, everyone spoke in hushed tones, almost in whispers.

Papa pulled five pennies from his pocket. "I'm going to lay these on the track," he told them. "When the wheel of the funeral train passes over them, it will flatten them. Each of us will have one as a treasure to keep through the years to remember this day. To remember this moment in history."

"Papa," Elise said, "would you please put a sixth penny on the track? Put one there for Verly, as well."

Papa smiled. "That's my Elise. Always thinking of others."

As she watched him place the coins carefully on the shiny wet iron rail, she thought about his remark. At times in the past, she'd felt Papa was too busy and that he never noticed her. But now she felt differently. He did notice her, and she knew he cared about her very deeply.

Her legs grew tired as they waited and waited. Finally, at around nine o'clock, they heard a long, low whistle as the train approached the station. Elise was so close, she could feel the steam rolling out from the sides of the engine as it chugged into the Springfield station. Bells throughout the city began to toll, and drums from a nearby band began to roll in a soft dirge.

A large portrait of the president framed by a wreath of evergreens was placed on the pilot beams of the locomotive. Smaller daguerreotypes were mounted between the high drivers. Evergreen boughs were strewn about the locomotive, along with yards and yards of draped black crepe. Crepe-trimmed Union flags fluttered from the front cowcatcher.

As the train steamed and hissed to a stop, Papa stepped forward and picked up the six pennies. He handed one to each of them. In Elise's palm, he placed two. She felt the warmth of the metal from having been flattened by the weight of the funeral train.

The funeral entourage got off the train, and the procession began. Men took off their hats, and everyone became silent. Solemnly, slowly, the crowd began to inch away from the station, moving down the street toward the state capitol building where Lincoln had served in the House of Representatives many years earlier.

Mama and Elise wore their rubber boots and stood under their parasols, but they were still getting wet from the steady gray rain. At the capitol, a podium had been erected. While the coffin was taken inside and readied, several officials and politicians spoke eloquently about their slain leader.

Between speeches, the bands played solemn hymns such as the "Doxology" and "Mine Eyes Have Seen the Glory." Tears burned in Elise's eyes as she listened to the sad, soft music.

When the speeches were over, the doors of the capitol were opened, and the crowds moved in that direction. By now it was nearly noon, and Elise's stomach was beginning to growl. Breakfast had been eaten many hours ago, but she didn't care. She was going to say good-bye to President Lincoln.

At long last they were inside, and she and Mama closed their parasols and shook the droplets out of their long, full skirts. It was even quieter inside than out. The only sounds were the rustle of hoop skirts and soft footfalls. Even a slight cough from someone in the crowd seemed noisy.

"You may speak a blessing," Mama whispered to her three children. "But remember, this vessel of clay is just an empty shell. Mr. Lincoln is rejoicing in heaven, set free from his heavy burdens."

The coffin was surrounded by mounds of flowers, evergreen wreaths, and drapes of white satin. Elise was near enough that she could actually see the coffin. The rows of people narrowed from the jumbled bunches into a single-file line. Peter was in front of her, Samuel behind her. Mama and Papa were behind Samuel.

As the line moved, Elise could see the thatch of dark hair and the beard for which Mr. Lincoln was so well known. A few more steps and she could see the rugged, angular face. His face held an expression of rest and total peace.

"Bless you, Mr. Lincoln," she heard Peter say, "for setting the captives free."

Now Elise stood right beside the coffin of President Lincoln. "Bless you, Mr. Lincoln," she said, "for extending forgiveness to the deserters and all those who started the war."

Behind her, Samuel whispered, "Blessings on you, Mr. Lincoln, for preserving our nation."

As Elise stepped down from the platform, she was weeping as she had the first day she received the news. Then Mama had her arms around her, holding her and comforting her and grieving along with her.

That afternoon, Secretary Chase came to the hotel where the Brannons were staying and visited with them. He stayed long enough to eat supper with them in the restaurant. He filled them in on many details of the final days of the war, as well as details of the assassination of the president. The next day, as Mr. Lincoln was buried in the Oak Ridge Cemetery, the Brannons stood near the front in the crowd of thousands, right next to Secretary Chase.

Hymns were sung, eulogies were given, sermons were preached, prayers were said. Rich green cedar boughs carpeted the stone floor of the vault. Flowers were placed in precise arrangements. Mourners carried flowers with them and heaped them on the coffin.

At last all the ceremony was finished. An era had ended. Abraham Lincoln was at rest.

Chapter 18

Friends Forever

As soon as Elise returned home, she saddled Dusty to ride to the Finney cottage and give Verly the special penny.

When Elise rode up, Verly came running out the front door to meet her. "Oh, Elise, I'm so glad to see you. Welcome home! I have wonderful news to tell you."

Elise jumped to the ground and tied Dusty to the hitching post. "After all the sadness of the past few weeks, good news would be most welcome," she said.

The May sunshine had finally broken through and was drying up the soggy countryside.

"The day after you left for Springfield, Papa received a letter. A special letter."

"From whom?"

"His son, Simon."

Elise looked at her friend. She remembered how intensely Verly hated anyone who fought for the South. "What did the letter say?" she asked.

"Since Papa didn't know if Simon was dead or alive, that was the first great news—he's alive, and he's well." Verly's pretty blue eyes were sparkling. "He wants to come home for a visit. Isn't that wonderful?"

"It is absolutely wonderful. Milt must be ecstatic."

"Oh, he is. We all are." Verly plopped down on the steps of the small front porch. Elise sat down beside her. "Just think," she said, "now I have a new older brother as well as a new papa. I have a whole new family! Isn't God good?"

"That He is, Verly. That He is." Elise had never seen her friend so joyful. Just then Elise remembered why she'd hurried over. Reaching into the pocket of her apron, she said, "I've brought you a little gift."

"A gift? For me? How kind of you."

"Hold out your hand."

Verly extended her palm. "This," Elise said, placing the flattened penny in her friend's hand, "is a coin that Papa laid on the track at Springfield. It was flattened by the funeral train of Mr. Abraham Lincoln."

Verly gazed reverently at the coin. "Thank you, Elise. Thank you for caring enough to share your special moment with me."

"Someday, when we are very old and we're surrounded by our grandchildren and our great-grandchildren, we'll have these coins as a memento of this moment in history."

Verly smiled. "And you know what? I bet we'll still be friends after all those years."

Elise laughed and put her arms about her friend to hug her. It felt wonderful to laugh once again. "Verly," she said, "I bet you're right!"

Janie's Freedom

Callie Smith Grant

A Note to Readers

Though Janie's story is fictional, her experience represents that of many African Americans following the Civil War.

In 1861, the United States of America were anything but united. Verbal battles between the states erupted into a bloody, all-out war. Fought on America's own soil, Northerner against Southerner, this "War Between the States" lasted from 1861 until 1865.

Many things were disputed in the war, but the most compelling issue was the existence of slavery in America. Much of young America was built by slave labor, and this was especially true in the Southern states. Early Southern plantations provided a wonderful life for wealthy whites, but this came from the unpaid labor of their black slaves who were either kidnapped from their homes in Africa and transported across the Atlantic Ocean or born into slavery to previous generations of captives.

Fortunately, many Americans believed that no one had the right to own other human beings. The Emancipation Proclamation was issued by President Abraham Lincoln in 1862 and went into effect on New Year's Day in 1863. This decree was to free Southern slaves, though it was largely ignored until the war was over. (Northern slaves were freed in 1865 by the Thirteenth Amendment.)

In the story that follows, you'll meet young Janie, a fictitious, freed Southern slave. It's two years after the end of the Civil War. Like many former slaves, Janie does not know where her family members are—they were separated and sold to different owners before the war began. And like many former slaves with their first taste of freedom, she finds a whole new world opening to her.

Contents

Chapter 1

Rubyhill

"Janie! Janie!" Aleta ran down the main path of the slave quarters. "Come quick! There's a carriage with horses! Something's happening!"

Eleven-year-old Janie stopped sweeping the dirt in front of the cabin she shared with old Aunty Mil. It was a lovely September morning at Rubyhill Plantation, and Janie had been making pretty patterns in the dirt with the broom. Inside the one-room cabin, Aunty Mil warmed herself by a fire. Janie propped the straw broom against the log wall of the cabin and trotted up the knoll toward seventeen-year-old Aleta.

Aleta was Janie's friend, even though they were not the same age. The older girl had taken Janie under her wing in the plantation kitchen when Janie first arrived at Rubyhill six years ago. Aleta acted like a big sister to Janie—even called her "little sis" sometimes—and that was fine. While Janie wore her hair in braids, Aleta covered her own hair with a bright scarf tied in back like a grown woman.

"Come on, Janie," Aleta said. "You got to see this." She grabbed Janie's hand and pulled her the rest of the way up the knoll, taking them both out of the quarters.

The two ran to the front of the Rubyhill Plantation's mansion, the place everyone called the Big House. There in the weedy horseshoe drive stood a fine carriage drawn by a handsome pair of matching gray horses. Janie had not seen such well-fed creatures in a long time, not since the war started and the master and his son rode off to fight in it. Even the Yankee soldiers who came through Georgia two years before had not ridden such fine horses.

She shifted her attention to the carriage itself. It was made of wood and shining leather. The wheels were straight, and their black paint showed through the red road dust. The driver, a white man, sat ramrod-straight, buggy whip in hand, eyes straight ahead. He looked uncomfortable, maybe from all the sudden attention he was receiving from the former slaves of Rubyhill. Janie noticed that he also looked quite well fed. She wondered where he was getting food.

Most of Rubyhill's twenty former slaves joined Janie and Aleta in the front yard, standing at a slight distance from the horse and carriage. It was some sight to see, these pretty horses and their stout, white driver sitting in the sun in the middle of the fire-scorched front yard. Janie and Aleta whispered to each other, but the others stayed silent and alert.

After nearly a quarter hour, the former slaves heard a noise behind them. Turning almost as one, they watched two men gently lead Miz Laura down what was left of the broken-down veranda stairs. Miz Laura was the mistress at Rubyhill, and she looked thin and old beyond her years. She wore a too-large, wrinkled black dress and a black straw hat that tied under her chin. Her shabbily gloved hands gripped the arms of the men flanking her as she slowly moved toward the carriage. *What's happening here?* Janie wondered, but she kept silent.

With some difficulty, Miz Laura climbed into the carriage, helped by the men who then swung up behind her. She placed a hand on the driver's shoulder. "Wait, please," she said in a soft voice. She turned in her seat to the crowd of freed slaves.

She took her time looking each person in the eyes, one by one. The strangeness of this hit them all; never had Miz Laura—nor any other white person—ever sought direct eye contact with the slaves. The group stood uncomfortably silent, but many, including Janie, returned her gaze.

The woman began to speak in a weary voice. "These men are my cousins from Pennsylvania. That is where I'm from." She paused and looked off in the distance for a moment. "It's become painfully clear that my husband and my son will not be returning to Rubyhill ever again. My family has sent for me, and as I'm certain you can understand, I've decided to return home with them." She paused again and sighed. "I want to thank you good people. You kept me from starving. I do not know how you did it. I even wonder why you did it. But I greatly appreciate it."

Miz Laura looked around her at the Big House, with its broken front pillars, collapsed roof, and blackened walls. She gazed at the stumps of the once-mighty oaks that had lined the long drive, the broken stone walls of the burned-out formal gardens, and the acres of overgrown fields, no longer blackened by the fire set by the Yankees but also no longer green with planting.

"I ask your forgiveness," she said suddenly. "I should have insisted my husband give you a better life while I could. I was wrong, and I regret it now, every moment of every day." She stared at her gloved hands for a moment then looked at the small crowd again. "Stay at Rubyhill as long as you like. Take whatever you can use from the house or from anywhere else on this land. My men won't be coming back. Neither will I. May God bless you all and keep you safe."

Miz Laura leaned back and placed one hand over her eyes. As one of the cousins draped a carriage blanket over Miz Laura's lap, Aleta called out a blessing to the white woman. The others murmured good-byes or remained silent as the driver flicked his buggy whip and the carriage rolled down the drive in a rosy cloud of Georgia dust.

The community of former slaves dispersed thoughtfully. Janie and Aleta waited until they could no longer see the carriage, then they walked quietly back to the slave quarters together. Finally Janie said, "What's it mean, Aleta? Miz Laura's never comin' back?"

"Looks like it," replied Aleta.

As they approached Janie's cabin, Aunty Mil's reedy voice came from the door. "What's going on, Janie-bird?"

Aleta waved to Janie and headed back to the yard. Janie waved back and ducked into the cabin. "Miz Laura's cousins come got her. They's goin' north."

"Mm-mm." This was Aunty Mil's response to many things in life. Arthritic and blind with age, she spent her days rocking in a broken chair, trying to keep her old body warm.

The rocker had come from the Big House. Janie had seen the Yankee general Sherman and his soldiers throw it through a glass window when they came through Rubyhill on their path of destruction. The chair had lost an arm and the tip of a runner in the process, but it still rocked. And it had a nice, thick, embroidered seat cushion.

Janie had watched it get rained on in the yard. Then it dried out. When a rainstorm approached again, she had asked the older slaves if she could take the chair to Aunty Mil. The elders had said yes. Janie had picked the glass out of the cushion; then she dragged the chair to the quarters all by herself. At the time, it had been almost bigger than she was. Aunty Mil liked the chair and now rarely left it.

"Wanna sit in the sun, Aunty Mil?"

"Yes, baby girl. Thank you so much."

Janie helped the old woman up, dragged the chair to the dirt path outside the cabin, and placed it square in the sun. Aunty Mil hobbled out and sank onto the now-worn cushion. Janie noticed the old woman's face was bathed in sweat.

"You all right, Aunty?"

"Yes. That fire in there kinda hot all of a sudden is all." Blindness had turned Aunty Mil's eyes light blue. Now she closed them and leaned back. "Ooh, that's a good breeze." She rocked a moment. "Now tell Aunty Mil all about what happened up there."

Janie told the old woman about the handsome carriage and matched gray horses and Miz Laura's speech. "Mm-mm," the old woman responded. "Change in the air." She was suddenly fast asleep. Janie noticed that was happening a lot lately.

Janie grabbed the broom and quickly finished sweeping the yard, swirling patterns in the dirt and thinking about what had just happened. Then she went about her daily task of finding food that Aunty Mil could eat without having to chew, since the old woman was missing many of her teeth. Janie had exhausted most of the plantation's possible stashing places, but she still managed to find some she hadn't remembered before.

And although she couldn't remember every place she had hidden food, Janie remembered the rest of the events of two years ago as if they had happened yesterday. That day was a milestone in her life, like the day her father was sold to the chain gang and the day a year later when little Janie was sold away from her mother and brought here to Rubyhill. The day General Sherman and his soldiers came to Rubyhill marked a line in the Georgia clay; there was life before the Yankees and life after the Yankees. And nothing nowadays was anything like it had been before.

Back then, a runner came panting into the slave quarters one day. He was from Bailey Meadows, a plantation several miles away, and he'd been sent to warn Miz Laura and the others that the Yankees were about thirty miles down the road and headed this way. The word was that they were stealing what they could and destroying anything else in their path.

Miz Laura already had her many valuable things buried in the fields and gardens in case the Yankees might come to Rubyhill. Now the slaves figured they had a couple days to take care of what really mattered, and they got to work.

First they slaughtered and cooked two pigs for the next couple days' food. Then they scattered the other pigs into the fields and woods. They found hiding places for hams and wheels of cheese.

Miz Laura had not given thought to the canned goods and other root-cellar items, but the slaves did. They sent the children to find places in the forest and fields to hide anything small and edible. For three days and two nights, Janie and the other child slaves carted glass jars of fruits, vegetables, and preserves out of the cellar and hid them in the nearby woods. They buried potatoes, carrots, and turnips in the dirt all over the fields. Whatever eggs the hens laid were boiled; after they cooled, the children covered the eggs in mud and tucked them into the slave-cabin fireplaces. Then they chased the hens into the woods.

It was late on the third day when the soldiers arrived. Indeed, they took any food they could find in the smokehouse and kitchen. They took the milking cows and whatever goats, sheep, pigs, and chickens had made their way back to the barnyards. There were no horses left at Rubyhill—they'd already been taken by Confederate soldiers for the war effort.

Now Sherman's men took anything they considered valuable from the house—big, thick rugs; paintings; even stacks of china dishes—and then they set fire to the house, the barns, the stables, the fields, and every tree they could torch, even the peach trees. The slaves were especially surprised by that part.

In the middle of the screaming and yelling, the Yankee general himself shouted the announcement that the slaves were free. "Every bit as free as I am," he emphasized. Then the troops moved east through the pungent black smoke, singing as they marched. They had not touched the slave quarters.

A few pigs and chickens wandered back during the next week or so. Some hams and cheeses had escaped detection, and potatoes buried in the burned fields tasted nicely roasted when they were dug up. The Yankees had avoided the plantation's beehives, so there was honey.

Soon enough, however, they ate all the hidden food that was easy to find. Except for a few chickens, the remaining livestock had to be killed for meat. The plantation's inhabitants lived off whatever forest edibles they could find and whatever fish and game they could rustle up, vegetables they could grow, eggs from the laying hens, and any food the children found from their many hiding places. It was plenty of work just keeping everyone fed.

Today, Janie thought she remembered where she had buried a jar of preserves, and she set out with a large spoon for digging. After digging in an area around a patch of rhubarb gone to seed, she did indeed find a glass jar of peach preserves. She cleaned it off with her apron then carefully cradled it to take back to Aunty Mil, eager to give her something sweet and soft.

On the way, she saw several of the former slaves gathered around the pump. Janie spied Aleta and headed for her side. Seventeen-year-old Blue, a well-liked young man, was saying to the others, "I believe it's time to go in the Big House and see if there's somethin' we can use."

An elder shook his head. “Miz Laura may think nobody comin’ back here, but sooner or later, somebody be back to claim this land, burned or not.”

After a long pause, Aleta spoke up. “Well, for now, I think Blue’s right. We ought to find what we can use around here. Miz Laura said we could—we all heard her. I say let’s go to the Big House.”

The Big House cook shook her head. “I want nothin’ to do with going in there. That house is haunted.”

Blue looked at her and laughed. “You been goin’ in there for years. Why you say it’s haunted now?”

“Miz Laura was there then. It don’t feel right going in there now. Too much misery.”

“Come on, Cookie,” said Aleta. “Miz Laura gave us her blessing. You heard her. Let’s you and me go in there together and see what we find. No need to fear an empty house. It’s just empty.” Aleta linked arms with the heavyset cook and pulled her along to the back door of the house. “Let’s go find us something good, Cookie.”

Janie hurried back to her cabin with the preserves and woke up Aunty Mil. “I found something soft for you, Aunty,” she said as she pried open the jar.

The old woman dipped a finger in and tasted the peachy sweetness. “Ooh, child, you done it now,” she cackled. “Tastes that good.”

“I’ll be right back, Aunty,” said Janie. “People going in the Big House like Miz Laura said we could. I’ll see if I can find something else for you to eat.” She handed a spoon to Aunty Mil.

“I thank you, Janie-bird.” Aunty Mil stopped dipping her finger into the preserves and began spooning little bites, savoring the syrupy fruit. “I thank you for many things, baby girl.”

Janie laughed and trotted through the quarters again. A slight girl but with strong legs and arms, Janie was always running or dancing about, and she was known as a good worker. She remembered a time when they weren't always trying to find food, but it seemed like that's all they did now. And Janie was always hungry.

Maybe there would be some surprises in the Big House. Maybe there was even food still hidden somewhere in there.

Janie hurried up to the Big House.

Chapter 2

Inside the Big House

Janie, Aleta, and Blue stood inside what was left of the main entrance hall of Rubyhill's Big House and looked up the charred spiral staircase to the hole in the roof. They had entered with the cook through the side door, and now the three young people stood in this front hallway. Miz Laura had called it the foyer.

It felt strange to Janie to be inside the Big House. In the past two years, Miz Laura had not moved much of anything since the day the Yankees destroyed so much of it. She'd ordered the others to leave things as they were for some unexplained reason. It was a mess.

"Dunno how that woman stayed in her right mind living like this," muttered Aleta.

"Seems she lost her right mind," offered Blue.

Aleta shrugged. "Sounded right in her mind to me when she left. Sounded sad is all."

Janie gazed around the foyer, which was a big room in itself. She vividly remembered the parties here before the war and how she'd peek in from the dining room. It was something to see, all those ladies in their great big hoopskirts, milling about, holding on to the arms of tall, well-dressed gentlemen. They had all fit in here just fine with plenty of room to spare.

Now this once grand entrance area was dark and dingy. The door to the front veranda was tied shut with baling twine. Scattered around the room were broken urns and glass from window panes and once-beloved possessions, sagging drapes, slashed paintings of previous Rubyhill inhabitants, and general filth. It plainly showed the two years of neglect that had followed the fire.

"Maybe we can use them drapes," Aleta remarked. She was a good seamstress. "I could make blankets out of 'em."

Janie hesitantly slid open the pocket doors to the parlor. Since the upstairs fire, this was where Miz Laura had been living, and she hadn't left the room much at all. One of the former slaves had continued to help her, cooking and doing her laundry. This was done for her strictly out of kindness, since slavery was over.

At any rate, it appeared that Miz Laura had been sleeping in this room on a once-fine couch, its velvet ripped open by a Yankee's sword. She'd left her blankets and bedclothes strewn around. Janie tiptoed over to them. She shook them out and set them aside to be used by the community of former slaves.

"I'm going upstairs," she heard Blue announce from the foyer.

"You crazy?" Aleta fussed. "Half the stairs is burned out."

Blue laughed. Janie hurried to the hallway and watched as he headed up to the charred area. Always nimble on his feet, Blue climbed and pulled himself from solid point to solid point and got to the upstairs balcony. Janie thought he looked like a cat climbing a tree.

Blue disappeared into the first bedroom. "Soldiers took this room apart, that's for sure!" he yelled from inside.

"Hey, Blue!" Aleta called up. "See if they went into the middle rooms where the clothes were! No windows on those, so it's gonna be dark in there!"

After a few moments, Blue showed up at the banister. "Nobody touched those rooms, Aleta. Must'a been too busy ripping apart everything else, but those rooms—the doors ain't even open. Most of the rooms burned through the roof, though."

"I want to go up there," said Janie.

"No, little sis," said Aleta. "Too dangerous."

Blue laughed. "For her? She's surefooted as a goat, and she don't weigh enough to make anything collapse. Come on up, girl. Follow what I tell you."

Janie listened to Blue and took every step and handhold he instructed her to take until she had made her way up to the second floor. "Wanna come up?" she called down to Aleta.

The older girl shook her head. "I'll go through what's down here. Let me know what you find."

Janie had never been upstairs in all her time at Rubyhill. She'd never climbed the circular staircase when it was intact. The kitchen was detached from the house, as were most plantation kitchens, partly because of the intense southern heat and partly as a safety precaution in case a cooking fire surged out of control. Because Janie was a kitchen worker, the only indoor rooms she'd been in were the pantry and the dining room.

The five upstairs bedrooms had doors off a U-shaped balcony that looked over the foyer downstairs. All the bedrooms had extensive damage from smashing, slashing, and fire, as well as from rain, since most of the roof had burned out.

Just as Aleta said, some of the bedrooms were connected by dressing rooms that ran between them. The soldiers had entered bedrooms by way of the hallway doors and, in their haste, hadn't disturbed the dressing rooms.

Blue and Janie discovered that the dressing room in what had been Miz Laura's bedroom was untouched by the fire. There was a smoky smell, but flames had not reached that small part of the roof. It was dark in there, but even in the dim light, they could see some clothes and wardrobe drawers.

Blue left Janie in Miz Laura's bedroom and ran to find candles. Janie sank down on her haunches and looked around, then up at the gaping hole in the roof. She could see straight up at the sky through the burned-out part. So blue, and not a cloud in it. *Hard to believe anything bad happened here when you look up high,* she thought. A family of goldfinches had built nests in the charred boards, and the birds were noisy and upset over Janie's intrusion. She spoke gently to the largest bird. "Don't worry, little momma, we won't be here long."

Momma. Janie had a quick vision of her mother back at Shannon Oaks, smiling at her in the rosy light of the cabin fire. She had strong memories of Momma stroking her head and singing songs about Jesus to her. Before Poppa was taken away on the chain gang, Momma used to laugh a lot. But nobody knew where Poppa had been taken. There wasn't much laughter after that day.

Janie'd last seen Momma at Shannon Oaks Plantation, the very place where Janie had been born on Christmas Day eleven years ago. Few slaves knew their birthdays. But since Christmas Day was the one day every year slaves did not have to work, it was easy to remember that day was Janie's birthday.

She sometimes wondered about going to find Momma, but Janie had never been away from Rubyhill since the day she was brought here six years ago as a small child. She had no idea how to get to Shannon Oaks. She wasn't even sure how far away it was.

Of course, Janie knew north from south and east from west like every other country child. But she really didn't have a clear idea as to where she lived in relation to the rest of the world. Rubyhill itself was her world.

The most disturbing thing, though, was that there was no telling where Momma might be now. Poppa was sold south the year before little Janie was sold to Rubyhill, and since then, Momma could have been sold, too. Besides, if Momma were still around, wouldn't she come find Janie?

This was the question that often nudged its way into Janie's young heart. It was a question that had left her hopeful after the soldiers told them they were free. But as time went on, she found that question made her heart ache. She didn't think she could go searching for Momma, but she sure wished Momma would search for her. If she could.

Blue crashed his way back into the room, holding a big torch and a couple of squat candles.

"How you get up them stairs with that fire?" Janie asked.

"Wasn't easy, girl, but here I am." He squatted down and handed Janie the candles. After lighting both candles, he walked to a smashed-out window and called down to the yard. "Ready, Nathan, Lucy?" Ten-year-old Nathan and his twin sister, Lucy, were good friends of Janie. They stood below the window, a waterlogged blanket stretched between them. Blue tossed the lighted torch out the window, watched as Nathan and Lucy caught and doused the torch with the blanket, and then turned back to Janie.

Blue took one lighted candle from her and approached the dressing room. "Come on, girl. Let's see what we got in here."

Shannon Oaks Plantation, Georgia

Forty miles away at Shannon Oaks Plantation, a former slave named Anna picked her final ear of corn for the day. She and the others dumped each of their heavy canvas bags full of corn into piles at the end of each row. There would be plenty to eat for a while.

The former slaves of Shannon Oaks were undoubtedly eating

better than many other Georgians. Food wasn't necessarily plentiful, but at least Shannon Oaks had not been in the direct path of Sherman and his men. Not all had been lost that day in Georgia.

And Anna had seen plenty of loss over the past few years. Her young husband had been chained up and taken from her before the war. One year later, her brown-eyed little girl was sold and taken away. Anna had been beside herself with grief.

But she held on. Every day Anna hoped and prayed the three of them would be together again. She didn't know where they were. George could be anywhere south of Shannon Oaks. Maybe Mississippi, she'd heard. And little Janie—really named Georgeanna after both her parents—was last known to be at a plantation called Rubyhill.

Anna sometimes thought about striking out for that place called Rubyhill. Only one thing held her back.

The day George was chained onto the chain gang and led down the long drive at Shannon Oaks, Anna had run alongside him, frantic. It was horrible to see her strong, handsome husband in chains. Anna had wept openly.

"Don't you cry, woman!" George called to her. His eyes flashed in a mix of anger, fear, and love. "You stay strong. You stay strong for Janie." He had held Anna's gaze with his own as he was pulled away, then said the words she would not forget: "I'll come back and get you. I'll come back."

Anna was holding him to it. The war had been over for almost two years now. When would George come back? And when could they go find their little girl?

Anna slipped two ears of corn into her apron pocket to roast later on. She kept her strength up by eating even when she'd rather do anything but eat. Because no matter where George had ended up, if he said he was coming back, he'd be back.

If he was still alive, that is.

Chapter 3

The Leather Box

In spite of the general smokiness, a sweet waft of cedar met Janie when she and Blue opened the wardrobe doors. They both worked quickly by candlelight, pulling out all the clothing they could find, first in one room and then in all the upstairs dressing rooms.

There were shirts and pants, dresses, skirts, blouses, nightgowns, robes, warm coats, lightweight jackets, and the real prize: shoes and boots. *Them Yankees were in some hurry to miss all this,* Janie thought. A few woolen items had started to get moth-eaten, but the cedar walls had protected most of them.

Piece by piece, Janie and Blue pulled clothing out of the wardrobes and hauled everything to an open window. There they dropped the items into the eager hands of former slaves who had gathered below.

On plantations, the only clothes slaves had were the ones on their backs, and technically they didn't even own those. Every year each person was issued one outfit of clothing and one blanket. Shoes were scarce even in better times, and it was not unusual to go barefoot all year long.

Since midway through the war, however, no clothing or blankets had been issued at Rubyhill. Everyone's clothing was looking threadbare. There hadn't been enough wool for winter for a couple of years, and even in Georgia, winters could be chilly. Janie recalled waking up to a dusting of snow on the ground once in a while.

At least now, she knew Rubyhill's ex-slaves would manage to stay dressed and warm for a long time with all these fine garments.

Eventually, Janie and Blue carefully made their way back down the burned staircase. The sun was lowering, and it was starting to give everything indoors an eerie shadow. Janie was eager to get out of this dark house and into the fresh air. She was also eager to join the other members of the community in sorting through the huge piles of clothes now at their disposal.

"Be sure Janie gets something nice," Janie heard Aleta reminding them. "She worked hard hunting and hauling for y'all."

Janie appreciated Aleta's big-sister ways. She was a little bossy, but nobody minded, simply because Aleta had the interests of them all at heart. She was wise beyond her seventeen years, and everyone saw it.

"Come over here, Janie," Aleta said.

Janie hurried to where Aleta rummaged through the huge piles of clothing. She pulled out a lovely calico-print dress and held it lengthwise in front of Janie. Aleta's experienced eye took in all of Janie's slender body. "Miz Laura's bigger than you, but not so much. I can cut this down some."

Aleta looked back at the pile. "Master and his son sure had a lot of clothes for menfolk. Most everybody should be able to find a coat here."

Janie began rummaging. She found a pair of warm slippers that would fit Aunty Mil. Then she pulled out a thick jacket that had belonged to the master's son, but on Janie it was a full-length coat. She rolled the sleeves up, over and over. Aleta looked over at her and laughed. "I'll trim that down, too, but you don't need that right away. We got a little time before cold sets in."

Janie rummaged until she found a pair of thick socks that would help Aunty's cold feet. Then she found some shoes that she could wear herself and a jacket that would fit Aunty Mil.

Janie straightened up and looked around. The rose trellises lay in pieces in bunches of weeds, never having been cleaned up. The many roses and other flowering bushes were long gone.

Only now did Janie notice a few of the other former slaves pulling at the weeds and digging with big spoons in and around the old flowerbeds. Both Nathan and Lucy sat cross-legged, digging at the ground in front of them with cooking spoons.

Valuables had been buried very well in the gardens, and plants were put in the ground right over them. The Yankees hadn't found a thing there, not that they didn't try. But back when Miz Laura was still giving orders, she had said to leave that sort of thing buried because there might be stray thieves roaming the countryside. So today was the first digging anyone had done in the gardens.

"Find anything?" Janie called out to Nathan and Lucy.

"Nah, not yet," Nathan replied. Lucy shook her head.

Old Joe, one of the elders, called out, "I got me something here." He pulled a dirt-covered box up out of the ground and set it in front of him. He squatted back on his haunches and brushed the dirt off the box. "This here box is made of leather," he commented. "I seen it before." He pried the box open, then gave a long, low whistle.

Janie sidled next to Old Joe and looked over his shoulder. The box, which was about the size of four loaves of bread laid out side by side, was full of paper money.

"Rebel cash," remarked Blue. "Ain't worth a thing no more."

"Rebel cash ain't worth a thing, all right," said Old Joe with a chuckle. "But this here works just fine."

Everyone became silent. Finally Aleta spoke. "What are you saying, Old Joe?"

"Only thing rebel money's good for is kindling, true enough. I'm saying this here's Yankee money. This here money works fine."

Blue squatted down next to Old Joe. Blue reached in the box and touched the money, then pulled his hand back as if he'd touched something hot. "How you know that?" he asked.

Old Joe stood, stretched, and shook his head. "You young'uns don't think I got a mind for nothin'. What you think I did all them years with Master?"

Nobody answered. Old Joe snorted. "I kept the books."

Still nobody responded until Nathan said, "You mean you can read?"

Janie was stunned by that possibility. It had been illegal to teach slaves to read, and as far as she knew, nobody among them had ever learned.

"No, boy, not them kinda books. I can't read any better'n you, son," said Old Joe. "But Master made sure I could figure. He taught me numbers so's I could keep the books for taking crops in and make sure he didn't get cheated at the mills."

Old Joe rubbed the small of his back. "So I know numbers. And I know what money looks like. I know when it turned rebel cash, what that looked like, too. And I heard talk about this here Yankee money. Master told Miz Laura to hide it in case she need it to go north some day. We all buried this two years ago, not knowing what we buried."

"Well, why didn't she have us dig it back up?" asked Blue.

Old Joe shrugged. "She never was right in the head after them Yankees—you know that."

The cook spoke up. "Nobody hurts for money in Miz Laura's family, even after all this war. You saw them horses, that big white man driver. Miz Laura probably forgot all about this money in the ground."

"Maybe she just wanted to get out of here as fast as she could," offered Aleta.

Janie stared at the box of money. She'd never had an occasion to see money except when the chain gang had come through to buy slaves, and even then it was never a box of money. Those memories were too hurtful to think about, anyway.

"How much you figure is there, Old Joe?" Janie asked.

"A whole lot. I can tell you that much," he said.

"Us black folks use that money 'round here, white folks gonna think we stole it," Blue groused.

Old Joe looked at Blue for a long moment. Then he looked around at the others. The lowering sun turned his skin a golden hue, it seemed to Janie, just like the fine oak furniture she used to polish in the Big House dining room.

"You most likely right on that part," Old Joe said. "We can use some of it now and then, here and there. But the rest, you gonna take, boy. You goin' north."

For once Blue was speechless, and so was everyone else. It was little Janie who finally spoke up. "What you mean, Old Joe?"

Old Joe placed his old, dry hand on Janie's head. "I mean this, child. . . You young'uns here got to go north. There's nothing down here for you. You got to get out of here, get work, learn to read and write. Nobody here can teach you that."

Janie felt sick to her stomach at the thought of anyone going anywhere. She'd lived on Rubyhill for more than half her life. For better or worse, Rubyhill was home, and these people had become her family. "But. . .why?" she stammered.

Old Joe tugged lightly on one of Janie's braids. " 'Cause that's how it's got to be, child." He looked out beyond the gardens. "I been places y'all never been. I been north, even. Master trusted me to go with him—everybody knows that. I woulda run, but I couldn't leave my wife and babies down here on their own, and Master knew it. I meant to fly out of here someday and take them north with me, but when my wife took sick. . .my babies gone. . .that war. . ."

Old Joe turned and looked around the silent group. "Any old ones want to go, that's fine, but I'm past that now. My woman's dead, my girls sold off." He paused. "I'm saying you young'uns got to have a chance. As long as you stay here, maybe you know in your mind you're free, but not in your heart. Never in your heart. You'll still think like a Georgia slave. Rubyhill still a plantation owned by white folks." He snorted and shook his head. "Crazy white folks, at that."

Janie noticed for the first time that Old Joe was getting filmy blue eyes just like Aunty Mil.

Blue finally recovered from being dumbfounded. "Old Joe, I ain't never thought about these things."

"Well, boy, time you did. 'Cause you the one gonna lead 'em north."

Blue's mouth dropped open again. "But where would we go?"

Old Joe looked off in the distance for a moment. "I been thinkin' 'bout Chicago. Way up north and mighty cold, but I hear tell there's work for everybody there, black or white. Big cold city. Sits on water big as a ocean—Lake Michigan. That lake don't belong to nobody, so's you can fish on it plenty and nobody'll bother you."

Old Joe went silent. Then he looked back at Blue. "I been there, son, plenty times. I can tell you how to get there." With that, Old Joe picked up the box of money and walked back to the quarters.

It took a long moment for the others to go back to work. Janie stood thoughtfully, worried about the changes that seemed to be happening no matter how she felt about them.

The cook snapped her out of her reverie. "Come here and help—I just found the silver."

The group moved over to circle around Cookie. Everyone pulled silver dishes and cups wrapped in newspaper and cloth out of the ground. They worked quickly, piling all the pieces on top of one of the flowerbeds. "We can sell this," the cook said. "Or trade it. Maybe we can get flour and rice and such."

Janie started when Nathan tapped her on the shoulder. "I found this, Janie," he said. "Want it?" He held out a cross on a long silver chain.

Janie took the cross. She placed it in the palm of her hand and looked it over while Nathan moved back to his digging. The heavy cross was made of pewter. There was writing on the back of it, but of course, Janie couldn't read it. She placed the chain around her neck, and the pewter cross dangled halfway down her chest. She didn't want the cross to get snagged on anything as she worked, so she tucked it inside her dress. She made her way over to Nathan and beamed at him. "Thanks, Nathan."

Nathan grinned, and he and Janie both went back to digging. As dusk fell, Janie gathered her haul of clothing and took it back to the cabin.

Aunty Mil was grateful for the slippers, which Janie put on her feet for her. "Older I get, seems the less my blood gets down to my feet," Aunty Mil said.

As for Janie, the day had been so full of excitement that she had trouble staying awake while she told Aunty Mil about it. Finally the old woman chuckled and told Janie to go to bed. "Let's talk in the morning, child."

Janie collapsed on her pallet next to the fire. Just before she fell asleep, she fingered the pewter cross. The thought came to her, *If you go north and learn to read, you'll know what it says on this cross.* Then she fell sound asleep.

That night, Janie dreamed she was eating a big jar of succotash. How good it tasted! When she woke up, she could still taste it. Only then did she remember that she'd buried that very thing two years ago under a floorboard of the detached kitchen.

Later she found it was right where she'd hidden it.

Chapter 4

"I Got to Go"

Janie stirred cornmeal mush and canned peaches around in the big black pot over the cabin fire. Aunty Mil rocked steadily in her chair, humming and moaning. Moaning was something Aunty Mil did sometimes when she prayed or thought about the past. It was just a way she had of expressing herself, and Janie had gotten used to it.

"Aunty Mil, you hungry now? I'll spoon this up if you're ready."

"Yes, Janie-bird, I'm ready."

Janie scooped the thick, sweet concoction with a big ladle Cookie had given her from the Big House kitchen. The mush dropped into a chipped bowl with a pleasant-sounding *splat*. Janie lifted Aunty Mil's hand so she could feel how warm the bowl was. Then she steered a spoon into the woman's other hand.

Aunty Mil thanked Janie and placed the bowl securely in her lap. She automatically said the meal's blessing, just as she did for all meals.

"Lord in heaven, we thank You for this food," Aunty Mil prayed. "Keep my Janie safe and sound in all her ways. I pray for traveling mercies for her and the others on their journey north. Amen."

Aunty Mil took a bite and made an appreciative noise.

But Janie sat silently. The prayer had unsettled her. She had not yet spoken to Aunty Mil about that part of yesterday's events. Janie had gone to sleep quickly last night, and this morning she had run out of the cabin very early. How did Aunty Mil know about all that talk from yesterday? And why did she pray that way? Janie wasn't planning on going anywhere.

Janie scooped out a portion of syrupy mush and squatted down to eat. But her stomach had twisted into a knot. She put her bowl down and watched Aunty Mil instead.

The old woman had a half smile on her face as she ate her soft food. She'd had to refuse the succotash Janie found earlier because the corn really needed to be chewed. But the old woman was very pleased with this soft meal, and she ate it happily.

"Aunty," Janie finally blurted out, "how you know people's fixin' to leave Rubyhill?"

Without missing a bite, the old woman chuckled and said, "Don't you know this place got no secrets? Ain't nothing strange about that, baby. Word just gets around—that's all."

Janie sat down on the cabin's dirt floor. "But I ain't going nowhere, Aunty. Not without you."

"Yes, you are, child," Aunty Mil said gently.

"Why you say that?" Janie was feeling even more unsettled.

" 'Cause it's your time, baby. It's time you took flight."

"But what about you?"

"Oh, child, it's time I took flight, too, but I'm not going with y'all."

Janie frowned. "Where you going?"

Aunty Mil stopped eating and aimed her sightless eyes in Janie's direction. "I'm going to heaven, baby."

"When?"

"When my Maker comes get me, that's when."

Janie sat very still. She felt afraid. "But when's that, Aunty?"

Aunty Mil didn't speak at first. All that could be heard was her spoon scraping the bowl. Finally she spoke. "Oh, that was good. Now come take my bowl, child. Let Aunty tell you about it." Janie scurried over to relieve the old woman of her dish and spoon.

"Now see here." Aunty Mil found Janie's head and rubbed on it with her bony fingers. Janie sank to her knees beside the chair and felt instantly comforted.

"Janie-bird, my time here is near about done. I know it. I feel it. I dream about it 'most every night. I don't know when my time to leave will be, but it will be soon enough. And then I got to go. Aunty Mil gonna fly right on outta this cabin, right up over this plantation, and right on up to heaven. You understand?"

Janie knew a little something about heaven. Her mother had introduced her to Jesus before Janie was taken to Shannon Oaks, and Janie believed that Jesus lived in her own heart. She hadn't given a lot of thought to heaven, though. She had heard songs about heaven sung all her life, first by Momma in their cabin, then secretly in the pine groves when she came to Rubyhill. During the frightening days of slavery, it had been illegal and dangerous for slaves to gather for any reason without the watchful eye of white men. Some slaves were even killed for it.

But most slaves believed in God, and many of them met together secretly for church. They gathered in groves of trees that would deaden the sound of their preaching and singing. That's where Janie mostly heard about heaven. She recalled hearing words much like Aunty Mil's, and there were plenty of songs about it. But Janie did not always know what those words meant exactly, even when she sang them herself.

The old woman went on. "Aunty Mil's been walking this creation a long, long time. This body's near about ready to give out. And when it's time, I'm leaving this old body behind. It will happen. You know this, Janie-bird. Heaven's my true home. I want to go home to my Maker and my family gone on before me. I don't want to leave you here, baby girl, but I got to go."

Aunty Mil turned to the fire. "And I been thinking on this for a long time, that you got to get north. You shouldn't stay here in Georgia no-how. Now you got your chance to fly on outta here with the others. I got to go where I'm going, baby girl, and I'll meet you on the other side. For now, though, you got to get north."

This was a lot for Janie to take in, and she felt afraid again. Ever since Janie was taken from Momma, Aunty Mil had been her family. "No, Aunty, I won't leave you."

Aunty Mil continued stroking Janie's head as if she were a cat. "Mm-mm-mm," she said. "That's all right, child." Janie could hear a smile in her voice. She leaned her face against Aunty Mil's apron. "Don't you worry," Aunty cooed.

The cabin became quiet with only the sounds of Aunty's rocking chair, the crackling fire, and the raspy breathing of the old woman.

"Sing me that song, child."

"Which one, Aunty?"

"The one about going to Canaan-land."

Janie began to sing the much-loved spiritual. She was known around the quarters for having a high, sweet voice, clear as a bird, according to Aunty Mil. Janie closed her eyes and sang her young heart out. When she was done, she saw Aunty Mil had dozed off. Janie watched the old woman's thin body rise and fall with the sounds of her breath.

Singing always helped Janie feel better. Now she felt hungry again. Aunty Mil was in the middle of her nap, resting nicely, so Janie took her own bowl of mush outside to eat it.

As she ate, Janie thought over what Aunty Mil had said about going to heaven. She'd heard other old ones talk like that but hadn't ever paid much attention to their words until now. When was Aunty Mil going away? Why did she have to leave at all?

Janie scraped her bowl with her spoon and tucked the dish inside the cabin door to clean later. She headed up the path toward the Big House. She needed to talk to Aleta.

When she reached the front yard, Janie heard her name called. She spun around to find Aleta hurrying toward her.

Aleta was excited. "Come on up here about dusk. Some of us are meeting by the kitchen to make plans for going north." Aleta's eyes looked very bright.

But Janie could not respond. She turned and ran back down the path. When Aleta called after her, Janie just ran faster, hurrying back to the warm security of the cabin and Aunty Mil.

Once inside, Janie saw that the fire needed tending. She rummaged for some small pieces of wood, keeping as quiet as possible for the sake of the sleeping Aunty Mil.

Janie stoked the fire and then grabbed a pail to fetch water at the pump. Only then did she realize there was no sound coming from the rocking chair.

Janie slowly walked to Aunty Mil and reached for the old woman's hand. It was cold.

"Aunty Mil?"

There was no answer.

Shannon Oaks Plantation, Georgia

Anna swept her cabin's dirt floor, steering the stray pieces of straw and chunks of mud to the small fireplace. She hummed softly to herself, a tune she'd learned from her own mother. Anna never knew the words to the song, but the melody always sounded hopeful to her.

And Anna lived daily with the hope of tomorrow. It was the best she could do. Hope was all she had left.

But at least the bondage was over, praise the Lord. She would never again be anyone's slave. And if there were any earthly way, George would find her again, he would.

After all, who would have believed Master would have had to let them all go free here at Shannon Oaks? Never would anyone have believed that could happen. And if that could happen all over the land, George could come back to her. And then they could go find their daughter.

She thought of George, whom she'd not seen now for seven long years. Big, strong George with skin the color of strong coffee with just a touch of milk stirred in. That's what she always told him. His dark eyes would light up every time she said that.

Anna sighed. How she missed George. And how she missed their singing, brown-eyed girl whom she'd not seen in six years. Anna prayed one prayer daily: "Dear Lord, I thank You for life for one more day. I ask for George and my baby to come back to me. In Jesus' name I pray this."

She went back to sweeping and humming. One day closer to seeing her loved ones again. That's what she had to believe.

Chapter 5

The Burial

Janie sat on the small woodpile outside the cabin she shared with Aunty Mil and pulled her knees up to her chin. She wrapped her arms around her thin legs and put her head on her knees.

Inside the cabin, two women prepared the old woman for her burial. They worked quietly. Everyone had loved Aunty Mil.

Aleta trotted down the path from the Big House. "Oh, Janie," she said, "I just heard." She grabbed Janie's hand.

Janie squeezed Aleta's hand for a minute then pulled her own hand back. Again she wrapped her arms around her legs.

Aleta sank down next to Janie on the woodpile. "You all right?" she asked in a gentle tone.

Janie shook her head. She could not speak.

That was a familiar feeling, the stark fear in her heart coupled with the inability to speak. She remembered when she'd first come to Rubyhill six years ago, how frightened and silent she had been.

Only five years old and ripped away from her home for the first time in her young life, Janie had been terrified by the time she entered the back drive at Rubyhill. All her life, she'd been safe and sound with Momma, or so she'd thought. But suddenly she had been yanked away by strange white people, thrown into a wagon full of other child slaves, taken away to a place she'd never seen, and thrust into the hands of more people she did not know.

When the black people at Rubyhill asked Janie her name that day, she stared back at them, too frightened to speak. They were very kind to the little girl. They understood all too well the shock of being pulled away from family, never to return. But when they asked her questions, Janie simply could not speak. She even opened her mouth to try. It was as if no sound would come out of her.

That's when Old Joe picked her up and carried her to Aunty Mil's cabin. The old blind woman had felt the top of Janie's head with her soft, dry hand. Then she'd stroked Janie's braids gently, cooing at her the whole time. Janie remembered it well.

"You just a little bit of a thing," Aunty Mil had said to her, chuckling softly. "You just a little dickens, ain't you? And they all say you can't talk. Well, old Aunty Mil thinks you just not ready. I can't see you or nothin' else, baby girl, so some time, you got to talk to me so's we can know each other. Meantime, though, you stay here in Aunty Mil's cabin, and you don't ever got to move again. Hear me?"

Little Janie had nodded. Only then did it dawn on her that the old woman couldn't see her nod. But Aunty Mil had felt Janie's head move under her hand, and she'd laughed out loud. "We gonna do just fine, you and me. You'll talk to Aunty when you's good and ready."

It had been months before little Janie had spoken. She had silently performed any chore asked of her. She worked hard for the cook at the Big House, fetching things from the root cellar, washing fruits and vegetables at the pump, climbing into low cupboards or up onto high shelves to get pots and pans the heavyset cook couldn't reach. And every night back at the cabin, Aunty Mil had stroked Janie's hair and prayed out loud as the child fell asleep.

One morning as Janie was waking up, Aunty Mil tripped on the broom in the cabin. The old woman fell and landed in the fireplace, and her skirt caught fire. Little Janie quickly beat the fire out with a small skillet, but Aunty Mil's legs were burned. "Quick, baby, go get someone!" the old woman told her.

Frightened, Janie had run outside in the quarters and not known where to go or what to do. It was still dark out. So she used her voice for the first time at Rubyhill. It was squeaky, but it worked. Little Janie stood in the middle of the center path and called out in her high voice: "Help! Help! Aunty's hurt!"

The other slaves poured out of their cabins and ran to her. Janie pointed inside the cabin, and Aunty Mil was quickly helped. The women in the quarters brought healing herbs and cooling salves to treat the burns. Before long, Aunty Mil's burns got better and went away, leaving only some raised scars on her leg.

But what truly made the old woman happy was that Janie had spoken out loud to help her. Janie never stopped talking after that. She even began to sing.

Of course, once Aunty Mil heard Janie sing, Janie had to sing all the time. Her sweet, high melodies filled the cabin, and on warm nights, the entire quarter was given the gift of her songs, traveling on the heavy air.

Aunty Mil often prayed out loud her thanks to God for having been burned because that's when Janie's sweet voice was "loosed." That's how Aunty Mil put it. And that's when she started calling the child Janie-bird.

Of course, it also meant the two could talk to each other at last. And talk they did! "You remember, child," Aunty Mil often said, "the Lord can make a way out of no way. Aunty Mil got hurt, but you and your birdsong sprung up out of it all. The Lord made it good."

Now Janie sat in silence with Aleta and let the memories stir around inside her heart and mind. What good could come of this? She couldn't believe Aunty Mil lay dead inside the cabin. It hurt so much.

Finally Aleta spoke. "Don't get quiet again, little sis. Don't stop talking and singing. Aunty wouldn't want that."

Janie stared at the ground and said nothing.

The two women came out of the cabin. One squatted down before Janie. "Baby, we gonna bury Aunty Mil pretty soon. We got her all nice and ready. You want to come in and sit a spell with her?"

Janie didn't move. Aleta gently pried one of Janie's hands away from clutching the other hand and pulled her up. "Come on, little sis. Let's say good-bye."

Aleta led Janie into the cabin where Aunty Mil lay stretched out on her pallet. Janie still stared down at the dirt floor. Aleta knelt next to the old woman and pulled Janie down next to her.

Janie felt the fire at her back. She was afraid to look at Aunty Mil.

"Come on, Janie," Aleta coaxed. "We got to say good-bye to Aunty Mil."

Janie finally raised her eyes to look at the old woman. Aunty Mil was lying perfectly straight and still, her hands folded on her chest. Janie stared, wondering what was so different. Then she realized that she had never seen Aunty's body straight or still. The old woman had had so many aches and pains that she could not even lie down. Aunty slept in the rocker. And even in her sleep, she moaned and moved about. Now she clearly was without pain.

Janie crept closer to Aunty Mil. The women had taken the kerchief off her head, and Janie saw Aunty Mil's long white braids spread out. She looked so young! It even looked like she was slightly smiling. Janie was amazed. Truly the real Aunty Mil had left her body and gone away, just like she said she would.

Aleta leaned closer to Janie. "You all right?"

Janie nodded. She still could not speak. She didn't know how she was going to get along without Aunty Mil, but she did know in her heart that the old woman was in a better place. She was glad about that. She reached out and touched the soft skin on Aunty Mil's cheek. Then she sat back and waited.

Soon the women came back in and wound long, white sheets around Aunty Mil. Then two men came in and picked up the ends of the sheets. They carried Aunty Mil's body outside and placed her on a cart drawn by a mule. The entire community of former slaves gathered behind the wagon. They followed the slow-moving mule and cart to the graveyard, where two men with shovels waited by a freshly dug grave. Aleta began to sing, and the others joined in.

Janie felt numb as she followed close behind the wagon. At the grave, she stood and held on to the white sheets at Aunty Mil's feet while Old Joe said a few words. She could feel the pewter cross under her dress, resting against her skin. It was a comfort to feel it.

Lost in her own thoughts, Janie didn't pay much attention to Old Joe until he addressed her directly. "Little Janie, you know Aunty Mil loved to hear you sing. You sing for her, would you now?"

Janie's heart felt like it would break. But Old Joe was right. And she knew Aunty would not want her to hide in silence ever again. So Janie began to sing, her high notes climbing and soaring over the pine trees. She saw Old Joe wipe his eyes. Then she closed her own eyes as Aunty Mil's body was lowered into the ground.

The men shoveled dirt into the grave. This was hard for Janie to watch. Again she felt the pewter cross press against her, and again, it was a comfort. She touched the outline of the cross through her dress.

When the grave was filled, a mound of dirt remained on top. Each of Rubyhill's former slaves found a rock nearby and placed it on the mound. Janie found a speckled rock, and she placed her rock on the pile, too.

When it was all over, the others moved silently back to work. Old Joe stayed behind and looked at Aunty Mil's grave for a long time. Then he patted Janie's head and turned down the path toward the quarters. Aleta stayed with Janie.

Janie finally spoke. "What am I gonna do now?"

"You know what you gonna do, little sis. You goin' north with us."

Janie looked at Aleta. "And leave her here in the ground?"

"Oh, Janie," said Aleta, "Aunty knew she was goin' on. And she knew we's goin' north. Don't you think maybe she and God worked it out so you don't have to stay and worry over her no more?"

Janie considered this. In spite of her sadness, she had to smile. "You might be right about that," she said to Aleta. "She wanted me to go north. And she was mighty happy about goin' to heaven. Said it was her time."

The two girls gazed at the mound of dirt awhile longer. Then Janie picked a nearby branch and laid it on the mound of dirt and rocks. "Good-bye, Aunty Mil. You sure been good to me. I will see you in heaven someday."

The two girls turned and walked hand-in-hand back to the quarters.

"Stay with me tonight, Janie," said Aleta. "Don't go back to the cabin by yourself."

Janie considered this. "I'll stay with you, Aleta—but first I got to go back to the cabin and get something."

"Want me to come along?"

"If you like. I thank you."

The girls trudged silently down the path to Aunty Mil's cabin.

Inside the cabin, Aleta busied herself rolling Janie's blanket and setting aside pans to take. Janie looked around. She knew she would not be back.

She spied the broken rocker. A wave of emotion swept over the young girl, knowing Aunty Mil truly was gone and would never rock in that chair again.

Janie walked over to the hearth and found the paring knife. Then she sliced a large square of fabric from the rocking chair. She cut it from the back ruffle so that more stuffing wouldn't come out. Surely someone else would want to use the chair. She folded the square of fabric and stuffed it into her skirt pocket.

"Lookie here," said Aleta. "You might want this."

Janie turned to see Aleta standing next to the hearth, holding out Aunty Mil's pale yellow head scarf. Janie took the scarf from Aleta, held it to her face, and breathed in the smell of Aunty Mil's hair.

A memory came to Janie, distinct and sweet. Every week, she and Aunty Mil would unbraid and rebraid one another's hair. Aunty Mil had taught her how to braid when Janie first arrived at Rubyhill. The old woman had placed her own cool, bony fingers over Janie's tiny ones and taught her first with string. It was awhile before she let the little girl braid real hair.

But Aunty Mil braided Janie's hair from the beginning, always telling her Bible stories, offering her a look at life that would train the child well. "Jesus walked this earth, child, so that He would know what it's like bein' a man," Aunty Mil instructed the girl. "He came down here to save us and free us. Then He went back to heaven to be with His Father. From up there, Jesus helps you. All you got to do is ask. You remember that."

Janie did remember it. Now she took the folded kerchief and placed it in her pocket next to the fabric square. Then Aleta and Janie stepped out of the cabin forever.

Chapter 6

A Harvest Moon

Janie woke up with a start. *Where am I?*

The full harvest moon shone so brightly that for a moment Janie thought it was dawn. But it was not. It only felt that way because she was sleeping outside in the light of that huge moon filtering through tree branches overhead.

Quickly Janie remembered why she was sleeping outside. She was part of the small party of Rubyhill's young former slaves who had left the plantation and were now moving north. They had just walked all day, resting only occasionally until they stopped at the edge of this cedar forest. There they'd eaten supper and fallen asleep as darkness came on. It was their first night away from home.

The fire was reduced to only coals. Janie sat up and listened to the sounds of the woods next to them. It was nerve-racking, hearing all those outdoor sounds so close by—owls hooting, small creatures scurrying, leaves rustling, and who knew what else—and nothing to keep any of it at bay. Janie hoped it was true what they said, that snakes don't crawl at night. She did wonder, though.

Janie wrapped her blanket tightly around herself and looked about. Sleeping around the fire wrapped in their own blankets were four others—Aleta, Lucy, Nathan, and Blue. When it came down to actually leaving, these five were the only ones who decided to go north.

Janie thought about why they were the only ones going. Maybe it was because none of them would have to leave family behind. Blue had been sold to Rubyhill from someplace in Virginia when he was very young. Aleta was born at Rubyhill, but all her kin were gone. Nathan and Lucy only had each other. They'd come to Rubyhill the same time as Janie, and they remembered little about their original family.

Janie's mind wandered to the events of the last week. So much had happened: Miz Laura's departure, Old Joe finding the box of Yankee cash, and then the death of dear Aunty Mil. The five young former slaves had waited only until the second day after the burial before venturing out.

Janie had dragged her feet at the thought of leaving so soon after losing Aunty Mil. So much was changing so fast. But the elders insisted that it was important to leave while the full moon offered so much light. Blue also reminded Janie that soon autumn would turn to winter. "We need to get as far north as we can before snow falls," Blue insisted. "Old Joe's told me how to go, and we got to go right away."

So Janie went along with it. They began making plans the day after Aunty Mil's death. All the other former slaves at Rubyhill prepared food for their young people for the journey—easy things to carry like hard-boiled eggs, pecans, boiled peanuts, and dried apricots. They distributed squares of cornbread and gingerbread to be stuffed into pockets for nibbling along the way. They even slaughtered and fried up one of Rubyhill's few chickens for their young people to take. Janie's mouth still drooled at the memory of how tasty that cold fried chicken had been at suppertime.

The five young ones also packed and carried a skillet, a boiling pot, a chopping knife, and some burlap bags of rice and cornmeal. Each one brought his or her own cup, bowl, and spoon. Blue wore a pouch around his waist and under his clothes in which he carried most of the Yankee cash. The rest of the cash was divided up among the other four and tucked deep into their pockets in case they somehow became separated along the way.

Early that morning, Aleta had distributed footwear and jackets taken from the Big House, items to be worn later when it turned cold. Each of the five young people rolled these garments up in his or her own blanket, which was about all any of them owned besides the clothes on their backs. They even slept in those clothes.

Janie brought along three more personal things. She wore the pewter cross under her dress, and she kept both the square of fabric from Aunty Mil's rocking chair and Aunty's pale yellow kerchief folded in her pocket.

Janie thought about how they left the plantation all in a line: Blue in the lead, Aleta at the end. All of Rubyhill's former slaves walked to the outskirts of the plantation with them to see them off. Some of the elders had begun to weep as Old Joe said a prayer over the five young people and sent them on their way.

As the five travelers began walking away, Cookie started to sing one of Janie's favorite songs, and the other former slaves joined in:

"If I could, I surely would
Stand on the rock where Moses stood.
Pharaoh's army got drown-ded,
Oh, Mary, don't you weep. . . ."

For a long while, Janie, Blue, Aleta, Lucy, and Nathan could hear the singing voices of those who had been the only family they had.

Now, by the light of the dying coals and the vibrant moon, Janie reached into her pocket and pulled out the yellow kerchief. She held it to her face and breathed in that familiar smell of Aunty Mil's hair. It was a living smell, sharp and sweet.

Janie placed the kerchief back in her pocket. She wrapped her blanket tighter around herself and rocked. She cried without making a sound.

Shannon Oaks Plantation, Georgia

Anna tended the supper fire in her cabin in silence. A full harvest moon had slowly made its way up and over Shannon Oaks.

It had been a long day of fieldwork. After supper, Anna intended to go right to sleep and rest up for another long day. Maybe she'd dream of her little girl again.

Georgeanna. Born Christmas Day and named after her parents. Her pretty little baby with the pretty name.

Back then, when Master's young wife had heard the new baby's name, she'd said, "That's too fine a name for a black baby. You call her Janie."

So Anna had no choice but to call her baby Janie. At least the woman liked Anna, or she, too, would have been sold south, probably soon after George was sold.

Word back then was that the soil at Shannon Oaks had become tired. That's how the men put it, anyway. They meant that the soil wasn't working as well as it used to, so the plantation wasn't producing the amount of quality cotton and tobacco it once had.

But Master was used to high living. And high living did not come cheap. To continue his standard of living, Master started dealing in and selling livestock, concentrating on horses. Then he concentrated on selling human beings. Even five-year-old Janie.

But not Anna. Master's wife absolutely would not allow it. And Master hated it when his young wife was unhappy. Nevertheless, he continued selling the other slaves, so that by wartime, not many were left at Shannon Oaks.

Anna's thoughts were interrupted by the loud bray of a mule outside. She didn't recognize this mule's bray, and it sounded like it was close by.

She stood and peeked out her cabin door. There in the bright moonlight stood a very thin man holding the reins of a mule in one hand and a bunch of sunflowers in the other. He stepped toward the cabin door.

Now Anna could see the man better. And—oh, could it be? Did he have skin the color of strong coffee with just a touch of milk stirred in?

The thin man's face broke out into a wide smile. "Anna?"

Anna's knees gave way, and she sank gently to the ground. It was George. Alive. He had come back to her, just as he promised he would.

George ran and dropped to the ground beside his wife, cradling her in his arms. Seven long years were over in one moment as both of them sobbed openly with joy.

Chapter 7

The Rubyhill Five

On the third day of the journey north, clouds filled up the sky. Soon enough, a cold rain poured on the little band from Rubyhill. *Seems like every step we take north, things get colder,* Janie thought. *Even rain.*

The plan was to reach Chicago before winter set in. That was a distance that should take them about forty days on foot, according to Old Joe. They would move north by northwest through Georgia, then into Tennessee, Kentucky, and Indiana. Old Joe pointed out that Chicago "sits right on top of Indiana." Janie didn't quite understand what that meant, and Blue explained that it meant it was at the northern point of Indiana.

Old Joe sat them down for a talk the day before they left. He warned them that there could be snow once they hit Indiana. "You might have to sit out a snowstorm but not too much, leastways not till after the first of the year. Remember, winter moves south faster than you can walk north. You got to keep moving and get to Chicago long before Christmas."

He warned them that once they got into Chicago, the cold wind would be brutal. "You young'uns ain't got the blood for that now, but you will by the next winter. The blood thickens up after you been in the cold awhile. First winter, though, y'all gonna feel the chill right down to your bones 'cause y'all from Georgia. But you remember Old Joe said it's gonna get better."

That had not sounded at all appealing to Janie. Already on this trip, she was feeling colder at night than she remembered ever being before.

The Rubyhill Five had skirted Atlanta and now found themselves close to Tennessee on this rainy third day of travel. They filed silently through an open pasture bordered by wooded hills and boulders. As they neared the tree line, Aleta spoke up. "We got to put off walking for now, Blue," she said. "Won't do no good to take sick in this wet cold."

Blue nodded and stopped in his tracks. Janie marveled at what a good team those two made. One made a suggestion; the other either agreed or reasoned out something else. Janie, Nathan, and Lucy rarely needed to express their opinions under the leadership of this almost adult teamwork. They just let themselves be led by Aleta and Blue.

Aleta spied a huge boulder with an overhang of rock. The grass under it was long and looked fairly dry. "Let's try that over there."

The five moved as one to duck under the rocky overhang. They slid down onto the grass together. "Move in closer," said Aleta. They huddled against one another until the rain could reach only their bare toes.

"Sure wish I'da thought to bring some kinda oilcloth for this rain," groused Blue. "All I thought about was snow."

"All I thought about was food," said Aleta. They both chuckled at that, and Nathan and Lucy giggled right along. Janie felt grateful that the group tended to stay in such high spirits even in the face of difficulties.

The route Old Joe had mapped out for them was working out so far. They were covering probably close to twenty miles each day, just as Joe thought they might. Over and over he warned them they should keep moving while both good weather and food lasted. The food was holding out so far, but they would have to start foraging for more in a couple of days.

The quiet chatter stopped eventually, and the youths leaned against each other for about half an hour. Janie felt herself getting sleepy in the gentle sounds of the rain. Her head dropped on Aleta's shoulder.

"Listen," she heard Nathan whisper.

It was the sound of thrashing grass. Someone or something was out there in the rain. Quite a lot of someone or something, it sounded like.

Aleta turned to Blue. "Deer?" she whispered anxiously.

Blue shook his head. "Men," he whispered back.

The five ex-slaves knew that avoiding contact with white people on this trip would be good. Yes, blacks were free now. But not all white folks were happy about that.

Janie had often heard the elders back at Rubyhill talk about the state of affairs these days. Rubyhill wasn't the only place where people had to scrape to get food to eat, they reported. Nobody fared all that well anywhere in the South, and some white people blamed black people for the hardships. Those white people sometimes took the law into their own hands to hurt black people. The elders had said that the law of the land had never protected blacks before, and there was still no reason to expect it to. "Maybe some day, Lord willing," Janie had heard Old Joe say. "But that day ain't here yet."

So the band of five moved fairly quietly most of the time, and they stayed away from main roads and houses. Besides, they didn't want to get accused of trespassing on anyone's land.

The thrashing came closer. Then voices. Deep male voices. Janie felt afraid. She closed her eyes and touched the outline of the pewter cross beneath her dress. *Please protect us, Jesus. . . .*

"You head on home, buddy, and start on those chores," she heard a man say. "We'll be along shortly."

A younger voice replied, "Yes, sir."

The thrashing moved away. Janie was so relieved she thought she'd faint. Instead, she opened her eyes and found herself looking straight up into the face of a tall white boy, maybe fifteen or sixteen. She could feel everyone else look up, too. The boy carried a rifle.

Seeing them gave him a start, and he stared back, mouth open. For a long while, nobody spoke. They could hear the voices of the other men fade into the distance, but nobody moved or said a word.

Janie took in the young man's appearance. Even in her fear, she noticed that his clothes were wool. He wore boots and a red hat, and hanging off his belt was a very fat rabbit he'd apparently shot. The boy's eyes were bright blue.

It was as if everyone, black and white, was struck mute. When they could no longer hear the men in the distance, the white boy finally spoke. "Y'all hungry?"

Nobody moved except Nathan. He nodded.

The white boy untied the rabbit and threw it to Nathan, who reached up and caught it in the air. "Y'all have to skin it yerself," the white boy said. Then he grinned, turned, and jogged off in the rain.

Nathan stood up. He triumphantly held the rabbit up high. Rainwater dripped off it.

"Well, I'll be," said Blue. "I'll be."

"Nice white boy, sure enough, but we still trespassin'," Aleta reminded him nervously. "We got to move on soon as this rain lets up."

So they did. Several miles later, the rain stopped completely. Blue spied a tobacco barn that appeared abandoned. "We'll sleep here tonight," he said.

"We best build a supper fire elsewhere," said Aleta.

Blue nodded and took off walking. "Start skinnin' that rabbit!" he called over his shoulder. "And find us some dry kindling, too! I'll be back."

Aleta worked on the rabbit, and the others silently foraged for dry firewood. By the time Blue came back, they were ready to cook. Then Blue led them a quarter mile away to the place he'd scouted out for the supper fire.

Aleta made an excellent rice stew with the rabbit. It was a welcome and rare hot meal for the weary travelers. By the time they'd trudged back to the tobacco barn, Janie thought she'd fall asleep on her feet.

Stomachs full of hot food, all five young people fell fast asleep in their blankets.

Shannon Oaks Plantation, Georgia

Anna stirred honey into a pot of oats that hung in the fireplace. She turned to her husband. "I still got to fatten you up, mister."

George sat on the cabin floor and grinned. His eyes sparkled in the firelight. "No complaints, woman."

"That's good," Anna replied. She bent over the fire and began dropping mounds of dough into a flat skillet on top of the coals.

George chuckled. "I been dreamin' about them biscuits for seven years now."

Anna flashed a smile at her once-strong husband. His complexion looked better after four days of rest and food, but he was still so thin. He'd arrived at Shannon Oaks weak and not able to keep any food down for the first couple of days. Once he was able to digest Anna's baked custard, he'd been improving ever since. Good thing he was still young. He would recover his strength.

Anna's gratitude at having George back could hardly be described. Her heartfelt prayers of thanksgiving were constant. She wondered what had happened in George's life all these years, but there was no hurry to share difficult stories.

Of course, they had right away talked about little Janie. George had understandably been stunned to hear his daughter was gone. Now he brought it up again. "I still can't get over it, Anna. What these white folks thinkin', sellin' off a little girl like Janie?"

Anna turned back to the fire and hung her head. The day her child had been taken from her was the most powerless day of Anna's life.

George reached over and grabbed his wife's hand. "Listen here. You couldn't do nothin' about it," he said. "You stayed strong like I asked." George stroked Anna's work-worn fingers. "Now I'll be your strength," he said. "We'll find our girl."

Anna sighed. "No telling where she is now."

George considered this. "You say they took her to Rubyhill. She might still be there. If not, someone there will know something. Let's you and me rest up a couple more days, and we'll head out for Rubyhill."

Anna looked into George's eyes. "You sure you up to it?"

George nodded. "We got to find our girl."

"Yes, Lord help us," said Anna.

Three days later, George and Anna left Shannon Oaks. A kind network of former slaves living in a dozen plantations along the way directed them in their journey to Rubyhill. It was two counties away in unfamiliar territory.

But along the way, each plantation's slave quarters opened up to the couple and showed them the best hospitality. At every turn, a community fed them and gave them a place to stay for the night.

By the time George and Anna reached Rubyhill three days later, they were anxious with anticipation and dread. Was little Janie here?

They approached the main grounds of Rubyhill slowly, steering toward the slave quarters. It was always best for black people to avoid white people when approaching a strange plantation.

"Don't seem to be no whites 'round here," remarked George.

Anna nodded. "Let's go to the kitchen."

Good smells wafted from the detached kitchen. As they drew closer, a heavyset woman stepped out and looked them over.

"How you folks?" she said. She gave the couple a friendly, gap-toothed smile.

Anna smiled back. George doffed his hat to the cook. "My name's George, and this here's my wife, Anna."

The women nodded to each other.

George continued. "We's looking for our little girl. She got sold from under us over at Shannon Oaks some six years ago. We heard she was brought over here."

"What's her name?" asked the cook.

"Her name's Janie," said Anna. "She's goin' on twelve years come Christmas—"

"Janie?" The cook looked stunned. "Oh, honey, Janie just left here, not even a week ago."

Anna grabbed George's arm. "What you mean?" she asked the cook.

"Five of our young'uns took off north to get themselves work. You just missed your girl, honey."

Anna's knees buckled. She felt George grab her up in his arms to keep her on her feet. She heard him say to the cook, "Ma'am, do you know where they's headed?"

"Chicago's what was said," the cook responded.

Anna no longer heard the conversation. She simply sank to the ground.

So close. So close, and so far.

Chapter 8

Maydean

Janie was weary. Bone weary. She concentrated on putting one foot in front of the other. Surely they would stop and rest soon.

Around thirty days had passed, and the Rubyhill Five had been on the road a long time—too long for Janie. It was late October, and she didn't know how much longer she could take it. But they still had to get through the whole state of Indiana.

The five young people had crossed the state line from Kentucky to Indiana just that morning. Every day they were closer to Chicago than they were the day before, but it seemed like every day they moved a little slower.

Janie was getting worried. Days were so cold and nights even colder. They were running into brief snow squalls here and there. They had begun wearing the heavy coats they'd found in the Big House. They were even wearing shoes and socks, and although the shoes felt uncomfortable to feet unused to footwear, everybody's feet stayed dry and warm.

Today the Rubyhill Five experienced autumn in Indiana as they'd never experienced it in Georgia. Everywhere the maple trees were vibrant with color. Janie had never seen anything like it—leaves that were bright yellow and red and some kind of color in between. She'd gathered a few at first but had since let them flutter back to the ground. There were so many.

But the thrill of all that beauty soon wore off. Janie was too cold and tired to care about nature's beauty. She was more concerned about how difficult nature was making it for them to get to their destination.

One of the biggest issues was food. Once again, Janie felt that constant, gnawing hunger. All the carrying food was gone, and foraging for food every day took time and energy. They worked hard for every bite they ate.

Fortunately, apples were in season and plentiful along the way, but how they all longed for—and needed—a good hot meal. *Maybe some chicken stew and biscuits,* Janie thought as she trudged along. *With boiled potatoes and carrots. Maybe some fried apple pie. Maybe. . .*

Janie stopped herself. This would do nothing but make her hungrier. She continued concentrating on taking each step.

There was one more worrisome thing, the most worrisome thing of all. Blue was coughing. It had started a couple days ago, and it seemed like every hour the cough sounded deeper and rougher.

Aleta fussed over him about it that morning. "Blue, that cough sounds evil. Let's take a day off and let you get some strength."

Blue showed a rare display of anger. "What we supposed to do, then?" he snapped. "All of us lay down 'til I get better? We ain't got that kinda time, and we ain't got nowhere to lay down. We got to keep going."

Aleta protested but soon said nothing more. Janie felt a little sick to her stomach to hear these two argue. She and Nathan and Lucy exchanged glances from time to time but remained quiet all morning.

The morning stretched on until Aleta insisted they stop at a maple grove and look for food. Blue said nothing. Instead, he stepped off the path and sank down onto the thick roots of a large tree. Janie saw that he was shivering.

As troubling as it was to see Blue this way, the three younger ones immediately circled out from the grove looking around for water and for something to eat. They left Blue with Aleta, who busied herself unpacking cookware and apples.

Nathan found some field corn, the kind livestock ate, but it would be better than nothing. They stuffed ears of it in their pockets. Then Lucy found mushrooms. After they determined the mushrooms were safe—they knew which ones were poisonous—the three picked lots of them. They also found hickory nuts and a creek from which they drew water with their boiling pots.

After an hour, they knew this would have to do. It wasn't a lot, but they could eat and still keep walking. They headed back to the maple grove. As they neared, Janie heard Lucy gasp. Janie looked up. Blue was stretched out on the ground. Aleta had wrapped him in his blanket, and he was shivering violently.

The three approached slowly. Aleta looked up and saw them. "Come help me keep this blanket on Blue. He's shakin' it right back off."

They all managed to get the blanket wrapped more tightly around Blue, who was indeed shaking terribly. Then Aleta had them all huddle around Blue to see if he could get warm enough to stop shivering. The five were used to huddling together by this point on the journey. But in this huddle, Janie could actually feel the feverish heat emanate from Blue.

Janie touched the outline of the pewter cross under her clothes as she did so often these days and began to pray silently. *Lord, help Blue. Help us all, Lord. We in trouble.*

They stayed together under the tree all afternoon. Nobody

talked, and nobody ate. Blue began to moan in his fever. Aleta looked terribly frightened, though she tried not to appear so. Nobody asked the question they all had on their minds: *What now?*

Dark came earlier every day this time of year, and it was fast approaching. Clearly there would be no more travel today. Still, nobody moved from huddling around Blue.

Finally Aleta spoke. "Each of you, one at a time, go fetch your blankets and come on back. We gonna stay close together tonight. We gonna get some water down this boy, and then y'all need to drink and eat what you found, right here in the huddle."

So that's what they did. Blue's fever actually kept them all warm throughout the night, but it was not a comfort by any means. Blue eventually became delirious, talking nonsense and even laughing in his feverish state. Nobody slept well under the circumstances.

Janie woke up with the cold morning sunlight touching her face. She looked around. The others still dozed, huddled up against Blue, who had finally fallen asleep. His breathing was loud and heavy.

Janie gently extricated herself from the sleeping tangle of the Rubyhill Five. She didn't want to wake anyone. But she was hungry. As she munched on mushrooms and hickory nuts from yesterday's food search, she decided to build a fire for boiling apples.

Moving quietly, Janie left the maple grove to search for kindling. At the edge of the noisy creek they'd found yesterday, she sensed she was not alone. She turned in a slow circle, her gaze darting about until she spied what she'd sensed was there.

Only a few yards away stood a white girl wearing a heavy jacket, men's pants, and big boots. She had the reddest hair Janie had ever seen. It was long and curly, and Janie saw that it was very matted. Janie had not heard this girl approach.

The two looked at each other for a moment. Then the redheaded girl spoke. "You're not from 'round here. Where you from?"

Janie was very startled by this. "Georgia," she replied.

"Where's that?" said the white girl.

Not sure how to answer, Janie paused. "Down south," she finally said.

"Who are you?"

On this journey, the Rubyhill Five had determined to keep information to a minimum when dealing with local whites and to keep on moving. They had not yet had anything frightening happen to them at the hands of locals, but it could happen. Janie told the redheaded girl her name and nothing else.

The girl spoke again. "You all alone?"

Janie paused, then shook her head.

The girl considered this. "My name's Maydean. I live down the holler with my granddaddy. He's drunk all the time and mean as a snake." She stopped talking, as if she'd said too much. "You movin' on through?"

Janie nodded. "Going north."

"Where 'bouts?"

"Chicago."

"I heard of it," the girl said. Janie saw that she was probably around her own age. The girl had the same shockingly blue eyes as that boy who had given them the rabbit. Janie noted wearily that it seemed like that had happened a long time ago.

The girl stepped forward. "What you doin' here?"

"Looking for firewood."

"I'll help you." And with that, the white girl tromped about in her pants and boots, briskly picking up small pieces of wood and stuffing them into her jacket pocket. Janie drew a little closer and noticed that the girl's clothes were filthy. She could see that the girl was very thin and that the dirty clothes hung loosely on her.

After about ten minutes, the two had enough wood to build a

fire and sustain it for boiling a pot of apples. Janie wondered what she should do now. Did she dare take this white girl back to her sleeping friends, especially when one of them was clearly sick?

Then it occurred to Janie that maybe this Maydean was the answer to the praying she'd been doing all night. The redhead seemed an unlikely answer to prayer, so Janie prayed one more thing silently: *Lord?*

Janie had the strongest impression that she should invite Maydean to eat with her and the others. Yet that was a very foolish thing to consider. Whites and blacks absolutely never, ever ate together. Janie could offer, but the girl would most likely refuse.

Nevertheless, Janie decided to invite her to share their food. "Maydean, are you hungry?"

Maydean's face was unreadable. Then she nodded. It suddenly occurred to Janie that if Maydean lived with a drunken granddaddy, she might be hungry a lot of the time.

"Come on, then," said Janie, and she led the redhead to the maple grove.

Rubyhill Plantation, Georgia

George and Anna never returned to Shannon Oaks. Instead, the hospitable Rubyhill residents took care of them for the next week and helped them plan their own trip to Chicago.

"You might as well stay here and get ready for your journey north," Old Joe had reasoned with George and Anna. "You cain't catch up with them others no-how. They all young and got a head start over you two. They say a black man live high as a white man up there in Chicago these days. I'll tell you everything I know 'bout getting up there, everything I told them children. You'll find your girl up there. But it's a mighty long way, and fella,"—Old Joe directed this to George—"I don't know's you should start it right away no-how."

Cook led George and Anna to Aunty Mil's now-empty cabin. The women had swept out the fireplace and the rest of the inside, and they'd dragged the rocker over to Old Joe's place.

Anna and George followed the cook inside. "This here's where my baby lived?" asked Anna.

"Yes," the cook replied, "and she lived a good life here with old Aunty Mil. She was a good granny to your girl. Got her to sing in that sweet voice and everything."

Tears ran down Anna's face as she gripped George's arm. How bittersweet it felt to be in Janie's home. How close Anna felt to her daughter.

For the next week, Old Joe sat with George by the hour and instructed him on the details of the journey north the same way he had the Rubyhill Five. Anna listened to all the stories about Janie that anyone wanted to tell her. George slept and ate, ate and slept, slept and ate. The day he told Anna he felt restless, they both knew it was time to head north.

Just as they had a couple of weeks before, the former slaves of Rubyhill gave a big send-off to the travelers. They sent them on their way with plenty of carrying food and the sounds of singing.

George squeezed Anna's hand as they walked down Rubyhill's drive. Anna squeezed back.

Chapter 9

Trouble

Nathan, Lucy, and Aleta were up and moving about when Janie and Maydean approached the maple grove. Janie saw that Blue was no longer thrashing or talking deliriously. He seemed to be in a deep sleep, his head resting on a big maple root. Janie wondered if Blue's deep sleep was a good thing or a bad thing.

Aleta stood quickly when she saw the two girls approach the grove. Janie could tell by Aleta's face and posture that she was nervous to see a white person. Now Lucy and Nathan stood, too, looking very concerned.

Janie spoke up right away. "This here's Maydean. She lives 'round here. She helped me find kindling. I want to boil us some apples, and I asked her if she's hungry."

This was quite a long speech coming from quiet Janie. The others stared at her, then at Maydean, then back at Janie. Bringing a white person to their encampment was absolutely the last thing they would expect any one of them to do. It was just too dangerous.

Janie understood the concern all too well. They'd been fortunate on the road so far. Nobody had really bothered them. Aleta prayed aloud for protection daily. Once they had stumbled upon a water moccasin while drawing water at a river, but it swam away without incident.

Even so, they would rather happen upon creatures of the outdoors than white strangers any day. Nothing good could come of letting white locals know the Rubyhill Five were traveling through.

But Janie's heart felt unusually light. Deep down, she knew it was good and right to offer this girl something to eat.

"Maydean, you any good at building fires?" she asked.

The white girl nodded and immediately started arranging kindling. Aleta continued to stare at Janie, a thousand unasked questions in her eyes. Lucy and Nathan stood together and watched.

Janie ignored Aleta's probing looks. Instead she pulled out the boiling pot, took the paring knife, and began coring apples. She stopped when she realized that Maydean had stopped moving.

Maydean had just noticed the sleeping figure of Blue. "What's wrong with him?"

"He's got the fever," said Janie.

"Fever, huh." Maydean still didn't move. "You got to get him indoors."

Nobody responded to that. Obviously that was not a choice they had.

Maydeen looked at Janie, then Aleta, then back at Blue. "He can't come to my house 'cause my granddaddy hates your kind." She said this without emotion, then went on: "But there's a doctor over the hill apiece. He'd fix him. I can take you there."

"A white doctor?" asked Janie.

Maydean nodded. "He ain't like my granddaddy, though. Him and his wife used to hide your kind. I knew it, but I never told nobody." She scratched her head. "They take in everybody. Feed 'em good, too."

Janie looked at Aleta. They certainly could use a doctor for Blue, and it sounded like this doctor might even treat black people. Maybe they should trust this girl all the way. Aleta shook her head and turned away.

But Janie felt strongly that Maydean was an answer to prayer. She grabbed Aleta's arm and pulled her away, out of earshot of the others.

"Aleta, we got to listen to her."

"Janie, you crazy? What you thinking? She's a white girl—and a mighty dirty one, at that."

"What's that got to do with anything? And I'm not crazy," Janie insisted. "Were we crazy when we took that rabbit from that white boy back then?"

Aleta shook her head. "But he was just one white person, and not a hateful one at that. The more white folks get wind of us here, the more trouble we get. 'Specially with one of us sick."

"She knows a doctor—"

"A white doctor," Aleta hissed, "and that ain't gonna do us no good. You know that."

Janie hissed right back. "If we don't get help for Blue, he gonna die right here."

Aleta's face fell. "I fear that, too, little sis. But if bringing in a whole lotta white people puts y'all in danger, too. . ." Her voice trailed off.

Janie could see the full weight of responsibility resting squarely on Aleta's shoulders. Together, Aleta and Blue could handle decisions for the five of them on this long, dangerous journey. Alone, it was a heavy load.

"Aleta," Janie said gently, "listen to me. I prayed 'bout this. I believe God sent this white girl to help us."

Aleta shook her head.

Janie continued. "Besides, she ain't got nothing. Look how she is.

We got to share food with her. She even helped with the fire."

"It's not that," Aleta said. "If she'll sit and eat black folk's food, she's welcome to it. It's pulling in more whites that's got me nervous. No, little sis, we can't do no more than feed this girl."

Suddenly it started to snow. Hard. If they hadn't had to live in it, this snowfall would have been pretty. But big, wet snowflakes were coming down fast and furiously. They made no sound.

There was, however, one sound that reached Janie and Aleta from the maple grove—the sound of deep, hard coughing.

But it wasn't coming from Blue. Aleta and Janie looked at one another.

It was Lucy.

Kentucky

In a dry, warm barn in the middle of Kentucky, George and Anna took cover from a morning rainstorm. The sounds of rain on the rooftop made them drowsy, and before long, both of them snuggled down into the hay and fell asleep.

Janie came to Anna in a dream. Janie was still five years old. She looked into Anna's face with those huge, cinnamon-brown eyes of hers, and she began to sing. *Oh, what a beautiful sound,* thought Anna. *Sweet and high-pitched like a bird's.*

Suddenly a hawk swooped down and snatched the little girl away and up into the sky. Anna woke with a start. Trembling, she shook George awake.

"We got to pray right now. Janie's in trouble."

Without any question, George rose up. The two knelt in the hay and prayed throughout the rest of the storm. By the time the rain stopped, Anna felt calm, and she and George continued north on their journey to find their daughter.

Chapter 10

Mrs. Hull's Kitchen

Janie stood next to Maydean on the long front porch of a big, white farmhouse. She gazed around the farm itself. The many handsome barns were painted white, and the barnyards were so clean that to Janie they looked as if they'd been swept with a broom.

Most of the animals were apparently taking shelter from the storm, although a few horses stood outside with their backs to the driving snow. Janie hoped she could take shelter soon, too. Walking through this snowstorm had left the two girls cold and wet.

Maydean knocked on the front door of the farmhouse. After a moment, a white-haired woman opened it. She wore a black dress with a starched white collar and stood no taller than Janie.

The woman's rosy face beamed. "Good morning, dear Maydean. Come in out of the weather!"

The door opened wide, and Maydean stepped in. Janie paused. She'd never in her life walked into a white person's home through the front doorway.

The white woman smiled directly at Janie. "Come in, child, before thee catches thy death of cold."

What a strange way she talks. Janie stepped inside and quickly took in her surroundings. A polished staircase on the right side of the hallway climbed straight up to the second floor. A banister curved around at the top. Downstairs, framed portraits hung all over the walls of the hall. An oil lamp caused shadows to dance over the images.

Indoors, Janie felt instantly warmer. Then a wave of guilt swept over her as she remembered the others huddling under their snow-covered blankets in the maple grove.

"This here's Janie," said Maydean.

The white woman took Janie's cold hands and rubbed them in her own warm ones for a moment. This was even stranger to Janie. She had never in her life touched or been touched by a white person. "Oh, thee is so cold," the woman said. "Come into the kitchen. There is hot food on the stove. Come."

The two girls stomped the snow off their feet and onto a thick rug beside the door before following the woman straight down the central hallway. A closed door opened to a huge kitchen. The kitchen was even warmer than the hallway.

"Sit down, girls," said the woman. The two girls pulled sturdy chairs away from a large oak table and sat. The woman looked directly at Janie. "I am Mrs. Hull, Janie. I am pleased to make thy acquaintance."

Not knowing how to respond, Janie simply nodded then looked at the floor, her hands in her lap. She felt shy in such a new and strange situation.

Maydean got to the heart of the matter. "Janie's people got caught in the snow in the maple grove on Uncle Willie's farm, Mrs. Hull. They come from down south, and they're headin' north. Some took sick—coughing fits and fever. They got to get inside."

Mrs. Hull looked instantly concerned. "How many?"

Maydean continued to speak for Janie. "Five all together, two of 'em sick."

"And how old is everyone, child?" Mrs. Hull spoke directly to Janie.

Janie cleared her throat. "Blue's seventeen, ma'am, and he's sick. The other sick one's Lucy, and she's ten. Nathan's ten, too. I'm eleven, and Aleta's seventeen." She stopped talking.

"Nobody elderly, then, and no babies?" Mrs. Hull said.

Janie shook her head.

"My husband will help them, child, and thee must not worry. Young people have a good chance of pulling through sickness of all kinds, and I'm sure thy long journey and the good Lord have made thee strong."

That sounded encouraging to Janie. Her toes were beginning to get warm. She could smell enticing odors in this kitchen. She looked around and spied chicken soup simmering on a back burner of a coal stove. The dregs of coffee were still warm and fragrant in a blue-speckled pot. Fresh baked bread sat on top of the sideboard. Janie's stomach growled out loud.

Mrs. Hull heard the stomach noises, and she smiled at Janie. "Thee is hungry."

"Yes, ma'am," Janie said. She quickly added, "But the others are out there in the snow. I can't eat when they can't." She stopped abruptly and looked down again. Had she been impolite? The words had just burst out of her.

But Mrs. Hull nodded vigorously. "Of course, child, I understand. I will fetch my husband immediately. That will take only a wee bit of time. While I do that, Maydean, please feed thyself and Janie, and please wrap food to take to the others. Get thy stomachs full and thy bodies warm so that both of thee are fortified for the outside."

Maydean hopped up and began fetching dishes from the sideboard. Janie surmised that perhaps this cozy, orderly farmhouse was Maydean's safe place from her drunken granddaddy. Janie felt better for Maydean.

She felt better about her own situation, too. It looked like help was surely on its way. *Thank You, Lord.*

Mrs. Hull pulled on a heavy black cloak and wool bonnet. Once more, she spoke to Janie directly. "Child," she said kindly, "thee must not fret. My husband is an excellent physician and will help the sick ones. Until I locate him in the barns, of course, we cannot leave. In the meantime, thee must take nourishment while I am gone. That is best for all concerned. Does thee understand?"

Janie nodded. "Thank you, ma'am."

Mrs. Hull left the room, and soon they heard the back door open and close. A draft of cold flashed through the warm kitchen.

Maydean ladled up a steaming bowl of soup and placed it with a spoon in front of Janie. "Eat," she said. She moved to the sideboard and cut two thick slices of bread and placed them right on the table next to the soup. Then she helped herself to the soup pot.

Janie waited. Should she eat—or not? The others back in the maple grove were cold and wet and hungry. . . .

"Eat, Janie," Maydean said again, as if reading her mind. "Mrs. Hull's right. We got to get warmed up while we wait. Then we can do better outside."

Janie nodded. She said a silent grace, picked up her spoon, and dug in.

Chapter 11

To the Rescue

Mrs. Hull was true to her word. By the time Janie had devoured her bowl of soup and a slice of bread with butter, Mrs. Hull had returned with her husband in tow.

"Janie, this is Dr. Hull." A short man with twinkling eyes nodded at Janie and Maydean. He was a powerfully built man in spite of his white hair, and he wore good wool clothing. Janie noted that his black clothes were clean, even though he'd just come in from farm work. He carried the good odor of fresh air.

Dr. Hull fished a large black valise out from under a worktable. "Virginia, dear, I'll hook up the team and bring the sleigh around front. Please give the young ladies as many blankets as they can carry."

"Yes, Otto," Mrs. Hull said, and she hurried into the room off the kitchen while the doctor headed for the back door.

Maydean had eaten quickly. Now she hopped to her feet, and Janie watched her spread two slices of bread with butter and wrap them in newspaper. "Only two of your friends gonna eat, I'll wager," she said. Then she put on her jacket and stuffed the food into her pockets. "Come on, Janie. Dr. Hull's gonna be ready in no time."

Mrs. Hull called to them from the side room. They found her in a storage room full of linens, pillows, and blankets. Janie had not seen so many linens since Rubyhill's Big House before the war. Mrs. Hull loaded both girls down with heavy blankets and quilts then led the way to the front door.

Before long, a team of two large, black draft horses pulled a long vehicle up to the porch. Janie had never seen such a thing as this sleigh. It looked like a passenger wagon, long with three wide bench seats, but it sat on runners instead of wheels. It was so big she could understand why two horses were needed to pull it. Dr. Hull occupied the driver's seat.

Blankets and girls were loaded onto the sleigh. Dr. Hull bundled each girl in an extra blanket, waved to Mrs. Hull, and started the huge horses down the snowy drive. Janie barely blinked, it all happened so fast.

Maydean called out directions to Dr. Hull. The sleigh was able to move quickly over the accumulating snow. Within ten minutes, they arrived at the maple grove.

Janie looked quickly for her friends. Finally she saw the pile of snow-covered blankets with Nathan and Aleta peering out from under. As she drew closer, Janie noted fear in their eyes.

Janie watched Aleta scrutinize the situation of a white man coming for them in a horse-drawn sleigh. Aleta frowned, but when she saw Janie wave at her from behind Dr. Hull, she stopped frowning.

Without further ado, Aleta sprang into action. She gathered the dry blankets offered her and wrapped them around Lucy and Blue, who both lay still. She helped Nathan brush the wet snow off himself then dried herself off. Janie jumped out of the sleigh, gathered all their gear, and threw it into the back of the sleigh.

Dr. Hull introduced himself to Aleta then made a quick

assessment of the sick youths. He took off one glove and pressed his fingers to each of their necks. He ran his bare hand over their feverish faces. He lifted their eyelids and looked at their eyes. Then he bodily picked up Blue and placed him in the sleigh. He stepped back and did the same with Lucy; then he tucked blankets around their deeply sleeping forms.

Janie's jaw dropped at the white man's strength and quick agility. He was a farmer, of course, used to hauling and lifting. But to Janie, he seemed kind of old for such strength. Of course Lucy didn't weigh much, and Blue had dropped weight in the past couple weeks. Still, Dr. Hull surely was a strong man.

Before long, the sleigh was loaded with people, and Maydean handed out the buttered bread. Dr. Hull slapped the reins, and off they went into the snow, the runners hissing as they traveled over the ground. Their return to the Hull farm was slowed only a little by the extra weight.

Once they arrived at the farm and unloaded the wagon, much to Janie's surprise, Mrs. Hull said there were beds ready upstairs for Janie, Aleta, and Nathan. She also had made up beds for Blue and Lucy in two back rooms on the first floor. "Dr. Hull and I sleep downstairs," she explained, "and we must be close to these two tonight. When they are well, they will move upstairs."

Janie and Aleta looked at each other quickly. *A white woman wants us to sleep in her house?*

Aleta offered to help Mrs. Hull with Blue and Lucy, but the older woman refused. "Thee must get into dry clothes, dear. Betsy will bring up warm water and towels so thee can bathe. We have clothes in the wardrobes upstairs, and something will fit. Betsy will help thee look."

A smiling young woman with blond braids pinned up appeared in the doorway. She wore an apron over her calico dress. "I'm

Betsy. Come on upstairs."

Mrs. Hull added one more thing. "We shall eat supper in an hour, and afterward I shall expect all of thee to take thy rest for as long as thee can. Thy friends are in Dr. Hull's capable hands and God's, as well."

Maydean moved to the kitchen while the others followed Betsy up the steep stairs. Aleta and Janie would share a big, four-poster bed in a large room in the front part of the upstairs. A smaller trundle bed was tucked underneath the high bed. Across the hall, Nathan would sleep on one of two single beds.

Each bed was made up with flannel sheets, warm quilts, and pillows—truly a new experience for the young former slaves. None of them had ever slept in such luxury. None of them had ever slept in a bed. None had even slept in an actual house before now.

Just as Mrs. Hull had predicted, the wardrobes held clean clothes that fit all three young people. Betsy chatted away as she handed out dresses, pants, shirts, nightgowns, and warm socks.

"Before the war, slaves escaping to the north stayed here, so Mrs. Hull always had good clothes on hand for them to wear in their new life," she said. "Sometimes they stayed a long time gaining their health before moving on. Dr. Hull is a gifted doctor. And Mrs. Hull is a wonderful nurse."

Nathan piped up. "Why do they talk that way?"

"They're Quakers," Betsy explained. "That's the way they talk. They believe it's a way of treating everyone equally under God."

"Aren't you their daughter?" asked Nathan.

"I'm a distant cousin—from the Methodist side of the family." Betsy laughed. "I work here for room and board and some money, which I'm saving. I plan to move to Detroit, Michigan, next year to attend teachers' college."

Janie felt a twinge of envy. How smart this young woman must be. And so kind. What a good teacher she would make. Janie noticed Aleta eyeing the young woman with approval as well. The two were about the same age.

"So now, does everyone have towels and dry clothes?" asked Betsy. "And nightclothes, too?" Of course Betsy couldn't know that the Rubyhill youths had never slept in nightclothes, only in their day clothes. And they never told her. They simply nodded gratefully.

"Fine, then. I'm going downstairs. During cold weather, we eat in the kitchen, so come there when you're ready." She smiled once more and headed downstairs.

Janie and Aleta looked at each other. They were too exhausted to say much. Besides, Nathan had been talking for everyone ever since they got to the Hull farm.

"Did you see them horses? They moved through that snow like it was shallow water. Big, healthy animals, too. What was that thing we rode in? It was so fast! Look at these pillows! Beds look so good, I may jus' sleep all day. Food smells good, too. Cain't wait to eat. . ."

And on and on. Finally Aleta shushed him and sent him to get ready in his own room.

Aleta was quiet at first as they washed at the basins of soapy water. Finally she spoke. "Janie, I sure am thankful you were listening to the Lord this morning. I don't know where we'd be. I don't know if any of us woulda lived 'til morning. I don't know. . . ." Aleta stopped and sighed.

Janie reached over and squeezed her friend's hand. "I'm thankful, too. These are nice people. And so's Maydean."

Aleta shook her head slowly. "I was wrong about her."

"How were you supposed to know?" asked Janie. "She looks a fright." Janie shrugged. "And she's white."

"Still no excuse to think the evil thoughts I was having," said Aleta. She pulled on a blue wool dress and a white pinafore apron over it. "Oh, this feels so good. Thank You, Jesus."

Janie dressed quickly in the warm, dry clothes Betsy had laid out for her. "Ready to go downstairs?"

"I sure am, little sis."

In the kitchen, the large oak table was set. There was a place for everyone who could sit and eat—Dr. and Mrs. Hull, Betsy, Aleta, Nathan, Janie, and Maydean, who had washed her hands and face, Janie noticed. Janie could see now that the girl had freckles.

Betsy placed a large, lovely serving dish of piping hot chicken stew on the table. The stew was loaded with carrots, potatoes, and onions. Mrs. Hull sliced bread on a wooden board.

As the supper table was being made ready, Dr. Hull filled everyone in on how the patients were. He kept it brief. "They both have fevers. We shall stay up with them, as fevers have the habit of rising at night. We will know more by morning. In the meantime, let us pray for thy friends."

Dr. Hull bowed his head and said grace, adding special prayers for Blue and Lucy. After the "amen," Janie glanced at Aleta. Janie realized once again the burden Aleta had carried all day and all the night before. Aleta's relief was clear. Having these kind people take that burden and carry it for now was a godsend.

At first, Aleta and Nathan stared at their dishes of bread and stew without touching any of it. This was the first hot meal they'd seen in weeks. But their awe did not last long. Soon both were devouring the delicious supper along with everyone else.

Mrs. Hull and Betsy replenished the food throughout the meal, and the youths—including Maydean—ate until they were satisfied. Even then, they mopped their plates clean with their bread crusts.

Now Janie's stomach was so full that it made her extremely sleepy. As the Hulls and Betsy talked, Janie caught herself nodding off. She jerked her head up and made herself keep her eyes open.

That's when she saw that both Aleta and Nathan had fallen sound asleep in their chairs.

Mrs. Hull smiled at her husband. He nodded and rose. The strong man picked Nathan right up off his chair and carried him upstairs. Betsy and Mrs. Hull pulled Aleta to her feet and helped her up the stairs. Janie managed to bid Maydean good night and get herself up the stairs, too, holding onto the banister the whole sleepy way.

In their bedroom, Janie and Aleta struggled into flannel nightgowns and fell into bed. Aleta rose up once more to put out the lamp, and the two girls were asleep within minutes.

It would be a long time before the Rubyhill Five traveled again.

Chapter 12

Wintering

"Janie, what you got there?"

Maydean pointed to the bodice of Janie's dress. It had become a bit of a nervous habit for Janie to trace the outline of that dangling cross through the fabric of her clothes. Since arriving at the Hulls, Aleta had frowned gently at Janie every time she saw her do it. But Aleta wasn't in the room right now.

Janie pulled out the cross. "Nathan found this buried with Miz Laura's silver, back at Rubyhill. Miz Laura told us to take whatever we wanted, so Nathan gave me this."

Maydean's blue eyes twinkled. "That makes Nathan your beau."

"What's a beau?" asked Janie.

Maydean tossed her red mane of hair and grinned. "Somebody who's sweet on you."

Janie shook her head. "No, Nathan's like a brother."

The two girls sat cross-legged on the braided rug next to a crackling fire in the front-room fireplace. The snow that had brought the Rubyhill Five to the Hull farmhouse had stopped, leaving behind a world of white. Maydean had gone home after supper the previous night but returned through the snow in the morning.

She had joined them all for hot oatmeal, and Mrs. Hull had invited her to spend the day.

The house had been quiet since breakfast. Mrs. Hull reported that Dr. Hull was in the back bedrooms, tending to Blue and Lucy. She said he would speak to everyone about it later.

Maydean reached out and gently touched the cross. “Can I look at it?” she asked.

Janie nodded. She took the chain off and handed it to the redhead. Maydean turned the pewter cross over in her hand. “What’s it say here on the back?”

“You can’t read?” Janie blurted out. She thought all white people could read.

A dark cloud seemed to spread across Maydean’s freckled face. She shook her head. She seemed embarrassed.

“I’m sorry, Maydean,” Janie said quickly. “I don’t know no black folks who can read, that’s for sure. But I just figured all white folks could.” She paused. “That wasn’t too smart of me.”

“My granddaddy won’t let me go to school,” Maydean said. “And he can’t read hisself.” She stopped talking. After a short uncomfortable silence, Maydean handed the cross back. “It’s real pretty, Janie,” she said.

“Thanks, Maydean,” said Janie. “You know,” she added, “your name’s real pretty, too.”

Maydean’s face lit up. “You think so?”

Janie nodded. “I never heard the name before.”

“I’m named for my mommy and daddy—May and Dean, see?”

“How come you live with your granddaddy and not with them?” asked Janie.

The cloud came back to Maydean’s face. “They’s both dead.”

It seemed Janie was bringing up difficult subjects for Maydean today. She said no more.

But a memory nudged her until it came full into the light. Suddenly Janie remembered something she'd forgotten for many years. "Oh my," she said aloud.

"What?" asked Maydean.

"I just recollected my momma telling me my name used to be Georgeanna. I was named after my poppa and her, too—George and Anna." Janie sat and let the memory sink in. "Georgeanna," she said again.

"That's real pretty. How's come you're called Janie then?" asked Maydean.

Janie thought hard until the reason finally surfaced. "I recollect what Momma said now. Master's wife said Georgeanna was too fine a name for a black baby. She's the one that named me Janie."

Maydean stared at Janie for a moment. "How come she did that if you wasn't her baby?"

"That's how it was in those days," Janie said. She looked at her new friend. "My momma didn't have no choice, Maydean. We was slaves."

The look Maydean gave Janie showed that Maydean had no clue what she was talking about. Janie wondered if maybe Maydean didn't realize what a slave was. Who did Maydean think the Hulls had been hiding all those years?

All Maydean said was, "You like being called Janie?"

Janie shrugged. "Never been called nothin' else."

A heavy curtain in the doorway was pulled aside, and Betsy stuck her head in. "Girls, come to the kitchen. Dr. Hull has some news."

The Hull kitchen was always so wonderfully warm that Janie loved simply walking into it. At the table sat Aleta, Nathan, and Dr. Hull. Mrs. Hull and Betsy scurried about making tea and scraping hot gingerbread out of a black skillet. Janie loved that part of being in the kitchen, too—the delicious, plentiful food. She and

Maydean slid onto chairs and waited.

Dr. Hull cleared his throat. "Good morning, everyone. I know all of thee must be worried about Blue and Lucy. Mrs. Hull and I tended to them throughout the night. The worst is over for young Blue; his fever broke as the sun came up." The doctor paused. "Little Lucy is still in a bad way, I'm afraid. I suspect all of thee have lacked good nourishment for some time now, and that has weakened Lucy considerably. She has little to fight with."

Will Lucy die? The thought took hold inside Janie, and she was instantly sick to her stomach. She looked quickly at Nathan. Lucy was his twin, the only blood family he remembered having. Understandably, Nathan was fighting back tears.

Mrs. Hull turned from the sideboard and spoke in her kind tone. "Dr. Hull and I are surprised that not all of thee fell ill the same way as Lucy and Blue, but we feel certain that possibility has passed. Praise God the fever did not spread further." She looked at each brown face at the table. "Dr. Hull and I want to invite thee to stay with us through the winter to rest and fortify thy bodies for the journey to Chicago. Will thee stay with us? Until spring?"

Numbly, all three Rubyhill youths nodded as one.

"Good," she said. She turned back to her tasks.

"The more fortunate news for Lucy," said Dr. Hull, "is that sometimes youths can handle a great deal more illness than adults. Lucy is ten, yes?"

"We'll be eleven soon, sir," said Nathan in a tiny voice.

Dr. Hull looked at Nathan a moment, then reached over and patted his shoulder. "Son, I assure thee that Mrs. Hull and I will do all we can to help thy sister pull through. In the meantime, let us all pray for Lucy's recovery."

With that, Dr. Hull lowered his head and began to pray aloud for Lucy's survival, as well as for the continued recovery of Blue. Then he excused himself and returned to his patients.

Except for the bustling noises Mrs. Hull and Betsy made, the kitchen was silent. Then Mrs. Hull sat down at the table.

"While thee young ones are with us," she said, "Betsy and I shall teach thee in the mornings. We shall meet here at the kitchen table."

Nathan looked up. "Teach us what, ma'am?"

Mrs. Hull smiled gently. "To read, young man. And to do arithmetic. How does that sound?"

Nathan slowly began to smile. Janie felt thrilled. She looked at Aleta, whose face once again wore a look of profound relief. Reading and working with numbers were skills they all knew they needed for the future in Chicago.

Betsy spoke up. "Mrs. Hull will teach you arithmetic, and I will teach you to read. Frankly, I will appreciate the opportunity to try my hand at actually teaching. I need the practice, so you'll be helping me as much as I hope to help you."

Janie looked at Maydean, but she could not read her facial expression. Should she ask if Maydean could join them? Would that embarrass Maydean, she being white? Janie decided to say nothing now but to approach Mrs. Hull about it later.

Betsy placed a plate of gingerbread squares on the table and poured glasses of fresh milk for all. Then she poured herself a cup of tea and sat down next to Janie.

"Miss Betsy," Janie whispered.

The blond girl looked at her.

Janie pulled the cross out of her dress and lifted it from around her neck. "What does this say?" She handed the cross and its chain to Betsy.

Betsy fingered the cross, smiled, and whispered back, "It says, 'Make a joyful noise.' It's from the Bible." She reached over and draped the chain back around Janie's neck.

Janie turned the phrase over in her mind. *Make a joyful noise.* The mystery was solved.

How she wished she could tell Aunty Mil.

Kentucky

An early November ice storm hit Kentucky as George and Anna traveled across the state. As a result, they found themselves spending the night on a horse farm near Lexington. They had made good time in spite of oddly frequent snow squalls, but they were not prepared for ice.

Nor was either of them really prepared for the hardship of the road. George's strength was not fully back, and neither of them were used to such cold. They weren't feeling very young anymore. Both of them were bone weary. Their love for their daughter had kept George and Anna moving northward, but it was starting to make sense to get off the road for winter and start up again in spring.

Good with horses since his days at Shannon Oaks, George sought employment at the Lexington stables of Mr. Albert DuPont. He was hired on the spot. The job provided a room over the horses, and Anna was allowed to stay, as well.

Since Mr. DuPont was a widower, Anna approached him with the offer to use her sewing and knitting skills to get him and his hired men ready for winter. A sensible man, DuPont happily hired Anna also.

So George and Anna decided they should spend the winter at DuPont Acres, put their money away, and start out again in spring. "We can take a train then, sugar," George promised. "We'll get to Chicago fast and in style."

Anna laughed. To her "in style" would simply mean staying clean and not sleeping out in the weather. And that sounded just fine to her. Initially, she was reluctant not to keep moving, but she saw the wisdom of shoring up their strength, earning money, and looking less bedraggled when they hit the sophisticated city of Chicago.

Besides, the recent nightmare about Janie had not returned. Anna felt a peace about her little girl, a peace for which she was grateful.

Chapter 13

Change in the Air

"Mrs. Hull?" Janie looked over the banister and spied the mistress of the house at the foot of the stairs. The white-haired woman looked up and beamed at Janie.

"And how was thy rest last night, Janie?" This was Janie's second day at the Hull farm.

Janie ran lightly down the stairs. "Very good, ma'am, thank you." She joined the woman in the hallway. Mrs. Hull was so short that Janie could look her straight in the eyes. "Mrs. Hull, did you know Maydean can't read?"

Mrs. Hull's mouth opened in surprise. "No, child, I did not know this. Why, there's a school not far from her house, and I assumed. . ." She looked down for a moment then back at Janie. "Is thee quite certain of this, child?"

"Yes, ma'am. Maydean told me herself. Her granddaddy won't let her go to school."

"Oh, I see." Mrs. Hull frowned. "Well, then, it is good of thee to bring it up. We should do what we can about that, shouldn't we, young Janie? Let us see if dear Maydean would like to join our little kitchen-table school. How does that sound?"

"That sounds real fine, ma'am," said Janie. She and Mrs. Hull smiled at each other.

"Now, dear Janie, I have a surprise. Come with me." Mrs. Hull led the way to the kitchen.

Indeed, the warm kitchen held the most wonderful surprise. Sitting at the table was the very thin figure of Blue, sipping from a cup of tea. In front of him sat a small dish of stewed pears. Blue's gaunt face made his eyes look as big as saucers. Aleta sat next to him, her eyes never leaving his face.

Seeing Blue sitting up and handling that dainty flowered cup made tears well in Janie's eyes. "Blue!" she called.

Blue looked up at Janie and grinned weakly. "Hey, girl. Come sit down here and help me eat them pears." His hand shook as he lowered the teacup. It rattled softly in its saucer.

Janie slid into the chair next to Blue. "Them pears is yours, Blue. You got to eat 'em."

"That's what I been telling him," Aleta fussed. "He's got to eat. That fever took the stuffin' right out of him."

Blue laughed softly. He placed his hand on Aleta's and left it there a moment. Aleta's face flushed, and her brown eyes sparkled.

Janie was surprised. She'd thought of them all as brothers and sisters, but clearly Blue and Aleta were—what had Maydean called it? Janie thought a minute. Oh yes—they were beaus. Sweet on each other. It looked that way to Janie, anyway.

Change in the air. Aunty Mil's favorite phrase drifted through Janie's mind. *Yes,* Janie thought, *lots of change in the air.*

Aleta pulled her hand away from Blue and looked self-consciously at Janie. "Blue's gonna be here at our kitchen school. He's gonna learn to read, too. Mrs. Hull says he can sit up for an hour at a time. Won't be long 'til we start our lessons."

"That's good," said Janie. She paused. "How's Lucy?"

"Nobody's saying nothing," said Aleta. "Dr. Hull's in there with her now. We got to keep prayin', little sis."

Blue looked at the tablecloth. It was hard to read his face. He most likely knew he had almost died, and he must be very worried for Lucy. Janie breathed a quick, silent prayer.

The kitchen door to the hall opened, and in walked Maydean and Betsy. They stopped at the sight of Blue.

Aleta introduced everyone who hadn't met, and Blue thanked Maydean for taking them to Hull Farm.

"I'm awful glad you're better," Maydean said. "Mrs. Hull will feed you good—I can tell you that." She turned to Janie. "Betsy's gonna braid my hair. You wanna come watch?"

Janie looked at Maydean's matted red mane. It would need a lot done to it before braiding would even be possible. Betsy certainly had her work cut out for her.

Janie glanced over at Blue. He and Aleta were looking shyly at one another again. Janie smiled inside. She hadn't seen that coming—Blue and Aleta together—but it made so much sense. They were meant to be together.

"Sure, Maydean," Janie said. "I'll come along."

The three girls headed into the front room, where the morning fire burned warm and slow. Maydean still wore men's pants, and she plopped down on the rug in front of the fire. She sat cross-legged, and Betsy sank down behind her. "What a marvelous head of hair you have, Maydean," Betsy said.

Janie thought that was a very kind thing to say. The fact of the matter was Maydean's long, curly hair was dirty and matted.

But Betsy didn't seem to mind. She brushed and brushed Maydean's hair. She worked oil through the matting with her fingers until she could brush every snarl free. Then she brushed some more.

Janie thought about Aunty Mil and how she used to comb Janie's nappy hair with only those long fingers of hers, then braid it nice and snug. Whenever Aunty Mil hit a snarl and had to work through it with her fingers, she would coo, "Little girl, you got the patience of Job."

The first time Aunty Mil had said this, little Janie had piped up, "How come you say that?"

" 'Cause you let Aunty Mil pull on this knot of hair, and you don't complain or cry or nothin'."

"Who's Job?" Janie had asked.

"A patient man o' God," was all Aunty said. But the next time—and every time—she untangled a snarl, she said, "Little girl, you got the patience of Job." Janie came to expect it and like it. Those hair sessions were some of the fondest memories Janie had.

It took a long time for Betsy to get Maydean's hair unsnarled. Throughout what had to be a painful process, Maydean simply sat quietly and looked straight ahead into the fire. She reminded Janie of the horses back in Georgia, how they looked when the groomsmen brushed their sleek coats. Those big creatures always stood perfectly still, looked straight ahead, and seemed to like how the brushing felt. That's how Maydean looked to Janie.

Before long, Janie could see that Betsy was right—Maydean did indeed have a glorious mane of hair. Now Betsy's fingers worked and worked some more until she'd braided two long, thick braids, snugly woven to stay put.

"Voilà!" said Betsy.

"What's that mean?" asked Maydean.

"It means I'm done, and you are beautiful. Turn around so Janie can see."

Maydean squirmed on the rug until she faced Janie.

"Oh, Maydean," Janie said, "you got to look in a mirror. You look so pretty."

Betsy pulled Maydean to her feet, moved her to the gilded mirror across the room, and placed her square in front of it. Janie watched Maydean's reflection. The redhead's jaw dropped.

"That's me?" she asked.

Betsy nodded. "I can help you keep it that way, too. I'm giving you this hairbrush to take home, and. . ."

Maydean's expression changed. "If it's all right, Miss Betsy, can I leave the brush here and just use it here?" Maydean's eyes looked anxious. "If I take it home, I might lose it."

Without a question, Betsy nodded. "Of course. I will find a special spot for it, Maydean. It will be your personal grooming spot in this house."

Maydean's shoulders drooped visibly. "Thank you, Miss Betsy," was all she said.

Mrs. Hull stuck her head in the room. "Girls, Dr. Hull wants to see us." Her eyes widened when she saw Maydean. "Why, look at that! How lovely thee looks, my dear." Then she hurried to the kitchen.

Everyone immediately gathered in the kitchen again—all except Blue, who was resting in his room, and Lucy, of course. Aleta, Janie, Nathan, Mrs. Hull, Betsy, and Maydean waited expectantly for news.

Dr. Hull was brief. "I want thee all to know," he began, "that in this past hour, our young Lucy's fever has broken." He looked at each of them. "She is still unwell. I do not know if any permanent harm has come from her days of fever, and I shan't know for a while. We must continue to pray for the child's health."

With that, Dr. Hull led a short, heartfelt prayer then returned to the back of the house.

It happened so fast that nobody said anything for a bit. Then Mrs. Hull spoke briskly. "I believe it is time to start our school. Betsy and I can give Lucy any special help she needs while she's recovering, and before long, she'll be caught up. Let us begin in the morning."

The Rubyhill youths nodded.

Mrs. Hull looked at Maydean. "Will thee be joining us as well, dear?"

Maydean looked at her hands. She shrugged.

"I shall take that as a yes," Mrs. Hull simply said. "Now Betsy and I shall see all of thee bright and early tomorrow after breakfast. We'll meet right here at the table."

With that, Mrs. Hull left to join the doctor at Lucy's side.

Aleta turned to Maydean. "You got the most beautiful hair," Aleta said.

Maydean simply squirmed in her chair and grinned.

Chapter 14

Christmas Eve

A rooster woke Janie up on the morning of Christmas Eve. She looked out the bedroom window to find the hills and fields covered in another heavy blanket of fresh snow and tinged with the pink of a soon-to-rise sun.

Janie sat up and hugged her knees under the warm, heavy quilts. Aleta was already up and out of the room, probably downstairs helping. The Rubyhill youths who had not taken sick offered to do any work they could at the Hull farm, and their help was appreciated.

Janie smiled. She felt happy these days, more content than she had been since Aunty Mil was alive and more hopeful for the future than she'd ever been in her whole life.

There were many blessings for Janie to count as she stayed snuggled under the quilts. First of all, Lucy was getting stronger every day. She would eventually move upstairs to Aleta and Janie's room, but right now the stairs were a bit too much for the very weakened Lucy. Dr. Hull said that he couldn't see anything deeply wrong with Lucy from the long fever, but he warned them that she would be quieter than she had been before being sick. That would last a long time, he said, most likely all winter.

Indeed, Janie found Lucy to be very subdued. She sat quietly at the kitchen table with everyone for meals and for short periods of schooling. Sometimes Janie caught Lucy watching her move about the room. Lucy's big dark eyes were expressionless until Janie made a funny face. Then Lucy's eyes smiled, but often her face did not.

"You all right, Lucy?" Janie would ask.

Lucy would nod and continue to watch Janie with those big dark eyes. After a while, Janie understood that Lucy had simply lost all her energy at those times and that watching the others was entertainment for the still-weak girl. When this happened, Janie would help her friend back to her room in the back of the house. Lucy would crawl into bed and fall asleep almost instantly. This happened every day, but the naps were getting shorter every day, too.

Of course, people had gotten sick before in Janie's world, but they usually got better faster than this. Janie sorely missed Lucy's friendship. Maydean was turning into a friend, but Lucy had been Janie's friend for many years. Aleta seemed preoccupied with Blue these days, and Janie didn't feel she should take up Aleta's time. And Nathan. . .well, Nathan was a boy.

At least Janie could see the baby steps Lucy's health was taking. And they were forward steps. She would be her old self soon enough.

On the other hand, Blue was back to his full strength and former sassiness. He and Nathan helped Dr. Hull and some hired hands with the farm work. Blue had early on returned to teasing Janie like a big brother, and everyone was relieved to see it.

And then there was the Blue and Aleta romance. It took a couple of weeks for Janie to adjust, but now she found herself happy to see how Blue acted with Aleta. He did not treat her as a sister anymore at all. He held Aleta's hand under the table, and he watched her cross a room as if nobody else were in the room with them. Janie figured that must be what love between a boy and a girl looked like.

These winter days found Aleta making a handsome quilt. She allowed Janie to help her with it. Lucy was too weary to concentrate on needlework, but she sat with them. Maydean had no interest in it. She preferred to help out with the chickens and cows outdoors or work in the kitchen on occasion with Betsy.

Maydean had truly blossomed from the dirt-caked, wild-haired girl Janie had met weeks ago. Maydean spent almost every day at the Hull farm. Janie watched the girl transform from dirty to clean, from what Blue called "half boy" to all girl. Maydean still wore men's clothing, but now Janie knew why. That was all her drunken granddaddy had for her to wear, and she didn't want him to wonder where she got new clothes.

Janie had also learned why the frightening man did not allow his granddaughter to go to school. "It's 'cause he cain't read," Maydean finally told her, "and he can't have nobody smarter'n him around. If he knew I could read, he'd beat the smartness right out of me."

Janie was horrified to hear this, but she said nothing else about it to Maydean. The Hull farmhouse door was always open to the child, so she had a sanctuary. She kept her books at the Hull farm along with the hairbrush and combs Betsy gave her. Maydean kept her hair braided, but she never worked on it at her own house, only at the Hull's. And every evening before dark, Maydean trudged on back to her grandfather's house. Now that Janie understood all that, it was an even happier thing to have Maydean around.

The Rubyhill Five's new reality still took some getting used to. All five of them now spent time each day with—even ate with—white folks. The strangeness of it never completely went away during their winter at the Hull farm. But Janie and the others had grown to love the Hulls, Betsy, and Maydean.

Mrs. Hull's and Betsy's good cooking filled out hollow cheeks and skinny arms. All the Rubyhill Five gained weight and soon looked hale and hearty. Even Maydean was no longer so thin, and her cheeks were rosy all the time. Janie appreciated not going to bed hungry. Every night she thanked the Lord for that.

Best of all, Janie and her friends could read. It had not taken long. Betsy said that they not only were more than ready to learn new things, they were also all very smart. The group progressed quickly under the kind and careful instruction of Mrs. Hull and Betsy.

Soon they could both read and perform tasks of basic arithmetic. Janie found she was particularly good at this, and it was fun for her. She now was learning multiplication tables and even fractions.

The young students also took lessons in proper spoken grammar. At first, none of them had been particularly interested in talking in any other way but their own. Deep down inside, they also didn't want to speak like a Yankee. Such ideas had been part of their rural Southern upbringing, though they never spoke any of those ideas aloud at the kitchen table.

But Betsy, who came from St. Louis, told them, "You're eventually moving to Chicago. If you don't change how you speak, the good citizens of Chicago will dismiss you as country bumpkins. Let me help you so that northern people treat you with respect when they hear you speak."

Of course, Maydean wasn't going to Chicago, but she was most excited about learning proper grammar. She confided to Janie that she was formulating a plan. "What I want to do now, see, is to be a teacher like Betsy. I'm talkin' to her 'bout it all the time in the kitchen. She says I can get caught up real quick. She thinks I can do it." Janie noticed that Maydean's face brightened with passionate energy when she spoke like this.

Another exciting benefit the Rubyhill Five and Maydean had during kitchen school was that now they could all read the Bible. Slaves had almost no access to the Bible since they were not allowed to read or gather for church. Janie was stunned at how much was in just one book.

At first it was difficult with all the old-fashioned language and complicated sentences. But Mrs. Hull and Betsy patiently walked them through the hard words to understand the thrilling stories of the Old Testament and the birth, life, and death of Jesus in the New Testament.

Now Janie knew where to find, "Make a joyful noise." She also knew that the Lord considered her singing such joyful noise.

Janie learned who Job was, the man Aunty Mil said had patience. That Old Testament hero had lost everything, and in some ways, Janie felt like him. But through it all, she read, he still loved the good Lord. Janie considered her own losses, and she came to see that all people went through pain in life, no matter who they were. Janie determined that no matter what, she would continue her love and dependence on the Lord.

There were two exciting things Janie thought about this snowy morning. One was that her birthday was tomorrow on Christmas Day.

The other exciting thing had to do with reading. Mrs. Hull had told them that on Christmas morning they would be reading aloud the story of baby Jesus as found in the Gospel of Luke. "We shall gather around the dining-room table, and thee shall take turns with the scripture verses," she said. "Dr. Hull and I shared the reading of the Christmas story with our own children, and we would feel privileged to do the same with all of thee."

At first nobody spoke. Then Mrs. Hull laughed gently. "Do not fear, young ones—we shall all share the difficult words!"

Of course, they had planned a succulent dinner, as well. A turkey stuffed with dressing would be roasting in the big black oven long before breakfast. Betsy and Maydean had been baking all week for the feast.

Janie had heard Mrs. Hull invite Maydean to come celebrate Christmas with them if her grandfather didn't mind. "It's just another day to him, ma'am," Maydean responded matter-of-factly. "I'll be here. Thank you, ma'am."

All these things turned over in Janie's mind as she watched the rising sun begin to color the fields a deep gold. She kicked back the quilt and gingerly slid to the floor. The wood planks were always so cold to her bare feet that she immediately hopped to the big rag rug a few feet away. There, Janie hopped from one foot to the other to get dressed. She still wore the pewter cross around her neck, and it bumped comfortably under her clothes as she hopped around.

Once dressed, Janie bounded down the stairs to the kitchen. Mrs. Hull turned from the stove. "Good morning, Janie. Thee is hungry?"

"Yes, ma'am, I am." A piping bowl of oatmeal was set in front of her, followed by a glass of milk. Janie bowed her head and silently said grace. She opened her eyes, took a deep breath, and smiled.

"Thee is happy this morning," Mrs. Hull observed.

Janie nodded. "Tomorrow's my birthday," she blurted out.

Mrs. Hull turned to face Janie. "Really, child? On Christmas Day?"

Janie grinned and nodded vigorously.

"Well, this is cause for celebration." Mrs. Hull sat down. "How is it that thee knows when thy birthday is, child?"

"Slaves didn't work on Christmas, ma'am."

Mrs. Hull's face made a quick flinch. "Ah," she said smoothly, "I see. How convenient to have been born on a day one can remember!"

Janie nodded again and poured corn syrup on her oatmeal.

"Does thee know the birthdays of thy friends, Janie?"

Janie stopped with her spoon in midair. Never had she even wondered about the birthdays of Aleta, Blue, or the twins. She simply accepted that they did not know. She always felt special, in fact, that she knew her own.

Janie set her spoon down. She looked at the tablecloth. "No, ma'am," she said softly, "I don't know their birthdays. The only birthday I've ever known is mine." Somehow it sounded selfish when she said it out loud.

Mrs. Hull looked at Janie thoughtfully. "And does thee think it matters to them?"

Janie pondered that for a moment. "I think it matters to Lucy and Nathan, 'cause they's twins."

"They *are* twins," Mrs. Hull gently corrected her.

"Yes, ma'am, that's what I meant. They have each other, blood and all, but that's all they know."

"What about Blue and Aleta?"

"I never heard them say nothin'—anything about it, ma'am."

"How old will thee be tomorrow, Janie?"

"Twelve, ma'am."

"We shall celebrate, young Janie." Mrs. Hull gave her a rosy-cheeked smile. "A birthday is a special thing. And to celebrate thy birthday on the same day we celebrate the birth of our Lord Jesus is special indeed." She stood and turned back to the stove.

An idea came to Janie. The twins knew they had been born in winter. Couldn't they share Janie's birthday with her? Couldn't they simply decide that was their birthday, too? They could all turn one year older together. They could celebrate together.

Janie dipped her spoon into her oatmeal. She said nothing about her idea to Mrs. Hull.

But Janie had a plan.

CHAPTER 15

"And It Came to Pass"

Momma sat on the floor next to a fire and gazed at Janie. Momma's eyes looked just as warm as the fire itself. She moved over next to Janie and completely encircled her in her arms. Then Momma took both of Janie's hands and counted each finger out loud. She reached down and took Janie's bare feet and counted each toe out loud. It tickled when she did that, and Janie giggled. Momma began to laugh along with her. . . .

Janie woke up slowly, smiling. She lay in bed for a minute, letting the dream run through her mind. *Momma.* She'd been as real as if she'd been in the room.

It had been years since Janie had dreamed about her mother. These days she dreamed about Aunty Mil or the others left behind at Rubyhill. Once she had even dreamed about the white boy back near Tennessee—that he gave her a big basket full of live baby rabbits to play with, his blue eyes twinkling.

But this rare dream about Momma felt so real. Janie lay in bed awhile longer, half-asleep, letting the feel of Momma's almost forgotten presence stay with her.

When she heard rustling in the room, Janie reluctantly got up.

Lucy lay in the trundle bed next to the high-poster bed. She had asked to sleep upstairs with Janie and Aleta just for Christmas Eve, so that night Dr. Hull had carried Lucy up the stairs and placed her in the trundle bed. Aleta had tucked warm quilts around her, and Lucy drifted off to sleep right away.

Now Janie leaned over and looked down to find Lucy's eyes open. "Good morning, Lucy. How you doing?"

"Good morning, Janie," Lucy responded. "I'll be up in a minute." But Lucy's eyes closed again. Lucy never bounced out of bed these days. Janie knew she still needed time to gain back her strength.

Aleta rolled over. "Hey, you two—ready to get up?"

Janie and Aleta hopped onto the rugs, avoiding the cold wood floor as always, and they cleaned and dressed. Then Aleta sat at the foot of Lucy's bed. "Hey, little girl, want me to help you get up and dressed?"

Lucy opened her eyes, nodded, and sat up.

"I'll go downstairs and see if Maydean's come yet," said Janie. She bounded out of the room and down the stairs.

Twelve! Janie thought as she opened the door to the warm kitchen. *I am twelve years old today!* Momma's face from the dream flashed in her mind, and she felt a momentary twinge of sadness alongside her excitement.

Betsy set down the blue-speckled coffeepot and looked up. "Merry Christmas, Janie," she said.

Blue stood at the door with his heavy clothes on, drinking from a mug of coffee heavily laced with cream and sugar. "Mornin', Janie-bird. Merry Christmas, girl. And happy birthday, too!"

"Yes," Betsy beamed. "Happy birthday to you!" She paused and added, " 'Janie-bird?' "

It had been awhile since anyone had called Janie that, and it was bittersweet. "That's what Aunty Mil called me," she explained.

Betsy smiled. "Because you made a 'joyful noise,' yes?"

Janie grinned and nodded.

Blue set down his mug. "I'll be back 'fore long. Got to help Dr. Hull with the snow." He headed for the back door.

"Maydean's not here yet?" asked Janie.

"Not yet." Betsy opened the oven and pulled out hot biscuits, which she dumped onto a linen towel. Then she stirred applesauce on the stove and added cinnamon to it. "Hungry?"

"Yes, ma'am." Janie sat at one of the table places set with dishes and silverware. "Betsy, I been thinkin' on something."

Betsy picked up the applesauce pan and poured its contents into a heavy dish. "What's that?"

"I want to share my birthday with Lucy and Nathan."

Betsy kept her eyes on the hot items. "How do you mean?"

"Well, nobody from Rubyhill knows their birthday 'cept me. It's not right that I'm the only one gets a birthday. I don't know when Aleta and Blue were born, and I don't know that they care all that much. But I do know Nathan and Lucy were born in wintertime just like me. I want to give them my birthday. We three can share it, can't we?"

Betsy stopped working and looked at Janie. "Why, I think that's a grand idea." She sat down across from Janie. "How do you want to do this?"

And plans were made.

That day, the Hulls, Betsy, and the Rubyhill Five did what Mrs. Hull had promised they'd do on Christmas morning. After breakfast, they gathered in the dining room, where a fire burned nicely. Mrs. Hull lit tall candles in the center of a fine mahogany table upon which sat a very large black Bible. Dr. Hull took a seat at the head of the table and invited the others to join him.

First Dr. Hull offered a short prayer of thanks. Then he opened to the second chapter of the Gospel of Luke and began to read, " 'And it came to pass. . . .' " The big Bible was passed around, and each person took his or her turn reading a few verses from the Christmas story.

The story unfolded of Mary and Joseph's difficult journey, the birth of baby Jesus, the shepherds, the angels—all of it very exciting to Janie. It wasn't easy for the young readers to pronounce all the words they came upon, but they did their best. Janie felt very special taking part in the reading.

As the reading went on, Janie marveled at how the very Son of God had been born in such a humble way, right in a barn among the animals. *Why, Aunty Mil's cabin would have been more comfortable than that,* thought Janie.

She wished Aunty Mil were right here so that Janie could read this exciting Christmas story to her. The dear old woman loved Jesus, but Janie wondered how much of this story—or any of the Bible—Aunty Mil really knew. Then the thought came to Janie: *Aunty Mil lives with Jesus. She knows all of this now.* It was a wonderful thing to consider.

When the reading was done, a comfortable silence settled over the group. The fire crackled, and candle flames waved gently in the house drafts as the meaning of the good words lingered.

Only one thing marred the reading of Luke this snowy Christmas morning.

Maydean had not come.

Chapter 16

Where's Maydean?

No doubt about it, Christmas dinner was the most delicious feast any of the Rubyhill Five had ever experienced in all their young lives.

Dinner was held at midday in the dining room, where the Bible reading had been. The long mahogany table was spread with a thick, lacy tablecloth, flowered china, and silverware Janie had not seen before. A vase of yew branches and holly graced the center. The table looked very handsome.

Janie was glad Betsy had taught them how to use silverware. None of the Rubyhill youths had ever held a fork before arriving at the Hull farm. They'd actually never even sat together around a table for meals before arriving here. Slaves did not have access to fancy silverware or table linens—or even dinner tables, for that matter. So table manners were taught kindly at the Hull kitchen school, right alongside reading and arithmetic.

After everyone was seated at the festive table, Dr. Hull offered grace. Then Betsy and Mrs. Hull served the meal. There was roast turkey, cornbread stuffing loaded with sausage and sage, potatoes and gravy, butternut squash, green beans cooked with bacon, side dishes of sweet pickles and succotash, and more flaky, golden biscuits than they could possibly finish. It came as no surprise that everyone was too full for dessert, so Mrs. Hull suggested they eat that later on.

Janie leaned back in her chair and stopped herself from fingering the outline of the pewter cross under her bodice. She felt so full she thought she would burst.

She thought about her wonderful day so far—the vivid dream about her mother, the morning Bible reading, the satisfying feast. In spite of it all, though, Janie found herself with one nagging worry.

Maydean still had not shown up.

Nobody had come up with any possible explanation for her absence, and this special holiday at the Hull farm was simply carrying on without her. Janie could not imagine Maydean intentionally missing that Bible reading on Christmas morning. And she certainly never missed meals at the Hull place, either—something Janie understood all too well. So where was Maydean?

Betsy stood and clapped her hands. "Everyone, we have a surprise for you!" Janie knew this had to do with birthdays.

But suddenly there was a knock on the front door. Betsy looked at the Hulls briefly then hurried out to the foyer. When the door opened, a gust of wind came into the dining room. In the hallway, they heard Betsy cry out.

Dr. Hull rose quickly and put up his hand to indicate that they were to remain quiet. He hurried into the hallway. "Oh, child," they heard him say. "Come in, come in."

Maydean? Janie abandoned her new table manners, jumped up from the table, and ran to the hallway.

Maydean stood in the hallway, covered with snow. Janie could see that she had no coat or boots on under that snow—just pants, a man's shirt, a sweater, and what looked like slippers. Her hair hung wild, no longer braided, and it, too, was covered with snow.

When Janie stepped closer, she saw that Maydean's face was swollen. Then she saw that one side was covered in deep purple bruises. Maydean didn't even look like Maydean.

"What happened, child?" said Dr. Hull in a kind but tight voice. Betsy cried silent tears as she peeled the snow-covered sweater off Maydean and dropped it onto the rug.

"He was out all night, drunk," Maydean said simply.

"Thy grandfather?"

The girl nodded. "I got up and around this morning like usual. I was gonna come here soon as I could. He was there, drunker than I ever seen him. He gets mighty mean, so I tried to stay outta his way." Maydean paused and touched her head. "I had my braids still pinned up on my head, like you and me did 'em yesterday, Miss Betsy."

Betsy began rubbing Maydean's red hands and said nothing.

"Kept hittin' on my face," Maydean continued. "Then he pulled on my hair 'til all the braidin' was gone. I guess I'm lucky I still got any hair left." Maydean sighed and touched her bruised face. She winced. "I got away and run here."

"Janie, please get Mrs. Hull," said Betsy.

Janie turned and almost collided with Mrs. Hull, who was carrying a crocheted blanket from the front room. Mrs. Hull draped the blanket around the shoulders of the shivering Maydean and squeezed her tightly. "There, there. Thee is safe now," she heard Mrs. Hull say.

Aleta and Janie ran upstairs and gathered warm clothes for Maydean. As they hurried about, they heard Dr. Hull ask Maydean if she'd been hurt anywhere else. She had not, but she was terribly cold.

When the girls started back downstairs, they saw Dr. Hull pick the frozen girl up and carry her to the kitchen. Then he pulled Mrs.

Hull into another room to talk to her, leaving Maydean in Betsy's care.

Janie and Aleta hurried into the kitchen where Maydean stood in front of the oven. Betsy began to peel the rest of her snow-packed clothing off. She wrapped Maydean in a big flannel blanket and rubbed the girl's arms and legs vigorously through that.

Betsy began toweling Maydean's hair, all the time chattering away. "We'll get that swelling down, and we'll get you into these warm clothes. I'll brush your hair out all nice, sweetie, and I'll braid it up for you again."

Maydean simply stood in silence, staring straight ahead. She looked wobbly to Janie.

Mrs. Hull bustled into the kitchen, a gentle smile on her face. "Maydean, child, thee shall stay here tonight. It's all arranged. Lucy goes back to her own room today, so thee can sleep in her bed upstairs."

Maydean turned to Mrs. Hull, her eyes wide and anxious.

Mrs. Hull seemed to understand. "Dr. Hull has decided to deliver Christmas food to thy grandfather, child. He and Blue are arranging this as we speak." She paused, then continued. "Alcohol is an evil thing, and it can overpower the goodness in any man. But the Lord has been known to break many a stubborn heart, so we shall pray for thy grandfather, Maydean. For now, thee shall stay here with us. Dr. Hull will not allow thee to be harmed again. And he will approach thy grandfather in peace."

Maydean's shoulders slumped and her eyes welled up with tears. Janie touched her friend's chapped hands. "You'll stay upstairs with Aleta and me, Maydean. You'll like it up there."

With that, Maydean sat down at the kitchen table and finally cried.

Chapter 17

A Happy Birthday

Dusk fell over the snowy fields of the Hull farm. In the warm, white farmhouse, dinner dishes had been washed and put away. Lucy and Mrs. Hull were taking naps in their rooms while Aleta finished tidying up the kitchen.

In the front room, Betsy turned on oil lamps for Nathan, Janie, and Maydean. The young redhead sat curled on a sofa. She was now clad in a warm flannel nightgown and robe, and she kept a heavy coverlet over her lap. It had taken a long time to warm Maydean up after her cold journey. Now all nice and snug with some hot food in her stomach, Maydean looked ready to go to sleep.

Nevertheless, Maydean's sleepy eyes followed the comings and goings of the others in the room. She seemed content to say nothing but to simply bask in the warm safety of the Hull home. She especially liked it when Nathan and Janie took turns reading aloud to her from the second chapter of Luke. They wanted her to hear the beautiful story in the Bible's own words while the day was still Christmas.

Aleta dashed into the front room. "They're back from your granddaddy's," she said to Maydean. "I ran out when I saw them come into the yard. Blue told me your granddaddy accepted the food from Dr. Hull and was even polite about it."

Maydean looked very relieved to hear this.

"That's not all," said Aleta. "Blue says Dr. Hull told your granddaddy straight out that his grandbaby's not safe, not while he's living with the bottle. Dr. Hull told him you'll stay here until your granddaddy's in his right mind again. Blue says the old man took it all right. Even thanked Dr. Hull!"

Maydean pulled the coverlet up around her neck and looked around the room. "I'm awful glad to be here," she said.

"And we're so very glad to have you with us," said Betsy. "Do you feel like having your hair brushed?"

Maydean nodded and turned so that Betsy could sit behind her on the sofa. Betsy pulled a brush out of her apron pocket and slowly, carefully ran it through Maydean's tangled mane. "We'll have you fixed up in no time," said Betsy.

Maydean leaned her cheek—the one without the bruises—against the back of the sofa. Before long, in spite of the hair-brushing, she fell asleep. Betsy continued brushing, then wove two thick braids and laid them gently on Maydean's shoulders.

Betsy gestured for them all to follow her. "Let's heat up some cider in the kitchen," she whispered. Everyone but the sleeping Maydean trooped to the kitchen table.

Mrs. Hull was one step ahead of them. Up from her nap, she was laying out Christmas desserts on big platters. Nathan's eyes lit up, and he watched each movement with sharp interest. Nathan loved sweets.

Betsy pulled Janie aside. "We'll do what we planned over dessert."

Janie glanced back toward the front room. "Are you sure?"

Betsy squeezed Janie's hand. "You know what I think? I have a feeling Maydean would like the attention to be directed away from her for a while. What do you think?"

Janie grinned and nodded. "I sure do think she'd like something happy to happen."

Betsy grinned back. "I agree with you, Janie. So let us conspire to launch our plan over dessert."

Dr. Hull and Blue came in from the snow. Lucy rose from her nap and wandered into the kitchen. Finally Mrs. Hull said, "Let's take our dessert to the front room and join Maydean. She should not miss a moment more of this holiday."

Treats and hot drinks were put on trays and moved to the front room. Maydean woke up and blinked. When she saw the cookies and candies, she smiled broadly.

"Is everybody here?" Betsy asked. "Let's all have a seat. Janie has something she'd like to say."

The adults settled into chairs and the youngsters onto rugs. Janie stood up and cleared her throat.

"Today's my birthday. Today I am twelve years old."

"Happy birthday, young Janie!" called out Dr. Hull.

"Thank you, sir," Janie responded with a short, funny curtsy—thanks to Betsy's coaching—in his direction. "But what I want to say is this. It's no fun to be the only one with a birthday to celebrate. I want to share mine." She turned to Nathan and Lucy. "Will you two share my birthday with me? Not just today but from now on?"

Nathan's eyes lit up. He turned to his twin. "I say yes! How 'bout you, Lucy? What do you say?"

Lucy blinked and smiled. Then she nodded with more vigor than anyone had seen her have since before the fever.

"Lucy says yes, too," said Nathan. "Thanks, Janie!" He thought for a minute. "Does that mean you're our big sister now?"

"I'd like that," Janie said, suddenly feeling shy and happy.

"Maybe not so big, though," teased Dr. Hull. Everyone laughed.

Nobody noticed Betsy had left the room until she rounded the corner with a gigantic birthday cake. She had written each of their names on top with buttercream frosting. And of course, each of them could read it. The room broke into applause.

"Well," said Mrs. Hull, clapping her hands, "isn't this wonderful? And all of it on the birthday of our Lord Jesus!" She turned to Nathan and Lucy. "This is a thrilling moment for both of thee. Thy family has increased today."

Mrs. Hull turned to Janie. "And thee has chosen to share what thee has with a glad heart. May our Lord bless thee, precious child."

Janie beamed. Dr. Hull stood and prayed over the group. When he finished, Lucy stood and came over to Janie. She hugged her.

That was a very nice gesture. But the best thing to Janie was that this was the most energetic movement Lucy had made in weeks.

Little Lucy was most certainly on the mend on this, her new official birthday.

DuPont Acres, Kentucky

Even in the middle of Kentucky, it snowed this Christmas Day. Anna made dinner for Mr. DuPont and all his hired hands. Then she retired to the room over the stable where she lived with George.

Anna wrapped her arms around her knees while she waited for George to finish feeding the horses. She had one thought on her mind. Today, like every Christmas, was her baby's birthday.

How many more Christmas Days must she wait to see her child again?

Chapter 18

Indiana Spring

Time passed quickly while the Rubyhill Five wintered at the Hull farm. It was a cold and snowy winter, more so than usual. But before long, the snow thawed and did not return.

Janie found that she loved the feel and smell of spring in Indiana. While spring was a vibrant time in Georgia, there was something about having weathered the cold and the snow that made an Indiana spring particularly beautiful.

It started with a sweetness in the air. Rain became warmer. Daffodils and tulips shot up next. Then came the fragrant lilacs and lilies of the valley, and soon just about everything was in blossom. Best of all, Janie was allowed to watch the births of lambs and calves. There was new life everywhere.

In the big farmhouse, another bed had been moved into the girls' room upstairs. Now Aleta, Lucy, Janie, and Maydean all shared the big bedroom. Betsy had a small room to herself at the end of the upstairs hall. Janie felt as if she had lots of sisters, and she liked the feeling.

All of the youths on the Hull farm had gained much-needed weight and strength over the winter, and they all looked good and healthy. Good nutrition and lifestyle added to the eagerness of all the kitchen-table students to learn everything they could. Mrs. Hull and Betsy continued to teach their students as much as they could handle and then pushed them to learn even more.

By spring, everyone could read and write fluently. They could perform any math task asked of them. They could write and deliver short speeches on any number of topics, their manners were beyond acceptable, and the Bible was becoming a familiar friend.

Janie never ceased to be amazed at how Maydean blossomed after moving in with the Hulls. She was turning into a bright and beautiful young woman. Betsy had taken the girl under her wing and taught her how to groom and dress herself and to polish the rough edges of her speech and manners.

Now Maydean wore her braids pinned up like Betsy's. Janie liked the way it looked and began to do the same. She liked to pin her braids in a spiral at the back of her head.

It thrilled everybody that Maydean was studying already to apply for teachers' college. She also practiced writing letters so that she could stay in touch with Betsy next year when Betsy moved to Detroit.

Janie was glad about the letter-writing in particular. She and Maydean planned to write each other many letters. Janie knew that the Rubyhill Five would be moving on soon.

There was no question as to whether or not all five Rubyhill youths would continue traveling north, even though it would be dreadfully hard to leave the Hull farm. But they were all committed to starting a new life in Chicago. The only question was when.

One morning in early April, Janie could hardly wait to finish her breakfast of sausage and biscuits with jam. Dr. Hull had told her only half an hour earlier that a foal would be born of her favorite mare that morning, and Janie didn't want to miss this for anything. She ate so fast she didn't even talk to Lucy and Nathan, who joined her at the table. Then Blue came to breakfast.

"Hey, y'all," said Blue pouring himself a cup of coffee. "It's one fine day outside."

"I'm a little late getting out there," said Nathan. "You already do your chores?"

Blue nodded and sat down. He stirred milk and sugar into his coffee then looked around the table. "Where's Aleta?"

"Don't you usually know?" teased Janie.

Blue grinned and took a sip of coffee. Then he cleared his throat. "Look, Janie, Nathan, Lucy. . ." He paused. "Aleta and I have been talking. Let me just come out and say that I know we're having a good life here. But it's spring. That means it's time for us to get moving again."

Janie stopped eating. Of course she always knew the day would come when she would have to leave these people she'd come to know and love. She felt sick to her stomach.

Nathan and Lucy were quiet, too. Blue waited. Then he said, "Anyone want to say anything?"

Nobody said a word.

"I'm thinking we could leave in a few days," Blue went on. "What do you think about that?"

"I—I guess that would be fine," stammered Nathan. Lucy's dark eyes grew wide, but she said nothing.

Finally, Janie spoke. "I don't want to leave yet, Blue."

Blue nodded. "I kinda thought you might say that. But, Janie-bird, but you might never want to leave if we don't get going fairly soon. You didn't want to leave Rubyhill, either, remember?"

Janie nodded. "How long you think we'll have to be on the road?" she asked. The thought of leaving the comforts of the Hull house was not a pleasant one.

Blue cocked his head and thought. "Oh, about a couple weeks, depending on how things go. Think you can do it?"

Janie looked at the tablecloth. "I don't know. I guess so."

Blue reached over and touched Janie's hand. "Hey, you. We're family, you know. We're all together in this. God's been good to us, leading us here to the Hulls. They've prepared us for near about everything. But I don't think we're meant to stay here forever. Do you?"

The days here at the Hull farm had been so full that Janie hadn't really thought about the future. But deep down inside, she had to agree. Their destination remained Chicago.

Janie looked at Blue, then at Nathan and Lucy. "I'd like it if we could stay until after Easter. That's two weeks more."

"Then we will," said Blue.

DuPont Acres, Kentucky

Anna brought the subject up first. They had just finished breakfast in their room over the stable. "When we headed for Chicago, George?"

George stopped cleaning his boots and looked at his wife, but he didn't answer. Instead, he went back to cleaning his boots.

"We got enough cash now," Anna said.

George looked up at her, then back down. "Well, sugar, the thing is, I promised DuPont I'd stay through foaling."

Anna stared at George. "We got enough cash now," she said again, as if he hadn't heard her.

"I promised him I'd stay through foaling," George repeated softly.

Anna's anger flared up, fast. "What you talking about?"

George answered his wife calmly and slowly. "I should've talked to you about it first, Anna. But I gave the man my word."

"You gave him your word?" Anna stood up. "And what about me, George? What about what you promised me, that we'd find our girl? What about that? What's your word worth there?"

George stopped working and looked at the floor.

Anna marched to the window and stood with her back to her husband until he left for work.

Nothing more was said about Chicago again for weeks.

CHAPTER 19

Chicago

Chicago sure is windy, thought Janie.

It was the middle of May, and the Rubyhill Five found themselves right in the center of the largest city they'd ever seen. Indiana seemed like a long time ago. Now instead of living with the Hulls, Betsy, and Maydean, the youths were encountering hundreds of strangers—black, white, Chinese, Indian, Mediterranean, rich, poor, and even in between. When the five of them first arrived in the city, they found it so curious and fascinating that they simply wandered the streets for two hours.

People hurried up and down the first sidewalks the Georgian friends had ever walked on. The many shopwindows showed merchandise that the young people had never dreamed of buying. Vendors cooked and sold food right on the street, and the smoky smells beckoned the Rubyhill Five on every block. The force from all those people was so strong that Janie felt she could reach out and touch it.

Then there was the Great Lake Michigan, its shores right in the city. What a powerful body of water, deep blue and full of whitecaps. Alongside the docks, dozens of fishermen displayed their wares.

In the distance, large ships sailed on the lake's long horizon. To Janie, they looked like strange, breathing creatures crawling along.

Here in Chicago, Janie at first battled instant fear. She had never been around so many people in her life—noisy ones at that. And she had never seen a body of water bigger than a wide part of the Ohio River. This water seemed to go on forever. She could not even see the other side of the lake.

Blue and Nathan were thrilled at seeing the city and the huge lake with its ships. Aleta praised the fashions the women wore. Even Lucy chattered excitedly about the fresh fish they'd fry. Janie simply stared at everything and made certain to stick close by the others.

The five young people had traveled through most of Indiana on foot. But several miles south of the outskirts of Chicago, they had decided to use some of their money and finish this journey by train. Thankfully, they'd never before dipped into that cash they'd found so long ago at Rubyhill. Now was the time.

So there was another first for the Rubyhill Five. They'd never boarded a train before. Fortunately, one of their lessons at the Hull kitchen-table school had been how to read train schedules. Mrs. Hull had also given them practice in using money and figuring change as part of their math lessons. Dr. Hull stepped in toward the end of their stay to teach them how to read maps and street plans.

The friends remained ever grateful for the help they had received in so many ways at the kind hands of Dr. and Mrs. Hull and Betsy. Never could the Rubyhill Five have entered this cosmopolitan city with confidence had they not wintered with the Hulls, receiving nourishment, education, and practical skills the entire time.

Back in Indiana, Dr. Hull had been positive and helpful about the upcoming journey to Chicago. He told them that as country people, they might find the city challenging at first, but there was no reason to fear the people there. He confirmed what had been rumored in Georgia, that a black person could live nearly as well as a white person in Chicago.

Dr. Hull had even written down the address of what he called a *benevolent society*—a place of goodwill that had helped runaway slaves get established in Chicago. Even though slavery was now abolished, the director of the society, a Mr. Solomon, would happily help them find lodging and possibly work.

The other exciting thing Dr. Hull wrote down was the name and address of a church pastored by a black minister, a Reverend Silas. This man had wintered at the Hull farm many years ago during his own escape from slavery. He had gone on to attend seminary and become a minister. Now he was pastor of a substantial Chicago church. "Go to that church straightaway," Dr. Hull told them. "Reverend Silas will help thee, as well. And it is a fine church community that will help thee in thy spiritual walk."

After allowing themselves time to gawk at the exciting things Chicago had to offer, the five young people circled back to the train depot so that they could follow Dr. Hull's written directions to the benevolent society. They headed down the sidewalk as directed by their notes.

Janie was grateful that these sidewalks kept dangerous, fast-moving horses and wagons at bay. While some of Chicago's streets were made of brick, many streets were still dirt and, at this time of year, muddy. Walking on the sidewalks was not only safer, but it also helped keep their clothes clean. The Georgian youths did not want to appear to be country bumpkins, and staying neat and clean was important.

It was an amazing thing to stand in the heart of the great city of Chicago, but it was even more amazing to have the ability to read. There were so many signs to read. Janie did not remember seeing signs with words in the South. Of course, she had never been to a southern city, but she figured maybe they had had signs. In the Georgia countryside, she'd heard there were crossroads markers, but those had been taken down during the war to confuse the Yankee soldiers. Janie had never seen them, anyway. She'd never left the plantation back then, and in their journey north, they had stayed off main roads.

So in Chicago, while the wind whipped down the sidewalks with a vengeance, Lucy and Janie read the shop signs aloud to each other, rolling new words and names on their tongues. JANSSEN'S BAKERY. CITY INSURANCE. CORNER BUTCHER. LIVERY. MRS. MILLER'S ALTERATIONS.

Finally, Blue called out, "Here's the street! Dr. Hull said the building numbers go up and down in order, so let's figure out which way to go for number 32."

"There!" called Nathan, pointing west. "The numbers go up that way."

They turned down the street until Blue halted in front of a handsome, four-story, brick building. He looked once more at his notes, then nodded. They all piled inside to a hallway where there was no wind.

People hurried in and out the door, barely taking notice of the youths. Clearly, people in this city were used to seeing strangers, and it looked to Janie like white folks and black folks seemed to mix and get along all right together.

"See if you can find Mr. Solomon's name on these doors," said Aleta. They moved slowly up the hall until Janie spied the man's name.

Inside the greeting area of Mr. Solomon's office, the atmosphere was homey. A fire burned low in a huge wall fireplace that was big enough so that Janie, Lucy, and Nathan could have fit inside it. They all stood in front of the fire.

"May I help you?" said a woman's voice behind them.

The five young people whirled around. A white woman had risen from behind a desk. She was tall, and her hair was gray. She wore tiny eyeglasses, and she gave what Janie sensed was a warm and genuine smile.

"Excuse us," said Aleta. "You have a nice fire. . . ." She stopped. An awkward silence followed as they stood at the fireplace.

The tall white woman nodded. "Enjoy it as long as you like."

Aleta spoke again. "We're here to meet Mr. Solomon."

The white woman nodded. "Do you have an appointment?"

"No, ma'am," said Aleta.

"Did anyone in particular send you?"

"Yes," said Aleta, "Dr. Otto Hull in Indiana."

"Ah, yes. You wintered there?"

All five nodded.

The woman continued. "A good man, Dr. Hull. How is he? And Mrs. Hull, is she well?"

None of the five from Rubyhill were used to talking to strange white people, even after living with the Hulls. To engage in casual conversation with white strangers was very new to them.

But Aleta carried the day, telling the woman any news she could think of regarding the Hulls. "And we have a letter of introduction from Dr. Hull," she finished.

"Excellent," said the white woman. "Let me take it to Mr. Solomon."

Aleta relinquished the letter to the tall woman, who said, "Please have a seat."

Janie realized that had they not spent time with the Hulls, they never could have approached this organization of white people, strangers all. But the Rubyhill Five had learned enough social graces to do just fine. Aleta had just shown them how it was done.

The five young people sat down on a row of straight chairs against the wall. As they waited, Janie thought about their last day at the Hull farm. How difficult it had been to say good-bye. Mrs. Hull had held her close and promised her they'd see one another again, and if not on earth, they'd meet in heaven. "Thee knows there will come a time of no good-byes, yes, child?"

Dr. Hull's face would have been unreadable had his eyes not been shining in an odd manner. Janie wondered if those were a strong man's tears. He hugged each of them tightly. "We thank God for sending thee to us, and we shall dearly miss thee all," was all he said.

Betsy cried openly as they readied their things on the last day. She packed lots of tasty carrying food for the group, and once they were on the road, they saw that she'd also wrapped and packed a Bible in with the food. It was a much-welcomed surprise, just as they knew Betsy intended it to be.

Maydean kept a stiff upper lip that last day, but her eyes betrayed her. Janie knew the bedroom would be especially lonely for Maydean once the girls left. She decided Maydean should have the pewter cross.

Before leaving that day, Janie draped the silver chain around her friend's neck without comment. Maydean clutched the cross in her hand. "Thank you, my friend," she whispered. She turned the cross over and read the inscription again, then looked up. "Make that joyful noise, Janie, no matter what. And write to me."

Janie had simply nodded, too full of emotion to speak.

On the day the Rubyhill Five started their last leg of the journey north, nobody stood at the gate and sang to them. The Quakers were not singers like those at Rubyhill. Just the same, the power of their love and prayers sustained the young people all the way to Chicago.

The tall woman's voice interrupted Janie's thoughts. "Mr. Solomon will see you now."

Chapter 20

New Places, New Faces

Mr. Solomon was a kind man and every bit as helpful as Dr. Hull had said he would be. Soon enough, the Rubyhill Five found themselves moving into a clean and respectable boardinghouse.

The three-story, solid-brick house sat in a neighborhood of mostly black and immigrant families. The boardinghouse was owned and run by Mrs. Babbs, a big woman with a big heart. The girls shared a room on the women's second floor, and Nathan and Blue shared a room on the men's third floor. They took meals with the other boarders in a long dining room on the first floor.

All five found jobs right away. Janie and Lucy worked in restaurant kitchens, and Aleta sewed for a tailor. Blue and Nathan both loaded cargo at the docks.

There were no laws to make children attend school in those days. There also were no laws against hiring children. Some businesses even preferred hiring children because they could pay them less. The Rubyhill Five did not know this. They only knew that as former slaves, they'd never earned money before at all, so to be paid for one's labor truly felt like a step up.

Other than the Yankee cash from Rubyhill, cash on hand was

still a new thing for the Georgia youths. Each earned enough money to pay room and board and have a little left over.

Fortunately Mrs. Hull had drilled them on how to handle money. She also had taught them to first give away ten cents of every dollar. This was a biblical habit called *tithing*, she informed them. Most people would give that tithed money to a church, but Janie also liked to look for people in need on the street and give to them, as well.

As soon as Janie could afford it, she bought her own Bible; the rest of her earnings, she saved. Janie took the worn piece of fabric from Aunty Mil's chair and stitched it into a drawstring purse, and that was where she kept her savings. She stuffed the purse deep into her pinafore pocket and carried it all the time.

Janie realized that Dr. Hull had been right about another thing. Living in the city was a lot different from living in the country. After the initial thrill of Chicago wore off, Janie found she had some adjustments to make. For her, city life was jarring—noisy, dirty, and laced with bad smells. Its intensity was a shock to her country-girl nature every single day. And the Chicago summer was horribly hot and muggy with no relief.

Eventually, however, Janie learned to find what she loved in the city. She missed the farm animals, but she got to know the slow-moving milk-wagon horses, the alley cats begging for scraps, and the many birds. Janie liked to watch and feed pigeons, cardinals, and sparrows, all flying free above the clamor and congestion of the city.

The other part of nature Janie soon learned to love was Lake Michigan, and she came to appreciate living beside such a rare and grand force of nature. She found the crashing waves exhilarating, the sound of the foghorns comforting, and the flocks of screaming seagulls great fun. In that first hot Chicago summer, the Rubyhill youths learned that spending evenings at the lake could cool them down for sleeping. Sometimes on Sundays, very early, Janie went to the lakeshore alone to think and pray.

Chicago offered other things Janie had never thought about before. Access to libraries where she could read and borrow books made her feel incredibly wealthy. Free concerts of music of all kinds cropped up in parks all over the city. She heard public lectures and speeches on all kinds of topics and issues. She did not want to spend the money to attend the theater, but once she and the twins splurged and attended a circus. Nathan talked for a while about finding work there until he learned that the circus people stayed on the road all the time. "I'm done with that kind of life," he said.

Unfortunately, Janie also observed that even though all kinds of people lived and worked together on these streets, Chicago did have whites who treated black people as inferior. And some blacks treated the immigrants as inferior. It seemed the many different kinds of people here did not necessarily like one another, Janie decided. They simply tolerated the situation of living together.

Nevertheless, the Georgian youths did sense a sure and certain freedom they would never have had back home, and they enjoyed every moment of it. Black people walked free and proud in Chicago. Black neighborhoods packed with black-owned businesses thrived. Chicagoans were not always warm, but they were helpful, and they respected hard work.

Best of all, Janie and her friends attended a big, beautiful church. Dr. Hull's friend Reverend Silas was pastor of a large AME church, which stood for the African Methodist Episcopal denomination. For Janie, who had no church background other than the quiet Quaker meetings in Indiana and the services in the pine groves back at Rubyhill, the reverend's church services were dramatic and thrilling. Especially the music.

To Janie, music at Reverend Silas's church was a little like the fieldworkers' music back home, only this was faster, more upbeat, and fuller of sound. There were women singers who could make the hair stand up on Janie's neck; they were that powerful. Janie loved singing with them, and she was grateful she could read the words in the hymnal. Some members played musical instruments—piano, drums, trumpets, and tambourines—during church. Reverend Silas pointed out that young David of the Old Testament was their musical example in this regard.

Chicago women, Janie observed, wore hats and other head coverings when out and about, and this appealed to young Janie. At age twelve going on thirteen, she felt like she was almost a woman herself. One day, she pulled Aunty Mil's faded yellow head scarf out from under her pillow and inhaled the comforting but fading scent of Aunty Mil's hair one more time. Then Janie tied the head scarf over her own pinned-up braids. She ran downstairs to look at herself in the hall mirror. She may still be small, but she looked grown-up. Janie wore the head scarf from then on.

So the days in Chicago were full and rich. Janie wrote long letters to Maydean, enclosing shorter ones to be delivered to the Hulls and to Betsy. She detailed every move the Rubyhill Five made in their new life and every decision as well. In August, Janie was elected to write to the Hull farm about the biggest news of all.

Blue and Aleta were getting married.

Train Station, Chicago

The Chicago-bound train huffed slowly into the station. George took his wife's hand, and the two of them stood with their faces in the open window of their passenger car. True to his word, George had put Anna and himself on a train for the journey from Kentucky to Chicago. There would be no more walking for his wife on this trip.

Neither of them had ever been in a city like Chicago before. George had finally told Anna how he'd spent his seven long years away from her. The chain gang that bought him at Shannon Oaks had marched him all the way to the hot Louisiana city of New Orleans, where he spent many painful years working as a slave. It had been a horrible life.

It had been hard for Anna to hear about it, but it drew them closer when George finally shared his story with her. Living as a slave in New Orleans was nothing like riding into the great city of Chicago as a free man. Praise the Lord, how far He had brought them!

George pulled Anna close to him. "I am so sorry I made you wait for this trip, sugar. You should never have to wait for anything again."

Anna laid her head on her husband's shoulder. The fight of last spring was over, forgiven and forgotten. "We'll find her, George," she said. "We're so close I can feel it."

The train rolled to a stop.

Chapter 21

Good News

Janie sat with Mrs. Babbs at the breakfast table and sipped her morning tea. It was early Sunday morning, and the other boarders were still sleeping. Fortunately, Mrs. Babbs, like Janie, was an early riser, so the two of them often enjoyed morning tea together.

"Miss Janie," said Mrs. Babbs, "I have been meaning to tell you about an experience I believe you might enjoy."

Janie loved listening to Mrs. Babbs speak. She had a deep melodious voice and spoke formally to everyone. It was part of her unique warmth and charm.

"Yes, Mrs. Babbs?" Janie carefully set her cup in its saucer then folded her hands in her lap as Mrs. Hull had taught her.

"A great speaker is coming to our fair city. On Saturday next, she will speak at the Temperance Hall."

"She?" said Janie. Even in Chicago, Janie had not heard of such a thing as a woman delivering a public speech. Janie didn't really count church testimonies in that category.

"Yes, dear, *she*. Her name is Sojourner Truth, and she is a powerful speaker. I have heard her before."

"Sojourner," Janie repeated. "What a beautiful name."

"She chose her name, Miss Janie. She had a slave's name, and she changed it to reflect her true mission in this world. She says she is but a sojourner through life, put into this world to speak only truth. She was an abolitionist prior to the war, and now she speaks of the rights of women."

Unfortunately Janie would have to miss this event. "I'm afraid I won't be able to attend, Mrs. Babbs. The restaurant is very strict about missing work on Saturdays."

Mrs. Babbs nodded sympathetically.

"But I'm glad you brought this up, Mrs. Babbs," Janie continued. "It's her name that impresses me. It makes me think that maybe I could change my own name."

"Yes, Miss Janie, you could. Sojourner Truth certainly did."

Janie thought back to when she and the others had filled out paperwork at Mr. Solomon's place that first day in Chicago. None of them knew their last names. If any of them had one, they'd never heard it. Janie had felt a sense of shame about this for the first time. It was one more indignity from having been slaves.

That day, the Rubyhill Five had excused themselves for a moment in Mr. Solomon's office. They had huddled in the hall and came to the decision to borrow the Hull name for the time being. Janie still called herself Janie Hull.

Mrs. Babbs brought Janie back to the present. "If I may be so bold as to ask, Miss Janie, what might you change your name to, if you were so inclined? And would you care for more tea?"

"No, thank you, Mrs. Babbs." Janie paused. "My given name was Georgeanna, but I've always been called Janie. As much as I like Georgeanna—those are my parents' first names—I'm used to being called Janie." She stirred her remaining tea thoughtfully. "You know, Mrs. Babbs, my last name isn't really Hull, either. Most of us here from Georgia aren't even blood family. We all took our last name from the Quakers we wintered with."

Before Mrs. Babbs could respond, they heard tromping down the stairs. Blue and Nathan appeared in the doorway. Blue snapped to attention and gave a slight bow to Mrs. Babbs, who always loved such a show of courtesy. Nathan immediately followed suit.

"Sit down, gentlemen," Mrs. Babbs cooed. "Will you both be wanting coffee this morning?"

"Yes, ma'am, that would be fine," Blue said in a charming tone. Nathan nodded, and they both sat.

When Mrs. Babbs rose and went to the kitchen, Blue turned to Janie. "Good morning, Janie-bird."

"That's it!" said Janie.

"What's what?" said Blue.

"That will be my new name. I mean, Bird will be my last name. Janie Bird. It will always remind me of Aunty Mil."

"I like that," Nathan said.

"You thinking on changing your name, Janie?" asked Blue. "Why don't you go back to Georgeanna?"

Mrs. Babbs moved into the dining room with coffee. She'd caught the tail end of the conversation. "If I may say," she said, "you might wish to use the name Georgeanna as your middle name."

"That's a whole lotta names," Nathan observed.

"But very proper," Mrs. Babbs assured them. "I am not sure how it is done in the South, but in Chicago, we do tend to give three names to newborns."

"Janie Georgeanna Bird," said Janie. It sounded pretty to her, like music. "I like that, Mrs. Babbs. Thank you. That will be my new name from this day on."

Blue grinned. "That's my girl. Good for you." He spooned sugar into his coffee and stirred it. Then Blue shared something he had never mentioned before. "I sometimes think about changing my name, too. Blue sounds like a slave name to me."

Nobody responded. Blue continued.

"My momma said I was named for my daddy, and I know my daddy was named for the color of his skin. They said he was 'blue-black.' "

Janie shuddered. Blue had beautiful coal-black skin. Apparently because of that, he had been named the same way people would name a horse—according to color. It was another shameful legacy from slavery.

"But you know," said Blue, "Aleta fell in love with me as Blue. And she and I think a lot of Dr. and Mrs. Hull—as if they were our own parents—so we might want to keep their name."

"You could give yourself a middle name," suggested Janie.

Blue considered that. "I could. I'll talk to Aleta about it. I can't say as I care much, but when we have children someday, it might matter then."

The table fell silent. Then the other boarders appeared for breakfast, and the subject was dropped.

Later at church, Reverend Silas announced the engagement of Blue and Aleta. The reverend congratulated the young couple from the pulpit and then surprised them by saying, "We are going to have a full worship service for these young people on their wedding day. It will be held on a Sunday morning and followed by the kind of feast this church knows how to fix."

The people of the congregation chuckled. Their church suppers were impressive indeed.

Reverend Silas looked directly at Blue and Aleta. "I am authorized by the state of Illinois to marry you legally, and I will do so with great joy. On that day, Blue and Aleta, you will be married in the eyes of God and in the eyes of the law."

Janie felt a shiver of excitement for her friends. Back in Georgia, when a slave had married, there was no church or law involved. Slaves had to ask permission to marry from their masters. If they were given approval—and there was no guarantee they would receive it—they followed a short ritual called *jumping the broom*.

In the ritual, the couple laid a straw broom on the ground, held hands, and jumped over it together. Then the couple was considered married. No minister, no paperwork. Freedom had not yet changed this ritual at Rubyhill. A black couple would still jump the broom to marry.

Janie looked over at Aleta and Blue. Their eyes were wide with wonder. This ceremony would be a lot stronger and more binding than merely jumping the broom. When they married, it would be a union approved by both God and the community, and nothing could tear them apart.

Nobody would ever be able to do to Blue and Aleta what had been done to Janie's parents.

Elsewhere in Chicago

George and Anna had a plan. They had saved enough money so that they did not need to find paying work right away in Chicago. Instead, they intended to spend all of their time and energy seeking out Janie's whereabouts.

Old Joe back at Rubyhill had suggested they try black-member churches and societies that helped people in need. He remembered those places from being in Chicago before the war, but he had no names or addresses for the couple.

It was of no consequence. George and Anna had worked hard to get north, and they would work hard now to find their daughter.

They started with the churches.

Chapter 22

A Wedding Day

Blue and Aleta's wedding fell on a sunny day in late September. One full year had passed since the day the five youths left Rubyhill. Whenever Janie thought about how much had happened that year, it made her head spin.

The week before the wedding, a handsome travel trunk arrived by train from the Hull farm. Inside were gifts for everyone, and there were exceptionally generous gifts for the happy couple.

A letter enclosed from Mrs. Hull explained that she and Betsy had seen this engagement coming a long time ago. Many weeks before they received Janie's letter with the actual news, the two Indiana women had begun to stitch a coverlet for the couple. That was finished and folded in the trunk alongside a new family Bible.

The wedding took place in the sanctuary of the AME church on a Sunday morning. True to his word, Reverend Silas conducted a beautiful worship service complete with lots of soul-stirring music, and he worked wedding vows into it all.

Janie, sitting with Nathan and Lucy in the front pew, was so happy she thought she'd burst. Aleta had never looked more beautiful, and Blue had never looked more handsome. Aleta wore a lovely deep blue dress she had sewn, and she carried a bouquet of colorful gladiolus from Mrs. Babbs's backyard. Janie wished the other former slaves from Rubyhill could be here to see this.

Janie's front pew seat was closest to the wall. She casually craned her neck to see who was in attendance behind her. There sat the choir ladies. Mrs. Babbs and some of the boarders were there. The Italian tailor who employed Aleta had come with his wife. Mr. Solomon attended, too.

The service started early and lasted a long time. When the wedding vows were finished, Reverend Silas raised his hand to pronounce Blue and Aleta as husband and wife. Janie heard a creak in the back of the sanctuary as the double doors to the entrance opened. She turned to see who had arrived so late.

A well-dressed man and woman stepped inside and looked around for a seat. Janie had never seen them in church before, and it didn't look like they realized a wedding was in process. Reverend Silas nodded at them and continued with his pronouncement, followed by a blessing. "Let us pray," he said then, and heads bowed.

But not Janie's. She couldn't take her eyes off the new couple who remained standing for the prayer. The woman's hand lay on the man's arm, and she kept it there as he removed his hat and bowed his head.

Janie took in their cinnamon skin and fine clothing. The way the woman cocked her head looked oddly familiar. Then for some reason, the woman raised her head and looked straight at Janie, showing her deep brown eyes.

When Reverend Silas said, "Amen," the congregation repeated the word and raised their heads. The pastor started to invite people to the wedding feast in the back room, but he stopped.

Little Janie Georgeanna Bird in the yellow head scarf was literally running down the church aisle to the back of the sanctuary. And

Janie didn't care who was looking or even where she was. She knew who those people in the back were.

Momma had found her. And Poppa, too.

It took some time for everyone to calm down after the initial excitement of the reunion of George, Anna, and Janie. Once Reverend Silas understood what was going on, he announced to everyone that today the lost had been found. Good preacher that he was, he also took this opportunity to remind them that Christ had performed His first miracle at a wedding.

But Janie wasn't really listening to Reverend Silas. Momma was holding her so tightly, Janie didn't think she'd ever breathe again. But she stayed put. Momma's arms around her felt so good, just like that dream on Christmas morning.

Janie peeked up at her tall father. She could see that she looked a lot like him. After standing in shock for a moment, he wrapped his arms around both his wife and daughter and openly sobbed.

At that point, the church people wept, too. Even formal Mrs. Babbs pressed her starched handkerchief to her eyes.

Emotion traveled over the room like a wave for the next several minutes. When it finally had settled down, Momma released her tight hold on Janie but continued to hold her hand. Janie pulled her parents around the room and introduced them to all her friends, old and new.

After introductions were made and eyes wiped, the newlywed Blue raised his hand for attention. "I want to say something to all of you. Aleta and I appreciate this wedding day so much. We are husband and wife now in a way we never could have been back in Georgia."

Blue turned to Janie's father. "I am a happy bridegroom today, sir," he said, "and I have an idea. If you and your wife only jumped the broom to get married way back when, why don't you make this *your* true wedding day, too?"

Reverend Silas's eyes brightened. "What a spectacular idea, Blue." He faced George and Anna. "May I offer to conduct the ceremony that makes you married in the eyes of God and in the eyes of the law?"

George and Anna looked at Janie, then at each other. "Yes," they each said at the very same time. And they both laughed.

Another wedding was held at the AME church that day. Janie's family was together at last.

Rachel and the Riot

Susan Martins Miller

A Note to Readers

While the Borlands and their friends are fictional, the Easter riots actually took place. After the Civil War, there was increasing tension between people who owned companies and the people who worked for them. Some owners did not care if their employees were working in dangerous places. They refused to pay their workers enough money to live on.

Because of these problems, workers formed unions. They thought if they worked together against company owners, they would have a better chance of getting more pay and safer working conditions. Sometimes they were successful. Many times they were not. And too often, violence erupted.

In most places, unions weren't legal. Sometimes company owners paid people to break up the unions. Many union members were killed, and some union members killed company supporters in return. This conflict went on for decades. It wasn't until 1935 that the federal government passed a law guaranteeing workers the right to form unions.

Contents

CHAPTER 1

Papa's News

"Pass me that knife, please."

Ten-year-old Rachel Borland wiped her hands on the white apron that covered her blue-and-white-checked dress and pushed her blond hair away from her blue eyes. Then she arranged six carrots on the thick butcher block next to the sink. Potatoes, onions, and shelled peas were already lined up along the counter.

Sam, her twelve-year-old brother, handed her the knife. "What are you making?"

"Stew." Chunks of beef simmered in a big black pot on the stove. Rachel was ready to add the vegetables. She checked the flame on the new gas stove.

"Do you have to put in onions?" Sam asked, making a sour face.

"Papa likes onions. You can pick them out."

"You sound just like Mama."

Sam lifted the lid on the pot and bent his dark head over it to inspect the meat. Sam took after their French grandmother. His hair and eyes were as dark as Rachel's were fair.

"Why don't you stir that, as long as you have the lid off?" Rachel handed her brother a spoon.

"Do you think Papa will be home on time?" Sam asked. "I don't like burned stew."

"He hasn't telephoned," Rachel answered. "He tries to call if he knows he has to stay late at the hospital."

Sam slumped into a chair at the kitchen table. "When your father is a doctor, you have to get used to unpredictable hours."

"That's what Mama always says." Rachel attacked the carrots and whacked them into bite-sized pieces. "But Uncle Ernest is a banker, and he works long hours, too," she added, using the title her parents insisted the children use as a sign of respect toward their older cousins.

"Downtown Minneapolis is a busy place to do business."

"Uncle Ernest says it's busier every year. He can hardly believe it's 1889 already."

"And Uncle Stanley works for the railroad," Sam added. "And his shifts change all the time." He glanced at the pot. "Just don't burn the stew."

Rachel rolled her eyes.

Mama came through the door from the dining room.

"How are you doing with supper?"

Rachel scooped up a handful of carrots and threw them in the pot. "Everything is on schedule. We just need Papa to come home." She added the potatoes to the pot and stirred the mixture vigorously.

"Put the peas in last," Mama said. "They don't take long to cook."

"I remember." Rachel added the onions and left the peas on the counter.

"I'm sure Papa will be here soon." Mama opened a cupboard and removed a stack of large bowls. "Sam, can you get the spoons, please?"

Sam stood up and crossed the kitchen. Just as he pulled open a drawer, they heard the front door open.

"There's Papa," Rachel said. She wiped her hands on her apron again and went to greet her father.

"Right on time," Mama said.

Mama and Sam followed Rachel to the front door. Eight-year-old Carrie was already there with her arms around her father's neck. He scooped up his youngest child and turned to greet his family.

"Something smells wonderful," Papa said.

"Rachel's making stew," Mama informed him.

Papa looked at Rachel. "You're becoming quite a cook, young lady."

"I made baking powder biscuits, too," Rachel said proudly.

"I can see that." Papa reached out and wiped a smudge of flour from Rachel's cheek.

"Will you sit next to me at supper, Papa?" Carrie asked.

Papa smiled. "Don't I always?"

"I was just making sure."

"We weren't certain that you would be home on time tonight," Mama said.

Papa put Carrie down and sighed. "I wasn't either. The streetcar drivers are threatening to strike."

"A strike?"

"Why?"

"What's a strike?"

"How would we get downtown?"

"One question at a time," Papa said, holding up one hand. "I'll tell you everything I know."

Rachel glanced back toward the kitchen and sat on the edge of a chair.

"You already know," Papa said, "that the streetcar drivers have formed a union. They think that if they bind themselves together as one voice, then they will have more power. They want a raise in their wages."

"They haven't had a raise in a long time," Mama said. "Your cousin Stanley reminds us of that all the time."

"But Thomas Lowry, the owner of the Minneapolis Street Railway, says the company is losing money," Papa said. "He can't even afford to pay them the wage they earn now."

Rachel pressed her eyebrows together. "Do you think that's true?"

Papa shrugged his shoulders. "I don't know. Some people think he is planning to electrify the streetcars, and that will cost a lot of money."

"Electric streetcars?" Sam asked excitedly. "No horses?"

Papa nodded. "It will happen before much longer, I'm sure." He sat down on a sofa.

"I remember when we all went downtown to see the first electric lights on Washington Avenue," Sam said.

Mama chuckled. "You were only five years old. Cousin Seth was sure he had explained everything so that you could understand."

"So if Thomas Lowry pays a higher wage now," Sam said, thinking aloud, "then he won't be able to afford to electrify the streetcar system."

Papa nodded. "I think that's right."

"Electric streetcars will be good for Minneapolis," Rachel said.

"But what about the drivers?" Sam protested. "Is it fair to make their families suffer so we can ride electric cars?"

"What's a strike?" Carrie asked, snuggling next to her father on the sofa.

Papa looked down at Carrie. "A strike would mean that the drivers would tell Mr. Lowry that they won't drive the streetcars."

"Would they get paid if they did that?"

Papa shook his head. "No, if they don't work, they don't get paid."

Carrie was puzzled. "Then they won't get any money. Isn't that worse than not getting a raise?"

Papa laughed. "Now you sound like Uncle Ernest."

"I do?"

"Yes, he says that Mr. Lowry is just making a good business decision. He doesn't force anyone to work for his company. If they don't like the wages, they can look for jobs somewhere else."

"They could work at the flour mills," Rachel suggested.

"A lot of people want to work at the mills," Sam said. "It would be hard to get a job there."

"That's exactly what Mr. Lowry thinks," Papa said. "He believes the drivers need their jobs. Not many of them can afford to go without being paid, and he says they won't find better jobs somewhere else."

"Even if they get other jobs," Mama said, "they might have the same problems."

"You're right," Papa added. "Already there have been two hundred strikes in Minnesota in the last ten years."

"But a streetcar strike will hurt a lot of people besides Mr. Lowry," Sam said. "That doesn't seem fair."

Carrie sat up straight and sniffed the air. "What's that smell?"

"My stew!" Rachel leaped up and flew to the kitchen. She snatched a spoon off the counter and stirred the contents of the pot quickly. The stew was just beginning to stick to the bottom of the pot, but it was not ruined. Thanks to Carrie's sensitive nose, supper was saved. Rachel sighed in relief. She would have to concentrate better than this, or Mama would not let her cook anymore. She stuck a fork in a potato and decided that the vegetables were tender. The peas, which she added now, would take only a few minutes to cook. It was time to bake the biscuits. Rachel was just putting the pan of biscuits in the oven when the rest of her family trailed into the kitchen.

"I told you I don't like burned stew," Sam said.

"It's not burned," Rachel assured him.

"You're not going to burn the biscuits, too, are you?" Sam asked.

Rachel made a face at him. But she glanced at the oven. She had never made biscuits all by herself before. She wanted them to be perfect.

"Can I have butter on my biscuits?" Carrie asked.

"Of course," Mama said. "Why don't you get the butter out and put it on the table?"

Mama had left the stack of bowls on the table. She resumed getting the table ready for the meal.

"Sam, we still need spoons for the stew," Mama said.

Papa sat down in his usual chair.

"I had lunch with Stanley today," he remarked.

"How are the Browns?" Mama asked brightly.

"They are doing well. Miranda is applying for a job at the Boston Clothing Store on Washington Avenue."

Mama chuckled. "She has loved that store from the time she was two. She would do a wonderful job working there."

"That's what Stanley thinks. Freddy is having a hard time settling down in school. His teacher has been sending notes home quite frequently."

Mama smiled. "Well, he is only seven years old. Even Carrie still has a hard time sitting still all day."

"The Browns are fine," Papa said. "But all this business about the streetcars is taking its toll."

"What do you mean?" Sam asked.

Rachel checked the biscuits and stirred the stew. All the while, she listened to what her father had to say.

"Stanley is barely talking to Ernest," Papa said.

"But Ernest is his sister's husband," Mama said. "How can he not talk to them?"

"Oh, he'll talk to Linda. I don't think anything can come between

Stanley and Linda. And of course Seth and Miranda are still the best of friends."

"Those two cousins have always been inseparable," Mama said.

Papa frowned. "It's just that Stanley finds it difficult to be around Ernest."

"Stanley and Ernest have always been able to see past their differences before," Mama said.

Papa shook his head. "This is different. Stanley didn't even want to hear me say Ernest's name."

"Is Uncle Stanley mad at Uncle Ernest?" Carrie asked.

"Let's just say they have a difference of opinion," Papa said. "They're having trouble understanding each other."

"What do the streetcars have to do with them?" Rachel asked. Carefully, she lifted the pot of stew from the stove and set it on the table.

"Stanley thinks that the streetcar drivers have a right to form a union and go on strike," Papa answered Rachel. "It's not only the question of higher wages. They also complain that the cars are too open to the elements. They have no protection against the rain, the wind, or the cold."

"And what does Uncle Ernest think?" Sam asked.

"Ernest thinks Thomas Lowry is a good businessman and makes decisions that are good for his company. And Ernest thinks Mr. Lowry has a right to do that. If the street railway company can't make enough money, all the drivers will lose their jobs."

"So maybe it's better if the drivers don't get a raise," Rachel said. "That's better than no job at all."

"But doesn't Uncle Ernest think the streetcar company should be fair to the drivers?" Sam asked.

"What if he can't be fair to the drivers and stay in business at the same time?" Papa countered.

"There must be another way to save money."

"Electric streetcars will be cheaper—once Mr. Lowry can afford to buy them and put in the electrical lines."

"Uncle Stanley and Uncle Ernest don't work for the streetcar company," Rachel said. "Why would they quarrel over this?"

"I asked myself the same thing," Papa said. "But Stanley is part of the railroad union, so he has a lot of sympathy for the streetcar drivers and their union."

"And Ernest is a banker," Mama said, "so he has sympathy for the businesspeople."

Rachel nervously took the biscuits out of the oven. Then she sighed in relief. They were a perfect golden brown and had fluffed up nicely.

"Those look absolutely beautiful, Rachel!" Mama said. "I should have let you make biscuits a long time ago."

"I'll put them in a basket," Rachel said, her pride showing in her blue eyes.

Mama put a ladle in the pot of stew on the table, and the family took their seats. Bowing her head, Rachel listened as her father thanked God for the food. Silently, she added her own prayer: *Please, God, help Uncle Stanley and Uncle Ernest be friends again.*

Chapter 2

Who's Right?

"Are you playing baseball today?" Rachel asked Sam the next morning.

"Yep. As soon as I'm done here." Sam pulled the broom across the linoleum kitchen floor as rapidly as he could.

"What else does Mama want you to do?" Rachel was folding laundry on the kitchen table. She had just brought it in from the clothesline in the backyard.

"Nothing. This is my last chore for the day."

"Is it a practice or a game?" Rachel asked, smoothing out one of her cotton skirts.

"Practice. We're getting ready for a game against the Seventh Street team next week." Sam parked the broom in the corner of the kitchen.

"I hope you hit a home run."

"Thanks. I'll be glad just to get a hit." A few minutes later, Sam was off to the baseball field with his bat propped on his shoulder.

After her brother left and Rachel finished the laundry, she got ready for her friends Janie Lawrence and Colleen Ryan. Janie and Colleen liked to cook as much as Rachel did, and the girls were going to look through recipes.

Rachel, Colleen, and Janie had been friends since they were five years old. They had played with dolls together, and now they were learning to cook together. Colleen was happy-go-lucky and always seemed to have a smile on her face. She liked to eat almost as much as she liked to cook. Janie was more serious. Her mother had been ill, so she had learned to cook in order to help out at home. Rachel liked learning to cook with both her friends.

Rachel pulled a plate from the cabinet and took out the jar of cookies that her mother had helped her make the day before. She put a pretty napkin on the plate and carefully arranged the cookies on the plate. She took three glasses from the cabinet so they could have milk with their cookies.

Just as she was going to go pick some flowers from her mother's garden, Rachel heard a knock at the door. When she opened it, her friends were standing there, but they did not sound very much like friends.

"Who says I don't know what I'm talking about?" Colleen said strongly. Rachel had never heard her jolly friend sound so intense.

"If you knew what you were talking about, you wouldn't say the things you are saying," Janie retorted.

"Haven't you heard of free speech? I can say whatever I want to." Colleen nodded to Rachel and pushed past Janie into the house. Janie followed, barely acknowledging Rachel's presence.

Rachel closed the door and looked at her friends. This was so unlike them, and she really did not know what to do. "Uh, what's wrong? Did something happen?" Colleen and Janie just looked at each other.

After what seemed to Rachel like hours, Janie walked over and handed her some papers she had brought. Rachel could see they were recipes that Janie had written out so carefully. Janie headed for the door.

"Janie!" Rachel called. "Aren't you going to stay? Aren't we going through recipes?"

Janie sighed. "I want to, but I don't know if I can." She looked over at Colleen, who was just standing in the middle of the room, arms folded across her chest. Colleen looked away.

Finally, Rachel could stand it no longer.

"What's the matter?" Rachel asked.

"Aw, nothing," Colleen snarled. "Just go look through your recipes."

"It's not nothing," Janie insisted.

"Then what is it?" Rachel asked again. "You're not acting like it's nothing."

"Janie's father works for the streetcar company," Colleen answered.

"I know," Rachel replied. "I've ridden in his car lots of times."

"The union is going to ask for a raise," Janie said. "My father deserves a better wage. He works hard."

"I know he works hard," Rachel said. "Sometimes it's cold and wet in those cars. And the drivers spend all day out in the weather, no matter how bad it is."

"And he works long hours. He's never home for supper. We hardly see him before we go to bed at night."

"I still don't understand what you two are arguing about," Rachel said.

Janie spoke up quickly. "Colleen doesn't want to admit that people like my father deserve to be paid for their work."

"He gets paid," Colleen muttered. "If he doesn't like his wage, he can find a new job. My father says that the streetcar drivers formed a union so they could bully the owners of the company."

"That's not true!" Janie replied. She moved closer to Rachel. "Unions protect the workers. When people stand together, they can do more than when they are alone."

"That's a good point," Rachel said. "It's like Sam's team. They all need each other, or they will never be able to beat that Seventh Street team. Let's go. I have cookies in the kitchen."

Rachel moved toward the kitchen. Neither Colleen nor Janie showed any sign of moving.

Rachel took a mental inventory of her friends. Colleen's father worked at the bank where Uncle Ernest worked. They lived in a nice house, and Colleen always had time to play once her chores were done. Janie's father was a streetcar driver who had to work longer hours to help cover his wife's medical expenses. Free time for Janie, like this morning, was rare. She had to spend a lot of time working around the house and helping to care for her family.

The girls hardly ever talked about what their parents did for a living. Somehow it had never mattered before. They had been together ever since they started school. They all lived within a few blocks of each other. Why should they worry about how their parents made a living? They had all ridden in the streetcar that Janie Lawrence's father drove. When they did, they enjoyed calling the driver by name. They were riding with a friend. *Why should that change,* Rachel wondered, *just because of a union?*

Rachel always looked forward to any time that she could be with her friends—but not because she wanted to listen to a dispute about unions. She wanted to have cookies with her friends and look through recipes. She remembered what her father had said the night before about her uncle Stanley and uncle Ernest.

"Let's do what we came here to do," Rachel said. She hurried past Janie and Colleen and went into the kitchen.

But Janie was not ready. "Unions are not a game," Janie said. "And Thomas Lowry, the owner of the streetcar company, is not interested in families. He just wants to make money."

"He has to run a good business," Colleen said, "or the whole company will go broke. Then no one has a job."

"He doesn't have to make himself filthy rich at the expense of all the drivers."

"Is that what your father says?"

"Yeah."

"He's just jealous of Thomas Lowry."

"That's the nuttiest idea I've ever heard."

Rachel stepped back into the living room. At first Janie and Colleen were both making good points. But now they were sniping at each other. And why did they have to discuss this now, when they were supposed to be having fun doing something they all liked?

"Come on," Rachel pleaded. "Let's go. We're wasting the whole morning."

"Yeah, you're right." Colleen walked into the kitchen and stopped in front of Janie. "I see those cookies. Let's go."

"Oh, okay. Mother was feeling better this morning, so I could come, but I don't want to stay too late. Let's not waste any more time." Janie looked reluctant, but she joined the other girls in the kitchen.

"Let's get started." Rachel put her arms around the shoulders of her friends. She put Janie's recipes on the table, and Colleen added hers to the collection.

"There's milk to go with the cookies. Janie, can you get it? I've got to go get my recipes." Rachel left the girls in the kitchen as she went to her room to get the recipes she had collected from her mother and grandmother.

Rachel was surprised that she did not hear a sound as she came back toward the kitchen. One of the things she had always been able to count on was having a good time with her friends. Yet today no familiar laughter came from the kitchen. No talking, either. With dread, she entered the kitchen. Colleen and Janie were sitting at the table just staring at each other. The milk was still in the pitcher, and the cookies hadn't been touched.

Janie slid her chair back and stood up. "I'd really better leave. I—um—don't like leaving my mother for very long." She picked up her papers and started to leave.

Quickly, Colleen picked up her recipes. "Oh, I forgot. I have plans with my family. How could I have forgotten? We'll have to get together some other time."

Colleen followed Janie to the front door. Slowly, Rachel joined them. "I wish you didn't have to leave," she said as she opened the door. "Please, can't you stay longer?" Both her friends shook their heads no and started down the sidewalk, Janie a few paces ahead of Colleen.

Rachel closed the door and returned to the kitchen. She sat at the table and looked at the plate of cookies she had so carefully prepared. She poured herself a glass of milk and took a cookie. Rachel leaned her chin on her hand. This was supposed to be a wonderful day—just three friends spending time together doing something they loved. What had gone so wrong? Would their friendship survive?

Chapter 3

A Friendship Ends

Monday morning came too soon. All day Sunday, Rachel wondered about Janie and Colleen. How long could they stay mad at each other? Neither of them could change what was happening in the streetcar company. But they could play together, just as they had since they were five years old. Rachel had dreaded Monday morning, when she would have to go to school and see Colleen and Janie.

Mama believed in observing the Sabbath. After church on Sunday, she liked the family to spend the afternoon together in quiet activities. Rachel usually read a book. She was in the middle of *Twenty Thousand Leagues under the Sea,* a Jules Verne novel. Her cousin Miranda had recommended the book to her. But even the fantastic imagination of a science fiction writer like Jules Verne could not distract Rachel. All day she wondered how Janie and Colleen could go from being best friends to enemies. Had they ever really liked each other—the way Rachel liked both of them?

Now Monday morning had come. Rachel and Sam entered the school yard. Rachel was further behind Sam than usual. She had a very small build and short legs, and she nearly always had trouble keeping up with Sam's long stride. Today she was having even more difficulty keeping up with him. With his book bag over one shoulder, he turned to look at his sister.

"Don't you feel well, Rachel?" he asked.

"I feel fine," she muttered.

"You look fine, too," Sam observed. "But you're not acting fine. What's the matter?"

"Nothing."

"I don't believe that for a minute. You've been acting strangely ever since Saturday."

"What do you mean?"

"For one thing, you sat still all the way through church yesterday, even when we sang that hymn that you think has such a funny tune."

Rachel shrugged. "So what?"

"So, I think something's wrong. Something happened with your friends. That's when it started."

Rachel gave in. She knew Sam would keep after her until she told him what was wrong.

"Janie and Colleen had a fight," Rachel said. "It's about the unions. They were so mad at each other that they didn't want to go through recipes."

Sam glanced across the school yard. "Here comes Janie now. Colleen is right behind her, but they're not talking to each other."

"See what I mean? They've been best friends since they were little, and now they don't want to talk to each other."

"It doesn't make sense." Sam sighed.

Rachel shifted her attention to another corner of the school yard. "Who is that new girl over there?"

Sam followed her gaze to a girl Rachel's age who sat timidly on a bench alone. "Oh, that's Annalina Borg. Her family just came from Sweden."

"How do you know them?" Rachel asked.

"Uncle Stanley told me about them. Mr. Borg was looking for a job. Uncle Stanley wanted to hire him, but he doesn't have any openings right now."

"So did Mr. Borg find another job?"

Sam shook his head. "I don't think so. But Uncle Stanley says that Mr. Borg wants Annalina to start right out getting an education. He made sure she would start school right away."

"I'll have to be sure to talk to her."

"Good luck." Sam chuckled. "She doesn't speak English."

"Not any?"

"No. They just arrived from Sweden last week."

"She's probably lonely, then. There aren't any other Swedish children in our school."

"Most of them don't live around here. But the Borgs are renting a house in the neighborhood until they find someplace to settle down."

A door on the front of the school opened, and a teacher came out. She pulled vigorously on the rope that moved the brass bell atop the building. The bell clanked, instantly commanding the attention of every student in the school yard.

Sam laughed. "There's your teacher. Miss Whittlesey means business today."

Rachel groaned. "She'll probably give us a math quiz."

"I'm glad I'm not in your class."

Inside the school door, Sam and Rachel separated. There were four different classes in the small building, covering eight grades. Rachel walked down the hall to her classroom. Standing at the back of the classroom, she wished she could choose a new seat. Miss Whittlesey had assigned her a seat behind Janie and across the aisle from Colleen. When the assignments were made, all three girls had been ecstatic. Now, Rachel knew, Colleen and Janie would feel differently. Reluctantly, Rachel took her seat. Janie came in and sat in front of her.

"Hi, Rachel."

"Hi, Janie."

Colleen was already sitting across the aisle. Janie did not say a word to her. But Rachel could not ignore Colleen.

"Good morning, Colleen," she said.

"Morning," Colleen muttered without looking up from her desk.

Miss Whittlesey had threatened to give a math quiz, but she didn't. Rachel was relieved. She was not sure she would be able to concentrate well enough to take a test, and she dreaded the thought of what might happen between Colleen and Janie during lunch.

Rachel spotted the new girl at the other side of her classroom, but there was no way to talk with her. Finally lunchtime came. The students burst out the doors of the school with their lunch buckets and scattered around the school yard to enjoy the April spring day.

Rachel was one of the last ones out of the building. She looked around, hoping to talk to Annalina—or at least try to. At last she spotted the fair-headed girl sitting on a bench on the far side of the school yard, unpacking her meager lunch.

Rachel approached her. "Hello," she said brightly.

Annalina looked up, confused. Finally, she forced a smile.

"I know you don't speak English," Rachel said, "but I want to be your friend."

Annalina wrinkled her forehead in concentration. Rachel knew she had not understood anything.

"You have to learn English," Rachel said, "or you won't be able to learn anything else at school."

"English?" Annalina said, finally recognizing a word.

"Yes, English. You must learn." Rachel sat down on the bench next to Annalina. "When my little sister was learning to talk, my mother said that the most important thing was that we all talk to her a lot. So that's what I'm going to do with you. I'm just going to talk until you understand."

Rachel smiled at Annalina, who smiled back blankly.

"I can't imagine what it must be like not to understand anything around you," Rachel said, as she unwrapped her sandwich. "But it can't be very pleasant. You're going to have to learn very quickly, because you don't want to be miserable forever."

Rachel peeled her sandwich apart and held up a slice of Mama's fresh bread. "Bread," she said slowly and distinctly. "Bread."

Annalina looked at the lunch in her lap. She had fruit and a sausage.

"No, you don't have any bread," Rachel said. "But you know what bread is. Just say the word." And she dangled the bread in front of Annalina once more.

"Brud?" Annalina said timidly.

Rachel was careful not to laugh. "Almost. Try again. Bread." She spoke as distinctly as she could.

"Bruad," Annalina croaked.

"That's better," Rachel said. "You just have to practice. Bread."

"Bruad. Bruad. Brrread."

"There you go!" Now Rachel pointed at the fruit in Annalina's lap. "Apple."

Annalina picked up the sausage and said, "Uppa."

"No, that one," Rachel said, pointing again. This time she had her finger nearly on the fruit. "Apple."

Annalina picked up the apple. "Appo?"

"Apple."

Rachel repeated the word as many times as Annalina needed to hear it before she could say it correctly.

"Eat," Rachel said, and she took a bite of her bread.

"Eat," Annalina echoed perfectly.

"That's an easy word, isn't it?" Rachel said. "There are lots of easy words. Maybe we should learn those first."

Annalina smiled and bit her apple. Rachel thought it was a true smile.

In between bites of her own lunch, Rachel continued talking.

"Is our teacher helping you at all?" she asked. "I suppose Miss Whittlesey knows that you don't speak English. But she has so many other students that she won't have time to teach you any words. That's all right, because I can do it. I'll have to find out where you live, though. We won't see each other enough at school."

Annalina smiled again. Rachel could see the anxiety in her blue eyes.

"You have no idea what I'm saying," Rachel said, "but I hope you know that I'm trying to be your friend." She reached out and touched Annalina's blond braid hanging over one shoulder. "I've always wondered what I might look like with braided hair. My mother says I have such beautiful hair that I shouldn't tie it up in knots. But I think you look very pretty."

Rachel twisted the ends of her own hair between her fingers. She and Annalina both had blond hair and blue eyes.

"Hair," Rachel said.

"Eeaare," Annalina croaked.

"Hair." Again Rachel repeated the word as many times as Annalina needed. She glanced across the school yard at Sam. "I wonder if you have any brothers."

Sam had settled under a tree by himself with his lunch. He could feel tension between his friends Jim Harrison and Simon Jones. They had acted kind of strange at baseball practice, as though they suddenly didn't like each other. Sam could see Jim coming toward him. He glanced around. Simon was off to one side, gently tossing a baseball between his hands.

"Hi, Sam," Jim said. "Are you finished eating?"

"Almost."

"We still have a few minutes before the bell rings. How about playing catch?"

Sam hesitated. Out of the corner of his eye, he saw Simon looking in his direction. What would Simon think if he tossed a ball with Jim? Sam was beginning to feel pulled between his two friends.

"I think I need to let my lunch settle," Sam finally said.

"Come on, Sam, just a few throws?"

"Maybe later." Sam stuffed a piece of cheese in his mouth and tried to look busy eating.

Jim shuffled off. But as soon as he was gone, Simon made a beeline for Sam.

"What did Jim want?" Simon demanded.

"He just wanted to play catch," Sam answered.

"But you didn't want to play with him, did you?"

Sam shrugged. "I said I wasn't finished eating."

Simon bent over and looked in Sam's lunch bucket. "It looks like you're finished now. Let's find a bat and hit a few balls."

Sam's stomach sank. He'd been afraid Simon was going to say that.

"Like I told Jim," Sam said, "I want to let my lunch settle."

"You never wanted your lunch to settle before," countered Simon. "You don't even like to eat lunch."

"Well, today I ate lunch, and I want it to settle."

"You're ignoring me, just like Jim. Are you on his side?"

"What are you talking about? What is going on between you two? I noticed it at practice. Simon, you almost hit Jim in the head with a baseball!"

Simon looked at Sam in disbelief. "How can you not know what is going on? Jim thinks the streetcar drivers should go on strike. That's just stupid. Why, Mr. Lowry will go out of business if he has to pay the drivers more. They get paid. If they don't like it, they can go get another job. They can work for Mr. Pillsbury."

Sam shrugged. This was the same thing that had caused the problems between Rachel's friends Colleen and Janie. And between Uncle Ernest and Uncle Stanley. It seemed as though everyone was taking sides.

"So, whose side are you on—mine or Jim's?" Simon prodded.

"I'm not on anybody's side," Sam said. "I just want to eat my lunch."

Across the school yard, Rachel saw the frustration rising in her brother's face. She wondered what Jim and Simon had said to Sam. She could see his tension in the way he held his head. Jim and Simon and Sam had been friends for a long time—just like she and Colleen and Janie.

"Don't worry," she said aloud to Annalina. "We'll be friends because we want to be. None of this other business will matter."

Annalina nodded seriously as if she understood. Knowing she did not, Rachel smiled.

As usual, Rachel was one of the last students out of the building when school was over. Sam hurried to catch up with his sister.

"Sam, what was going on with you, Jim, and Simon at lunch? I saw them talking to you."

Sam looked at Rachel and sighed. "It's the same thing as what's going on between Colleen and Janie—the unions. Jim thinks the streetcar drivers should go on strike, and Simon thinks they shouldn't. I guess it started at baseball practice, but I ignored it and just practiced. Now they want me to choose between them. I just want to be friends—with both of them."

Rachel smiled and nodded at Sam. She knew exactly how he felt. When did being friends and having things in common stop being enough? When did it start to matter whether their fathers were in unions or not?

Chapter 4

On Strike

"Why didn't you call me when you were ready to start cooking?" Rachel lifted the lid on one pot to see what Mama was fixing. "I would have come to help you."

"You were doing homework," Mama answered. "I don't like to interrupt you when you're studying."

"I would rather cook."

"Studying is important. You can slice some cheese to have with the soup."

Rachel opened the icebox and removed a chunk of cheddar cheese. Picking up a knife, she asked, "Mama, do you know any Swedish words?"

"Swedish?" Mama was puzzled.

"Don't you have any Swedish friends?"

"Well, yes, I know a couple of Swedish women at church, but they've been in Minneapolis for several years. They speak English."

"Don't you ever hear them speaking Swedish to each other?"

"Sometimes they do. I never paid much attention to what they were saying. Why are you suddenly so interested in Swedish?"

"There's a new girl at school. She's in my class, and she doesn't speak any English."

Mama smiled. "Are you going to try to teach her English?"

Rachel nodded. "She seems like a very nice girl. I sit with her at lunch some days. But I wish I knew a few words that she could understand."

"Why don't you ask her?"

"What do you mean?"

"When you teach her the English word for something, find out the Swedish word."

Rachel thought about her mother's suggestion. "I should have thought of that. I've been too busy teaching her to pronounce 'sandwich.' "

Sam appeared at the back door off the kitchen.

"Oh, good," he said, pulling the door open and dropping his book bag to the floor. "You haven't served supper yet. I was afraid I was late."

Mama glanced at the clock. "As a matter of fact, you are late—very late. But so is your father. I've been waiting for him." She picked up a wooden spoon and stirred the bean soup.

"Is it sticking to the bottom?" Rachel asked.

"It's starting to. If he doesn't come home soon, we'll have to start without him."

"Oh, no, let's wait," Rachel pleaded. "I like it when we all eat together."

"I don't want to eat burned food," Sam said.

"You won't." Rachel stirred the soup some more.

Carrie came in from the dining room. "I'm hungry," she grumbled. "When will supper be ready?"

"It's ready now," Sam said.

"Good." Carrie climbed into a chair. "Let's eat."

"We're waiting for Papa," Rachel said.

"Do we have to?" Carrie whined. "I'm *sooo* hungry."

Mama glanced at the clock again. "I don't understand why he didn't telephone if he was going to be this late."

"That is strange," Sam agreed.

"Maybe there was an emergency," Rachel suggested.

"Yes, I suppose so," Mama murmured.

For another ten minutes, they stirred the pot of soup and speculated about why Papa was so late.

"I'm starving to death!" Carrie declared dramatically. "We can save some food for Papa. Please, let's eat."

Mama sighed and glanced at the clock once more.

"I suppose we might as well," she said. She reached for a stack of bowls and started dishing up the soup.

Carrie carried hers to the table and picked up her spoon.

"Wait until we give thanks," Mama said.

Carrie sighed and put down her spoon.

A few minutes later, Mama, Rachel, Sam, and Carrie sat before their steaming bowls of navy bean soup with bread, meat, and cheese on the platter in the middle of the table. Mama gave thanks to God for the food. Rachel prayed silently that Papa would be safe.

"Finally!" Carrie said, as she plunged her spoon into her soup and slurped up the first mouthful.

Just then the back door opened.

"Papa!" Rachel cried.

"Donald, are you all right?" Mama asked. She rose to her feet to greet him.

Papa kissed Mama's cheek. "I'm sorry I didn't call," he said. "By the time I realized I should call, I wasn't anywhere near a phone."

"You look exhausted," Rachel said.

"What happened, Papa?" Sam asked.

Papa took off his coat and hung it over the back of a kitchen chair.

"Just let me get settled, and I'll tell you all the whole story," Papa said.

Mama dished up Papa's soup, and they all sat down again.

Papa took a bite of bread and then began his story.

"I was so busy today that I hardly noticed what was going on downtown," he said. "I saw nearly two dozen patients at the clinic this morning. Then, after lunch, I went over to the hospital to make my rounds. I thought it was odd that there were no streetcars around. But I didn't have far to go, so I paid no attention. Later, another doctor told me that Thomas Lowry had announced a cut in the wages of the streetcar drivers—two cents an hour!"

"But the drivers already make so little money," Sam said. He thought of Jim Harrison and wondered how his friend would take the news. Rachel worried about how Janie Lawrence's family would get along with a cut in her father's wages. Rachel and Sam glanced at each other, their concern evident in their eyes.

Papa nodded. "I know. I knew Mr. Lowry would not want to give the drivers the raise they wanted. But I did not think he would cut their wages even lower."

"What will the drivers do now?" Rachel passed the platter of meat and cheese to her father.

"They won't drive the streetcars, that's for sure," Papa said. "They went on strike." He took a bite of the cheese Rachel had sliced.

"Strike?" Carrie asked.

"Yes, a strike. The drivers refuse to drive until Mr. Lowry gives back their wages."

"So that's why there were no streetcars when you went out," Mama said.

Papa nodded. "As word spread around the city, the drivers turned back to the car barns. They stabled the horses and hung up their reins. By the middle of the afternoon, no streetcars were running anywhere in the city."

"None at all?" Sam asked.

Papa shook his head. "None."

"But there are over two hundred streetcars."

"Not today. Not even one."

"It's hard to imagine Minneapolis without streetcars," Rachel said.

"We'll all have to get used to it," Papa said. "I don't think this will be settled easily." He chewed on his cheese. "Of course, I didn't realize when I left the hospital that the streetcars weren't running. When I set out for home, I thought I would pick one up along the way. As I said, by the time I realized there were no streetcars, I was far from a telephone. I had no choice but to walk the rest of the way home."

"It's a long way," Mama said. "No wonder it took you so long."

"At least I wasn't alone." He folded a piece of bread around a chunk of cheese. "Everyone who works downtown was in the same situation. We all had to walk."

"What about Uncle Ernest?" Rachel asked. "He has a lame leg. It's hard for him to walk that far."

"I thought of him," Papa said.

"Did you see him leaving the bank?"

"No, I didn't see him. And there was nothing I could do for him anyway. We don't own a carriage."

"No," Mama said. "We've always depended on the streetcars."

"Uncle Ernest doesn't have a carriage, either," Rachel said. "How will he get to work every day without the streetcars?"

Papa shrugged. "I'm not sure what Ernest will do. But I know he thinks Mr. Lowry did the right thing."

"Perhaps we should think about getting a carriage and a horse of our own," Mama said.

"Surely the strike will be settled soon," Sam said.

Papa shook his head again. "I wouldn't count on that. As I walked home, I listened to what people were saying in the streets. Mr. Lowry is a very stubborn man. No one believes he will negotiate with the drivers. Either they do things his way, or they don't work."

"But that's not fair," Sam said. "He should at least talk to the drivers. Maybe if they understood each other better, they would figure something out that would make both sides happy."

"That's not likely."

Rachel and Sam had stopped eating. Only Carrie continued to happily slurp her way through the meal.

"What will happen now?" Sam asked.

Papa sighed. "I'm not sure. I don't think anyone can say. Mr. Lowry might hire other men to drive the streetcars."

"Can he do that?"

"Yes, he can. It's his company. He doesn't have to do what the union tells him to do."

"That doesn't seem fair to the drivers," Sam said.

"Mr. Lowry is not concerned about the drivers. His concern is for his company."

"But the drivers are his company," Rachel said emphatically.

"He doesn't see it that way," Papa said. "His income comes from the passengers. He has to keep the cars running, or he won't make any money at all."

"If he gave the drivers their wages back, he wouldn't have any trouble keeping the cars running," Mama reasoned.

Papa shook his head. "I don't think he will do that."

Sam twirled his spoon in his soup and stared absently at the bread platter.

"Sam, Rachel, you must eat," Mama prodded.

"I've lost my appetite." Sam put his spoon down.

"You must eat anyway," Mama said. "I know this strike will upset a lot of people, but that's no reason to starve yourself."

"Papa," Sam said, "did you happen to see Mr. Harrison downtown? You know, Jim's father."

"No, Sam, I'm sorry. I didn't see him. He must have gone home earlier in the day."

"Oh."

"You'll see Jim tomorrow at school, won't you?"

Sam nodded.

"You can ask him how his father is."

Sam did not answer. Rachel wondered if he was thinking about what Simon would say to Jim.

"And Janie's father. The Lawrences really need the money." Rachel's father nodded at her.

"Papa, I wonder what Uncle Stanley thinks about all this," Rachel said. "I know he likes the unions. He belongs to one."

"I'm sure he supports the strike," Papa said. "He knows how businesses can take advantage of employees."

"It's not fair," Sam said.

"No, it's not," their father agreed.

"It's not fair of the company to cut the wages of the drivers. But it's not fair for the drivers to go on strike, either."

"What good will the strike do?" Rachel asked. "If Mr. Lowry finds other men to drive the streetcars for less money, how does that help people like the Harrisons or the Lawrences?"

"It doesn't," Sam said. "That's why it's not fair. Nobody is helped. Everybody is hurt."

"It sure seems that way to us," Mama said.

"I can't understand why Mr. Harrison would go on strike," Sam said. "He needs his job. And I think he even likes his job. He's always telling stories and joking with the passengers."

"Oh, I know he likes his job," Papa said. "I've heard him say so. But he's a member of the union. If the union votes to go on strike, then all the members go on strike."

"Even if they don't want to?"

"The strength of the union comes from everyone banding together," Papa explained. "If some of the drivers cooperate with Mr. Lowry, then the rest of the drivers will suffer even more. They have to act together, as if they were one person. That's the only way the union can have any power against the company."

Sam nodded. "I know. I've heard Uncle Stanley explain about unions. But it still doesn't make sense to me. Even if all the union members join together as one big person, they are still not as powerful as Mr. Lowry. He owns the company."

"Yes, but he cannot operate the company without drivers," Papa said.

"So they need each other," Rachel said.

"It just might take awhile before both sides realize how much they need each other."

"I hate to think what this will do to Stanley and Ernest's relationship," Mama said. "Agnes and Linda will be pulling their hair out trying to find ways to make their husbands get along."

Papa sighed heavily and pushed his empty plate away. "Let's just pray that someone finds a solution to the strike very soon."

Chapter 5

The Union Prepares

"Come on, Sam," Rachel said urgently. She stood near the front door, ready to go. "Annalina will be waiting. Let's go."

"Tell me again what we're doing," Sam said. He looked up from the book he was reading in the living room after school.

"I told Annalina I would take her downtown. She hasn't even seen Bridge Square yet. And I want to show her the shops."

"But it's getting late. The shops will not be open much longer."

"That's all right because we're not really shopping. We're just looking. But Mama says I can't go alone."

"That's right." Mama glanced up from the newspaper. "I'm not sure you should go at all."

"Aw, Mama!" Rachel grumbled.

"There's an article right here in today's newspaper talking about the strike," Mama said. "A lot of people out on the streets are angry. The police have had to break up several fistfights."

"We'll be careful, Mama," Rachel promised. "I already promised Annalina, and she hasn't got a telephone. I don't want to disappoint her."

"What do you think, Donald?" Mama asked.

Papa put down the business section of the paper and looked at Rachel. "I think," he said slowly, "that Rachel should have talked to us before she made a promise to Annalina."

"Please, Papa," Rachel pleaded.

"I understand your mother's concerns," Papa said. "You will have to be extra careful. Can you promise me that?"

"Yes, yes! We'll be so careful!"

"Donald, are you sure about this?" Mama asked doubtfully.

"They're just children," Papa said. "They're not members of any union. I don't think anyone will bother with them."

"But they could get caught in the middle of something."

"That's why we're sending Sam along," Papa said. "Between the two of them, Sam and Rachel have enough sense to stay out of trouble."

"So we can go?" Rachel asked hopefully.

"Yes, you may go," Papa answered.

Rachel looked at Mama.

"If you insist on going," Mama said, "at least take a jar of preserves to Mrs. Borg."

Outside, Sam and Rachel walked for several blocks.

"This isn't the way to Bridge Square," Sam said after a few minutes.

"I know. But it's the way to Annalina's house."

"How far away does she live?"

"About a mile, I think."

"So we have to walk a mile in the wrong direction?"

"It's not the wrong direction. It's the way to Annalina's house."

"But then we have to walk all the way back again, and then the rest of the way to Bridge Square. And then we have to come all the way back to bring Annalina home. That's going to be at least four miles."

Rachel shrugged. "We have time."

"Under the circumstances, I think Annalina would understand if you did not show up at her house."

"There's no reason to disappoint her," Rachel said with determination. And she walked a little faster.

"If we could ride the streetcar, I wouldn't mind," Sam said.

"Look!" Rachel pointed. "There's a streetcar. And it's going our direction." She put out her hand to hail the driver.

Sam grabbed Rachel's arm and yanked her back from the edge of the street.

"Ow!" she protested.

"What do you think you're doing?" Sam hissed.

"You said you wanted to ride a streetcar. And here's a car now. The driver must not be part of the strike."

"All the drivers are on strike," Sam said emphatically. "This driver is a scab."

"A scab?"

"One of the men Thomas Lowry hired to drive the cars in place of the regular drivers. He makes the new drivers promise not to join a union."

The streetcar rattled closer to them. The driver glanced at them hopefully. Sam pulled Rachel farther away from the road. The car rumbled on.

"No one was riding in the car," Rachel said.

"That's right." Sam nodded.

"But why is Mr. Lowry paying men to drive empty cars?"

"He hopes people will get tired of walking and start riding."

"But you don't think so, do you?" Rachel asked. "Just a few minutes ago, you were wishing you could ride a streetcar, but when you had the chance, you wouldn't get on."

Sam shook his head. "It's not safe. I promised Mama and Papa I would look out for you."

"What would happen if we got on a streetcar?" Rachel asked. "If no one else is in the car, how could we get hurt?"

Sam glanced around. "Do you see those people at the next corner?"

Rachel nodded. One block away stood a woman and three young men who looked like they had nowhere to go.

"If we get on," Sam said, "they'll get on. They'll call the driver names and lecture us all the way downtown about destroying everything the union has worked for."

Rachel looked at her brother. "How do you know all this?"

"I talked to Jim."

"I thought you weren't getting along with Jim."

Sam shrugged. "I have nothing against Jim. I don't understand why he's fighting with Simon, but I'm trying to be friends with both of them."

Rachel nodded. She knew how hard that could be. "So what did Jim tell you?"

"His father is thinking about going back to work, because Jim's mama is worried they won't have enough money to pay their bills." Sam started walking again. "Besides, it doesn't matter now. There won't be another car along this way for a long time."

It took Sam and Rachel almost an hour to walk to Annalina's house and then retrace their steps to go to Bridge Square. As they approached the downtown area, Annalina's blue eyes lit up with a fresh glow. She raced ahead of Sam and Rachel, her braids bobbing over her shoulders. Every few steps, Annalina glanced over her shoulder to make sure Rachel was behind her, but she could not make herself slow down.

Knowing that Annalina could not understand him, Sam said to

Rachel, "I've never seen someone so excited about seeing a bridge."

"Bridge?" Annalina said, repeating the word Rachel had taught her a few days ago.

"We've always lived in Minneapolis," Rachel said. "We've seen the bridges our whole lives. If we visited Sweden, we'd be interested in things that other people think are ordinary."

"I suppose so," Sam muttered.

They were on Hennepin Avenue now, heading for the heart of downtown Minneapolis. In a few minutes, they would be at Bridge Square. From there they could look at the huge Pillsbury mill across the river. Sam hoped there would be trains on the stone arch bridge that carried Jim Hill's railroad across the surging Mississippi River.

Annalina's blue eyes were bright with excitement. She darted from one shop to another, pointing and questioning with her eyes. Smiling, Rachel answered as many questions as she could.

Suddenly, Rachel stopped and pointed.

"Sam, look! Isn't that Uncle Stanley?"

Sam peered down the street. "Yes, and it looks like Seth is with him."

Rachel quickened her steps. "Let's go say hello."

As they got closer, they saw that Uncle Stanley and his eighteen-year-old nephew, Seth, were not just out for an afternoon stroll. Their hands were full of pamphlets, and they were handing one to every person who passed by.

"What is it?" Rachel asked.

"Union literature," Sam answered. He slowed his steps. "Why don't we just go on by? They look busy."

"Don't be silly," Rachel said. "We can't pretend that we didn't see them."

"They haven't noticed us yet," Sam countered.

Just then, Seth waved a long arm.

"Now they have." Rachel started toward her cousins.

Annalina looked confused, but she followed where Rachel led.

"Hello, Uncle Stanley. Hello, Seth," Rachel said cheerfully. "I would like you to meet my friend Annalina."

"Glad to meet you, Annalina," Uncle Stanley said. "What brings you downtown on this fine afternoon?"

"She doesn't speak English," Sam said.

Seth's eyes widened slightly. "Not at all?"

"Only the words Rachel has taught her."

"Oh, I understand." Uncle Stanley turned to Rachel. "So I'll ask you what has brought you downtown today."

"Annalina just moved to Minneapolis two weeks ago. I wanted to show her around." Rachel gestured toward the stack of papers under her older cousin's arm. "Why are you here?"

"We have a union meeting in a few minutes," Uncle Stanley explained. "We're asking people to come inside and hear a speaker."

"Is it about the strike?" Rachel asked.

Uncle Stanley nodded. "The strike will not be settled if people cannot learn to listen to one another."

"I suppose that's true."

Rachel wondered if Uncle Ernest knew that his son Seth was passing out union literature. Surely Uncle Ernest would not approve. He was already unhappy that Seth had taken a job with the railroad while he got ready to go to college. But Rachel decided not to ask about Uncle Ernest.

"Are there many people in there?" Rachel asked instead, pointing to a brick building.

"There is still room for more." Uncle Stanley reached out and handed a pamphlet to a man passing by.

"We'd better go in soon," Seth said.

"All right," his uncle replied. He handed a pamphlet to Sam.

"Here, take this home to your father."

"My father is not a union man."

"But he's not against the union, either," Uncle Stanley said. "He might be interested in what we have to say."

Uncle Stanley and Seth disappeared inside the brick building.

"What does the pamphlet say?" Rachel asked.

Sam turned it over and looked at the front. "Stand together," he read. "The strength of many, the mind of one."

"The strength of many, the mind of one," Rachel repeated. "I like that."

Sam looked up from the paper into his sister's blue eyes.

"Are you thinking what I'm thinking?" Rachel asked.

Sam nodded slowly. "But just for a few minutes. After all, you promised to show Annalina the bridge, and soon it will be time to take her home."

Rachel nodded. "I just want to see what it's like."

Once again, Annalina did not understand what was happening, but she followed where Rachel led—into the brick building.

Inside, they crept down a dark stairwell and came to a set of double doors.

"It must be in there," Sam whispered, peeking through the crack between the two doors. His jaw dropped. "There must be three hundred people in that room."

"Open the door," Rachel urged.

"Are you sure?" Sam asked.

Rachel nodded. Annalina looked from Sam to Rachel and back again.

Sam opened the door, and the three of them slipped into the back of the room.

In the front of the room on a makeshift stage, a man stood on a chair. "The mayor is making promises he can't keep," the man shouted. "He promises to protect the drivers. He threatens to arrest anyone who gets in the way of the smooth operation of the streetcar system."

The crowd booed and rumbled.

"This city does not have enough police officers for the mayor to keep that promise," the man shouted, thrusting his fist in the air. "We have people standing on every corner watching the cars. We know who is riding and who is not."

"See?" Sam whispered. "Isn't that what I told you?"

"Shh!" Rachel wanted to hear more.

The man on the chair continued. "This is not the first strike in Minneapolis, and it will not be the last. Organized labor will grow in strength, grow in numbers, grow in influence."

The crowd cheered. Sam spotted Uncle Stanley in one corner. He was starting to applaud.

"The day of management's power is past," the man said. "We are entering a more humane era. In the future, a man who gives an honest day's work will get an honest day's wage. He will use that wage to care for his family, to bring up his children in dignity."

The crowd roared and chanted, "Stand together, stand together."

Annalina clutched Rachel's arm so tightly it hurt. "What mean?" she said. Her blue eyes had lost their glow and become frightened.

Rachel sighed. "If only I could explain it to you. Your father would understand. It's the same reason he brought you here—the reason he wants you to go to a good school."

Annalina searched Rachel's face with questioning eyes.

"We'd better go," Sam said.

Chapter 6

Annalina's Problem

We sit here?" Annalina asked hopefully.

"Very good!" Rachel exclaimed. "Yes, we'll sit here." With a cotton handkerchief, she dusted off a wooden bench. "Now, I know you've never seen a baseball game before, so I'll try to explain the rules."

Annalina peered at the baseball diamond, with the shapeless white sandbags evenly spaced around it.

"One team will try to hit the ball and run all the way around," Rachel explained. "They have to touch all the bases. The other team will try to stop them. Each team gets three outs, and there are nine innings."

Annalina looked at Rachel, completely confused.

"I never realized how complicated it is to explain baseball." Rachel loved baseball games. "You'll get the idea when they start playing a real game."

Sam had talked for weeks about playing the team from Seventh Street. Apparently many of the other players had, too. Quite a few family members had turned out to watch the match. Rachel was surprised to see some of her friends from school. Some of the girls had brothers on Sam's team. Colleen and Janie were supposed to come with Rachel to the game, until. . .

Rachel turned and waved to a row of girls behind her. No one waved back. Instead, Rachel saw several of them put their heads together. She could tell from the way their shoulders were moving that they were laughing. Katherine Jones glanced up at Rachel. But instead of catching Rachel's eyes, she quickly turned her head back to the huddle.

"Baseball," Annalina said very distinctly. She gestured as if she were throwing a ball.

"Very good," Rachel said. She gestured as if she were swinging a bat and said, "Bat."

"Bat. Bat." Annalina echoed.

Behind them, Rachel heard another echo. She twisted around to see her friend Mariah Webster saying, "Baht, baht. Ja, ja, dis ist baht."

Mariah and Katherine burst into giggles. "Ja, ja."

Rachel stared at Mariah. Mariah stared back.

"Mariah Webster, you stop that!" Rachel demanded.

Mariah and Katherine giggled even harder.

Rachel turned to face the field again, her arms crossed on her chest. "Never mind them," she said to Annalina. "We have a ball game to watch."

Both teams were finishing their warm-ups. Soon it would be time to begin playing. Sam did not seem to be concentrating on the warm-up, however. His eyes were raised to the outfield. Simon had not shown up for the game. Rachel knew Sam must be hoping that Simon was just late. But as the minutes dragged by, Rachel realized that Simon might never come to play on the team again. Simon was their best hurler. Without him throwing the ball, the team could be in for a great deal of trouble on the field.

"I'll be right back," Rachel told Annalina. She made her way between the benches to the edge of the field where she could hear the boys' voices.

"He's not coming, is he?" she heard Steve Jones say to Sam.

Sam shook his head. "I guess not."

"Maybe he's sick," Steve said.

"Naw," said another boy, "I saw him on Bridge Square this morning. He's fine."

"Maybe his parents wouldn't let him play today," Sam speculated. "Maybe they had relatives visiting or something."

"Naw, they come to all the games. More likely they wouldn't let him play because they don't want him on this team anymore."

"That's ridiculous," Sam said. "He's played on this team for three years. They never minded before."

"It's different now."

"No, it's not. It's the same team."

"Now Jim's father and Simon's father are on opposite sides of the strike."

"So what?" Sam said. "That doesn't mean they can't play baseball together."

"Yes, it does." It was Joe Rugierio's turn to speak. "My parents didn't want me to come, either. Most of you are management families."

"We're just families!" Sam insisted. "And we're the same team we've always been."

Rachel sighed and made her way back to her seat beside Annalina. The game should have started by now, but most of Sam's team was still standing around talking. And Simon, the star pitcher, wasn't there. Of all games to miss, this was the big one with the Seventh Street team.

"I'm sure the game will start soon, Annalina," Rachel said.

"They're just planning their strategy."

Annalina nodded, but Rachel could tell that she didn't understand. Rachel hunched forward, hoping that the game would start soon.

"Hey!" called the captain of the other team. "Are we going to play ball or what?"

"We're almost ready!" Sam called back. He turned back to his teammates. "So, who is going to hurl today?"

Rachel watched while they chose Larry Lerner to take Simon's place on the pitching mound. They would be short one player in the outfield. They scattered to take their positions.

Rachel leaned on her knees to study the first batter. Her stomach sank as she recognized this batter. Sam's team would not be able to get anything past him.

Larry let the first pitch go. It was so far out of the strike zone that the other team burst into laughter.

"It's okay, Larry, just keep your focus," Sam called out. He clapped his hands in encouragement.

Larry wound up again. The pitch was straight this time, but not very fast. The batter had plenty of time to get a good look at it and swing hard. He whacked the ball right over Sam's head and into left field. Steve Jones scrambled after it. By the time he chased it through the grass and heaved it to the infield, the batter was standing on second base, grinning at Sam.

Larry looked lost. Rachel saw Sam go to the mound to speak to him. She knew he was trying to make Larry feel better.

The second batter came up to the plate. The runner took a generous lead off second base. It was as if he knew what would happen next. Larry only threw one pitch. The batter swung. Rachel groaned. She could tell from the sound that the hit was a home run. The batter whooped his way to first base and then kept going. While the outfielders retrieved the ball, the two players from the

Seventh Street Spades trotted around the diamond victoriously. The score was two to nothing, with no outs in the first inning.

Larry walked the next two batters, with eight very wide pitches in a row. Sam crouched in his position. There was still hope for a double play if the batter hit the ball to Joe. Joe could snap the ball to Sam on second, who would throw it to Jim. Rachel knew it could all happen in one smooth motion they had practiced a hundred times. She held her breath.

But the next ball did not come to shortstop. It went to right field. The runner on second base scored easily, and now there were runners on first base and third base—and still no outs. Rachel sighed. Three to nothing. This was going to be a long game. And they were getting killed in the first inning.

She turned to Annalina. "Sam's team is not doing well yet. Three members of the other team have touched all the bases, including home plate. That means they're ahead three to nothing. But, Sam's team hasn't come to bat yet."

Again, Annalina nodded, but Rachel was sure she didn't understand what Rachel was trying to explain to her. As Rachel searched for words to better explain what had happened, she thought she caught a glimpse of Simon standing at the edge of the park. When Rachel looked back, though, Simon was gone.

Rachel turned her attention back to the game. Larry walked another batter. The bases were full. Rachel watched as Sam put his hand up for a time-out. The team gathered on the pitcher's mound. "Just a minute," Rachel whispered to Annalina. She slipped down to the front of the benches again where she could hear what was going on.

"We have to help Larry out here," Sam was saying.

"You mean we have to get him out of there," Joe said.

"That's exactly right." Sam took the ball from Larry and slapped it into Joe's hand. "You're the pitcher now."

"But who's going to play shortstop? What about the double play ball?"

"Look, you're used to throwing at me and hitting the mark in double plays. You have to do the same thing throwing at the plate. Larry can cover second, and I'll play short."

"It seems to me that we need help in the outfield," Steve said. "That's where all the hits are going."

Sam shook his head. "Not anymore, right, Joe? From now on, the ball doesn't leave the infield."

Joe nodded seriously.

"But the bases are full," Steve reminded everyone, "with no outs. We've got to watch the play at the plate."

"Come on," chided the captain of the Seventh Street Spades. "Are you going to play or not?"

The boys on the Spades howled with laughter. "Maybe they're too weak from their desk jobs," one of them said. "Baseball is too much like physical labor. You actually have to move your muscles to play."

"That must be it!" another one scoffed. "They're in no condition to play against a union team."

Joe snapped his head around to Sam. "Are you going to let them get away with saying that?"

"The only thing to do," Sam said calmly, "is to pull ourselves together and prove we're the great team we know we are."

Rachel felt proud of her brother as she made her way back to her seat. Clearly, though, the team was in a lot of trouble. She saw Sam move the ball from Larry to Joe. But she also knew that no one was as good as Simon. They needed Simon more today than they ever had before.

"Hit ball," Annalina said. "Boy hit ball."

"That's right," Rachel said. "We just didn't want so many boys to hit the ball."

"Hit ball," came the snickering voices behind them.

Rachel turned around and glared at Mariah again. Mariah laughed aloud.

"You're sitting with a scab," Mariah said loudly. "Did you know that, Rachel Borland? You're sitting with a scab. I saw her father driving a streetcar yesterday."

Rachel glanced at Annalina. "Is that true, Annalina? Is your father driving a streetcar?"

"Drive? Ja, Papa drive."

So it was true. Mr. Borg was driving one of those empty streetcars rattling around town.

It was all Rachel could do to keep from edging away from Annalina. But it would do no good, and Rachel did not want to hurt Annalina's feelings. She glanced at Annalina's face. Her new friend did not look as excited as she had a few minutes earlier. *She understands,* Rachel thought. *She understands what Mariah is saying and what those other girls are doing.*

The game had to get better. Rachel could not imagine that it could be any worse.

She watched as Joe got ready to throw his first pitch. He took a long time, and he looked over his shoulder at Sam two times. Finally, he threw the ball. It was a good pitch—right into the strike zone. The batter let it pass. But at least Joe Rugierio had thrown the first strike of the game.

Rachel sighed in relief. If only Joe could do that a few more times. Once again, Joe got ready to hurl the ball. Another strike! The Seventh Street team had stopped laughing.

On Joe's third pitch, the batter swung. It was a weak hit and took a long time to dribble to shortstop. Sam fielded it easily, but it was too late to throw it to home plate. He had to settle for throwing the ball to Jim at first base. One run scored, and the other runners advanced. But at least there was one out. The score was four to nothing, with runners on second and third.

The next batter got a good hit. Both runners scored, and the batter ended up on second base. Six to nothing. Then Joe struck out a batter. It took eight pitches, but he did it. Two out.

Rachel just wanted the inning to be over. They were down by six runs, but it was only the first inning. The Spitfires had some good hitters on their team. If they could just get a chance to bat, they might be able to even the score.

Glancing across the field, Rachel was sure she saw Simon leaning against the fence with his hands stuffed in his pockets.

By the time the inning was over, the Seventh Street team led by eight runs. Now Rachel just wanted the game to be over. She was certain Sam must feel the same.

Chapter 7

A Fight in the Family

"I'm so glad you stopped by, Linda." Mama poured three cups of tea: one for herself, one for Aunt Linda, and one for Rachel. Mama usually did not include Rachel in the grown-up tea talks. Rachel was going to be on her best behavior so Mama would do it again sometime.

"Easter is just a few days away," Mama said. "We need to make plans for dinner after church."

"It's my turn to have the family over," Aunt Linda said. She dropped a sugar cube into her tea.

"Are you sure?" Mama asked. "I would be happy to have Easter dinner here."

"Nonsense," Aunt Linda said. "You've had the last two birthday parties. Let me do it."

Rachel did not care where Easter dinner would be. But she did care what they would eat and hoped it would be something she could help prepare. Rachel sat down at the kitchen table next to her mother and across from Aunt Linda. Sam was at the end of the table. Mama had not offered him any tea. Rachel knew he would not drink it anyway.

"Can we have that currant glaze on the ham?" Sam asked.

"Do you mean the one that Agnes makes?" Mama asked.

"That's the one. I love that glaze!" Sam smacked his lips.

"I'm sure she will be willing to make the glaze—just for you."

"I'll get the ham, of course," Aunt Linda said, "and the sweet potatoes."

"What will we make, Mama?" Rachel asked.

"What would you like to make?"

"Pies," Rachel answered. "I want to learn to make a good pie crust."

"Ugh!" Sam groaned. "Do you have to experiment on the rest of us?"

"Hush, Sam," Mama said. "Your sister is turning into a fine cook. You should be glad to have her around. I know I am."

Rachel beamed.

"What kind of pies?" Aunt Linda asked.

"Peach, apple, strawberry, cherry." Rachel listed all her favorites.

Mama chuckled. "We'll see what kind of fruit preserves we have in the cellar."

"Can we use Pillsbury's Best flour for the crust?" Rachel asked.

"Of course. How could we live in Minneapolis and not buy the best flour in the country?"

"Where's Ernest?" Mama asked. "Maybe he has some suggestions for the menu."

"He's in the living room going over some papers," Aunt Linda said. "If we ask him what he'd like, the list will be far too long to accomplish."

Mama laughed.

A knock on the front door brought the menu planning to a halt.

"Sam, please go see who that is," Mama said.

He darted off to answer the door. Rachel cocked her ear toward the voices that drifted into the kitchen from the hallway.

"It's the Browns!" Rachel jumped to her feet. "I wonder if Freddy is with them."

Mama glanced at Aunt Linda. "I'm sorry, Linda, I had no idea they would be coming by."

"It's all right. You didn't know Ernest and I would drop in, either. We're all here. I'm sure everything will be fine."

Aunt Agnes appeared in the doorway. Her seven-year-old son Frederick was right behind her.

"Is Stanley with you?" Mama asked.

Aunt Agnes looked over her shoulder nervously. "I left him in the living room with Ernest and Sam."

"Have Ernest and Stanley seen each other lately?"

Aunt Agnes and Aunt Linda both shook their heads emphatically.

"Then they'll have a lot to catch up on," Mama said optimistically.

Rachel was not so sure it was a good idea to leave Uncle Stanley and Uncle Ernest in the same room.

"What do you have to eat?" Freddy demanded.

"Frederick!" his mother scolded.

"I'm sorry. Cousin Dorthea, might I have a bit of a snack?"

Mama smiled. "Such a little gentleman. Of course you may have a snack. Rachel, why don't you see what we have?"

Rachel got up and went to the icebox. "How about leftover chicken?" she suggested.

"White meat or dark?" he asked suspiciously.

"It's a leg."

"Good. I'll take that."

"Freddy," his mother coaxed.

"Thank you, Rachel, I would like the chicken leg."

"We were just discussing Easter dinner," Mama said. "Linda has offered to have everyone at her house. And Sam has put in a request for your currant glaze."

Aunt Agnes sighed and glanced toward the door that led to the living room. "A family dinner would be nice. We haven't done that for a long time."

Rachel put the chicken leg on a plate and set it in front of Freddy. Aunt Agnes had a strange look on her face.

"What is it, Agnes?" Mama asked.

Aunt Agnes hesitated. She glanced at Aunt Linda.

"It's all right," Aunt Linda said. "I can see that you're nervous about Stanley and Ernest being together. To be honest, I am, too."

"I hate to create a situation where they might quarrel," Aunt Agnes said.

"But we can't stop bringing the family together because Stanley and Ernest don't agree on unions and management. Stanley and Ernest have known each other a long time. I believe they are genuinely fond of each other."

"I'm sure they are, too," Aunt Agnes said. "And they both love you, Linda. But lately Stanley is so edgy about this union business. I can't predict how he will behave."

"They seem to be doing just fine right now," Mama said. "You left Stanley in the living room with Ernest, and we haven't heard a peep out of them."

"That's not necessarily good," Aunt Agnes said. "It means they're not speaking to each other at all."

Just then, Sam entered the kitchen. He slumped into a chair. "I'd rather listen to you talk about recipes," he said, "than sit in there with the two of them."

"What's going on?"

"Nothing. That's the problem. They're just sitting there staring at each other. Uncle Ernest pretends to be working on his papers, but I don't think he really is. And Uncle Stanley is making me crazy, jiggling his leg all the time."

"Jiggling his leg?" his wife said in alarm. "That means something is on his mind." She turned to Sam. "Didn't he say anything at all?"

Sam shrugged. "He asked me about my baseball team. But I don't think he heard a word I said."

"Is he twitching his moustache?" Freddy asked, his mouth full of chicken.

Sam nodded.

Freddy and Aunt Agnes looked at each other.

"Papa's going to be angry, isn't he?" Freddy said what they were all thinking.

Just at that moment, the voices in the next room exploded. Rachel's heart raced as she jumped out of her chair. Sam was ahead of her, bounding into the living room. Mama and the other women were right behind them. They stood at the edge of the living room. The men seemed not to notice anyone had entered the room.

"You're an intelligent man, Stanley," Uncle Ernest was saying. "I do not understand why you are behaving like such a simpleton on this matter."

The color was rising in Uncle Stanley's face. "You see the world one way, Ernest, and I see it another way."

"You see the world the way you want to see it," his brother-in-law retorted. "You want the unions to be powerful, so you inflame the average person. You fill their heads with ideas that can never come true."

"The unions will make their ideas come true—and life will be better for the average worker."

Uncle Ernest slapped the table next to his chair. Rachel jumped back.

"When will you understand that the people who own these businesses have something to say on these questions?" he shouted.

"You want to create a perfect world for the average worker, but you want the owners to pay for it—men like Charles Pillsbury and Thomas Lowry. They've worked hard to build up their businesses."

"They've made themselves rich by keeping their workers in poverty!" Uncle Stanley stood up and towered over Uncle Ernest.

"Mama?" Rachel whispered. "Shouldn't we do something?"

"I'm not sure what to do," Mama answered.

"Don't do anything," Aunt Linda said. "Stanley and Ernest are grown men. Eventually they have to work this out."

Sam was not convinced. "What if they don't?"

Carrie tumbled down the stairs from her room and ran to her mother. "Mama, why are they yelling?"

Uncle Ernest pushed his papers aside and pulled himself out of his chair. He was not as tall as Stanley, and his cork leg made him unsteady for a moment. But he stared up at his opponent and continued his side of the argument. His jaw was set, and his words were clipped.

"Am I to believe that you think getting no pay at all is better for those workers than the pay Mr. Lowry offers?"

"The wage cut is only part of it. The strikers are standing on a principle, Ernest."

"And their children are going hungry for the sake of that principle," retorted Uncle Ernest. "Does the principle justify the way they terrorize the new drivers or the way they taunt anyone who tries to ride a streetcar?"

"They are doing what they believe they must do."

"And what if they are wrong?"

The front door opened and Papa came in. Instinctively, Rachel flew across the room and snuggled against him.

Papa put down his medical bag next to the door and looked around the living room.

"What in the world is going on in here?" Papa demanded. "I could hear you halfway down the block."

The two men did not answer. They continued to glare at each other.

"Don't bother to answer," Papa said, "because there is no good answer. There is no excuse for the way you two are behaving. I don't care what is going on in the streets, and I don't care what the politicians are saying. You will not bring your arguments into my home."

Uncle Stanley broke his stare and turned to Papa. "I'm sorry, Donald. Of course you are right. We let things get out of hand."

But Papa was not finished. "Stanley, Ernest is married to your sister. I would think that out of respect for Linda, you would make an effort to be civil to him. And you, too, Ernest. Do not forget that Stanley is Linda's brother."

"You are quite right, of course." Uncle Ernest turned around and picked up his papers. "Linda, I believe we should leave now." He moved toward the door without so much as glancing at his brother-in-law.

Rachel watched Aunt Linda's face. Whatever she was thinking or feeling, she did not show anything in her face. Aunt Linda turned to Mama and Aunt Agnes.

"I'll telephone you," she said. "We'll finish making our plans for Easter dinner over the phone."

"Are you sure we should get together?" Aunt Agnes whispered, glancing up at her husband. "It could be very unpleasant."

Linda kept her voice even. "Easter Sunday celebrates the resurrection of our Lord—victory over sin. That includes family arguments. I will not let this union business destroy our family."

"Linda," Uncle Ernest called as he opened the front door.

"Don't forget the glaze, Agnes," Linda said over her shoulder as she headed for the door.

As soon as the couple had gone, Uncle Stanley said, "Agnes, perhaps we ought to be on our way as well. We only meant to stop in for a moment."

"Yes, of course," she replied. "I'll just get Freddy."

In another moment, they were gone as well.

Rachel looked up at Papa. "Will Uncle Stanley and Uncle Ernest be friends again?" she asked. "When the strike is settled, will they stop fighting?"

Papa sighed. "I hope they stop fighting no matter what happens with the strike. They are both bigger and stronger than this petty arguing."

"But they don't think it's petty," Sam said. "They're on opposite sides, and they both think they're right."

"Then we must help them to see the truth," Papa said. "Both Mr. Lowry and the unions have some good arguments. They have to learn to listen to each other—and that includes Ernest and Stanley."

Chapter 8

Lost!

Can we go? Can we go?" Eight-year-old Carrie twirled to make her new pink Easter dress spin.

"What's your hurry?" Sam asked. "Easter dinner is not for two more hours."

"I want to play with Freddy," Carrie said.

"Be careful of your new dress," Mama said. "Perhaps you should take an old frock along to play in later."

"No!" protested Carrie. "I want to keep my new dress on. I've hardly worn it at all—just to church this morning." Carrie twirled around the kitchen. The wide skirt of her new pink cotton dress spun in a perfect circle.

"Everyone looked beautiful in church today," Rachel said. "Cousin Miranda should always wear that color of green. And Molly looked so wonderful sitting next to her beau."

Mama took a pie from the oven and set it on the counter. "Carrie, please stop spinning. You're going to knock something over."

"I'm being careful!" Carrie protested.

Mama warned her with a raised eyebrow, and Carrie screeched to a halt.

Rachel gently touched the top of the pie, testing for doneness.

"Mmm." Sam smacked his lips loudly. "Maybe we should have a snack now."

"Don't you touch my pie!" Rachel said.

"It looks perfect, Rachel," Mama said. "You should be proud of yourself."

Rachel was proud. "Let me wrap it up, Mama." She pulled open a cupboard and reached for a towel. "I want to carry it."

"Mama, is Freddy really going to be there?" Carrie asked.

"Of course he is. The whole family will be there."

"Everyone?"

"Everyone. The Browns, the Stockards, everyone."

"Even Uncle Stanley?"

"Why, of course Stanley will be there."

Carrie stuck her lower lip out thoughtfully. "Freddy's family did not sit in front of us today at church. They always sit in the row in front of us."

Mama started wrapping up a basket of biscuits. "Church was very crowded today because it was Easter. Freddy's family had to find a seat in the back."

"No, they didn't," Carrie said. "They were there early. I saw them. Freddy said his father did not want to sit near Uncle Ernest."

Rachel watched Mama carefully. How would she explain why the two men were angry with each other?

"What else does Freddy say?" Mama asked casually. She laid a linen napkin over the top of the biscuit basket.

"He says that his papa says Uncle Ernest doesn't understand about the streetcar strike. He says Uncle Ernest is being too stubborn for his own good."

Mama nodded. "Yes, that's what Stanley thinks."

"Is he right, Mama?" Carrie seemed to genuinely want to know.

"It's very complicated, Carrie. Why don't we talk about it another time? But I promise you that Freddy will be there today, and you can play with him all afternoon."

"Then let's go!" Carrie cried.

"I believe we are ready," Mama said.

Rachel's stomach was a little nervous. If her two older cousins sat down at the same table, how long would the family dinner last? Aunt Linda had a long table, and there would be fourteen people there—fifteen if Molly brought her new beau. Uncle Stanley and Uncle Ernest would not even have to talk to each other. But would they be able to control themselves? Would they want to?

Mama and Carrie were ready to go.

"Shouldn't we wait for Papa?" Rachel asked.

Mama shook her head. "He had to see a patient at the hospital. I told him just to meet us at the Stockards'."

"I suppose it would be silly for him to come all the way back here first." Rachel buttoned her new sapphire cloak under her neck.

"Especially with no streetcars running," Sam added.

They gathered their things and started out. Rachel carried the cherry pie, while Mama carried the apple pie and corn pudding. Carrie had the biscuits. Sam lugged a sack of potatoes destined to be peeled, boiled, and mashed at the Stockards' house.

As they walked, Carrie chattered about her new dress and the new wooden top she carried in her pocket to show Freddy. Rachel concentrated on keeping the cherry pie level. Even through the thick towel she had wrapped around the pie plate, she could feel the warmth and smell the sweet cherry filling. Her stomach growled.

Sam scanned the neighborhood. "A lot of people are out walking today," he observed. "Most people stay home on Sunday afternoons."

Rachel could see that Sam was right. A lot of people were in the streets. "Maybe they are out for the same reason we are," she said.

"Waiting for their Easter dinner."

Sam squeezed his eyebrows together. "I don't think so. They're not carrying food. And most of them are not really walking. They're just standing around."

Once again, Sam was right. Rachel was starting to feel nervous.

"Mama?" she said quietly.

"I'm sure everything is fine," Mama said. "People are a bit restless with the strike, that's all."

Rachel was not convinced. She looked at Sam. He seemed to be watching the street carefully.

"We're walking too slow," Carrie announced, paying no attention to the conversation. She proceeded to skip.

"Carrie," Mama warned. "Don't get too far ahead of me."

"Here comes a streetcar," Carrie said, pointing.

The car was empty, of course. Rachel could see straight through it. The car was headed toward downtown.

"Isn't that Annalina's father?" Sam asked.

"Where?" Rachel's eyes darted through the crowd.

"In the streetcar," Sam said. "I think he was driving."

The car stopped at the next corner, and an elderly woman boarded. Immediately two young men swung aboard. Even from down the block, Rachel could hear them heckling the driver.

"Scab!"

"Management sympathizer!"

The car rumbled down the street. Rachel could see the two young men hovering over the driver. At the next stop, the elderly passenger got off.

"She's an old lady," Sam said, disgusted. "Why don't they leave her alone and let her ride?"

"Do you really think that was Annalina's father?" Rachel asked.

"I didn't get a good look," Sam said, "and I've only seen her father once. But she told you he had started driving streetcars."

"Do you think we could catch up with it?"

"Now, Rachel," Mama said, "I understand your concern about your friend's father. But you cannot put yourself in danger. He made his own choice to drive a streetcar."

"I just want to know if it was him."

The car had stopped again, three blocks up. Rachel peered down the street, trying to focus on the driver's profile.

"Carrie!" Mama called. "Wait for me."

Rachel did not turn around at her mother's voice. Why couldn't Carrie just be patient and walk with the rest of the family?

Try as she might, Rachel could not see the driver clearly. He was too far away.

"I can't see him," she said, disappointed. No one answered her.

Now she whirled around. Where was Mama? And Carrie and Sam?

In the last few minutes, the street had flooded with dozens of people. Where had they all come from? And what were they doing? They seemed to move like the current of the Mississippi River toward downtown Minneapolis. Caught up in the pressure of the growing crowd, Rachel stumbled along for a few feet, clutching her still-warm pie. She examined the crowd for her mother's bright blue shawl or Carrie's new pink dress. They were nowhere to be seen.

"Sam!" she cried aloud. "Mama!" Rachel could feel tears of panic springing to her eyes.

A couple people passing by turned to glance at her. But there was no flicker of recognition in their eyes. They were strangers.

Stay calm, Rachel told herself. *They can't have gone far. You only turned your head for a moment.*

Against her will, Rachel was moving down the street with the flow of the crowd. Cradling her pie, she pressed her way out of the mainstream. Mama always told her that if she got lost, she should stay where she was and someone would find her. She was lost now. Rachel determined to get out of the crowd and stay put.

Rachel pressed herself up against a fence. She recognized the well-tended home before her. It was Mariah Webster's house. The picket at the top of the fence was poking into Rachel's back. But she hardly felt it. She poured all her energy into looking for her family in the throbbing mob.

The murmurs of the crowd had swelled to a roar. Mumblings had become shouts. Rachel could hear what the people were saying.

"We'll teach them a lesson they won't forget!"

"We'll show that Thomas Lowry that he needs us more than he thinks he does."

"We have to get rid of those scabs."

Get rid of the scabs? What do they mean? Rachel wondered.

Three men charged down the middle of the street, shoulder to shoulder, marching in step.

Over the noise of the crowd, Rachel cried out, "Mama! Sam!"

"Rachel!"

Relief swept over Rachel at the sound of her brother's voice.

"I'm here, Sam, here!"

She still could not see him.

"I'm coming!"

And then he was there.

"What happened?" Rachel asked.

Sam shook his head. "I'm not sure. Mama chased after Carrie, and when we turned around, you were gone."

"But I didn't go anywhere!"

"Never mind. I found you."

"But where are Mama and Carrie?"

The crowd around them thickened by the moment. Dozens had

turned into hundreds, perhaps even thousands.

"I've never seen so many people," Sam said, "except at the ballpark or a parade."

"Sam, where are Mama and Carrie?" Rachel asked again, more urgently this time.

Sam turned to look at his sister and sighed. "I don't know."

"Are they waiting for you somewhere?"

"I don't know. Mama was worried about you, and I said I would find you. And now—"

"And now it will be impossible to find them."

"Let's not give up yet." Rachel could see the concentration in her brother's dark eyes. "We haven't even started looking yet."

Rachel swallowed a sob. "I never did like crowds."

Still carrying the sack of potatoes, Sam offered his elbow. "Here, hang on to me. Whatever you do, don't let go."

"Believe me, I won't!"

"Let's go back to the corner where you saw the streetcar," Sam suggested. "That's the last place we were all together."

Rachel thought that was a good idea. But it was harder than it sounded. Everyone else was swarming down the street in the other direction. With one hand, she held her prized pie. With the other hand, she squeezed Sam's elbow. Together, they forged their way against the ever-growing stream.

Men of all ages filled the street, and women and children, too. The men marched with determination toward a goal Rachel could not see. The children whooped and hollered. Rachel heard the edge of her new cloak rip when someone pulled on it. She jerked herself away and held on to Sam's arm even more tightly.

"Sam, what are all these people doing?"

"What did you say?" Sam shouted.

"I said, what are all these people doing?"

Sam shook his head in confusion.

"Do you think Mama and Carrie are all right?" Rachel asked anxiously.

They had arrived at the corner where they had seen the streetcar, but there was hardly room to stand there. Hundreds of people flooded the intersection. But Rachel could see no sign of a bright blue shawl or a new pink dress.

"Sam, what if we don't find them?" Rachel said. "Mama always says to stay put when you get lost."

"We can't stay here," Sam said. "Even Mama would say that this is dangerous."

Rachel's heart raced. Where was Mama?

"We have to get out of the way of this mob," Sam said.

"But what about Mama and Carrie?" Rachel pleaded.

Sam hesitated only a moment before answering. "Mama will do whatever she has to do to keep Carrie safe. And she would want us to keep ourselves safe."

Rachel nodded. Sam was right. "But where will we go?"

Chapter 9

The Easter Riot

"Come on," Sam said. "This way."

"Where are we going?" Rachel asked.

Sam must not have heard her. He did not answer. Rachel held on to his arm a little tighter. She thought how silly they must look carrying a sack of potatoes and a cherry pie through the mob.

Rachel realized Sam was leading her straight into the heart of the crowd. "What are you doing?" She tugged on his elbow.

Sam shouted over his shoulder, "Trust me!"

Rachel got bumped from the back. The cherry pie started to slide. She jerked her arm from Sam's elbow and gripped the pie more securely with both hands.

Sam turned around to see what had happened. "I told you not to let go of me."

"I'm sorry. The pie started to fall."

"Forget about the pie." Whatever calm Sam had managed to hang on to was disappearing. His dark eyes darted back and forth, alert to every movement of the crowd.

Rachel took Sam's elbow again, but she kept her grip on the pie. They were carried along by the crowd until they came to the next corner. Sam steered them down a side street where they rested.

Rachel swallowed the lump in her throat.

Sam was breathing heavily. "We have to figure out what we're going to do."

Rachel watched the crowd around them and wished she were somewhere else, anywhere else. She kept looking for Mama and Carrie. Everything looked brown and gray. Nothing was blue or pink.

"We should keep going to the Stockards'," Rachel suggested. "Everyone will expect us there."

Sam shook his head. "It's too far—at least another mile."

"But Mama will go there."

"I'm not sure what Mama will do. If she's trapped in the crowd like we are, she won't be able to get to the Stockards' either."

"We could go home. It's closer."

"We'd have to go against the crowd," Sam said.

That seemed like an impossible task.

"We'll take the back streets," Rachel said. But even the back streets were filling up.

"I know!" Sam said suddenly. "The hospital. It's only a few blocks from here."

"Yes, and Papa might still be there."

"Even if he's not, we could use a telephone."

"All right, let's do it."

With new determination, they turned to join the still-swelling crowd.

"Sam, how many people do you think are here?"

"Must be thousands," Sam answered. "They just keep coming. The crowd goes on for blocks and blocks."

They walked a block toward the hospital. Rachel felt as though they were going only a few inches at a time. It was hard to keep the pie level. Cherry filling had started to seep through the towel wrapped around the pie tin. It stuck to Rachel's hand and dampened her sapphire cloak, turning it a deep purple that reminded her of blood. She shivered.

They came to a standstill, pressed in on every side.

"What's happening, Sam?" Rachel shouted. She could hardly breathe. "I can't see."

A tall man next to her leaned toward Rachel. "I'll tell you what's happening. We're going to teach that Thomas Lowry a lesson once and for all. You can be proud to be here today. This will be a day Minneapolis will not soon forget."

Rachel did not answer the man. Without looking up at him, she moved even closer to Sam.

Sam was craning his neck, trying to see through the crowd.

"I think there's a streetcar up there," he said. "I saw it a minute ago, but I can't see it anymore."

Rachel was too short to see anything. A jolt from behind pushed her into the woman in front of her. The pie oozed some more.

"Wait!" Sam cried. "The streetcar is still there. It's just covered with people."

"People are riding the streetcar?"

"No, they're climbing all over it."

"Climbing?"

"Yes, standing on top of it, hanging out the windows."

Rachel's stomach was flipping. "Sam, I'm scared."

Then she remembered the streetcar they had seen earlier. "Sam! Is it the same streetcar we saw earlier?"

"Probably. There haven't been any others going by."

"Annalina's father! What if that was Annalina's father driving the streetcar?"

Sam was silent.

"Sam, we have to find out!"

"I never said I was sure it was him. It just looked like him. It could have been another Swedish immigrant."

"Or it could have been Mr. Borg."

"We don't know that for sure."

"You're the one who thought it was him!"

"I was probably wrong," Sam insisted. He pushed Rachel in front of him and pointed through an opening in the crowd. "Look, see for yourself what is happening."

The crowd had parted just enough for Rachel to spot the streetcar. Men, women, and children of all ages were scrambling up the sides of the car and hoisting themselves to the top. Those on top offered their hands to pull more people to the top of the car. Rachel could not imagine how there was room for one more person up there. Still they climbed.

"I don't see any horses to pull the car," Rachel observed.

Sam stood on his tiptoes and craned his neck. "I don't either. They must have unhitched them."

A man with a bullhorn leaned out the side of the car.

"Thomas Lowry, if you are out there," he shouted, "take note. You cannot ignore us. You cannot simply hire more drivers. What will happen when you have no more streetcars?"

"What does he mean, Sam?" Rachel asked.

"Rachel, I think we have to get out of here. Now!" Sam pulled Rachel forcefully along. She stumbled as she tried to keep her balance. "We have to get to the hospital."

But to get to the hospital, they had to pass the streetcar. Sam wound his way steadily through the crowd.

"People are getting out now," Rachel said as they got closer to the streetcar.

"Don't pay any attention," Sam said. "Concentrate on the hospital."

"But why are they getting out? Are they finished?"

"How would I know?" Sam snapped. "I just want to get out of here."

"But, Sam—"

Sam spun around. His mouth opened to speak, but then he saw what Rachel was looking at. A row of men had lined themselves up along one side of the streetcar. Bracing their feet solidly, they leaned into the car. It rocked from side to side. Whooping, more men joined the effort. Dozens were pushing on the side of the streetcar. The car rocked some more. They pushed again. Now the car was tipping.

Sam jerked Rachel back. The car tumbled over on one side. With a mighty groan, the joints on one end gave way, and the top of the car splintered off. A wheel broke loose and skidded through the crowd. Once again, the mob scrambled to stand on top of the wreckage. In only a few seconds, it was impossible to see what they were standing on. A mountain of people had arisen in the middle of Minneapolis. The horses had been unhitched. Now they thundered down the street, whinnying and thrashing their hooves. The crowd parted to let them pass. No one tried to catch the frightened animals.

"You are destroying private property!" The shout came from the middle of the street. Four men, their fists raised in the air, charged toward the buried streetcar.

The man with the bullhorn laughed. "If you are Mr. Lowry's men, you are too late."

"Have you no respect for something that doesn't belong to you?"

"Just like Mr. Lowry respects us, eh? He thinks he owns us. Well, he doesn't. He won't even come to the arbitration table. When will he show us the respect we deserve?"

Lowry's men hurled themselves toward the man with the

bullhorn. He toppled over backward. Rachel could hear fists smacking flesh. Blood spattered faces and clothing. The mob on the top of the streetcar moved like an avalanche down to the street. It was too late for words. Fists were swinging in every direction.

"Rachel, we have to get out of here now!" Sam shouted. He took a firm hold of her arm and pulled her along.

Suddenly a man in a brown coat fell backward right into Sam. Sam lost his balance—and his grip on Rachel—and was swallowed up into the mob. His sack of potatoes hit the ground and split open. Seizing the opportunity, some teenagers scrambled to pick up the potatoes and began heaving them into the crowd.

Still clutching her crumbling pie, Rachel searched for Sam. Everything was happening so fast! The crowd swirled around her. Rachel was getting dizzy. She was afraid she would fall down, too.

"Sam!"

"Rachel!" came the muffled response.

"Sam, where are you?"

Then she spotted his boots. Sam was sprawled across the middle of the street. In their rush to join the fracas, people were stepping on him or stepping over him. No one stopped to help him. Rachel forced her way into the flow of traffic and jerked to a stop in front of Sam. A woman hurtling past knocked the pie out of Rachel's arms. The pie landed upside down. Cherries oozed through the towel. Then someone stepped on the pie tin, smashing it beyond repair.

"My pie!" Rachel moaned.

Sam was on his feet. "Forget the pie."

"Sam, are you all right?" Rachel examined her brother. She saw footmarks on his jacket, and his face was bruised. Blood trickled from a cut on his left cheek.

"I don't think it's anything serious," Sam said, "but I'm glad we're headed to the hospital."

"I wish Mama was here," Rachel moaned.

"I just hope Mama and Carrie are all right."

With their elbows linked, they started off again. Inch by inch, they edged their way to the outskirts of the crowd. Finally the hospital was in sight. But Rachel knew it would take them a long time to go even a few blocks.

Whoever had been driving the streetcar had long ago abandoned it. Rachel found herself scanning the faces in the crowd, looking to see if Mr. Borg was there.

Tripping and jostling their way through the crowd, Sam and Rachel made slow but steady progress. When they reached the hospital door, Sam pushed it open and they tumbled in.

Chapter 10

At the Hospital

Inside the main hospital door, Sam and Rachel stopped for a moment to catch their breath. They dropped into a pair of empty wooden chairs away from the door.

"Are you all right, Sam?" Rachel asked. "You look pale."

Sam raised one hand to the side of his head. "I have an awful headache. I think I got kicked."

"I couldn't even see what happened to you," Rachel said.

"I got knocked over, that's all. I should have been paying better attention to what was happening."

"Don't be silly," Rachel said. "You couldn't help what happened."

Sam leaned his head back against the wall behind him and closed his eyes.

"Maybe you need a doctor," Rachel said. "The cut on your cheek is still bleeding." She reached into the pocket of her pastel plaid skirt for a handkerchief and dabbed at the cut.

"I'll be all right," Sam responded, wincing a little bit. "But we should try to find out if Papa is still here."

Rachel surveyed the lobby. It was crowded. Sam and Rachel were not the only ones who had come to the hospital to escape the chaos of the streets. They had gotten the last two empty chairs.

"You stay here," Rachel said, "and I'll try to find out if Papa is still here."

Across the congested room was a large wooden desk painted green, and behind the desk was a flustered nurse. Nearly two dozen people swarmed around her trying to ask their questions. Some of them were scraped and bruised and probably wanted a doctor. Others were just asking a lot of questions. The nurse kept looking down the hall as if she wanted to escape.

Rachel went and stood at the desk. She knew that the nurse at that desk would have a big black book that would show whether her father had signed out and left the hospital. Ordinarily it was a simple thing to approach the desk and ask about Papa. But Rachel could not get anywhere near the desk that day. The nurse would not pay attention to a small ten-year-old when twenty adults were pressing in on her. Rachel tried to figure out if there was a line so she could get in it. Three times she was pushed away by someone much bigger than she.

Finally she turned back to Sam. He had not moved the whole time she was gone.

"The nurse is too busy," Rachel reported. "I think I'll go up to the ward on the third floor. That's where Papa usually sees his patients. You can stay here."

"No," Sam said, "we should stay together."

Inwardly, Rachel was relieved Sam wanted to stay with her.

Sam pulled himself to his feet, and they started down the hall to find the dark stairs that would take them to the third floor. At the top of the stairs they turned left and continued on to the ward. Sam cautiously pushed open the door to the large room. Sixteen beds were arranged in neat rows down both sides of the ward. Several nurses made their way swiftly from one bed to the next to make sure the patients were comfortable.

"I don't see Papa."

"I don't, either," Sam said. "Where else should we look?"

"We can check the other wards," Rachel suggested.

"You'll do no such thing!" barked a voice behind them.

Sam and Rachel spun around to find the ward's head nurse scowling down at them. "This is a hospital, not a playground," she said.

"We're looking for Dr. Borland," Sam said. "He's our father."

"I'm aware of that, but children do not belong in a hospital ward."

"We have to find him," Rachel said.

"There!" The nurse pointed to a small, dark room across the hall. "You may wait there. When I see Dr. Borland, I will tell him where to find you."

"My brother is hurt," Rachel said. "He needs to see a doctor."

The nurse narrowed her eyes and studied Sam's face. In the same harsh tone, she said, "That's a nasty cut. I'll send in a cold pack. But you must wait in there!" She pointed emphatically to the small room. Sam and Rachel shuffled across the hall reluctantly.

The room was furnished with four wooden chairs and a small table. A round window high in the wall provided the only light.

"Do you think she will really tell Papa we're here?"

"I hope so," Sam answered. "And I hope she sends that cold pack."

"Does your head hurt very much?" Rachel asked softly.

Sam nodded.

They waited in that room for what seemed like hours. Sam laid his head down on the table. Rachel went to the doorway and looked out. The third floor seemed much busier than it usually was. Nurses moved down the hall with quick, purposeful steps. Their crisp uniforms swished and rustled with every step. Doctors in white jackets hung their stethoscopes around their necks and looked worried.

Suddenly Rachel jumped out into the hall.

"Papa!"

"Rachel! What are you doing here?"

Rachel took her father's hand and pulled him into the small room.

"Sam! Are you all right?" Papa put his hand on Sam's flushed cheek.

"He got kicked in the head," Rachel explained.

Then she told Papa the whole story of how the family had started out for the Stockards' for Easter dinner and Mama and Carrie had disappeared.

Papa made Sam sit up so he could look in his eyes. "I don't see any sign of serious injury."

"I just have a headache," Sam said. "I'll be all right. But what about Mama and Carrie?"

"There's a telephone down at the end of the hall," Papa said. "We'll go call the Stockards and see if Mama and Carrie made it over there."

But Mama and Carrie were not at the Stockards'. No one but the Stockard family was there. Aunt Linda had heard about the tipped-over streetcar and the riot. In fact, she told Papa that two streetcars had been tipped over, not just one. But she had not heard from Mama.

"That means they are still out there somewhere," Rachel said.

"They could have gone in another building," Sam said.

Papa looked worried—very worried. "I want to look for them."

"But Papa, the riot!" Rachel protested.

"I'll settle the two of you in a safe, quiet place. Sam, maybe we can find you a bed to rest on until your head stops hurting. Then I'm going to go out to look for your mother and sister."

"Dr. Borland, come quick!" It was the head nurse. "They need you down on the first floor."

"What happened?"

"Several more men have just come in, and they are hurt quite badly."

Papa sighed. "All right, I'll be right there."

"Papa, don't leave us here," Rachel pleaded.

"Come with me," Papa responded, "but stay out of the way. I don't want you to get hurt."

Papa thundered down the stairs. Rachel and Sam did their best to keep up with him. Sam groaned with every step. The lobby was even more crowded than it had been earlier. Papa made his way to a corner of the room and ducked through a door into a room behind the main lobby.

Rachel gasped when she saw the first patient. "It's the man with the bullhorn!" she said to Sam.

"I don't think he thought anyone could hurt him," Sam said.

The man's left arm did not look right. The skin was scraped off one side of his face, and his right eye was bruised and swollen.

"What do you think happened to him?" Rachel asked.

"It was probably those management men," Sam answered. "Remember? The three men who ran up right after the streetcar fell over?"

Rachel nodded. "But there were only three of them—three against the whole crowd."

"They must have had other friends with them. Besides, with a baseball bat or a heavy stick, all it would take is a couple of swings."

Careful to stay out of the way, they watched their father at work. He set the broken arm and gave the nurses instructions about the other injuries.

"When can I get out of here, Doc?" the man asked.

"I'd like you to stay a couple days," Papa told the man.

"I can't do that. I have no money to pay you. I'm a streetcar driver."

"We'll worry about that later," Papa said. "I think you have two broken ribs. You must be taken care of." He turned to the nurse. "Make sure he gets a bed in one of the wards."

"Here comes the next one," the nurse responded, as an orderly wheeled in another patient.

"I know this man," Papa said.

Rachel's heart leaped. Mr. Borg? She lurched forward for a better look. No, it was not Mr. Borg.

"I've treated him before," Papa continued. "He's one of Thomas Lowry's managers."

"Then he's a dog!" growled the first patient.

"Orderly," Papa said, nodding his head at his first patient. "I think you can take him upstairs now."

"Dog, he's a dog!" shouted the man as the orderly wheeled him away.

Papa turned his attention to his new patient, who was unconscious. With a thumb, Papa pushed one of the man's eyelids open. "I don't like the way his pupils look," he told the nurse.

The nurse from the front desk stuck her head in the room.

"Doctor, there are two more coming in now."

"Aren't there any other doctors around?" Papa asked.

"Dr. James is upstairs with a critical patient. Dr. Michaels is delivering a baby."

"Is there no one else?"

"It's Easter Sunday, Doctor," the nurse responded. "Most of the doctors did their rounds hours ago and went home to Easter dinner."

"We need help," Papa insisted. "Get on the telephone and call Dr. Lee and Dr. Sheridan. Now!"

"Yes, Doctor."

The man on the gurney in front of Papa began gasping for air. Papa held the man's mouth open and pushed down on his tongue with a flat wooden stick.

"His airway is blocked! We'll have to intubate!"

Nurse Howard flew into action and produced a narrow tube.

"Hold his mouth open," Papa ordered as he started forcing the tube down the man's mouth. The patient thrashed. Two more nurses came in to help hold him down. In another moment, Papa had the tube down the man's throat, and he was breathing steadily.

Rachel could hardly bear to watch. She scrunched up against the wall as tightly as she could. Sam had found a spot in the corner where he could sit down and lean his head against the wall.

Papa stepped back from his patient just as the orderlies brought in two more men.

"What do we have?" Papa asked.

The nurses gave the best report they could on the injuries they had observed. Blood and broken bones filled the small room.

Sam and Rachel pressed themselves up against the wall, hardly able to take in what they were seeing.

"Doctor, perhaps your children would be more comfortable somewhere else," Nurse Howard suggested.

"No, they're fine," Papa said without looking up.

"It's okay, Papa," Rachel said. "We can go wait in the lobby."

Papa glanced up for just a second. "Don't go anywhere else, do you understand? And if any fighting breaks out, you come right back in here."

"Yes, Papa."

"Miss Howard, please make sure that my son has a place to sit down."

"Yes, Doctor."

Nurse Howard ushered Sam and Rachel back out to the main lobby.

When they were alone in the crowded lobby, Sam said quietly, "They are all the same."

Rachel turned to him, puzzled.

"When they are hurt," Sam said, "they are all the same. They need a doctor. They all have the same broken bones and bloody faces. And Papa helps them all. He doesn't care if they are union or management."

Rachel scanned the lobby. Sam was right. Everyone was the same. She could not tell just by looking whether the woman in the green coat was waiting for a union husband or a management husband. She could not tell if the children playing in the corner belonged to a union father or a management father.

She found herself looking for Mr. Borg once again and praying that he was safe.

Chapter 11

Where's Mama?

In the lobby, Rachel picked up a newspaper someone had abandoned. The headlines for Easter Sunday 1889 cried out: "Strike Continues. Lowry Says No Negotiations." "Restless Drivers Threaten Action." "Union Demands Heighten."

Rachel scanned the beginning of one article: "Thomas Lowry, owner of the Minneapolis Streetcar Company, insists that he will not submit to arbitration to settle the streetcar strike. 'In the future,' said Lowry, 'the Minneapolis Street Railway will run its own business instead of having it run by a union.' Although the business has suffered greatly during the strike, Lowry continues to hire replacement drivers. He has brought in a hundred men from Kansas City to drive the routes abandoned by union drivers. If Lowry continues to refuse arbitration, drivers are threatening further action to force his cooperation."

Rachel tossed the paper aside. The news was already old. The drivers were no longer threatening action. They had taken action that morning. Their action had brought Rachel and Sam to the hospital lobby instead of to the Stockards' house for a scrumptious Easter dinner. Rachel's stomach was starting to growl. She thought about the cherry pie, and her eyes filled with tears.

Where had Sam gone? Rachel glanced around the lobby, searching for her brother. They had promised Papa not to wander off. Her eyes darted from person to person until at last she found him.

Sam had shuffled up to the big green desk. The lobby was just as full as it had been before, but the crowd seemed more organized. A different nurse was on duty. She seemed less flustered and more in control. "The line forms to the left," the nurse called out every few minutes. She answered questions and passed out forms for people to fill out. Every once in a while, someone wanted to ask a question without waiting in line. But the nurse firmly said, "The line forms to the left."

Papa had been out to the lobby to check on Sam and Rachel two times in the last two hours. No new emergencies had come in for more than an hour, and Dr. Lee and Dr. Sheridan had finally showed up to help Papa. Rachel thought that things ought to be settling down. She wondered where Papa was now. She supposed he was at the bedside of the patient he had intubated.

She knew Papa had read a lot of articles about intubation before he ever tried it. But finally he was convinced that the only way to help some patients breathe was to intubate—to put a long tube down their throats so they could get air to their lungs. Then Papa would make sure the patient was all right and breathing on his own before he would relax.

Papa was a good doctor. Rachel was sure of that. But she wanted to know how much longer the good doctor would have to stay at the hospital.

Rachel eyed the long line ahead of Sam at the green reception desk. She did not want to stand in that line with him just to ask if the nurse knew what her father was doing. How could that nurse know? She had been in the lobby the whole time. Rachel got to her feet and moved toward the door that led to the examination room behind the lobby. Maybe Papa was still there.

As she got closer to the room, Rachel cocked her ear. She did not hear any noises coming from the room. *Probably all the patients have been moved to the wards,* she thought. But she wanted to check the room just to be sure Papa was not there. With her hand on the doorknob, she turned to look around. She did not see Nurse Howard anywhere. Still with her back to the door, she turned the knob and leaned back on the door and pushed it open.

The clatter that followed told Rachel that the room had not been empty. When she got the door open, she saw a dismayed Nurse Howard scrambling to pick up a tray. Medical instruments had scattered all over the floor.

The nurse scowled at Rachel. "Look what you did!"

"I'm sorry," Rachel exclaimed. "I'll help you pick everything up." She stooped to the floor and retrieved a pair of steel tongs.

"Don't touch anything," Miss Howard said. "Some of these are delicate instruments. Now they'll have to be cleaned all over again."

"I–I'm sorry," Rachel muttered.

"Perhaps you haven't noticed that we are rather busy around here today."

"Of—of course," Rachel stammered. "I was just looking for my father."

"As you can see, he's not here. Now scat."

Rachel scurried out of the room and back to the lobby. Sam had taken a seat again, and Rachel sank into the chair beside him, her heart pounding.

Sam chuckled. "Something tells me you've been doing something you shouldn't have been doing."

Rachel was not amused. "I was just looking for Papa."

"He said to wait here. The nurse said he's busy setting a broken leg."

"He told us to wait a long time ago. Why isn't he finished?"

"A lot of people were hurt in the riot," Sam said. "Papa is a doctor. He has to take care of them."

"But what about Mama and Carrie?" Rachel asked. "Papa was going to look for them."

"They haven't shown up here," Sam said. "That probably means they are all right."

"How can you be so sure?"

"I'm not sure. But it makes sense."

"I'm getting hungry," Rachel said. "We were supposed to eat hours ago. I didn't eat any breakfast because I wanted to be sure I had room for pie."

"I'm sorry about your pie," Sam said softly.

"Right now I would settle for burned toast."

"Me, too."

Rachel stood up again.

"Sit down, Rachel," Sam said. "Just relax. There's nothing you can do but wait."

"I can't. I'm tired of sitting. I'm tired of this room. I'm tired of this day!"

"It has been a long day," Sam agreed.

Rachel started pacing. The crowd in the lobby was thinning out. People with minor injuries were being released, and their families took them home. Rachel stood and looked out the window on the side of the building. *The street looks better,* she thought. Not so many people were roaming around. As the afternoon gave way to evening, people took shelter in their homes.

Suddenly Rachel lurched forward. She had been pushed from behind. Remembering the feeling of being pushed in the middle of the mob earlier in the day, she panicked for a second. Then she spun around. As she did, Carrie grabbed her around the waist.

"Carrie! You're all right!" Rachel exclaimed. "Where's Mama?"

"Right here," came Mama's voice.

Rachel threw herself into her mother's embrace. Sam joined the reunion.

"I'll go find Papa," he offered. Off he went, before Rachel could tell him not to bother looking in the examination room behind the lobby.

In almost no time, Sam was back with Papa. Rachel smiled, relieved, as her parents embraced, and then Papa gave Carrie a messy kiss on the forehead.

"Over here," Papa said, and he herded his family to an empty corner of the lobby. "I'm so glad you're all right. But where have you been?"

"I didn't know what to think when I lost track of Sam and Rachel," Mama said. "I had to trust that the Lord would take care of them. It was all I could do to keep track of Carrie in that mob."

"Papa, there were millions and millions of people," Carrie said.

Mama smiled. "Thousands at least. I've never seen such a mob, even on a parade day."

"So where did you go?" Rachel wanted to know.

"We stayed to the edge of the crowd as much as we could," Mama answered. "I tried to look for you at the next corner from where I lost you. But there were too many people! And they were doing crazy things!"

"We went shopping," Carrie blurted out.

"Shopping?" Rachel was confused.

"Not exactly," Mama said, "but we saw Mr. Johanssen in the crowd, and he opened up his shop for us. He kept going on to find any women and children who needed help."

"That's a relief," Papa said. "Remind me never to charge him for medical care again!"

"We saw women and children in the street," Sam said. "But some of them were helping with the riot."

"I know," Mama said sadly. "Some of the children didn't understand what was going on. They either got scared, or they got excited and joined in."

"Mama," Rachel said, "I never found Mr. Borg. If all the trouble is over, maybe I could go see if he's all right."

"Rachel, you are sweet and thoughtful to want to do that," Mama said, "but we can't be sure the streets are safe yet."

"Sam could go with me."

Mama shook her head. "We'll have to find out about Mr. Borg another way."

"This is the nearest hospital," Sam said. "If he didn't come here, he's probably not hurt."

"He wouldn't come here," Rachel said, "because he doesn't have any money to pay doctors."

"If he were seriously hurt," Papa said, "someone would have brought him here anyway."

"I'm hungry," Carrie complained. "When are we going to have Easter dinner?"

Mama and Papa looked at each other.

"It looks like we'll have to skip Easter dinner with the family this year," Mama said. "But we can have a simple meal with our own family."

"What will we eat?"

"Let's see what we have."

"I dropped the cherry pie," Rachel said sadly. "I hung on to it as long as I could."

"I'm sure you did," Mama said.

"And they were throwing the potatoes in the crowd," Sam said.

"That's all right," Mama answered. "The potatoes were not cooked anyway."

"Then what do we have?" Rachel asked.

"I have biscuits!" Carrie proclaimed. "They're a little squashed, but I still have them."

"And I've got corn pudding," Mama said, "and apple pie. I'm sorry it's not the pie you made, Rachel, but it is a pie."

"Can we eat now?" Carrie said. "I'm too hungry to wait until we get home."

Mama and Papa looked at each other again. It was well past suppertime. No one had eaten since before church that morning.

"Certainly," Papa said. "I'm sure I can find some of the trays they use to feed the patients."

While Papa went to find the trays, Mama pulled a little table out of the corner of the room and set the food on it. The bread really was squashed. Rachel figured Carrie must have been holding it tightly when she was frightened. Rachel did not blame her little sister for squashing the bread.

When Papa returned, they gathered around the little table on their knees.

"It's not much of an Easter dinner," Papa said, "but we have a lot to give thanks for."

They held hands as Papa prayed. "Lord, we are grateful that You have protected our family during the danger today. Thank You for bringing us safely back together. And on this Easter Sunday, we give thanks for the power of the resurrection, when Jesus Christ was raised from the dead so that we could have peace with God. May You grant peace to our city tonight. Amen."

Mama started tearing the bread into chunks. Papa had brought forks for the corn pudding and apple pie.

"Dr. Borland," called the nurse from the desk, "they need you in the back again."

Papa sighed. "Go ahead and eat. I'll be back as soon as I can."

Rachel watched reluctantly as Papa disappeared once again.

Chapter 12

A Birthday and a Baseball Plan

A few days after the riot, Rachel and her mother were working about the house. Sam had left for baseball practice, and Carrie was with friends. As usual, Papa was not expected home from work until late.

"Rachel, don't you have a birthday coming up?" Mama said, brushing a stray strand of hair out of her eyes. "How would you like to celebrate this year?"

Rachel put the towel that she was folding onto the pile of freshly laundered linens. "You know, I think I would like to have just a small party with a few friends."

Rachel had been giving her birthday some thought. She was finding it harder and harder to be in the middle of the conflict between Colleen and Janie. They were her oldest friends. She could barely remember a time when they hadn't played together. Now she was torn between the two—and she didn't like the feeling.

And then there was Annalina. Rachel enjoyed being with her and teaching her English. If only she could bring Annalina and Colleen and Janie together! Rachel felt frustrated that the other girls in her class still did not want to be friends with Annalina. If they just got to know her, Rachel was sure they would like her as much as she did. But how could she help the other girls understand Annalina?

Maybe she could start with Colleen and Janie.

"Who would you like to invite?" Mama seemed relieved that Rachel wasn't asking for a big party.

"Just Annalina—and Colleen and Janie. I'll invite them tomorrow. Could we have a cake and some ice cream?"

Mama smiled. "Sure."

As she went back to folding her laundry, Rachel could not help but worry a bit about her plan to bring her friends together.

The next baseball practice, on the Saturday after the riot, Rachel tagged along with Sam. She loved watching baseball, even practice baseball, and the boys never seemed to mind if she was there. She settled on one of the wooden benches at the edge of the field and leaned forward, anxious to see how things would go today.

The practice did not start out very well. The players straggled to the field late; some of them never arrived at all. Simon came, but no matter how many questions the others asked, he would not explain why he had not played in the game against the Seventh Street Spades.

Rachel knew that her brother had an idea for making his team better. They needed a coach. All the "real" teams had a coach. Sam and Rachel had talked it over, and they knew just who would be the perfect guy for the job—their cousin Seth.

"We've been playing together since we were nine," Rachel heard Sam tell his teammates, "and we do pretty well."

"That's right!" exclaimed Steve. "We're the best."

"The best," echoed Elwood.

"But I think we could be better, don't you?" Sam challenged his team.

Heads started bobbing.

"I know just what we need," Sam said. "We need someone with experience to work with us, to teach us, to help us figure out some good plays."

"Are you talking about a coach?" Joe asked.

"That's right," Sam answered. "We could get our own coach. Some of the other teams are starting to do that."

"I heard that the Oak Lake team has a coach," Elwood said.

"Why can't we have a coach, too?" Sam asked. "What do you think, Joe?"

Joe shrugged. "We're doing all right on our own, but we could probably do better with a coach."

"That's exactly what I was thinking," Sam said.

Simon was starting to warm up to the idea. "We could find someone older than we are—but not too old."

"It has to be someone who really loves baseball," Steve said. "When you're trying to win a game, attitude counts more than anything else. You can have all the skill in the world, but if your attitude is not right, you'll get nowhere."

"Do you really think a coach could help us?" Jim asked.

"Sure!" Sam responded. "We'll find someone who knows how to throw pitches that are hard to hit, someone who can help us with our swings."

"Someone who can hit long fly balls for us to practice catching," Steve added.

"Exactly!"

"But where would we find someone like that?" Simon asked. "Who is going to have time to help a boys' team?"

"I think I know someone who would do it," Sam said. He held his breath, getting ready to speak the name he had in mind.

"Who?" Simon asked.

"Yeah, who?" Jim wondered.

"Seth Stockard."

"Who's Seth Stockard?" Elwood asked.

"I know who that is," interrupted Simon. "That's your cousin."

"He's my second cousin, actually," Sam clarified. "He loves baseball, and he's really good at it."

"Has he ever been a baseball coach before?" Steve asked. "We need someone with experience, lots of it."

"I don't think he's ever been a coach," Sam said, "but he goes to professional games all the time. He understands the strategies they use. He could teach them to us."

"And you really think he would do it?" Jim was still skeptical.

"I think all we have to do is ask him."

"Wait a minute," Simon said. "How old is Seth Stockard?"

"He's eighteen."

"Does he go to college?"

"He's going to go in the fall," Sam said. "He's going to be a scientist."

Simon still looked doubtful. "What does he do now?"

Sam took a deep breath and gave the answer he had hoped to avoid. "He has a temporary job at the railroad station."

"So he's a union man," Simon said flatly.

Sam remembered the day he had seen Seth passing out union leaflets. "The important thing is that Seth understands baseball," Sam insisted.

"Attitude is everything," Steve said. "We don't need someone coming in here and spreading union propaganda."

"Who said anything about the unions?" Sam countered. "We're talking about a baseball coach. Seth would be perfect."

"Well. . ." Simon leaned on a bat. "You did say his job at the railroad was just temporary. He probably hasn't joined the union himself."

"So what if he has joined the union?" Jim snapped.

"We have to be careful who we have around here," Simon said.

"What is that supposed to mean?" Jim pressed.

"Yeah, what is that supposed to mean?" Tad echoed.

Rachel thought Tad seemed eager for Simon and Jim to go nose to nose.

"Take it easy," Sam said. "We're talking about baseball, remember?"

"Doesn't Seth's father work at a bank?" Simon asked.

"Yes, that's right."

"So he doesn't come from a union family."

"That's not what matters. We need a coach, and he can help us."

Elwood was watching Steve carefully. Joe shuffled around the edge of the circle acting like he was not interested in the discussion. Rachel could see that Tad's eyes were bright with the hope of an argument. Hank was so nervous his chin twitched.

"I say we give it a try," Steve said finally.

"Me, too," Elwood immediately added.

"I don't suppose it could hurt," Jim conceded.

Rachel was watching Simon. His jaw worked back and forth while he thought about the question. Rachel clasped her hands nervously in her lap, hoping that Sam's plan would succeed.

"All right, we'll give it a try," Simon finally said. "But the minute there is any talk about union nonsense, he leaves the team. Agreed?"

"Agreed." Sam nodded.

Rachel sighed and sat back on the bench. It was a fair compromise.

CHAPTER 13

A Special Supper

"I hope Annalina likes chicken," Rachel said, as she turned over a drumstick in the simmering lard.

"I'm sure she will like anything you cook." Mama glanced over Rachel's shoulder at the frying chicken.

"I tried to ask her what she likes," Rachel continued, "but she didn't understand. The other girls were laughing at me when I was squawking like a chicken."

Mama chuckled. "It probably was funny."

"Annalina still did not understand. So I don't know if she eats chicken. I don't know anything about what Swedish people eat."

"What does she bring for her lunch at school?" Mama whacked the ends off a bunch of carrots.

"She usually just brings bread. Sometimes she has a piece of fruit."

"Then I'm sure she'll enjoy your biscuits and apple pie."

The biscuits were already out of the oven and wrapped in a cloth to keep them warm until dinner.

"Annalina's mother makes the most beautiful bread. It's not just a loaf or biscuits. She twists the dough into braids, and the crusts look shiny."

"She probably brushes the top with an egg mixture," Mama said.

"I want her to teach me how to make Swedish bread."

"Why don't you ask her?"

"I will—as soon as I learn enough Swedish or Annalina learns enough English to translate."

"That won't be long," Mama said, "considering how much time you spend with her working on English."

"I'll be so glad when she learns enough English to really talk. On the day after the riot, I tried to ask her if her father was all right. But she didn't understand. It was so frustrating!"

"I'm sure it was frustrating for Annalina, too," Mama said. "But at least you found out that it was not Mr. Borg driving that streetcar on Sunday."

"I was so relieved. He was home safe. It was someone who looked like him."

Mama glanced at the perfectly formed pie on the counter next to her daughter. Rachel followed her mother's eye.

"Is it time to put the pie in the oven?" Rachel turned over another piece of chicken. The hot lard sizzled and splattered.

"Yes, put the pie in," Mama said. "That way it will be fresh and warm at just the right time."

Rachel opened the oven, which was still warm from the biscuits, and set the apple pie in the middle.

"Don't forget to watch the time." Mama tossed the carrots she had chopped into a pot of boiling water. "Linda and Agnes were disappointed that they didn't get to taste your pie on Easter."

"Me, too! It was my first pie, and it was perfect, but no one got to take even a bite."

"I'm sure this one will not go to waste."

"Mama, are we going to have another family dinner?" Rachel asked. "Can we make up for missing Easter dinner?"

"Agnes has suggested that. We all want to do it."

"Even Uncle Ernest and Uncle Stanley?"

Mama sighed. "Ernest and Stanley have finally found something to agree on. They have different opinions about the strike, but they both think that turning over a streetcar and starting a riot was not necessary."

"Does that mean they're ready to be friends again?"

"It might be a first step."

Someone knocked on the front door. "Annalina!" Rachel snatched up a towel and tried to rub the grease off her hands.

By the time Rachel got to the front door, Carrie already had it open. Annalina looked relieved to see Rachel.

"This is my sister, Carrie." Rachel took Annalina's hand and pulled her into the living room. Annalina smiled nervously.

"And this is my mother," Rachel continued.

Annalina nodded her head politely. With one hand, she clutched a small bundle close to her chest.

"Carrie," Mama said, "run and find Papa and Sam. Tell them our guest is here."

"Come in and sit down." Rachel led Annalina to a chair. "Sit." She demonstrated by sitting in the chair next to Annalina. The Swedish girl sat down, still clutching her bundle. Her faded yellow calico dress hung down over her scuffed brown boots. But her eyes were bright with anticipation.

"I'm going to check on the chicken," Mama said.

Rachel was tempted to flap her elbows and squawk but decided against it. It was too late to change the menu. Either Annalina would eat chicken or she would not.

Carrie returned with Papa and Sam. Annalina smiled at Sam, whom she recognized.

"This is my papa," Rachel said.

Papa extended his hand. "I am pleased to meet you."

Annalina put her small white hand in Papa's big hand. "Nice." Now she thrust the small bundle toward Rachel.

"What is this?" Rachel asked.

"Give," Annalina said.

"Give? Is it a gift?"

Annalina nodded. "I give."

Rachel laid the bundle in her lap and began unwrapping it. Annalina's family was very poor. What kind of gift could she have brought? Rachel gasped in delight when the package lay open in her lap.

"Dolls!" Carrie squealed.

Three small painted wooden dolls lay in Rachel's lap. They were only a few inches tall, but they were painted with exquisite detail in bright colors and a glossy finish.

"These are beautiful!" Rachel exclaimed. "Look, Mama." She held up the dolls as her mother came back into the room. "Look what Annalina brought."

Mama picked up one of the dolls. "Look at that little face! Why, Rachel, it almost looks like you."

Rachel turned to her friend. "Annalina, where did you get these?"

Annalina did not understand.

"Buy?" Rachel said. "Store?"

Annalina shook her head. "No. No store. I make."

"You made these?" Somehow the dolls seemed even more beautiful now.

Annalina gestured as if she were holding a carving knife. "Papa."

"Your papa carves the dolls?"

Now Annalina moved her fingers delicately as if she were painting. "Annalina."

"Your papa carves the dolls, and you paint them?"

Annalina nodded vigorously.

"They are a beautiful gift," Rachel said. "Thank you."

"I think supper is just about ready," Mama said.

"Great!" Sam said. "I'm famished."

Rachel showed Annalina the way to the kitchen. When they had all sat down around the table, Annalina bowed her head along with all the Borlands, and Papa gave thanks for the food and for Rachel's new friend. Mama had put the chicken on a platter, and she started passing it around the table. The boiled carrots followed, along with a bowl of mashed potatoes.

"Where are the biscuits?" Carrie asked.

"We almost forgot." Rachel popped over to the sideboard and fetched the basket of biscuits.

Carrie took two biscuits and passed the basket to Sam.

Rachel watched Annalina carefully as she took a small portion of everything that was passed. When the platter of chicken came to Annalina, she started giggling.

"What's so funny?" Rachel asked.

Annalina covered her mouth in embarrassment. But she could not stop giggling. Then she flapped her elbows in the air and squawked.

The whole Borland family burst out laughing.

"Yes," Rachel said, flapping her elbows, too. "Chicken."

"I think she understands now." Mama smiled.

"Chicken," repeated Rachel.

"Shikeen," said Annalina.

"Chicken. Do you like chicken?" Rachel asked.

Annalina picked up the chicken leg on her plate and took a big bite. Rachel leaned back in her chair, relieved.

"The chicken is delicious," Papa said. He helped himself to a second piece.

"Thank you." Rachel glanced at Annalina, and they almost started giggling again.

After a while, Mama said, "Don't forget to check the pie."

Rachel scooted her chair back and crossed the kitchen to the oven. Peeking in, she said, "I think it's done." Protecting her hands with two folded dishtowels, she removed the pie from the hot oven and set it on the sideboard.

"It looks perfect!" The crust had baked to a golden brown. Steam rose through the holes Rachel had pricked in the top of the pie.

Carrie pushed her plate away. "I'm ready for pie."

Mama inspected Carrie's plate to see that she had eaten all of her supper. "All right," Mama said, "but don't take more pie than you can eat."

Rachel took a stack of plates down from a shelf and started serving the pie. Mama cleared the dinner plates from the table.

Rachel set a slice of pie in front of her little sister and another in front of her brother. "You two have the privilege of being the first tasters."

Carrie stuck her fork in the pie and shoveled a piece into her mouth. Sam did the same.

As Rachel brought plates to the table for Annalina and her father, she saw Carrie spitting out her first bite of pie.

"Carrie!" Mama scolded.

"I'm sorry, Mama, but it doesn't taste like your apple pie."

"She's right." Sam's face was contorted, and his cheeks puffed out as he tried not to spit out the bite of pie. With a great effort, he forced it down his throat. "This doesn't taste like anyone's apple pie."

Rachel's heart started pounding. What was wrong with her perfect pie?

Papa gingerly took the tiniest piece of pie on the end of his fork and put it to his lips. Even before he put it in his mouth, he knew what was wrong. He started laughing.

"Rachel, how much sugar did you put in this?" Papa asked.

"One cup, just like the recipe called for."

"And where did you get the sugar from?"

Rachel whirled around to look at the canisters on the counter. Then she groaned. "I used salt!"

"A whole cup of salt!" Sam grimaced and put down his fork.

Rachel snatched away the plate she had just set in front of Annalina. Her friend was confused.

"No good," Rachel said. "No good."

"Annalina like pie," her friend said.

Rachel shook her head hard. "Not this pie. This pie is bad." She made a sour face. Rachel nudged the platter of chicken toward Annalina. "Have some more chicken."

Annalina started giggling all over again. Carrie and Sam flapped their arms. Mama and Papa roared. The kitchen full of human chickens almost made Rachel forget about her disastrous pie.

Still laughing, Mama took the plates from Sam and Carrie. "Rachel, you go visit with your friend. Papa can help me clean up tonight."

In the living room, Rachel pouted for a few minutes. She dropped her first pie in the Easter riot. Now she'd put salt in the next one. Would she ever make a pie that anyone could eat? She pushed her straggling blond hair away from her face and sighed.

Annalina's hair was neatly tied in tight braids. Rachel's hung loose around her shoulders, with two floppy bows on top of her head. She touched the end of one of Annalina's braids.

"This is pretty," she said.

Annalina reached out and took hold of Rachel's hair. With skilled fingers, she started braiding.

"Can you braid my hair?" Rachel asked.

Annalina's finger's kept moving.

"Wait," Rachel said, "I want you to do all of it." She pulled a straight-backed chair away from the wall and sat in it. Annalina combed her fingers through Rachel's hair, making it do exactly what she wanted it to do. After she had made two tight, neat braids, she moved the bows from the top of Rachel's head to the bottom of the braids. Finally, she stood back, satisfied with her work.

Rachel got up and stood in front of the brass-rimmed looking glass next to the front door. Annalina stood next to her. They smiled at their matching blond braids and blue eyes.

"You two could be sisters!" Sam had come into the room and looked at their reflection in the glass. "Rachel, you really look Swedish!"

Rachel smiled. "I think it would be fun to go to another country. Maybe someday I'll go to Sweden."

Annalina stepped away from the mirror and peered out at the darkness beyond the front door. "I go," she said quietly.

"Already?" Rachel moaned.

"Papa said he would walk Annalina home," Sam said. "She shouldn't go by herself now that it's dark."

After Papa and Annalina were gone, Mama said, "Your friend is very nice, Rachel. And you're doing a wonderful job teaching her English. She understands quite a bit."

"At least now she knows what *chicken* means! I don't understand how anyone could not like Annalina."

Chapter 14

Annalina's Gift

When Rachel went to school the next morning, she still wore her hair in braids. She liked the braids, and she did not mind one bit if she looked Swedish.

"People are going to get you confused with Annalina," Sam told her.

Rachel simply tossed her braids over her shoulders and said, "I don't care."

They got to school early, twenty minutes before the bell would ring. Carrie scampered off to play with girls her own age.

"I'm going to go find some of the boys from the team and let them know Seth is coming to practice tomorrow," Sam said.

Rachel scanned the school yard for Annalina, but she was not there yet. Shifting her bundle of books to the other shoulder, Rachel started over to the corner of the school yard where Annalina liked to sit. She would wait for her friend there.

Instead, she nearly ran into Mariah Webster.

"Rachel Borland, what have you done to yourself?" Mariah laughed loudly.

"What do you mean?" Rachel responded, even though she knew

what Mariah was talking about.

"Your hair! It's in braids!"

"So? Haven't you ever seen braids before?"

"Of course I have—just not on you."

"I never tried them before, but I like them."

"You look like you just got off the boat from Sweden."

Mariah had dark hair and dark eyes. No one would ever mistake her for a Swedish immigrant. Like Rachel's family, the Websters had been in America for generations.

"We all have to come from somewhere," Rachel said.

"Why do you want to be Swedish? What's wrong with being American?"

"What's wrong with being Swedish?" Rachel countered.

"Rachel, why are you so crazy lately? I never see you anymore. You always eat lunch with that new girl."

"Her name is Annalina. And there's plenty of room on the bench for you to sit with us."

"Now you're acting just like her, even fixing your hair the way she does. Are you going to stop speaking English?"

Rachel lifted her chin. "*Tack sa mycket.*"

"Stop it, Rachel!"

"Mariah, Swedish is just another language. Annalina is just like you and me and all the other girls. She's smart and funny and works hard. When she learns more English, you'll find out for yourself."

Mariah looked doubtful. "We've all known each other all our lives. I have enough friends already."

"But Annalina doesn't," Rachel said. "What if your father decided to move your family to Europe and you had to leave all your friends?"

Mariah was not sure what to say. "My father wouldn't do that," she muttered.

Rachel saw Annalina come through the gate. "There's Annalina now. Let's go talk to her."

"Um, you go," Mariah said. "I see Katherine coming in at the other gate, and I need to talk to her."

Mariah hurried off to Katherine and her familiar cluster of friends. Shaking her head, Rachel crossed the yard to greet Annalina. At the same moment, they put their elbows in the air and flapped and squawked.

"Chicken good," Annalina said.

"I'm glad you liked it."

Annalina smiled. "Pie not good."

"Shh. Don't tell anyone about that."

Behind them, Mariah snickered. Rachel glared at Mariah. Apparently talking to Mariah had done no good at all. Katherine, however, had stopped giggling. Rachel saw her looking at Annalina as if she was really interested in her.

They moved to a bench and put their books down. Rachel reached into the roomy pocket of her skirt and pulled out two of the dolls Annalina had given her the night before. She set them on the bench.

"These are beautiful," Rachel said. "I couldn't stand to leave them home."

Two other girls had joined Mariah and Katherine. Mariah was pointing at Rachel and Annalina.

Rachel had an idea. She held the dolls up in the air. Loudly, she said, "You did such a beautiful job painting these dolls. I hope that you will teach me how to do it." She turned the dolls in several directions. Their bright colors gleamed in the sunlight.

Annalina was puzzled.

Rachel pointed to Annalina and then herself. "You," she said slowly, "teach me." And she held her fingers together as if she were holding a paintbrush. She glanced at the other girls. They were watching.

"Painting the dolls is very difficult," Rachel said loudly. "You have a special talent. Not everyone could do such beautiful work."

Rachel knew she was talking too much—and too loudly. Annalina was not understanding. But Mariah and Katherine and the others understood. She had their attention now. In a group, they were slowly walking toward the bench where Annalina and Rachel sat. Rachel watched them out of the side of her eyes while she continued to talk to Annalina. When the four girls were close enough to cast a shadow on Annalina, Rachel turned to speak directly to them.

"Would you like to see my new dolls?" Rachel said to the girls. "Annalina gave them to me. She painted them herself."

Unsure, the other girls looked at each other. Finally Mariah nodded her head. "Okay. We'll look at them."

They gathered around the bench. Rachel passed around the two dolls.

"I've never seen anything like this," Katherine said. "Did she really paint them herself?"

"Of course she did," Rachel said. "She brought three of them to my house last night, all different sizes."

"Where does she get the dolls?"

"Her father carves them."

Mariah's eyes widened in interest. "Her father carves the dolls, and she paints them?"

Rachel nodded.

Mariah looked at Annalina then asked Rachel, "Does she understand what we're saying?"

"Slow down, and use short words," Rachel suggested.

"Are you sure?"

"Go ahead," Rachel urged.

Mariah turned to Annalina. "Very pretty," she said, holding one of the dolls.

"Dank you." Annalina smiled.

Rachel smiled, too. The beautiful dolls were a language of their own. Girls from across the ocean could enjoy the same beauty. Annalina was going to do just fine.

As the other girls all tried to talk at once to Annalina, Rachel stood up. She was hoping to share the good news with Sam. But when she tried to catch his eye from across the school yard, she saw that things were not going as well for him this morning as they had for her. "See you in class," she told the other girls, and then she moved closer to Sam and his group of friends, hoping to hear what was going on.

"It was crazy to turn over a streetcar," Steve was saying. "The people who did that should be arrested and locked up."

"All ten thousand of them?" someone asked.

"There were ten thousand people at the riot," Steve said, "but not all of them turned over the streetcars. Only a few did that."

Rachel could still picture the faces of the men who had rocked the streetcar till it toppled.

"Steve, I thought your father was in the union," Tad said. "Why are you siding with the streetcar company?"

"I'm not siding with anybody," Steve said. "I'm just saying they didn't have to turn over two streetcars."

"They had to do something to get the attention of Thomas Lowry. My father says that Lowry won't even talk to the union leaders."

Steve made a face. "Do you really think that destroying a streetcar is going to make Lowry give the drivers back their wages? Lowry is not the kind of person to be frightened by something like that. In fact, it's likely to make him even angrier."

Rachel thought Steve had a good point. She watched as Jim Harrison could not hold his feelings in any longer. "If Lowry can do whatever he wants to do with the drivers' pay, then the drivers can do whatever they want with the streetcars."

Simon made a face. "Cutting the drivers' pay was a business decision. Lowry wasn't trying to hurt anybody."

"Maybe he didn't try to hurt anybody," Jim said, "but he did. All he cares about is making himself richer."

"It's his business. He has a right to make a profit."

Jim's face was flaming red now. "Does he have a right to take food away from my little sisters?"

"He didn't do that."

"Yes, he did!"

"No, he didn't."

Simon swung at Jim, who ducked just in time.

"Get 'em!" cried Tad. Rachel shook her head. That boy was always ready for a fight.

"Stop!" Hank shouted. "Please don't hurt each other. Please stop!"

But Jim's right fist connected with Simon's left eye.

Rachel gasped and jumped forward, but her brother was ahead of her. "Jim Harrison, stop this nonsense!" Sam grabbed Jim's arm and twisted it behind his back.

"He started it." Simon glared at Jim.

"No, I didn't."

"Yes, you did."

The bell rang just then. All across the school yard, students started shuffling their way into the building. Rachel joined them.

"We're not finished," she heard Simon mutter at Jim. Rachel looked over her shoulder and saw that Simon's eye was swelling up and had turned an angry red.

Jim scoffed. "Just remember who punched you."

A shadow fell across the ground in front of Rachel. She looked up to see Mr. Martin, the principal, looming over the students.

"I understand some of you boys were just involved in a dispute," he said in his deep, grave voice.

Rachel looked back at the boys. Jim and Simon stared straight ahead. Neither of them said anything.

"It is my understanding that this dispute centered on the riot last Sunday. Is that correct?"

Again, no one spoke. Mr. Martin frowned.

"Mr. Borland," the principal said. "And Miss Borland. I believe you both were present during the riot. Is that correct?"

Rachel swallowed hard. "Yes, sir," she heard Sam say, and she nodded silently.

Mr. Martin looked at Sam. "Were you participating, young man?"

"No, sir! We were on our way to Easter dinner, and we got trapped."

"So I understand. Perhaps you would like to comment for the other students on what you saw."

The mass of students had fallen silent. Rachel felt as though everyone was staring at her and her brother. She saw Sam gulp. "People were angry," he said softly.

"Please speak up, Mr. Borland," the principal said. "I want everyone here to be able to hear what you have to say."

Sam squared his shoulders. "People were angry," he repeated, almost shouting now. "They were saying mean things about each other—about their own neighbors. A few weeks ago it didn't matter that one friend was a manager at the mill and another friend drove a streetcar. But now, people are choosing their friends based on how they earn a living."

"And do you find this reasonable?" Mr. Martin asked.

Sam shook his head. "No, sir. It's not fair." Rachel saw him look at Simon and Jim. "A friend is a friend, no matter what."

Jim spoke up now. "But what if the friend you trusted does

something to hurt you? Is he still a friend?"

Rachel watched as Sam thought for a moment. "I think that it is not always easy to understand why a person does something. And until we understand, we shouldn't get all riled up."

"Thank you, Mr. Borland," the principal said. "That is a very reasonable opinion. I would like everyone to spend some time today thinking about what Mr. Borland just said. And now, would you all please proceed immediately to your classrooms?"

Sam looked relieved to have attention shift away from him. Rachel caught his eye and smiled. "Good job," she mouthed, so only he would know what she was saying.

As the students jostled their way into the school building, Rachel noticed that Simon and Jim still did not look at each other. Had they listened to anything Sam said?

Chapter 15

A Birthday Blessing and a Tense Practice

Rachel woke up all at once on the first day of May, excited because of her birthday and yet a little worried because of her party. She had asked Annalina, Colleen, and Janie separately, and all had agreed to come. Colleen, Janie, and Rachel had spent their birthdays together in the past. Of course the cloud of the strike hadn't hung over them before.

"Happy birthday, Rachel!" Carrie screamed as Rachel came into the kitchen for breakfast. Carrie ran over and gave her now-eleven-year-old sister a big hug.

"Happy birthday, Rachel," Sam echoed, in a quieter, more dignified manner.

"Yes, honey, happy birthday," Rachel's parents greeted her in unison.

As Rachel sat down to her breakfast, she found two gifts at her place. "May I open them now, please?"

Her mother shrugged, "Well, I suppose so. But you must eat

breakfast before you leave for school."

Rachel carefully pulled the paper from the first gift. "That's from Sam and me," piped up Carrie. She seemed more excited than Rachel. Inside the package was the most beautiful book Rachel had ever seen.

"It's a journal. The pages are all blank so you can write down all of your thoughts," Sam explained. "There's something else in there, too."

Rachel lifted up the journal and found a lovely pen. "Oh, Carrie and Sam. It's beautiful. I will think of both of you every time I write in the book."

Next she opened the gift from her mama and papa. It was a small package, but the paper and ribbon were so fancy.

"Oooh, it's so beautiful." Inside the package was a gold necklace with a small locket. Inside the locket was an even smaller lock of very fair-colored hair.

"That's your hair, Rachel. From when you were first born," Papa said.

"I've been saving it to give to you," her mama added. "To remind you how small you once were and how far you've come."

Rachel thought she was going to cry. "I love them all—I love you all. Thank you so much." She got up and walked around the table, hugging each member of her family.

Bringing everyone back to the present, Mama reminded everyone, "It's getting late. Now everyone eat your breakfast."

After what seemed to Rachel like forever, school finally ended for the day. Annalina came home with her, and Colleen and Janie arrived not long after. As Rachel had requested, her mother had made a small cake just for the girls.

All of the girls seemed a bit nervous, and Rachel thought that

Annalina looked as though she felt out of place. "Let's eat cake first!" Rachel suggested. The others agreed, and they went into the kitchen. Mama had set the table with the nice plates, and she watched as Rachel cut the cake. After the girls got their cake, Mama left them alone for their own party.

"Annalina, this is 'cake.' Say it: 'cake.' "

"Cake!" Annalina said, smiling. Right the first time!

"That's right, Annalina. Colleen, Janie, she said 'cake.' " Rachel could not hide her enthusiasim.

Colleen and Janie looked at each other. Then they started giggling.

"Stop it!" Rachel said sharply to the two of them. "Annalina works hard to learn English. You shouldn't make fun of her." What Rachel had hoped would be the start of a renewed friendship was not off to a good start.

Colleen and Janie laughed harder. This time, Annalina joined them.

"What's going on?" Rachel could not believe what she was seeing—and hearing.

"It all right, Rachel," Annalina reassured her. "Colleen and Janie help me learn to say 'cake' to surprise you. We friend, too."

Colleen and Janie nodded. "Rachel, Janie and I decided that our friendship was too important to lose over something we could not control."

"Colleen and I agreed to disagree about the unions. After all, it's our parents' jobs, not ours. And we decided," Janie continued, putting her arm around Annalina, "that we should give Annalina a chance. After all, if you like her, there has to be a reason. Now, let's open your presents!"

For the second time that day, a gift had made Rachel feel like crying. She knew that what was in those packages could not be better than what Colleen, Janie, and Annalina had just given her.

That Saturday, Rachel followed Sam and her older cousin on their way to baseball practice.

"This is a terrific idea, Sam." Seth Stockard strode down the street next to his young cousin with a bat propped over his shoulder. At eighteen and a half, Seth was tall, with lanky legs and a long stride. His dark hair often looked like it needed to be combed.

"I promised the team you would say yes," Sam said, "so I'm sure glad you did."

"How could I say no to coaching a baseball team?"

"I thought you might be too busy. You have a job, and I know that you're really a scientist."

"I'm glad you recognize that, Sam, because I think it's time I started teaching you about science as well as baseball."

"Do you mean that?" Rachel saw the excitement on Sam's face, and she felt a twinge of jealousy. Sometimes it seemed like boys got to have all the fun. Then she remembered all the fun she and her friends had had at her birthday party, and she changed her mind. She knew her brother had had a tough time with his friends lately. He deserved to have some fun, too. "Can we work in your lab together?" Sam was asking Seth.

"Absolutely. But there's always time for baseball. You have a sharp team. I've seen you play. So I know this will be fun."

Sam sighed. "The last game was a disaster. I'm glad you weren't there. It was so embarrassing."

Seth chuckled. "I heard about it. It seems you lost your hurler. Has he come back to the team?"

"He was at practice on Tuesday, but I don't know if he'll come back today." Sam winced at the memory of Jim's fist hitting Simon's eye.

They turned a corner to head in the direction of the field.

"I know you can help us," Sam said. "But I have to warn you. Not everyone may want your help."

"Every coach has to win over some players—even on professional teams." Seth moved the bat to the other shoulder. "A good coach has to prove himself. I know I have to show that I understand baseball from the inside out."

If only it were that simple, Rachel thought. *If only the boys on the team would think about baseball and not unions and strikes.*

"You seem a little nervous," Rachel said, almost running to keep up with them.

Sam shrugged. "Getting a coach was my idea. Asking Seth was my idea. If—"

"If this doesn't work out, you'll look bad to the boys on your team." Seth finished Sam's thought. "Don't worry, Sam. I can make this work."

"How?"

"I'll just approach it scientifically. I'll make a hypothesis about what I think will happen then I'll try some ideas to see if the hypothesis is true."

Rachel and Sam laughed.

By the time they arrived at the practice field, most of the boys were there already. Sam got their attention and signaled that they should gather around home plate. Rachel took her usual place on the bench.

"This is Seth Stockard, our new coach," Sam said proudly.

"Hello, boys."

"This is Jim. He plays first base." Sam pointed his finger at each boy in turn. "And this is Steve and Joe and Elwood and Larry, Tad, and Hank." Sam scanned the field. "I don't see Simon. He's the hurler."

"He's probably not coming," Joe said.

"He's just late," said Hank.

"No, he's not coming," Joe insisted.

Seth jumped in. "Let's give him a few minutes more. In the meantime, why don't we get started?"

"Just a minute." Steve was leaning on a bat with a suspicious expression on his face. "I have a few questions to ask the new coach."

"Sure," Seth said. "Ask anything you'd like."

"Have you ever coached a baseball team before?"

"No, but I've played baseball all my life. I taught Sam everything he knows."

That seemed to impress Steve. Rachel knew Sam was a good player.

"What position did you play?" Steve continued asking.

"Most of the time I played in the outfield. I have a pretty good arm for throwing the ball back into the infield."

"Can you hit?"

"Better than average," Seth said confidently. "I can get a hit when I really need one."

"How many professional games have you seen?"

"Oh, dozens, maybe hundreds," Seth answered. "I go whenever I can with my uncle Stanley."

"He's a railroad man, isn't he?" Joe asked.

"Yes, he is."

"Is he in the union?"

Rachel's stomach tightened. But she could see Seth was not flustered. "Hey, are we here to talk politics or to play ball?"

"Play ball!" exclaimed Tad.

"Then let's get to it." Seth clapped his hands several times. "You're going to have to show me what you can do today. Then we can work out some plays."

"What do you want us to do?" Sam asked.

"Set up a batting practice rotation," Seth answered. "I want to see your swings."

Sam nodded.

"Jim, go on over to first base," Seth said. "I'll pitch. The rest of you can get in the hitting rotation."

The boys set up their formation. Elwood batted first. Seth threw him an easy pitch, but it was a little high. Elwood let it pass.

"Good eye, good eye," Seth said.

He threw the next ball. This one was right down the center of the strike zone. Elwood swung. The ball bounced through the infield, an easy ground ball.

Seth stood behind Elwood. "Let's work on that swing for a minute," Seth said. They grasped the bat together. "You have a lot of power, Elwood. But your swing is not quite even. You're hitting the top of the ball. That's what makes it become a grounder."

Seth moved the bat to show what he meant.

"Keep your swing even, and you'll get the ball into the air." They swung together again. "It'll take a lot of practice, but you'll get it."

Rachel relaxed on her bench. The team seemed to be interested in what Seth had to say. But Simon was still missing. *Joe is probably right,* Rachel thought. Why would Simon come to play baseball after Jim had given him a black eye?

When she turned back to the boys, she saw that it was Tad's turn to bat. He grasped the bat at the very bottom and stood poised with his arms over the plate. Seth threw the pitch. Tad swung and hit the ball on the center of the bat. It was a line drive that lost its energy and plopped to the ground at second base.

"Good swing," Seth said. "Nice and even. But try stepping back from the plate a little bit. Then you can hit the ball with the end of the bat. It will have a lot more power and go farther."

Seth showed Tad where to stand then pitched again. This time, Tad swung and belted the ball into right field. The team whooped its encouragement, and Rachel cheered, too.

In right field, Sam scooped up the ball and threw it back to Seth on the pitcher's mound. Tad had run safely to second base—something that almost never happened to Tad.

Rachel spotted Simon leaning against the fence. She waved and caught Sam's eye then pointed toward Simon. Sam started to wave to Simon and seemed about to call him over. Then he apparently changed his mind. Rachel nodded to herself. If Simon wanted to play baseball, all he had to do was join the team.

Jim picked up a bat. Rachel knew that Jim had a straight, even swing. She wondered what Seth's comment would be.

Jim hit the first pitch. He threw the bat down awkwardly and started to run. The ball went to second base, where Hank snatched it up and threw it to first base. In a real game, Jim would have been out.

"Nice try, Jim," Seth said. "You have a nice swing. Let me just suggest one thing." He picked up a bat to demonstrate. "As you swing, start taking a step with your left foot. After you connect with the ball, let the bat swing around in your left hand and let it go. Don't worry about it. If you lift your foot on the swing, you'll be one step on your way to first base. You might have been able to beat out that throw."

Jim nodded. "I'll try that next time."

The batting practice continued. Steve and Joe and Hank took their turns. Seth diagnosed the swings of each player.

Rachel was keeping an eye on Simon. The hurler's hands had come out of the pockets of his trousers, and he had moved along the fence closer to the infield—closer to Seth. Rachel saw Simon listening carefully to everything Seth said.

"Now I want to see how well you can field," Seth called out to the team members. "I'll hit some fly balls. You try to catch them and throw them back in."

The team spread out around the field. Simon left the fence and joined the practice. He stood deep in left field only a few feet away from the fence. But he had definitely joined the practice.

Seth tossed a ball in the air and swung. The ball sailed into left field. Jim scrambled to get under the ball and held his hands high. Judging the arc of the ball carefully, he took a few steps back. The ball plopped into his hands. Grinning, he heaved it back to the infield for Seth to hit again.

"That was pretty good," Steve called out. "For someone who usually plays first base, you do pretty well in the outfield."

"Thanks!" Jim called back.

Rachel smiled to herself. If dolls and a birthday party could build a bridge between enemies, maybe baseball could do the same.

When practice was over, Rachel trailed behind the boys as they walked off the playing field toward their homes. "Your cousin is really good," she heard Jim say to Sam. "I never noticed how I wasn't taking a step with my swing. That's really going to help."

"I've learned a lot from Seth," Sam said.

"You're lucky to have a cousin to teach you," Jim said.

"Jim is right." Simon had drifted over. "You're lucky to have Seth teaching you, and now we're all lucky to have him coaching our team."

Rachel held her breath, watching as Simon and Jim started to talk to each other.

"How's your eye?" Jim muttered.

"Not too bad."

"We thought you weren't coming."

"I thought about not coming."

"But you're here."

"This is my team," Simon said. "Where else am I going to go to play?"

Jim shrugged. "The Seventh Street team would be happy to have you."

"Naw. They don't have a coach."

Jim nodded. "You're right. We're the best. We have a coach."

"Even if he's a union man?" Simon asked.

"He's a ballplayer, through and through. That's what matters."

"Heads up!" Seth shouted. He tossed the ball toward the group. Rachel raised her eyes to the sky and tried to follow the path of the ball. She wanted to catch that ball, just to show the boys, but she knew she shouldn't spoil the moment by interfering.

Simon and Jim were also following the ball's arc, their heads tipped back. Neither of them were watching what the other was doing. Both of them jumped to catch the ball. Instead, they smacked into each other and tumbled into a heap. The ball dropped to the ground and dribbled past them.

The two boys broke into laughter. Untangling themselves, they lay on the ground, rubbing their heads where they had rammed into each other.

"I think you tripped me," Jim said, laughing.

"I'll probably have two black eyes now," Simon responded.

Rachel and Sam exchanged looks over the two boys' heads. Brother and sister smiled. Things were finally getting back to normal.

Chapter 16

A Disappointing Party

The doors opened and the children poured out of the school building into the bright sunshine of a May afternoon. Sam and Rachel met each other in their usual spot and looked around for Carrie. Rachel had promised Mama she would walk Carrie home.

"Rachel, look!" Carrie cried as she ran up to join them. "A streetcar!"

Rachel turned to look, and indeed a streetcar was rumbling past. At least ten passengers were riding inside. Now it was Rachel's turn to get excited.

"Sam, it's Janie's father. Mr. Lawrence is driving the streetcar!"

Sam looked carefully. "You're right. The strike must be over."

Mariah Webster was nearby. "The strike definitely is over," she informed them. "The drivers did not get their two cents an hour back. They have to work on Mr. Lowry's terms or not at all." Mariah tossed her hair over her shoulder haughtily.

"You don't have to be so excited," Sam said. "A lot of families got hurt during the strike."

"They caused all that trouble for nothing," Mariah retorted.

"The important thing is that it's over," Rachel said. "Everyone can go back to work, and things can go back to normal."

"I want to find Jim and talk to him," Sam said.

"You go ahead," Rachel said. "I'm going home. I have to finish getting ready for Annalina's party."

"Can I come to the party?" Carrie pleaded.

"I'm giving a birthday party for Annalina," Rachel said. "It's not for little kids."

"I'm not little, I'm eight."

"You'll have to be on your best behavior."

"I can behave, I promise."

"All right, then, but we have to hurry. I don't want Annalina to get there before we do." She turned and waved at Mariah. "See you at the party, Mariah."

Mariah did not answer.

Rachel and Carrie scurried toward home. They hadn't gotten far before they met Janie.

Janie was talking with some of the other girls in her class. Even Colleen was there.

"I saw your father driving," Rachel said. "I know he would never go against the union, so I guess this means the strike is over."

"It's over all right," grumbled Janie. "And Thomas Lowry won."

"I heard that the drivers didn't get the wage cut back."

"That's right. They got nothing. Thomas Lowry got it all, so he can stuff his fat, filthy pockets." Janie did not seem at all relieved that the strike was over.

"At least your father is working again," Rachel said.

"And the streetcars are running!" Katherine Jones was excited. "I was getting really tired of walking everywhere. I'm going to go downtown right now. I'm going to ride a streetcar all the way to Bridge Square and back."

"If you do," Janie said, "you're just putting more money in Thomas Lowry's pockets."

Rachel looked at Colleen, who had not said a word. *She could be gloating,* Rachel thought. *She could be boasting about the victory of Thomas Lowry.* But Colleen said nothing.

"A birthday pie?" Carrie asked, giggling. "I think that's silly!"

"It's what Annalina wanted," Rachel said. "Since she didn't get to eat pie when she came for supper, I promised to make her one for her birthday."

"Are you going to put candles in it?"

"Of course."

Carrie giggled again.

Rachel ignored Carrie and continued her preparations for the party. She had made the pie early in the morning before school, but she had not baked it yet. She wanted it to be fresh and hot from the oven for the party. Now it was time. She opened the oven and put the pie inside.

Then she turned her attention to the dining room. Mama had agreed to let Rachel have the party in the dining room. Annalina had never had a real birthday party before. Rachel wanted this party to be one Annalina would remember for a long time.

After the girls at school discovered Annalina's talent with the painted dolls, they seemed to welcome her a little more warmly. Rachel did not hear so many of them snickering behind Annalina's back. Katherine, especially, was intrigued by the dolls and wanted to learn to paint them herself. So Rachel had invited Mariah and Katherine and Phoebe and Beth to the party. Rachel had also invited Colleen and Janie, but they couldn't come. It was Colleen's father's birthday, and she had to spend the evening with her family. Janie was helping her mother. Janie told Rachel that her mother was getting stronger but was still too weak to make dinner without her help.

Pink was Annalina's favorite color, so last night, Rachel had decorated the dining room with as much pink as she could find, from the tablecloth to paper streamers tied to the lights. A big sign propped up on the buffet read HAPPY BIRTHDAY, ANNALINA. Rachel's gift for Annalina was wrapped in pink tissue paper and placed in the center of the table.

A knock sounded at the front door. Carrie jumped up. "I'll get it."

"I early?" Annalina asked. Her cheeks were pink.

"Did you run all the way?" Carrie asked.

Annalina nodded.

"You're right on time," Rachel answered. "The others will be here soon. Now close your eyes."

Annalina looked puzzled. Rachel put her hands over Annalina's eyes, making her friend giggle. She led Annalina into the dining room. There, she removed her hands. The Swedish girl gasped. "Pretty! For me?"

"Yes, it's for you," Rachel said smiling. "Happy birthday, Annalina."

Annalina spun around and hugged Rachel. "Dank you, dank you, Rachel."

Carrie nudged her way in between them. "Where are the other girls?" she asked.

"They're coming," Rachel said confidently. "We just got out of school. They probably had to go home and get their gifts for Annalina."

"Will you braid my hair while you wait?" Carrie asked Annalina.

Rachel looked to be sure Annalina had understood. Annalina was already separating Carrie's hair into the strands that would become twin braids.

The clock in the hall ticked loudly. Rachel tried not to look at it too often. She was no longer sure the other girls were coming.

Rachel watched as Annalina nimbly braided Carrie's hair. Carrie was sitting perfectly still. It would not be long at all before the job was done, but for once, Rachel wished that Carrie would wiggle a little bit. But Carrie had promised to be on her best behavior, and she was.

The clock ticked.

Finally someone knocked on the door. Rachel leaped out of her chair and ran to open the door.

"Katherine! Hello!"

"Hello, Rachel." Katherine stood on the front porch awkwardly holding a small package. She wore an emerald green satin dress that highlighted her eyes beautifully. Rachel had never seen her look so lovely, but she had not expected Katherine to change from her cotton school frock into such a fancy dress.

"Come in." Rachel opened the door wide. She glanced over her shoulder at the dining room, grinning. "Where are the others?"

Katherine shuffled into the house. "I'm not sure," she muttered.

Rachel was puzzled. "Didn't you talk to Mariah today—or Phoebe or Beth? They were all in school today."

Katherine licked her lips nervously. "I don't think they're coming," she said quietly.

Rachel closed the door and leaned against it. "What do you mean?"

"I asked them all if they were coming," Katherine said, "because I can't stay. I wanted someone to bring my gift."

"You can't stay?" Rachel asked.

"My mother says I have to go have dinner at my grandmother's house. My aunt just got engaged, and they're having a party for her tonight. Mama's waiting out in the carriage."

"So that's why you're in your best dress."

"I'm sorry, Rachel."

"It's all right, Katherine. You have to do what your mother wants you to do."

"I'm sorry about the others, too."

"That's not your fault," Rachel said.

"Here, please give this to Annalina." Katherine put the small package in Rachel's hands.

"Don't you want to say happy birthday to Annalina yourself?"

"My mother is waiting. We have to go look for my brother, Steve."

"But, Katherine—"

"I'm sorry. I have to go."

Then she was gone. Rachel turned back to the dining room. Determined not to let Annalina see the disappointment she felt, she marched into the room.

"Look what Katherine brought for you," she said brightly.

"Where is Katherine?" Carrie asked.

"She couldn't stay," Rachel explained. "She had to go to her aunt's engagement party."

"Katherine go?" Annalina looked puzzled.

Rachel nodded. "She wanted to stay, but she couldn't."

Annalina did not respond. Her lower lip quivered.

"I think it's time we get this party started," Rachel said.

"But no one's here," Carrie commented.

Rachel shot her sister a pointed look. "We're here," she said emphatically. "We don't need a whole roomful of people in order to have a party."

"They're not coming, are they?" Carrie said. "They didn't want to come to Annalina's party."

Rachel wanted to give her sister a good shake and send her out of the room. "That just means more pie for us," Rachel said.

But Annalina was not fooled. She had understood enough of

what Carrie said to know that no one was coming to her birthday party. She sank into a chair. "Girls not come," she said sadly.

Rachel said quietly, "No, the other girls are not coming."

Annalina set Katherine's gift on the table next to Rachel's. "They not like me."

"They don't know you," Rachel insisted. "If they would get to know you, they would like you as much as I do."

Annalina stared at the floor.

"Let's open the gifts," Carrie suggested.

"That's a wonderful idea." Rachel sat down next to Annalina and once again put the package from Katherine in her hands.

Slowly, Annalina unwrapped the box and opened it. Inside lay a neat row of six bright paint colors and two new brushes. Annalina's face brightened. "New paint! I need!"

"That was a thoughtful gift," Rachel said.

"Open Rachel's present," Carrie urged. From the other side of the table, she nudged the package toward Annalina.

Annalina gently removed three layers of pink tissue paper and opened her mouth in delight. "Pretty!" She held up one of twelve colorful ribbons, two each of six different colors.

"I got them from Mr. Johanssen's shop," Rachel explained. "I'll have to take you there. But maybe you already know him. He's Swedish, too, after all. He has lovely things in his shop. He might even like to sell your dolls. Your father could carve them, you could paint them, and Mr. Johanssen can sell them." She clapped her hands in delight at her own idea. "I'll talk to him right away."

Annalina laughed. She had not understood much of Rachel's speech. "Rachel talk much," she said.

"How is the party going?" Mama had just appeared in the doorway.

Annalina smiled at Mama. "Presents nice."

"I'm glad you like them."

"Is it time for pie?" Carrie asked eagerly.

Rachel glanced at the clock. "It should be just about done."

Mama sniffed the air. "It doesn't smell like you're baking a pie."

Rachel's stomach sank. Mama was right. By now the house ought to be filled with the aroma of sweetened fruit. She jumped out of her chair and dashed into the kitchen.

Pulling the oven door open, she looked at her pie. It was formed perfectly. But it was still pasty white and raw. She groaned.

"I forgot to ask you to light the oven," she said to Mama. "It should have been baking all this time."

"I'll light the oven now," Mama offered.

"It's too late," Rachel said. "Annalina has to go home soon."

Carrie and Annalina came into the kitchen.

"What's wrong with the pie this time?" Carrie asked.

Rachel's face crumpled.

"The pie is perfect," Mama said, "it's just not baked."

"No pie?" Annalina asked, confused.

Rachel shook her head. "No pie." She opened the oven door and showed Annalina. Instantly, Annalina understood. She started giggling.

"Why are you laughing?" Rachel said. "I've ruined your party. We don't have a cake or a pie or anything."

Annalina giggled some more. Carrie started laughing, too. And then Mama started.

"What's so funny?" Rachel demanded.

"If this were a baseball game," Carrie said, "you'd be out on three strikes. This is the third pie you've made that no one got to eat."

Now Rachel started laughing. "Three strikes or not, I'm not quitting," she said. "Someday I will make a pie, and we will all eat it!"

Chapter 17

Friends at Last

Rachel arrived at the baseball field early. She was one of the first spectators to claim a seat, so she made herself comfortable on the wooden bench along the first-base line. She arranged her blue calico dress so that it fell evenly around her knees and ankles and tucked in her shawl so it would not flap in the breeze. Her hair, braided carefully that morning, featured matching white ribbon bows.

Rachel leaned forward to study the activities of the players. The Spitfires were warming up on the field, while the Oak Lake Boaters were having batting practice.

Gradually more people came to watch the game. A few parents settled themselves on benches or quilts in the grass. Many of the spectators were brothers and sisters of the players.

Out of the corner of her eye, Rachel saw Mariah Webster strolling across the field beside Beth. Rachel turned her head to watch them more closely. Usually Mariah and Beth and Phoebe came to baseball games with Katherine Jones. Katherine came to watch her brother Steve, but Katherine was not with Mariah today.

Mariah tossed her hair haughtily as she approached Rachel. The bench was empty except for Rachel, who sat perched at one end, but Mariah and Beth did not pause.

"Hello, Mariah. Hello, Beth," Rachel said in her sweetest voice. "It's a fine day for a game, don't you think?"

Mariah rolled her eyes. "I suppose." She kept walking right past Rachel. Without speaking to Rachel, Beth followed Mariah to a patch of grass behind first base. There they put their heads together and giggled.

Rachel was determined not to be annoyed. She turned her attention back to the field.

Sam fielded a ball Seth had tossed toward him. In one smooth motion, Sam scooped it out of the dirt, twisted, and snapped the ball to Jim, waiting on first base. Jim grinned and delivered the ball to Simon on the pitcher's mound.

Abe signaled that the team should gather together. With his arms around the shoulders of Sam and Larry, Seth smiled proudly at all the Spitfires.

"You boys have been working very hard," he said. "In a few minutes, all your hard work is going to pay off."

"That's right," Elwood said. "The Oak Lake Boaters will not even know what hit them."

"Simon and Jim," Seth said, "do you remember the play we went over?"

Simon nodded enthusiastically. "If I see a runner taking a lead off of first base, I fire at Jim."

"And I keep my foot on the base so I'm always ready," Jim added. "We won't let any base runners get past us."

"Joe and Sam, are you ready for the double-play balls?" Seth asked.

"Better than ever," Sam answered.

"And you've all been working on your swings. Keep your eye on the ball and stay steady."

Hank and Elwood practiced swinging imaginary bats.

"Hey," Hank said, "where's Steve? We need him to help cover the outfield."

The whole team turned to scan the playing field.

"There he is," Larry called out, pointing at left field.

Rachel saw Steve trotting across the field with Katherine dragging behind him.

"Sorry I'm late!" Steve called out.

"We're just glad you're here," Jim said. "We need everybody today."

"Let's play ball!" Seth said, clapping his hands. The team scattered to take their positions.

Katherine hurried to get out of the way of the players. "Hi, Katherine!" Rachel called. "Come sit with me."

Mariah and Beth burst into laughter. "Of course she's not going to sit with you," Mariah said. "What makes you think such a thing? Come on, Katherine, there's plenty of room for you over here."

Rachel paid no attention to Mariah. She kept her eyes fixed on Katherine, whose steps were slowing down.

"I'd like to hear about your aunt's engagement party," Rachel said. "I'm sure everyone loved the dress you wore."

Katherine hesitated for just a moment. Then she turned her steps toward Rachel. She came and sat on the bench. Rachel could hear Mariah gasp in the background.

"Don't pay any attention to her," Rachel advised.

"I won't," Katherine said. "I should have stopped following Mariah Webster around a long time ago."

"How was the engagement party?"

"It was nice. There were lots of sweet cakes and punch. But I kept wishing I was at Annalina's birthday party."

"Really and truly?"

"Really and truly. You're right about Annalina. She's nice. I like her. I'm sorry for making fun of her."

"She'll be glad to hear that," Rachel said. "She's supposed to meet me here later."

Katherine turned her eyes to the field. "It looks like the game is about to start."

Rachel turned toward the field as well. She saw that Simon was studying the batter. With his left arm, he leaned on his knee. His right arm, with the ball in his hand, was tucked behind his back. Finally, he stood up straight, wound up, and threw the first pitch of the game.

It was a strike, straight and true. The batter swung and missed. The ball smacked into the hands of Tad Leland, the catcher. With a whoop, Tad threw the ball back to Simon.

From the sideline, Seth caught Simon's eye. Rachel held her breath as Simon nodded, indicating he had understood Seth's secret message. Simon got ready for the next pitch. The batter swung again, scraping the top of the ball with his bat and sending it dribbling into the infield. Sam easily stopped the rolling ball and threw it to Jim before the batter could get to first base.

Seth paced along the sideline, clapping his hands. "That's the way to do it, boys!"

"It looks like they're off to a good start," Katherine commented. "Steve was a little worried on the way over here."

"That's because they lost so badly the last time," Rachel said. "Simon wasn't here to hurl. But with Simon pitching and Jim Harrison playing first base, the other team doesn't have a chance."

Katherine smiled. "I hope you're right. But it's only the first inning."

"Go Spitfires!" Rachel shouted.

"Beat the Boaters!" screamed a voice just behind her. Rachel turned to see Mariah Webster standing behind the bench. Rachel stared up at Mariah with questions in her eyes.

"The ground is cold," Mariah said. "You said there was plenty of room on the bench."

"There still is."

Katherine scooted closer to Rachel. Mariah and Beth sat down.

"If you're going to sit here," Katherine said, "you have to promise not to be mean."

Mariah tilted her head, puzzled.

"I don't want you saying anything nasty about Annalina or Rachel or anybody."

Mariah didn't seem to know what to say. "I promise," she finally said.

"Here comes Annalina!" Rachel cried. "We have room on the bench for one more, don't we?"

"Of course!" Katherine responded.

But Annalina wasn't alone. Colleen and Janie were with her.

Annalina's steps slowed as she approached the first-base line. Now she stopped. She caught Rachel's eyes with her own worried ones.

Rachel waved to Annalina. "It's all right, Annalina. Come and sit with us."

Annalina did not move.

"What's the matter with her?" Mariah asked.

Katherine scowled. "Would you want to come and sit with people who have been as mean to you as we've been to her?"

Mariah hung her head. "No, I guess not."

Biting her lower lip, Annalina looked from Rachel to Katherine to Mariah. She still did not move her feet.

Rachel waved her arm in a big circle. "Come on, Annalina,

Colleen, Janie. Come and sit."

Colleen and Janie took seats on the bench. Still Annalina did not move.

Katherine stood up. "I'm going to get her."

Rachel grinned and watched. Katherine marched over to Annalina and took the Swedish girl by the hand. She pulled so hard that Annalina had no choice but to follow. Katherine led Annalina to the bench and pointed to the open spot between Mariah and Beth. Gingerly, Annalina sat down. She looked around nervously.

"It's all right," Katherine said. "We want to be your friends."

"Friends?"

"Yes, friends, just like Rachel is your friend."

"Rachel is friend."

"Yes, Rachel is your friend. And so am I."

Annalina smiled nervously. Katherine glared at Mariah and Beth.

Awkwardly, Mariah leaned over and put a hand on Annalina's shoulder. "Sit with us whenever you want to. We're glad to have you."

Confused, Annalina turned to Rachel for reassurance.

Rachel was smiling so big she could hardly talk. "It's all right, Annalina. It's not a trick. We all want you to sit with us, to be our friend." It felt right. Her old friends had joined with her new friend. Now they were all just friends, the way it should be.

The crack of a bat made them turn their heads back to the game. The ball sailed to center field. Steve Jones was under it and snatched it out of the air.

Chapter 18

Peace in the Family

Carrie twirled to make her pink dress spin. "Do you like my pretty dress, Papa?" she asked.

"You look spectacular." Papa sat on the sofa in the living room, Rachel next to him, and Sam in the chair across from him.

"I didn't get to wear my new Easter dress to Aunt Linda's for Easter dinner, so I decided to wear it today."

"You made a good choice," Papa said.

Rachel watched Carrie's spinning dress and thought of her own new sapphire cloak. It had not survived the Easter Sunday riot as well as Carrie's dress had. She only got to wear the new cloak one day. Then it was so tattered that it went straight to the rag pile. Still, Rachel was happy that Carrie was enjoying her new dress.

"Are Uncle Ernest and Uncle Stanley going to argue?" Carrie asked somberly. "Are they going to shout and be mad like they were when they were here?"

Papa pulled Carrie onto his knee. "I can't promise you what anyone will do. But I do think Stanley and Ernest are trying to get along better these days."

"The strike is over, so they don't have to fight about that," Carrie said.

Papa nodded.

"Freddy says that his papa quarrels with Uncle Ernest all the time."

"I don't think they quarrel all the time," Papa said slowly. "But they do have different opinions about many things."

"They can get along if they want to," Sam said. "Look at Jim and Simon. A couple weeks ago they were so angry they were hitting each other. But now they get along again."

"And Mariah and Annalina are starting to be friends," Rachel added. "Mariah thinks Annalina is really smart. Once she stopped making fun of her, she found out how much she likes Annalina."

"And Ernest and Stanley like each other, too," Papa said. "I'm sure of that. They've known each other for a long time."

"I'm glad we're going to have a family dinner to make up for Easter," Carrie said.

Mama entered the room. "Rachel, your pie is ready to come out of the oven. As soon as you wrap it up, we can be on our way to the Stockards'."

Sam snickered. "Are we going to get to eat this pie, Rachel?"

"This pie is perfect," Rachel declared. "I was very careful with the recipe."

A few minutes later, the Borland family was walking down the street, laden with their part of the family dinner. Rachel, of course, carried her cherry pie carefully and proudly. It was wrapped in two towels to keep it extra safe. Carrie swung a basket of biscuits, Sam lugged a sack of potatoes, Papa had the corn pudding, and Mama had the apple pie.

"Are we going to ride a streetcar?" Carrie asked.

"Here comes one now," Sam said.

"It's Mr. Lawrence's car." Rachel waved her arm to signal that the car should stop for them.

They clambered aboard and settled into seats right behind Mr. Lawrence.

"How are you all?" Turning to Sam and nudging the horses forward, Mr. Lawrence said, "I hear you hit quite a long ball against the Oak Lake team."

Sam smiled proudly. "It was a triple. Two runs scored on my hit."

"How is Mrs. Lawrence?" Mama asked.

"Well, it seems as though she has turned the corner. She's doing much better, thank you." Glancing at Rachel, he added, "I suppose Janie will have more free time for recipe swapping."

Rachel smiled. "Well, the last time we tried it things didn't go so well. I'm willing to try again."

"Why are you carrying around half a market?" Mr. Lawrence asked, eyeing their food.

"We're going to have Easter dinner," Carrie explained.

Mr. Lawrence chuckled. "Well, that's a fine idea. There was quite a bit of excitement that day, wasn't there?"

"We're going to the Stockards'," Carrie said.

"Ah, yes, I hear their son Seth is coaching your team," Mr. Lawrence said to Sam. When he saw the puzzled expression on Sam's face, he laughed. "When you drive a streetcar you hear all kinds of things."

They got off the streetcar in front of the Stockards' house. Carrie scampered up the steps and knocked on the door ahead of the rest of them. When it opened, she hurtled through, calling for Freddy.

Aunt Linda stood in the open doorway with Aunt Agnes right behind her. They both laughed at Carrie. Mama shook her head.

"When she gets excited," Mama said, "there's just nothing I can do to control her."

"Is everyone here?" Rachel asked.

Aunt Linda nodded. "Molly and Miranda are upstairs. No doubt they're talking about their latest beaus. Seth and Gage are out back in Seth's old lab."

"What about Uncle Ernest—and Uncle Stanley?" Rachel was almost too nervous to ask.

"Hmm," Aunt Linda said, puzzled. "I'm not sure where they disappeared to."

"These potatoes are heavy," Sam complained.

Aunt Linda took them from him. "Let's put the food in the kitchen. Rachel, your pie smells delicious. I can't wait to taste it."

Rachel and Mama followed Aunt Linda into the kitchen, where Aunt Agnes was stirring her currant glaze in a pan on top of the stove. She smiled to welcome them.

"The ham smells wonderful!" Rachel said as she set her pie down on the table and began unwrapping it.

Aunt Agnes bent over and peeked at the ham in the oven. "It will be done in just a few minutes."

"I'll start peeling potatoes." Mama took the sack from Aunt Linda.

"Agnes," Aunt Linda said, "do you know what happened to Stanley?"

"He was headed for the study the last time I saw him," Aunt Agnes replied.

Aunt Linda raised her eyebrows. "Ernest's study?"

"Yes."

"Ernest was in there reading the last time I saw him."

Mama and Rachel exchanged a worried glance.

Aunt Linda read their minds. "Perhaps I'll just go check and see how things are in the study."

"I'll go with you," Rachel said.

As they approached the open study door, they heard rising voices.

"What on earth made you think to do such a thing?" Uncle Stanley exclaimed.

"I'm simply using the mind that God gave me," Uncle Ernest answered. "I suggest you do the same."

"Oh, no!" Rachel said. By now, Mama and Aunt Agnes had heard the voices and followed them into the hallway. Papa and Sam left the living room and joined the growing huddle in the hall.

"Should we go in?" Mama asked.

"They have to work things out themselves," Aunt Linda insisted.

"They may need a little help." Papa stepped through the doorway. Then, he tilted his head back and roared with laughter.

"Papa, what is it?" Rachel asked anxiously.

Papa gestured that they should all come in. The two men sat across the desk from each other. Between them was a chessboard. Most of the white pieces had been captured, and the king was checkmated. Uncle Ernest had the smirk of victory on his face.

"We haven't been playing more than ten minutes," Uncle Stanley complained, "and already he's thrashed me."

Rachel laughed in relief.

Uncle Stanley pointed a finger at his brother-in-law. "This is not the end of it, my friend. I learn from my mistakes. You will not win so easily the next time."

"We all learn from our mistakes," Uncle Ernest said quietly. "Let us pray that the city of Minneapolis—even the whole country—can learn from its mistakes."

Uncle Stanley nodded. "This nation has too much potential not to learn from its mistakes. If Jim Hill can build a railroad that reaches all the way to the West Coast, the rest of us can learn to solve our problems together."

Uncle Ernest chuckled. "May I remind you that Jim Hill has not reached the West Coast yet?"

Uncle Stanley grinned in response. "It won't be long, now."

Rachel caught Sam's eye and saw the smile on his face. The two men were bantering the way they always had. But the lightness in their tone and the twinkle in their eyes made everyone relax.

"I'd better get back to the potatoes," Mama said.

"Oh, the glaze is probably boiling by now," Aunt Agnes added.

"Rachel, I'm saving room for a piece of your pie," Uncle Stanley put in.

Rachel smiled. "I'm afraid it's only one pie. It's not enough for fourteen people." She turned and headed for the kitchen.

"Well, I'm having a piece," Sam declared. "After all, you've made four pies and we haven't gotten to eat any of them yet."

"This pie made it all the way over here, safe and sound." Rachel pushed open the kitchen door. "As soon as dinner's over—"

White-faced, Rachel gasped and spun around to Sam.

"What is it?" Sam pushed past his sister and burst into the kitchen.

Freddy and Carrie sat at the table with cherries smeared on their faces and soiled forks in their hands.

"We were hungry," Freddy explained.

Rachel was too shocked to speak. Her beautiful pie was half-eaten. The remaining half was so crumbled that no one would want to eat it.

Sam roared with laughter. "I guess I'll have to wait for pie number five!"

Emily Makes a Difference

JoAnne A. Grote

A Note to Readers

The Allerton and Kerr families are fictional, but the events they find themselves in actually happened. During 1893, the United States celebrated the four hundredth anniversary of Columbus arriving in America. A huge world's fair in Chicago was dedicated in 1892 and opened to visitors in 1893. One of the major attractions was the first Ferris wheel, which towered over everything else on the grounds.

But many people weren't in the mood for a party. One of the worst financial disasters to ever hit the United States threw hundreds of thousands of people out of work. Banks closed. Railroads went out of business. People faced starvation. And in Minneapolis, a major fire destroyed businesses and homes.

The idea that Emily and Ted think of to help so many poor families actually was thought of by children in Minneapolis at the time. They played a large role in making adults aware of how big the problem of hunger in their city was.

To Donna Winters, friend and fellow writer.
Thank you for your assistance in researching
the Columbian Exposition.

Contents

Chapter 1

Danger at the Bank

Twelve-year-old Emily Allerton leaned close to her cousin Ted Kerr, who shared the double wooden school desk. "What do you think the teachers keep meeting about?" she whispered in his ear.

Ted's almost-black eyes turned toward tall, lanky Mr. Evans and short, stout Mr. Timms where they stood in the doorway. Mr. Evans shoved his round, wire-rimmed glasses up his skinny nose, all the time whispering furiously to Mr. Timms. Mr. Timms pressed his lips tightly together and shook his head, his round cheeks bouncing.

"I don't know," Ted whispered back. "This is the third time Mr. Evans has come to our room this morning."

One of Mr. Evans's long arms shot out, and he pounded a fist in the air between himself and Mr. Timms. His pointed chin stuck out defiantly. Emily couldn't hear everything he said, but one phrase reached her ears.

She whipped her head toward Ted. He stared back at her, his eyes as wide as she knew her own must be.

"Did he say 'Farmers' and Mechanics' Bank'?" she asked.

Ted nodded. "That's where Uncle Enoch works."

"Why would Mr. Evans be upset about the bank?"

"I heard Father and Mother talking after church yesterday about the bank. They said there was a rumor in the city that the bank doesn't have enough money."

"How can a bank not have enough money? Doesn't money come from banks?"

Ted shrugged, his shoulders lifting the brown jacket that covered his white shirt with its round collar. "I don't know, but the rumor said the bank was going to close."

Fear tightened Emily's stomach. "Will Uncle Enoch lose his job?"

Ted rolled his eyes. "Uncle Enoch isn't going to lose his job. It's just a rumor. Father says the bank is solid as rock."

"Whew." Emily's stomach felt normal again. She'd heard her parents talk about hard times in the country. Money was tight and people were losing their jobs. She didn't want Uncle Enoch to be one of those people.

The lunch bell rang, cutting off her thoughts. Mr. Evans dashed away. The students rushed toward the door, eager for the freedom of the lunch period and a chance to talk and laugh with their friends.

In the crowded hallway, Emily saw Mr. Evans again. He was shoving his black bowler hat over his straight, dark hair and pushing his way through the students. *Where is he going?* she wondered. The teachers usually ate with the students and made sure the children didn't get too rowdy.

"Hi, Emily. Want to eat lunch together?"

Emily turned to her fourteen-year-old sister, Anna. "Sure." She immediately forgot all about Mr. Evans.

Half an hour after lunch, the principal came into the room and whispered in Mr. Timms's ear. Emily turned to Ted again. "This is getting stranger and stranger."

Mr. Timms shook his round head as the principal left the room. With a sigh, he turned toward the class. "Will all of you please move closer together in your seats? Mr. Evans hasn't returned from lunch. His business must have taken longer than he planned. Some of his students will be joining us until he returns."

Mr. Evans's class began filing into the room as Mr. Timms finished explaining. Emily scooted closer to Ted.

"You're right," he whispered. "This is strange."

Emily didn't like being crowded in between Ted and the blond-haired boy from Mr. Evans's class. *It's only until Mr. Evans returns,* she reminded herself.

But Mr. Evans didn't return.

After school, Anna told them that her teacher, too, had left for lunch and not returned. "Another teacher, Miss Truman, told me that my teacher and some others went to the Farmers' and Mechanics' Bank at lunchtime. They were going to take out all the money they had at the bank."

"Why?" Emily asked. "Are they going to buy something with it?"

Anna shook her head. The brown curls so like Emily's brushed the shoulders of Anna's blue school dress. "No. They want to take their money out because they don't think the bank is a safe place to keep it anymore. Miss Truman says there's a run on the bank."

A chill shivered up Emily's spine. "A run," she repeated. She didn't truly understand what a run was. All she knew was that she'd heard her parents and Uncle Enoch talk about runs that happened on other banks. When there were runs on banks, people who kept their money in the banks lost their savings, and people who worked at the banks lost their jobs.

"Mother and Father keep their savings at that bank," she said to Anna. "Uncle Enoch works there. Wouldn't he have told them if their money wasn't safe?"

"I'm sure he would have." Anna's voice sounded positive, but her eyes looked troubled.

Anna left to walk home with a friend, and Emily went looking for Ted. They were cousins, but they'd also been best friends all their lives. She told him what Anna had said about the bank.

Ted drew his eyebrows together in a frown beneath his red hair. "Let's go down by the bank and see whether Anna is right. Maybe it's only another rumor that there's a run on the bank."

Emily and Ted had strict orders to go straight home from school each day, but she didn't think twice before agreeing.

When they reached Fourth Street where the bank stood, they couldn't see the doors and windows of the buildings for all the people.

"We'll never get close to the bank in this crowd," Ted complained. He climbed up on a bench that stood beneath a streetlamp. "Maybe I can see what's going on from up here."

Emily climbed right up behind him. She stared in amazement. "So this is what a bank run looks like."

"Looks like a sea of men's suit coats and hats to me," Ted said. They were across the street from the bank. "There's hardly an inch of space between the people."

"I don't think the trolley car can move." Emily pointed at the top of the colorful car that stood in the middle of the street.

She didn't stare at it long. The bank was what interested her. There were three huge, round-topped archways two or three stories high across the front of the tall stone building. The entryway through the middle arch was mobbed with men.

A man with a large camera jumped up on the bench beside them. Emily gasped and grabbed the light post. Ted grabbed onto Emily with one hand and the hat covering his red hair with the other.

The man didn't seem bothered by the rocking bench. He pointed the large black box toward the bank and waited until the bench stilled. *Pouf!* A small black cloud appeared as he snapped his shot.

Ted peered around Emily, squinting. "You a newspaper man, mister?"

The man grinned at him and winked. "Yep. I'm a photographer for the Minneapolis *Tribune*."

"The people in the bank's doorway don't seem to be moving," Emily said. "Do you know why not?"

The photographer nodded sharply. "That's because inside the bank, people are packed as solidly as they are out here in the street."

Emily looked back at the bank building. "It doesn't seem like any bank in the world could have enough money to pay all these people in one day."

The photographer grunted as he jumped down from the bench. "This one might not have enough, either. A bank down the street had a run this morning. Closed their doors at noon when they ran out of money."

Emily thought his voice sounded awfully cheerful to be telling such bad news. She watched, amazed, as the young man started off through the crowd with a bounce in his step and a whistle on his lips.

"Do you see either of our fathers?" she asked Ted.

He shook his head. "Not a chance of seeing them in this crowd."

"I hope they got our families' savings out. It would be awful if the bank paid out all its money before our fathers got here."

"Maybe we'd better get home and make sure they know about the run." Ted jumped down from the bench. Emily was right behind him.

They tried to hurry through the crowd, but hurrying was impossible. "I think I've said 'Excuse me, please' one hundred times in the last twenty feet," Emily complained.

Ted grinned. "I quit after the first dozen. No one seemed to be paying any attention to us anyway."

A few feet farther along, a tall man with a gray handlebar mustache stopped a younger man with a brown mustache that turned down along the sides of his wide mouth. "Hi ya, Fred. Are ya here to get yer money out of the bank?"

Fred gave his friend a grin. "Well, I came to get my money out, but a funny thing happened. I was in the lobby of the bank and feeling like a sardine squeezed into a can for all the people. Then a fellow pokes me in the arm and says, 'Mister, I'll give you fifty dollars for your place in line.' "

"Did you give it to him?" the friend asked.

"For fifty dollars? You betcha!" Fred chuckled. "I only have thirty dollars in my savings account. I figured I'd made good money for the day. I been standing in this crowd since ten this morning trying to get into that bank. I took the fifty dollars, and I'm going home."

Emily and Ted exchanged looks. Emily thought Ted looked as worried as she felt. Imagine paying someone fifty dollars just for his place in line! Things must be even worse than she'd thought.

Slowly they continued making their way through the crowd. As they walked farther from the bank, the number of people thinned. Soon they could walk easily along the boardwalk without bumping into people.

Ted hurried across the street. Emily followed, dodging business wagons with tall, white, wooden covers. Names like "Hodge's Emporium," "Olsen's Meat Market," "Himmelsback's Furniture," and "Zuckerman's Dry Goods" were painted in large letters on the sides of the wagons.

"Yuck!" She jumped to one side just in time to miss a smelly pile left by one of the horses pulling a wagon.

Watching the road carefully for more piles, she caught the heel of her shoe in the rail for the trolley cars. "Oof!" She landed flat on her face in the street, her shoe still caught by the rail and her foot stuck in her shoe. She tried to push herself up but couldn't. She couldn't even breathe.

I just knocked the air out of my lungs, she thought. *I'll be all right in a minute.* She fought down her fear, trying to stay calm even though her chest and throat ached from lack of air.

Suddenly she became aware of a familiar clanging sound. A trolley car bell! She twisted her head. A trolley car was only a block away and headed right for her.

Her gaze darted toward Ted. He had reached the other side of the street and was starting down the boardwalk. He hadn't even noticed that she wasn't beside him.

She opened her mouth, gasping for air, and struggled to sit up. The clanging grew louder. She glanced in its direction. Fear spun through her. The trolley was almost on top of her!

Chapter 2

The Accident

From behind, strong hands grabbed her beneath her shoulders and tugged. Emily's foot wouldn't budge from the rail. "My foot!"

The bell's clang and the clatter of the wheels of the electric trolley car banged in her ears like cymbals. She turned her head away from the trolley barreling toward her. She felt a hand on her ankle. With a strong jerk, her foot was free.

"Ugh!" She heard a groan burst from the person who yanked at her arms, pulling her—almost throwing her—from the path of the trolley.

Emily could feel the wind created by the trolley car as it whizzed by. "Thank you, God," she whispered.

"Are you all right?" a boy's voice asked.

She looked up. A boy about her age with straight, dark brown hair beneath a brown bicycle hat stared down at her with dark eyes. His face was tanned, but his lips looked almost white. She wondered if that was because he'd been afraid, too. "Are you. . . are you the one who helped me?" she asked in a shaky voice.

He nodded. "Are you hurt?"

Emily wasn't sure. She ached everywhere. Her ankle hurt, and she wondered whether she had twisted it. Her arms felt like they'd almost been pulled from her body when the boy grabbed her. The palms of her hands smarted from the gravel that had been driven into them when she fell. Still, she wasn't hurt so badly that she needed a doctor. "I. . .I'll be all right."

Suddenly Ted loomed over her. "Are you all right? I turned around just in time to see this guy pull you out from in front of the trolley."

"I'm all right," she repeated. She glanced up at the boy. "Thank you. I guess you about saved my life."

Ted looked at the boy with admiration shining from his eyes. "That was mighty brave of you."

The boy stood up and kicked at a pebble with the toe of a worn shoe. "Aw, it wasn't so much. Anybody would have done the same thing."

"Not anybody," Ted said. "Plenty of people wouldn't have risked their life for someone else like that, especially for someone they didn't know."

The boy held out his hand. "I'm Erik Moe."

Ted shook his hand. "Ted Kerr."

"I'm Emily Allerton, Ted's cousin."

Erik grinned. "So now we know each other, and we're not strangers anymore, so you can quit gushing all over yourselves thanking me."

They all laughed.

Emily tried to stand up, pushing against the paved street with her scraped hands. "Oooh!" Her ankle buckled, setting her down hard.

Ted and Erik both grabbed for her. "Is it your ankle?" Erik asked.

Emily nodded, holding her ankle above the buttoned shoe. She bit her bottom lip and blinked hard, trying to keep back the tears in her eyes.

"Is it broken?" Ted knelt down and tried to feel it. "Move your hand, Emily, and let me see."

Emily didn't move her hand. "I'm sure it's not broken. I think it's only twisted. It will be all right in a few minutes."

A wagon rumbled by. The horse pulling it snorted in their direction.

"You can't keep sitting in the street," Erik said. "How about if we help you over to the boardwalk?"

With one of the boys on each side of her, Emily made her way to the boardwalk, trying not to cry out at the pain in her ankle. She was glad to sit on the edge of the boardwalk with her feet in the street and lean against the bottom of a telegraph pole.

She glanced back at the tracks where she'd fallen. "My schoolbooks!"

"I'll get them." Ted hurried across the busy street. He was back in a minute with the books. "Your geography book looks all right, but I think you'll need a new arithmetic book." He held it up. The trolley's wheels had completely destroyed it.

"You should be more careful crossing the trolley tracks," Erik said.

His scolding tone embarrassed Emily. "I was watching where I was going. The heel of my shoe got caught in the track. I couldn't help that, could I?"

Ted nudged her shoulder. "If it weren't for Erik, your leg would be smashed like your arithmetic book."

She wrinkled her nose at him.

Erik set down the bag he'd been carrying slung over one shoulder. He leaned against the telegraph pole and looked down at her. His brown eyes were serious. "Trolley tracks can be as dangerous as railroad tracks. You have to be careful around them. My pa worked for the railroad. He saw a lot of people hurt there. He. . . he even lost four fingers off one of his hands in an accident at the railroad yard near here."

Emily saw pain flash through Erik's eyes as he told of his father's accident. Ted exclaimed, "That's rough!" then murmured, "I'm sorry, Erik."

Hearing about Erik's father made Emily suddenly ashamed of the way she'd snapped at him a moment ago. "I'm sorry, too. You were right about the trolley tracks being dangerous. I'll be more careful after this."

"My father works for the railroad, too," Ted said. "He's an engineer for the Great Northern Railroad."

"Has he ever been hurt in an accident?" Erik asked.

Ted shook his head. "No, but I always worry about him when he's working."

Emily glanced at him in surprise. "You never told me that!"

Ted shrugged. "Lots of people are killed in railroad accidents each year, both railroad workers and passengers. Father has been in some accidents, but only small ones. No one has ever been killed on any of the trains he was driving."

"What railroad does your father work for?" Emily asked Erik. Lots of different railroad companies had stations in Minneapolis.

Erik plunged his hands into the pockets of his worn brown corduroy trousers. The wooden boardwalk thunked as he knocked the heel of his shoe against the side of it. "He doesn't work for any railroad anymore. The railroad he was with is having hard times, so they fired some of their workers. Since Pa lost all the fingers on one hand and only has a thumb left, he was one of the first people the company fired."

He kicked the boardwalk again, so hard that Emily could feel the boards beneath her bounce slightly. "He'd been with the company fifteen years, and they threw him away like a piece of garbage."

The bitterness in his voice made Emily uncomfortable.

"That's tough," Ted said in a low voice. He cleared his throat. "Uh, what kind of accident was your father in when he lost his fingers?"

"He didn't lose all of them in one accident. He was a brakeman."

Emily and Ted glanced at each other. "It takes courage to be a brakeman," she said. Lots of brakemen lost fingers, Emily knew. Sometimes they lost entire hands or even their lives.

Erik flashed her a look of gratitude. "Pa lost two fingers in an accident three years ago, but he could still work. He lost the other two this winter."

"Was he trying to use the coupler?" Ted asked.

Erik nodded. "The last time, he was trying to attach a boxcar to the train with the link-and-pin coupler. He was standing between the cars, like the brakemen always do when they're attaching cars. He was steering the iron link into the socket so he could drop in the pin that held the cars together. But the boxcar was moved at the wrong moment, and his fingers were crushed in the link-and-pin coupler."

Emily blinked back tears at the thought of what it must have been like for Erik to have his father lose his fingers. "My father is a doctor," she said. "He's seen a lot of accidents like your father's. Too many, he says."

Erik's brown eyes grew darker with anger. "Everybody says there's too many accidents, but no one does anything about it."

Ted and Emily glanced at each other but said nothing. What could they say? Erik was right.

Ted cleared his throat. "Where does your father work now?"

Erik stared at the road. "Nowhere. He hasn't been able to find a job because of the hard times." He nodded at the bag at his feet. "That's why I had to quit school and go to work as a newsboy."

Emily couldn't imagine needing to quit school to make money

for her family. She knew there were children who had to do that, but she didn't know any. She thought it must be scary.

"Is your ankle feeling any better?" Erik asked.

"It still throbs," she said. "My shoe feels tighter than before."

Ted's eyebrows drew together in a frown. "That's not a good sign. Maybe your foot is swollen. Can you stand on it?"

He and Erik each took one of her arms and helped her stand. She held her breath as she put her weight on her injured foot. "Oooh!"

The boys' hands tightened on her arms.

"We'd better help you home," Ted said.

Erik nodded.

"You don't have to help, Erik," Emily said. "You have to sell your papers. I've kept you from your work too long already."

"That's all right," Erik answered. "It'll take you and Ted hours if you try to walk leaning on him."

Erik slung his bag over his shoulders. Ted put Emily's schoolbooks with his and fastened his book strap around them. Then he and Erik made a chair with their arms for Emily.

Emily still thought it took a long time to get home. The boys had to stop and rest a few times along the way. The closer they got to the house, the more Emily dreaded reaching it.

She glanced down at the ruffle that ran along the bottom of her green dress, just below her knees. It dangled below the hem now. The white stocking that came up over her knee was torn, and her leg and knee were scraped like the palms of her hand. "Mother will be upset about the dress," she said to Ted.

He laughed. "You are always doing something to upset your mother."

"I bet she'll be so glad you weren't hit by the trolley car that she won't be upset at all," Erik told her.

She shook her head. "You don't know my mother. She'll say,

'Emily Marie Allerton, why must you act so impulsively? Young ladies cross streets carefully and slowly. Why can't you be more like your sister, Anna?' "

Erik smiled at Emily's tone.

Ted laughed. "She sounds just like her mother," he told Erik.

Emily glanced at Erik and bit back a groan. How could she have let Erik help her home? Her parents and Ted's parents had warned them many times not to have anything to do with the city's newsboys. The adults thought the newsboys tough and were sure they would drag well-raised children into trouble.

Emily took a deep breath as the boys carried her up the front steps and across the wide wooden porch to the door of her house. Her parents weren't going to like a newsboy coming to their house with her and Ted!

Chapter 3

The Surprise

"Whatever happened to you, Emily?" Mother rushed out of the parlor and down the hallway toward the front door when the children entered the house.

"I hurt my ankle," Emily said. Ted and Erik set Emily down on one of the bottom steps of the stairway leading to the upstairs.

"I'd better go," Erik said. "See ya." He lifted a hand in a small wave and backed toward the front door. He nodded at Emily's mother, touching his fingers to the brim of his bicycle hat. "Ma'am." A second later he was outside and closing the door.

Mother frowned after him. "Have I met him before?"

"I don't think so," Ted said. "We just met him today."

Emily groaned and darted Ted a sharp glance. Surely he knew better than to say that! Her mother was going to be upset enough when she discovered Erik was a newsboy.

"Where did you meet him?" Mother asked.

"When I hurt my ankle." Emily leaned down and rubbed her ankle, groaning slightly.

As she'd hoped, her mother forgot about Erik instantly. She knelt in front of Emily and began unbuttoning the shoe. "What happened?"

Emily's father and Ted's parents came out of the parlor as Emily started to tell the story.

When Emily told of catching her heel on the rail, Mother sighed. "Emily Marie Allerton, why must you act so impulsively? Why can't you be more feminine, like your sister, Anna? Young ladies cross streets slowly and cautiously. They don't race across like boys. And just look what you did to your pretty new school dress."

Emily glanced at Ted and tried not to groan. Ted put his fist up to his face and gave a funny little cough. Emily knew he was trying not to laugh. She looked away to keep from laughing herself and continued her story.

When she told of Erik pulling her to safety, her mother asked, "Is that the boy who came home with you?"

Emily nodded. "He probably saved my life, or at least my leg."

"Yes, he probably did," her father said, kneeling in front of her. "We'll have to thank him properly." He ran experienced fingers lightly over her ankle. "Swollen but not broken. It will likely hurt for a few days. I'll bandage it so it will be easier to walk on. Marcia," he turned to his wife, "could you get some ice? It might be too late to stop the swelling, but we can try it."

Mother hurried down the hallway and through a swinging door into the kitchen.

Father helped Emily into the parlor, where she sat in his favorite stuffed chair, which was covered in green velvet, and rested her foot on a matching footstool. In a few minutes, Mother was back with a chunk of ice wrapped in a linen towel.

Emily flinched when her father pressed the cold towel against her ankle. "It will help," he said, holding it in place.

Mother stood behind him, shaking her head.

Ted's mother came to stand beside her. "Tell us more about this brave lad who helped you."

Emily was glad Aunt Alison had changed the subject from Emily's shortcomings, though she was sure her mother wouldn't think Erik so brave when she discovered he was a newsboy. She wished her own mother were more like Aunt Alison. Her aunt never got as upset as her mother over the small scrapes Emily and Ted's impulsive acts got them into.

Before she could say anything, Ted jumped in eagerly and told how Erik had risked his own safety to help Emily.

"I wish he would have stayed so we could thank him in person," Mother said.

Emily glanced at her in pleased surprise. "He's very nice."

"Even though he is a newsboy," Ted added.

Mother's face swung toward Ted. "A newsboy?"

Emily leaned her head against the back of the chair and closed her eyes.

"What were you two doing with a newsboy?" Mother asked.

Ted fidgeted, shifting his weight from one foot to the other. "We weren't with him when Emily fell. We didn't even know him until afterward. He helped Emily even though he didn't know her."

"That was brave and honorable of him," Emily's father said, "but you know we don't want you making friends with newsboys."

"Yes, sir," Emily muttered.

"That goes for you, too, Theodore," Aunt Alison said.

"Yes, ma'am," Ted muttered.

"Erik isn't a newsboy because he wants to be one," Emily told their parents. "He has to work because his father lost his job."

"That's right," Ted added from his seat in a tall-backed oak rocking chair on the other side of the room. He told how Erik's father lost his fingers and then his job.

"It's terrible that men like Erik's father have had to lose their fingers and their lives doing their jobs," Uncle Charles agreed.

"About twenty-five years ago, when I was younger than you, a man named Eli Hamilton Janney invented a new kind of coupler to connect railroad cars. It automatically connects, or couples, the cars when the cars are pushed together. It's much safer than the old way."

Ted's almost-black eyes flashed. "Then why don't the railroads use the new coupler?"

"The railroad companies thought it was too expensive to add to the railroad cars. Only the Pennsylvania Railroad used it. They thought it worked well. Then a few years ago, Iowa made a law that all railroads in Iowa had to use both Janney's coupler and a safer kind of brake called an air brake."

Emily sat up straighter. Anger, more powerful than the pain in her ankle, swirled through her chest. "I think it's *awful* railroads are more worried about money than about people like Erik's father! Why don't all railroads in all the states have to use the safest brakes and couplers?"

"Soon they will," Uncle Charles said. "The United States has a new organization called the Interstate Commerce Commission. It makes rules for companies that do business in more than one state. This spring they made a rule saying all railroads have to use Janney's coupler and the air brake."

"Hurrah!" Ted leaped to his feet. The chair rocked like a boat on one of Minnesota's wind-blown lakes.

His mother raised her eyebrows and shook her head. "Theodore, don't let the chair hit the wall."

Although Aunt Alison's words sounded like scolding and the children always knew she was serious when she called him Theodore, Emily could hear a laugh behind her aunt's voice.

While Ted slowed the chair's rocking and sat down again, Emily said, "I'm glad about the new rule, Uncle Charles, but the rule came too late for Erik's father."

"Yes," he admitted, "and that's a shame. But he probably helped get the new rule passed."

"How could he do that?" Ted asked.

"Yes, how?" Emily repeated. "He was only a brakeman, not a rich man."

"The brakemen have a union. Through the union, the brakemen work together to try to get railroads to do things in ways that make their work safer. The brakemen's union told the Interstate Commerce Commission how safe Janney's coupler is."

Ted frowned. "Is the brakemen's union like the railroad engineers' union that you belong to, Father?"

Uncle Charles nodded. "Yes. There are lots of different unions. There's a plumbers' union and a carpenters' union and a tailors' union. Each one tries to make working conditions better for their own kind of jobs."

"There are unions that try to help all working people, too, no matter what their jobs," Father told them, looking up from Emily's ankle, which he'd just finished wrapping in a bandage. "One is called the Knights of Labor. Another is the American Federation of Labor, which most people call the AFL."

"I've heard of them," Emily said.

Uncle Charles smiled at her. "In addition to trying to make work safer, they try to get better wages for their members—and shorter work hours. Those are some of the reasons your brother Walter thinks unions are so important, Ted."

Ted grinned. "Walter is always talking about unions and going to union meetings."

Father stood up. "Better wages and shorter hours are nice for the working men, but I think that helping make things safer is the most important work they do. I suppose that's because I'm a doctor and treat so many people hurt in unnecessary accidents. Some bosses make things as safe as they can for their workers without laws, but not all."

"That's right," Uncle Charles agreed. "The new law about couplers and air brakes will make trains safer for both workers and the people riding the trains. About 6,400 people were killed in railroad accidents last year, and almost 30,000 were injured."

"Wow!" Emily stared at Ted. His eyes were as big as hers felt. "No wonder the new rule was made."

"Sometimes people have to see how bad things are before they do something to change them," Father said.

"Erik's father isn't the only railroad man to lose his job this year," Uncle Charles said. "A number of railroads are declaring bankruptcy. They owe more money than they can make."

Ted stared at him. "Is. . .is your railroad in trouble?"

Ted's voice sounded high and tight. Emily felt suddenly sick to her stomach. Would Uncle Charles lose his job? What if Ted had to quit school and go to work like Erik?

Uncle Charles shook his head. "The Great Northern Railroad is in good shape. James Hill is too good a businessman to let the company get in trouble."

Emily's stomach felt instantly better, and she saw a grin on Ted's face. Then she remembered the bank run. She sat up with a jerk that bumped her sore ankle against the shoe on her other foot. She winced but ignored her pain in order to deliver her message. "We almost forgot to tell you why Ted and I were in such a hurry on our way home."

She and Ted interrupted each other again and again telling the story of the bank run.

"Have you talked to Uncle Enoch?" Ted asked when they were done.

"No," said Uncle Charles.

"No," Father added, "but—"

"Maybe you should take your money out of the bank and put it somewhere safe," Emily interrupted.

Father and Uncle Charles exchanged looks. "I think we'll wait until we talk with Enoch," Uncle Charles said slowly.

Father nodded.

Emily thought it looked like there was something almost like fright in their eyes, but she wasn't sure. She'd never seen any of their parents afraid before.

"But. . ." She licked her lips. Her parents usually didn't take advice from their children. She took a deep breath and started again. "What if all the bank's money is gone by the time you talk to Uncle Enoch? There were a lot of people there."

Ted sat on the edge of the rocker and nodded.

"I'm sure Enoch would have told us if our money wasn't safe," Father said with a small smile.

Is that a true smile, Emily wondered, *or a smile to make me and Ted feel better?*

Ted rubbed his hands over his knees. "Emily's right. You should talk to Uncle Enoch right away."

"We will, son," Uncle Charles said. "We promise."

"Enoch and his wife are joining us for dinner this evening," Mother said. "Your fathers can ask him about the bank then."

Emily and Ted glanced at each other. She wasn't at all sure that would be soon enough.

Aunt Alison stood up. "I'm tired of all this dreary talk. I think we could all use a dose of something more cheerful. Ted, Emily, I think Emily's parents have a surprise for you."

Emily looked at her mother expectantly.

"A surprise?" Ted's grin grew.

Father went to stand by the dainty upholstered chair where

Mother sat beside the fireplace doing needlework. He put his hand on her shoulder and asked, "What do you think? Should we tell them yet or make them wait?"

Mother put her needlework down and leaned her head to one side. She looked at Ted, then at Emily. "I'm not so sure. Perhaps they've had enough excitement for one day."

Emily could see her father's eyes sparkling with mischief. Excitement bubbled inside her. "Tell us now!"

Father laughed. "How would you two like to go to the fair?"

Emily frowned. "The state fair? That's not until fall."

Mother smiled.

Father shook his head. "Not the state fair. The World's Fair. The Columbian Exposition in Chicago."

Chapter 4

An Unexpected Meeting

The World's Fair? Oh, yes!" Emily grabbed the arms of the green velvet chair and pushed her feet from the footstool to stand up. "Ooooh!" She sank back down.

"Whoopee!" Ted leaped from his chair. It banged against the wall.

"Theodore!" Aunt Alison's voice held a sterner tone than usual. "If you let that chair hit the wall one more time, you will have to repaint and paper your aunt and uncle's parlor before you go to the fair—if we allow you to go at all."

Ted grabbed the arms of the chair, stopping it. "Yes, Mother." He couldn't stop grinning though. He knew his mother would never keep him away from something as important as the World's Fair. "When do we leave?"

"Not until after school lets out for the summer," Uncle Charles said.

Ted pretended to be disappointed.

Father laughed. "Besides, we have to wait until Emily's ankle is better. We'll be doing lots of walking at the fair. It's as big as a small town."

"Are Richard and Anna going, too?" Emily asked. It would be more fun with her sixteen-year-old brother and fourteen-year-old sister along. She was glad when Father said they would be going.

While their mothers prepared dinner and their fathers read the evening newspaper, Ted sat on the large velvet-covered footstool beside Emily, and they made plans for their trip. They were so excited about it that they completely forgot about Uncle Enoch and the bank run.

When Uncle Enoch and Aunt Tina arrived for dinner an hour later, Emily and Ted looked at each other. They both remembered the bank run.

Aunt Tina went into the kitchen with the other women. Uncle Enoch hung his stylish black bowler hat on the hat rack beside the other men's hats. Then he went to speak with Ted and Emily's fathers.

The men were across the room from Ted and Emily. They spoke in such low voices that the children could only hear a few words. The cousins stopped talking and tried to hear the men.

"We won't be able to take the trip if our fathers lose all their money," Emily whispered.

Ted didn't answer.

Finally, Uncle Charles looked over toward them. "You two may as well hear what your Uncle Enoch has to say, since you already know about the bank run."

The men moved closer so Emily wouldn't have to move with her sore ankle.

Uncle Enoch sat on the edge of the small beige and pink flowered chair Mother had sat on while doing her needlework. He looked very big on such a dainty chair, but it was the closest chair to Emily.

He leaned forward with an elbow on his good knee. The jacket of his business suit hung open. "The Farmers' and Mechanics' Bank, where I work, has more than enough money to pay all the people who keep their savings there." He held up his right hand, palm out. "I give you my word: Your parents' money is safe."

Emily wanted to believe him, but it was hard after seeing all those people at the bank earlier. She was glad when Ted asked, "Then why was there a run on your bank?"

Uncle Enoch spread his hands and lifted his eyebrows. "We aren't certain, but we have an idea. We think people mixed us up with another bank. The Farmers' and Merchants' Bank sounds a lot like my bank, the Farmers' and Mechanics' Bank, doesn't it?"

The two cousins nodded.

"Well," Uncle Enoch continued, "the other bank—the Farmers' and Merchants' Bank—had a run on it this morning. That bank hadn't as much money as we do in our vaults. They locked their doors at noon because they didn't have any more money to pay to the people who kept their savings at that bank."

"Why doesn't the bank have the people's money?" Emily asked.

"Yes, why?" Ted repeated. "When people put money in the bank, isn't the bank supposed to put their money in the vault to keep it safe until the people want it back?"

"Not exactly." Uncle Enoch pushed his round, wire-rimmed glasses into place. "When people put their money in the bank, they are called depositors. The bank pays depositors interest for putting their money in the bank."

Ted and Emily nodded.

"Why do you think the bank pays people for bringing their money to the bank?" Uncle Enoch asked.

Emily shook her head. "I don't know."

Ted frowned. "I don't know, either."

Uncle Enoch smiled. "The bank pays people interest for letting the bank use their money."

Surprise jerked Ted up straight. "You mean the bank doesn't keep the money in the safe?"

"Not all of it," Uncle Enoch said. "Much of it is loaned to people and businesses."

"Like when a man needs a loan to build a house?" Ted asked.

"Yes." Uncle Enoch smiled. "Or when a businessman needs a loan to add on to his business. When the bank loans someone money, *they* pay the *bank* interest."

"I see now!" Ted threw his hands in the air. "It's simple. The people with the loans pay the bank interest. Then the bank uses that money to pay interest to the depositors."

"That's right," Uncle Enoch agreed.

"I understand now," Emily said.

Uncle Enoch leaned forward to explain more. "When there's a run on a bank, like there was on our bank and the other bank today, it doesn't cause any trouble if the bank hasn't loaned out too much money. Understand?"

Ted and Emily nodded.

"What happens to the depositors who wanted to take their money back out of the other bank but couldn't get it today?" Ted asked.

"That depends," Uncle Enoch said. "If the people the bank loaned the money to pay it back, the bank can pay the depositors but not right away."

"What if the people with the loans don't pay back the bank?" Ted asked slowly.

"Then the depositors might lose their savings," Uncle Enoch said soberly.

"Are you sure the people *your* bank loaned money to will pay it back?"

Uncle Enoch nodded. "We believe most of them will. We're very careful about who we lend our depositors' money to."

"I hope so," Emily said, pointing a finger at Uncle Enoch and wiggling it playfully, "because I want to go to the World's Fair in Chicago!"

Ted and the men laughed. "Me, too," her father said, his eyes sparkling with laughter.

Ted and Emily hoped to leave for the fair as soon as school was out for the summer, but that didn't happen. They grew restless waiting for the end of July, when Father said they would leave.

In the meantime, they read everything they could find on the fair. The Minneapolis *Tribune* had many articles about it. Emily's brother and sister, Richard and Anna, and Emily's parents read the articles as eagerly as Ted and Emily. They spent many evenings in the Allerton parlor planning their trip and deciding which exhibits each most wanted to see.

"Can't we leave this week?" Emily asked at the end of one such evening. "This waiting is terrible. Why, I'm going to be an old maid before we get there!"

Everyone laughed.

Mother smiled primly. "Planning a trip is half the fun."

Emily and Ted exchanged exasperated looks.

Emily sighed and flopped down on her stomach in the middle of the flowered parlor rug, her arms folded across the newspaper where she had been reading about Minnesota's building at the fair.

"Do sit up, Emily," Mother said, shaking her head. "I wonder if I shall ever make a young lady of you. If you continue to flop around on the floor like a boy, you may be an old maid one day after all."

Emily sat up, the corners of her lips bent down and her cheeks red.

"At least there's the Hill parade later this week," Ted reminded Emily.

"Yes." Emily smiled at him, grateful that her cousin was trying to ease her embarrassment.

The parade was to celebrate the arrival of James Hill's Great Northern Railroad at Puget Sound on the Pacific coast. James Hill had started out as a young man in St. Paul, the sister city of Minneapolis. The two cities thought his accomplishment was their accomplishment, too.

"It sounds like the parade is going to be gigantic," Richard said. "One of the biggest affairs ever held in the Twin Cities."

"It should be." Father's newspaper crackled as he lowered it and looked at them over the top of it. "Mr. Hill is thought by many to be the greatest man in the United States."

"Not by Uncle Enoch," Emily reminded him. "Uncle Enoch thinks Mr. Hill takes foolish risks with his money."

Ted laughed. "He has a lot of money to take risks with. The newspaper says he has twenty-five million dollars."

"Someone with that much money could never go broke," Emily said.

Ted nodded, smiling.

Richard rested his elbows on his knees and spread his hands. "Still, hundreds of railroads are going broke this year. The panic is causing money trouble everywhere. And it must have cost James Hill a lot of money to build the railroad all the way from Minnesota to Puget Sound."

"People did call it Hill's Folly," Father agreed.

Emily glanced at Ted and noticed a frown on his face. Was he afraid that the Great Northern Railroad could be in trouble? What would happen to Ted if Uncle Charles lost his job?

That Saturday, Ted went to the railroad yard to meet his father and walk home from work with him. As he headed toward the yard, he remembered the conversation at the Allertons'. His stomach tightened. Angrily he pushed the scary thoughts away.

"Hey, there! Ted! Wait up!"

Ted turned at the call, glad to see Erik running toward him across the wooden platform in front of the station house. He dodged through the people who were always streaming from the large station. Erik carried his bicycle hat in one hand, and his straight brown hair flopped as he ran. A grin spread across his friendly face.

Ted grinned back. "What are you doing here? Shouldn't you be working?"

"I've sold all my papers. The railroad station is always a good place to sell them. People arriving want the latest news. People leaving want something to read on the train." He fell into step beside Ted. "What are you doing here?"

"I'm meeting my father." Ted hesitated. He didn't want to seem unfriendly, but he remembered his parents' warnings not to become friendly with newsboys. *If they knew Erik, maybe they'd like him,* he thought. "Would. . .would you like to come along and meet him?"

"Sure!"

Ted had been sure Erik would want to meet his father. Most boys he knew wanted to meet him. Engineers had exciting, good-paying jobs. Many men started work on the railroad as brakemen, like Erik's father. Even though the job was dangerous, the men did it in hopes of one day becoming an important engineer.

The boys stopped to watch a train steaming into the station. Ted held his breath while a brakeman ran across the top of the railroad cars and grabbed the round wheel at the back of a car. The man braced himself and turned the wheel to brake the car. The train slowed. Steam hissed from behind the wheels.

Ted grinned at Erik. "Your father must be brave to have been a brakeman. Running across the top of the cars looks exciting, but I wouldn't want to do it at night or in a snowstorm or when a train is flying down the track at forty miles an hour."

Erik didn't smile back. "I'll be glad when the trains all have the new air brakes. Then engineers like your father will be able to stop the trains safely from the engine."

Ted didn't know what to say.

When they reached Ted's father's engine, the train's fireman was holding a large copper can with a long, skinny spout. Ted knew he was using it to oil the bearings on the drive wheels, which were taller than the fireman.

"Hello, Mr. Thomas," Ted said, touching his fingers to his baseball hat. "Have a good trip?"

"Yup. Glad to be back, though."

Mr. Thomas's face was red and wrinkled. It seemed to Ted that the man's face was always red. He supposed it was from shoveling coal to make steam for the engine hour after hour during the train trips. It was one of his duties to make sure the train was kept in safe running condition, too. The safety of the passengers depended on Mr. Thomas doing his work well.

Through the engine's side window, Ted saw his father. "Hello, Father!"

Father turned and waved, smiling. Ted saw his gaze dart to Erik then back. His smile went away. "I'll be with you in a minute," he called.

Ted pushed his hands into the pockets of his brown knickers. He didn't want Erik to see how nervous he was. What if his father was angry at him for being with Erik? Would he tell Erik to go away? He hoped not. Erik was a nice boy. Ted didn't want his feelings or his pride hurt.

Ted could see his father was talking with another train worker. He turned to Erik. "Did you see the parade Wednesday?"

Erik nodded and laughed. "There wasn't any reason to be anywhere else. I think all of Minneapolis and St. Paul were there."

"My family and Emily's were there, too. Wasn't it great?"

"Sure was. What was your favorite part of the parade?" Erik asked.

"All the different kinds of transportation: the Indians with their horse-drawn drag, the voyageurs in their canoe, the dogsled, the Red River cart with its two large, solid wooden wheels—"

Erik's laugh interrupted him. "Did you ever hear anything as awful as those wheels screeching? I bet when those carts crossed the prairie, you could hear them for miles."

"The wheels could have used Mr. Thomas's oilcan, that's certain," Ted agreed. "Let's see, what came next? Oh, yes. The model of the first steamboat that came up the Mississippi. Then the prairie schooner with the two cows tied behind and the stovepipe sticking out the back."

"My father remembers seeing them a lot when he was young," Erik said. "He called them covered wagons."

"My father, too. Then came the stagecoach." Ted shook his head. "Hard to believe there are still parts of the country where people can't travel on trains, isn't it?"

"Must be awful slow traveling any other way," Erik agreed.

Just then, Father came down from the engine to greet the boys.

"This is Erik Moe, Father," Ted said. He clasped his hands behind his back, hoping they weren't shaking. Would his father like Erik, or would he be rude to him? "Erik is the newsboy who helped Emily when she tripped on the trolley rails."

"It's nice to meet you, Mr. Kerr," Erik said.

Father hesitated. His gaze seemed to study Erik's face. Then he held out his large, calloused hand. "A pleasure to meet you, Erik. Your bravery saved my niece's leg, if not her life."

Erik shrugged, his shoulders lifting his worn, once-white shirt. "Anyone would have done the same, sir."

Ted's breath came out in a *whoosh* of relief.

Before Father could reply, a booming voice came from behind Ted and Erik. "Why, it's Mr. Kerr, isn't it? Charles Kerr."

Ted turned around and looked at the man with the cheerful voice. The man was stout, with a chest that looked like a barrel covered by a fine, tailored suit jacket. The top of his head was bald, but the hair on the sides of his head was so long that it almost touched the collar of his double-breasted jacket. In one hand he held a stovepipe hat. A full, neatly trimmed beard and moustache covered his chin and lower face.

Ted's jaw dropped. "James Hill!"

CHAPTER 5

Mr. Hill's Story

"Ted, mind your manners," Father scolded in a low voice. Gulping, Ted closed his mouth.

Mr. Hill looked Ted in the eye. He held out his hand. "James Hill, it is. I came down to look over my trains. And you are?"

Ted shook his hand. "Ted. . .that is, Theodore Kerr, sir." He knew that Mr. Hill lived in a grand house in St. Paul, but he certainly had never expected to meet the great man.

"Ah, then you must be Charles's son." Mr. Hill looked at Erik. "And is this another of your boys?"

Father shook his head. "No, sir. This is a friend of my son's, Erik Moe."

Mr. Hill shook hands solemnly with Erik then held out his hand to Father. "A pleasure to see you again. Glad to see you are working for my railroad now. You were working for another line years ago when we met."

Ted swallowed his surprise. His father had never told him he'd met the famous railroad builder!

"I'm surprised you recall our meeting," Father said. "It was many years ago."

A smile gleamed in the midst of Mr. Hill's graying mustache and beard. "Many years ago, but I always remember men who love the railroad as much as I do."

Ted saw the pleasure in his father's eyes. "I remember you took over your first railroad in 1879, only three years after I moved here from Cincinnati."

Mr. Hill nodded. "Wonderful years, those were. Minneapolis wasn't much more than a frontier town then. Only about 35,000 people. Now it's a true city, with 167,000 people."

Father smiled. "In large part due to the railroads and men of vision, such as yourself."

"And men like you. Without good engineers and other railroad workers, my dreams could never have been realized."

"My dad worked for a railroad," Erik said. Ted glanced at him and saw his chin jut out in an angry, proud manner. "He was a brakeman. He lost his fingers, and now he's out of work."

Mr. Hill's sharp eyes stared at Erik a minute. Then he rested a hand on Erik's shoulder. "I'm sorry, son. Did he work for the Great Northern?"

"No."

"Has he found other work?" Mr. Hill asked.

"No."

Ted watched uneasily. How had Erik dared speak so angrily to such an important man? He watched Mr. Hill study Erik's face.

"Are you helping support the family then, Erik?"

Erik crossed his arms over his chest and glared at Mr. Hill. "Yes. I had to quit school and find a job. I'm a newsboy. Some of us aren't as lucky as you."

Mr. Hill's head jerked in surprise. "Lucky, is it? Don't you know that luck is only another name for hard work? Let me tell you a little about my life. We're not so different as you think."

Erik snorted.

Ted swallowed a groan. Father was glaring at Erik. He would never let Ted be friends with Erik after this!

"I was born in Canada," the great man began. "I went to school from the age of seven until I was fifteen. Then my father died, and I had to leave school."

Surprise pushed the anger from Erik's eyes. "I. . .I'm sorry. I didn't know."

Mr. Hill once again put a hand on Erik's shoulder. "Never stop learning just because you've quit school. Over the years, I've gathered enough books to have my own library. And I listen to others who are more knowledgeable than I am."

Erik nodded.

"I always loved travel," Mr. Hill continued, "so when I was eighteen, I left home and came to St. Paul. There were no railroads crossing Minnesota then, but goods had to be taken between Winnipeg, Canada, on the Red River and St. Paul on the Mississippi River."

"I bet I know how the goods were transported," Ted said. "By those screeching old Red River carts."

Mr. Hill threw back his head and laughed. "You've described the carts well. And you are correct. Goods traveled by Red River carts and by steamships. I wanted to find a better way. So in the middle of winter, I took a dogsled and traveled across country. Only Indians, fur traders, and missionaries lived in that part of Minnesota then."

"Dogsled!" Ted leaned forward. "That sounds exciting!"

"Don't interrupt, Ted," his father reminded him quietly.

Mr. Hill smiled at him. "It was exciting, but mostly it was cold."

Ted laughed. He decided he quite liked this man.

"I and some friends bought a small, struggling railroad," Mr. Hill continued, "and laid lines across Minnesota from St. Paul to the Red River. It took us ten years. That was the beginning of my transportation business. Later I had bigger dreams."

"Like the Great Northern line from St. Paul to Puget Sound—Hill's Folly," Ted said.

"Ted!" Father roared.

Ted clasped a hand over his mouth. How could he have repeated that awful name for Mr. Hill's railroad? He slipped the hand from his face. "I'm sorry, sir. I didn't mean to—to. . ."

"I've heard others call my plan a folly," Mr. Hill said calmly. "Although other railroads had been built across the country to the West Coast, no one had ever built one without the government giving them the land. People thought that was the only way a railroad could be built, because it takes so much land."

"But you did it," Ted said. "And you had to cross the mountains, too."

Mr. Hill smiled. "Yes. I see you know a bit about my railroad."

Ted shrugged his shoulders, feeling embarrassed and pleased at the same time. "My father has told me a lot about it."

Mr. Hill folded his hands over his chest. "Let me tell you about crossing the mountains. It's difficult to build a railroad over a tall mountain, you know."

Ted and Erik nodded.

Mr. Hill brushed dirt from the iron step leading to the engine's cab. Mr. Thomas jumped forward, whisking a large red handkerchief from his back pocket. "Let me do that for ya, sir. You'll be gettin' yer hands dirty."

"I've been dirty lots of times before," Hill said, but he let Mr. Thomas wipe the step. "Thank you, sir," he said, sitting down.

"You were going to tell us about the mountains," Ted reminded him.

"Well, when the Great Northern's line neared the Rocky

Mountains, I remembered a lost pass I'd heard about years ago."

"Lost pass?" Erik repeated breathlessly.

Mr. Hill nodded, his long, trim beard rubbing the front of his shirt and jacket. "Indians had told of a low point between the mountains that their people used. No one had used the pass in over forty years, so no one knew for sure where it was."

"What did you do?" Erik asked.

"I sent my chief engineer, John Stevens, to find it. It took him weeks and weeks, but at last he succeeded. He crossed the Divide on snowshoes. Then he started back. It was very cold. He couldn't sleep that night because he was afraid he'd go to sleep in the cold and never wake up."

"Why didn't he build a fire?" Erik asked. "Weren't there any trees? Didn't he have any matches?"

"There were trees and he had matches. But the snow was too deep to build a fire."

Ted and Erik stared at each other. They both knew what very cold weather felt like. The temperature was often below zero in Minneapolis. But Ted couldn't imagine there being too much snow to build a fire. "What did Mr. Stevens do?" he asked.

"He walked all night to keep from falling asleep. He went back and forth on the same path so he wouldn't get lost in the dark. In the morning, he went down the mountain to his camp. The pass is called the Marais Pass because the Marais River runs through it. Mr. Stevens's brave work shortened the Great Northern route by one hundred miles."

"Wow!" Ted shook his head.

"We weren't done with the mountains yet," Hill continued. "We still had to get over the Cascades."

"Aren't they the mountains near Puget Sound?" Ted asked.

"Very good!" Hill congratulated. "They are indeed."

"Did you have to find another lost pass through them?" Erik asked.

"No, but it was hard work. Stevens looked for the best way over the Cascades. I wanted to be sure I agreed with his plan, so I took the Northern Pacific Railroad as close as I could."

Ted and Erik and the railway men laughed at the thought of Mr. Hill using his competitor's train.

Mr. Hill smiled. "Then I took a buckboard and went to look over Stevens's planned route. I took my own bedding and slept out under the stars or stopped at the engineers' camps. Had to give up the wagon when I came to the Cascades. Went through them on horseback."

Erik shifted his feet. "I guess you meant it when you said luck is hard work."

Hill winked at him.

"Are the trees in Washington as large as the one in the parade yesterday?" Erik asked.

Ted remembered the log Seattle had sent to the parade. It was only a piece of a pine tree, but he'd never seen one so big around. It was on a large wooden flat wagon pulled by four strong horses. A man sat on the top—a logger, Ted guessed. He'd looked like an ant on top of that big log.

"The trees are truly that big," Hill told him.

"Why did you want to build the Great Northern all the way to Seattle," Erik asked, "when there were other railroads already at the Pacific?"

"Because of the trees you asked about," Hill said. "The trees have been sent by ships to other parts of the country. But people between Minnesota and the Rocky Mountains need trees to build houses and farms and towns. A railroad is the quickest way to get the trees to the people. Many people haven't moved to these lands because they don't have lumber."

"I hadn't thought of that," Ted said.

"And there's the farmers' crops. They have to get them to market. The flour mills in Minneapolis wouldn't employ so many men if farmers couldn't get their wheat to the mills to be ground into flour."

Mr. Hill took a deep breath and let it out. "The Great Northern. Hill's Folly. People have laughed at a lot of things I wanted to do—said they couldn't be done. But I've done them. Never let people tell you that you can't do the things you dream. Do you have a dream, Ted?"

Ted shook his head. "I don't know what I want to be yet. There're so many things to choose from."

"What about you, Erik?" the man asked.

Erik looked at the worn toes of his shoes. "I want to be. . .I want to be a newspaper reporter, but I guess that'll never happen. Not when I had to quit school."

Ted glanced at his friend in surprise. Erik hadn't mentioned his dream before. He wondered if Erik had ever told anyone about it.

"Believe in your dreams and a way will open," Mr. Hill told him. He bounced a thick index finger in front of Erik's face. "But don't think they will happen without lots of hard work. Do you read the newspapers you sell?"

"Every day," Erik answered promptly.

"That's good. Do you know what makes a news story good?"

"I. . .I'm not sure. I think so."

"I'm interviewed by lots of reporters," Mr. Hill told him. "You asked good questions when I told you about building the Great Northern line."

Erik smiled.

"Ask some of the reporters at the newspaper you work for how to write a good story," Mr. Hill suggested.

"Yes, sir," Erik said. Ted thought Erik didn't look like he believed there was any chance he'd ever be a reporter.

"What is your father's name, and what railroad did he work for?" Mr. Hill asked Erik.

Erik told him. Mr. Hill nodded then turned his attention to Ted's father. The two men spent a few minutes talking about the Great Northern, and then Mr. Hill went on his way.

When the important man had gone, Ted asked his father, "Do you believe what he said about dreams?"

"Well, the Bible says that God gives us the desires of our hearts. I believe God can put desires in our hearts to show us what He wants us to do with our lives. I certainly believe that making our dreams come true takes hard work."

Ted looked at him thoughtfully. "When you were a boy, you had a dream of working on the railroad, didn't you?"

"Yes."

"Your dream came true."

"Yes, with a lot of hard work. It wouldn't have come true if I had gone into some other kind of work." Father stepped into the engine for a last look around then jumped to the ground. "Ready to go home?"

Ted walked alongside his father and Erik. His father had had a dream when he was Ted's age. Erik had a dream, too. *Will I ever have a dream?* he wondered.

Chapter 6

The Adventure Begins

Ted entered the huge station house with his parents. His ears filled with the rumble of waiting trains, the calls of conductors hurrying passengers aboard, and the clattering of wheels as porters dashed about with luggage.

Ted and his parents tried to locate Emily's family in the crowd. Ted noticed a girl jumping up and down. Brown curls flowed over her shoulders beneath a straw hat. She was helping the hat pins keep the hat in place with one gloved hand as she bounced. With the other hand, she waved furiously.

Ted laughed as he recognized his cousin. "There they are," he told his parents. He hurried across the large room.

Emily grabbed his hands, squeezing them. "Isn't it wonderful? I thought the end of July would never come! We're going to the fair! We're going to the fair!" She started jumping up and down again.

Ted laughed. "Your eyes are as big as your hat!"

"Emily Marie Allerton," her mother said in a prim voice. "Stop leaping around like a. . .a toad and behave yourself."

Emily whirled about. "But it's so exciting, Mother!"

"Try to be excited in a more ladylike manner." Emily's mother folded her gloved hands in front of her waist.

"Yes, Mother," Emily murmured. She glanced at Ted and rolled her eyes.

"That dark green dress brings out your pretty green eyes," Ted's mother said to Emily. "Is it new?"

"Yes." Emily beamed a smile and turned all the way around to show off her outfit. "I love the leg-o'-mutton sleeves with the huge puffs at the shoulders, don't you, Aunt Alison?"

"They're lovely," she agreed. "I like the huge lace collar, too."

"I wanted new shoes," Emily told her, lowering her voice and glancing over at her mother to be sure she wasn't overheard. "But Mother said new shoes would only give me blisters at the fair."

"I'm sure she's right," her aunt replied. "The newspaper articles say that a person would have to walk 150 miles to see everything at the fair."

Ted laughed. "I guess your mother was right, Emily."

Emily joined in his laughter. "I have another new dress, too," she said, "and so does Anna."

Ted ran a finger beneath the stiff starched collar of his white linen shirt. "Mother insisted on buying me new clothes, too. Wish she hadn't."

His mother and Emily laughed together at him, but he was serious. "Old clothes are always more comfortable," he said, yanking at the too-tight buttons below the knees on his navy blue knickers.

"Do you have a new traveling satchel, too?" Emily asked. "Mother bought me this red one." She pointed to the bag at her feet.

Ted shrugged one shoulder, scratching at his neck where the new collar bothered him. "I'm using one of Father's old ones."

Emily's father turned from the porter who was loading their larger bags onto his cart. "Anything else that goes in the baggage car?"

Her mother shook her head. "I believe we'll need all the smaller bags on the sleeper car tonight."

Uncle Enoch and Aunt Tina walked up while Emily's father tipped the porter.

"How nice of you to see us off!" her mother said to them. "I only wish you and Ted's parents were coming with us."

Ted's father shook his head. "Train tickets are $16.30 each. Then there's the cost of the hotel and food and tickets to the fair and the special exhibits. The tickets to enter the fair are fifty cents per person! Too much in these hard times for a poor railroad engineer."

A sliver of fear slipped up Ted's spine. There was a teasing grin on his father's face, but his voice sounded serious. "I thought the Great Northern wasn't in any danger of going bankrupt," Ted said. "I mean, with Mr. Hill so rich and everything. . ." His voice trailed off.

Father squeezed his shoulder and smiled. "Mr. Hill is a good businessman. The railroad is in fine shape."

Ted wanted to believe him. He hadn't thought to wonder before this why his parents weren't going to the fair. Was his father afraid of losing his job?

Uncle Enoch leaned on his cane to take the pressure off his one good leg. "The Northern Pacific Railroad has gone bankrupt."

Ted darted a scared glance at Uncle Enoch. The Northern Pacific had reached the Pacific Ocean at Portland about ten years before James Hill's railroad reached Seattle. If that huge railroad couldn't make money, how could the Great Northern?

"James Hill is planning to buy the Northern Pacific," Uncle Enoch continued, "and join it with his Great Northern Railroad."

Father laughed. "And you thought Hill was foolish to build the Great Northern across the continent."

Uncle Enoch didn't join in Father's laughter. "Hill hasn't paid for the Northern Pacific yet, and the panic isn't over. A lot of railroads have gone under. Hill's roads may, too."

Emily grinned up at him. "At least you were right about your bank, Uncle Enoch. Our fathers' money is safe, and we're going to the fair!"

"That you are." Uncle Enoch winked at her.

"But the other bank you told us about closed," Ted added. "Its depositors lost their money, didn't they?"

Uncle Enoch nodded.

"Boarding for Chicago! Boarding for Chicago!" A uniformed boy a little older than Richard passed by.

Excitement pushed away Ted's fears. Emily grabbed one of his arms. "I can't believe it! It's finally time to go!"

Ted shook hands with his father and Uncle Enoch. He let his mother kiss his cheek without even making a face. He didn't care to have her kiss him in public, but he knew she was going to whether he liked it or not.

He and the Allertons went through the gates and into the train house. His uncle Daniel handed their tickets to a porter, who told them where to find their seats.

Ted's heart raced as he entered the car. Since his father was an engineer, he'd been on many trains. He'd even taken short train trips, sometimes riding in the engine with his father. But he'd never ridden in a fancy Pullman car with velvet-covered seats and beds that folded down from the walls.

He and Emily shared a seat. Across the aisle, Richard and Anna took a seat that faced their parents.

"It's as pretty as a parlor in here," Emily said. "I didn't know there would be carpeting on the floors or wood paneling on the walls. And the seats are as comfortable as a chair at home."

Ted knew his uncle Daniel had paid more money so they could

ride in the comfortable car. Passengers in other cars would be sitting up all night on hard seats.

The porter made a last call for passengers. Finally, the car doors were closed, and the train chugged out of the huge train house. Ted and Emily watched as they rode past other trains then past business houses.

Soon they were on the large, curving stone bridge that crossed the Mississippi River just above the Falls of St. Anthony. James Hill had built that bridge for his railroad, Ted remembered.

"Isn't it great to ride in one of Mr. Hill's trains across Mr. Hill's bridge?" Emily asked, her eyes shining.

Ted nodded.

"It was fun watching his parade," she went on.

Ted shifted uncomfortably on his seat. "Seattle planned a big parade and celebration for him, too. It was supposed to be held a month after the St. Paul parade."

Her green-eyed gaze darted to his face. "Supposed to be? What happened? Wasn't Seattle excited about the railroad?"

"The city had invited lots of important businessmen from across the country to take part in the celebration. Too many businessmen were too broke to come because of the panic, so the city canceled it."

Emily heaved a sigh that lifted the shoulders of her new traveling outfit. "I'm glad we're going to the fair. I'm tired of hearing adults talk about money and bank runs."

"And bankrupt railroads," Ted continued her list, "and stock market trouble."

"I don't even know what a lot of the words mean," Emily said, "except that adults are afraid of losing their money and their jobs."

Ted nodded. "Seems all the adults are going about with long, worried faces and whispering about money problems."

"Fairs are fun places. At least there no one should be sad and worried."

Ted hoped Emily was right. He tried to forget about James Hill and the country's money troubles. Instead, he watched out the window with Emily as the train left the city and traveled along the river through countryside and small towns.

"I'm glad it's summer and the days are long," Emily said. "I want to see as much as I can before it gets dark."

"We'll be in Wisconsin before long," he told her. "We have to cross the entire state before we reach Illinois."

"How long will it take us to get there?"

"Let's see. We left at 5:15 this evening. We get there at 7:45 tomorrow morning. But it's really 6:45 our time. So I guess that's—"

"Thirteen and a half hours," Emily said promptly.

"Right. I read in the newspaper that it takes four days to get to Seattle from St. Paul."

"That must be an awfully long ways away, but I think it would be fun to go someday. Ted, why isn't the time in Chicago the same as in Minneapolis?"

"Because the railroads needed time they could count on." Ted couldn't help feeling a bit proud that he knew something Emily didn't. "It used to be that towns could have whatever time they wanted. Wisconsin had thirty-eight different times."

"All for the same hour and minute?" Emily asked.

Ted nodded.

"That must have been confusing."

"The railroads needed to be able to tell what time it was easily so the trains would arrive when people expected and to prevent accidents. But the whole country couldn't have the same time."

"Why?"

"Because the earth rotates. That means the sun rises earlier on the East Coast than on the West Coast. So the railroad people decided to have four different time zones in the United States to make travel easier. That was ten years ago."

"What time will it be in Seattle when we reach Chicago tomorrow morning?" Emily asked.

"Four forty-five."

Emily laughed. "That seems silly, but I guess it's no sillier than having thirty-eight times in one state for the same minute!"

After a couple hours, Ted grew tired of watching the small towns go past. He pulled his leather bag down from the brass bars above the seat and dug out a book.

"That's a good idea," Emily said. "I brought a book, too. I'm reading *David Copperfield.* What are you reading?"

"Swiss Family Robinson." It was an exciting story, but Ted found himself looking out the window every few minutes anyway. When twilight faded into night, he was amazed at how huge the sky looked and how bright the stars shone away from the city.

The conductor lighted lamps inside the car. It was time to get ready for bed. Porters pulled down sections of the walls and made them into beds. The children used a tiny room at the back of the car to wash their faces and slip into their bed clothes.

Ted crawled into the berth above Emily's. He reached to shut the curtains that hid his bed from other people in the car.

"This is the most fun I ever had going to bed," Emily whispered as she closed her own curtains.

Ted didn't think he'd be able to sleep on the train, but he did. Soon, Aunt Marcia was waking him.

After using the small room to dress, wash, and comb his hair, he joined the others in the dining car for breakfast. Excitement spilled through him, though he tried not to show it. In just a couple hours, they'd be in Chicago!

Chapter 7

At the Fair

"Wow! The fair is as big as a town!" Ted peered out the window of the cigar-shaped car.

"This was a good idea you had, Ted," his uncle Daniel said from the seat across the aisle. "This train is built high enough so we can see all the buildings. It goes around the entire fairground. We'll be able to decide what to see first when we're done."

Ted grinned. "I wish Father could see this train. A train that travels on runners over water instead of on wheels over railroad tracks!"

Emily turned from the window. "Do you remember the Pledge of Allegiance, Ted?"

Ted nodded. Together they put their hands over their hearts and repeated: "I pledge allegiance to my flag and the Republic for which it stands; one nation, indivisible, with liberty and justice for all."

Aunt Marcia's eyebrows met in curiosity. "What is that verse?"

"It's the Pledge of Allegiance, Mother," Emily told her eagerly. "Our teacher taught it to us. She said that the day the World's Fair was dedicated last October, all the schoolchildren in the United States were going to say that pledge. That way, all of us had part in the World's Fair, even those children who don't get to come like we do."

"Now we say it every day," Ted told her.

The train started, and the children immediately forgot about the pledge. They were too busy pointing out all the wonders they saw from the window—including Lake Michigan.

"Are you certain it's a lake?" Aunt Marcia teased. "It looks more like an ocean. I've never been to a lake where I couldn't see the opposite shore!"

After the train had been around the entire fair, Ted said, "Let's go to the Transportation Building first. I promised Father I'd go. It's right by one of the train stations, so we wouldn't have to walk far."

Everyone agreed. "Though I don't know what could be displayed in the Transportation Building that could be more exciting or newer than this water train," Uncle Daniel told Ted.

Richard was studying a large paper. "This says the building covers eighteen acres."

"Oh, my!" Anna looked down at her shoes with their pointed toes and groaned. "We're just starting, and my feet are already tired at the thought of all that walking."

Inside the huge building, the group went from exhibit to exhibit. One showed how railroad steam engines had been invented in the early 1800s and had changed over the years.

"Look at this train," Emily called to the others. "The cars look like stagecoaches!"

Richard pointed to the engine. "The engineer is standing at the back of the engine, and there isn't any cab. Your father wouldn't like that during a snowstorm, Ted!"

"He sure wouldn't," Ted agreed. He read a sign by the display. " 'This is a replica of the first railroad train in America, 1831, on Hudson and Mohawk line from Albany, New York, to Utica, New York.' Wow!"

"Wow!" Ted said again a few exhibits further. "New York Central's Engine No. 999!"

Emily gave a puzzled frown. "What's so special about it?"

Ted gaped at her. "What's so special? It only goes one hundred miles an hour!"

"Nothing goes one hundred miles an hour, Theodore Kerr!"

"This does," her father said, reading the signs beside the huge engine.

Ted leaned against the brass railing that kept the engine and visitors apart. "I wish I could touch it. Look at all that polished steel. It sure looks modern."

Emily tipped her head to one side, her brown curls spilling over her shoulder. "I like the colorful, painted engines like we see in Minneapolis better."

"Not me." Ted shook his head. "I think it's exciting to see things that are new."

Trains filled most of the Transportation Building—old trains and new ones. Ted and the Allertons saw most of them, and it took most of their morning to do so.

After the last train, Anna sat down on a step and rubbed her ankle. "I wish we could ride one of these trains through the building!"

Ted thought the last exhibit was the strangest. "An automobile. It only carries a couple people. Why would anyone need one of these when they could hire a carriage?"

Uncle Daniel shook his head. "I think this will be nothing but a toy for rich people."

Ted nodded solemnly.

"Let's visit the Agricultural Building next," Uncle Daniel suggested as they left the Transportation Building.

Emily groaned. "Must we, Father? Farming exhibits don't sound like much fun."

"Farming is important in Minnesota," her father said. "We need to see what Minnesota is telling the world about it."

"First, let's find something to eat," Aunt Marcia said, "or we won't have strength to see any more exhibits."

There was a restaurant right on the way to the Agricultural Building. Ted had never been so glad to see food!

When he was done eating, Richard studied his map of the fair. "The Agricultural Building is built on the Grand Basin. The view of the basin is supposed to be beautiful." He was right. When the basin came into view, they all stopped dead in their tracks.

"The White City," Aunt Marcia said in a low voice filled with wonder.

Emily seemed to be trying to see everything at once.

"Did they really build all these buildings just for the fair?"

"Yes," Richard told her, "and all the fair buildings that aren't on the basin, too."

The basin was about a third of a mile long. The buildings along it were covered with fake white rock and marble. The noon sunshine glistened off the buildings, making them shine.

Huge white pillars stretched across the opposite end of the basin. In the middle of them was an opening where small boats could float out into the harbor of Lake Michigan.

But right in front of them was Ted's favorite place on the basin: the Columbian Fountain, the largest fountain he'd ever seen. In the middle was a barge with four oarsmen on each side and a man operating a rudder in the rear. In the front was an angel-like creature with a trumpet. All around them were smaller statues of people and horses.

Ted leaned close to Emily and whispered, "I'd sure like to wade out in that fountain and climb up on one of those horses!"

Emily's face lit up with mischief. "Wouldn't that be fun? It would feel good, too. The sun is hot."

They didn't stay in the sunshine long. The Agricultural Building faced the basin and was almost as long as the basin itself. Soon they were inside.

Threshers, mowing machines, and other important farm machinery filled the bottom floor. Ted and Emily soon tired of them and went upstairs.

"I wish we could see something more exciting than this old ag building," Ted grumbled.

Emily yanked on his sleeve and pointed. "Look! It's the big flour mill from Minneapolis!"

Sure enough, there was a complete model of the Washburn-Crosby flour mill. Small flour barrels formed a barrier between visitors and the model. Ted and Emily went right up to the barrels so they could see as much as possible.

"It's just like the real thing." Emily's voice was filled with excitement. "All the company's mills and elevators are here."

"And their warehouses," Ted added, "and even the railroad tracks that run by the mills to carry grain to them and flour away when the grain is milled."

"Just think. Everyone who comes to the fair from everywhere else in the country—from all over the world, even—will see a piece of our own city."

Ted lifted his nose and sniffed. "It smells like fresh baked bread."

They followed their noses to the next exhibit. A mill made flour while visitors watched. Beside it, women in dresses covered with neat white aprons made bread. Ted's mouth watered at the golden loaves they pulled from the ovens. When visitors were offered samples, he and Emily eagerly accepted. It seemed hours since they'd had lunch.

A boy about their age with curly blond hair and a round chin stood beside Ted. He helped himself to a sample, too. Ted noticed the boy carried his threadbare jacket over his arm.

Ted and Emily ambled along the aisle. A man passed them wearing a jacket heavy with braid and a tiny hat with a strap under his chin.

"He looks like he's wearing a band uniform," Emily said with a laugh.

"He's one of the Columbian Guard," Ted explained. "That's what they call the fair police."

"Hey, lemme go!"

At the yell, they whirled around. The boy they'd seen a couple minutes ago was yelling. The policeman had one of the boy's arms in a tight grip. In the other, the policeman held a camera.

"No pictures allowed," the policeman said firmly. "That's the rule."

"Lemme go!" the boy yelled again. The policeman dragged him, kicking and screaming, down the aisle past Ted and Emily. "I ain't hurtin' nothin'!"

Why is the boy being arrested? Ted wondered. He'd only tried to take a picture of the miniature mill. Ted tried to forget the incident as he and Emily continued down the aisle.

A young woman at another exhibit was handing out samples. "Would you like to try our cereal?" she asked the cousins.

Ted frowned. "I thought cereal was oatmeal."

"This is a new kind of cereal," the woman told him. "It's called Shredded Wheat."

Emily looked into the small bowl the woman held out to them and made a face. "It looks like straw."

"Taste it," the woman urged.

Emily shook her head back and forth so quickly her curls flew beneath her straw sailor hat.

"You aren't going to be a chicken, are you?" asked a tall young man beside them.

Ted reached out slowly and took a small piece.

"How is it?" Emily asked.

"Not bad. It's crunchy."

"With milk, it turns soft," the woman told them. "And sugar makes it sweeter, just as it does oatmeal. This cereal will save housewives time because it doesn't need to be cooked."

Emily grinned. "But it's not warm like oatmeal. I like warm cereal on a cold Minnesota morning."

"Then you would like our other new cereal, Cream of Wheat," the woman said. She spooned some into a small bowl from a pot on the stove behind her, added a little sugar, and handed it to Emily along with a spoon.

Emily hesitated.

"Chicken?" Ted asked, teasing.

Emily's chin shot up. "I guess if you could try something, I can, too." She spooned a tiny bit of the creamy white mixture and blew on the spoon to cool it. Taking a deep breath, she popped the spoonful into her mouth and swallowed it quickly.

"Why, it's good!"

Ted and the woman laughed at her surprise.

But their favorite new food was a few exhibits away: a new sweet called Juicy Fruit Gum.

"Too bad we can't have this for breakfast!" Ted said to Emily as they walked away, chewing it.

A minute later, Emily's family joined them. Ted and Emily told them about the boy who had been arrested.

"There are only a couple men who can take pictures at the fair," Uncle Daniel explained. "They paid a fee for the right. If people want pictures, they have to buy them from those men. Even newspapers and magazines can't take pictures. That's why the boy was arrested."

"I guess I understand," Ted said slowly, "but it doesn't seem fair.

The boy was only our age."

"We've seen enough for one day," Uncle Daniel said.

"It's almost dinnertime. Let's catch a beach cart back to the hotel."

Disappointment swamped Ted. There was still so much to see!

But when they walked out onto the boardwalk that separated the fair from Lake Michigan, he forgot to be disappointed. Here was a magnificent lake that put the ten thousand lakes of Minnesota to shame. The cool breeze off the lake felt good after the hot summer sun that had beaten down on the concrete walks.

In an inlet, three wooden ships bobbed. They looked very old, but small. "What are those ships?" Emily asked.

Richard knew the answer. "They are copies of the three ships Columbus brought over in 1492: the *Santa Maria,* the *Nina,* and the *Pinta.* They were built in Spain."

"I wouldn't want to cross the ocean in these ships," Ted said. "They're small!"

Ted remembered that the real name of this World's Fair was "The Columbian Exhibition." The fair had been dedicated in the fall of 1892, even though the buildings didn't open until the next spring. It was named after Columbus, who had reached America four hundred years earlier.

"I guess that boy should have taken pictures of Lake Michigan instead of the mill," Emily said to Ted in a sad voice.

Ted nodded.

Chapter 8

Mr. Edison Arrives

Be sure to act like a young lady today," Mother admonished Emily the next morning as they entered the fairgrounds.

Emily rolled her eyes. "No one here knows us, so I don't see why it matters how I act."

"Many important people from all over the world are visiting the fair," Father reminded her. "You never know when one of them might be standing beside you."

"Yes, Father," Emily said quietly.

He's right, Ted thought, remembering some of the important fair visitors they'd read about in the newspapers. Even a princess from Spain had come.

"Electricity Hall is the first place we'll visit today," Uncle Daniel said.

"Hurrah!" Ted grinned. "There's lots of things I want to see there."

Electricity Hall was much lighter than the buildings they'd visited the day before. The electric lights at the exhibits, along with the huge windows and skylights, made the building bright.

In the middle of the downstairs display area, General Electric had built the Tower of Light, designed by Thomas Edison. Pillars taller than people surrounded the tower's base. The tower was covered with five thousand lightbulbs blinking on and off. On top of the tower was an eight-foot model lightbulb made of tiny prisms that reflected the light and made the light seem even brighter than it was.

"Have you ever seen so many lightbulbs?" Aunt Marcia asked, staring up at the tower, which reached almost to the ceiling.

"Mercy!" Anna shielded her eyes. "It's so bright I can barely look at it!"

"The tower is seventy feet high," Richard said. It seemed to Ted that Richard knew more facts about the fair than the rest of them put together.

"Oh!" Emily pointed past the nearby exhibits. "Look, Ted! That must be the Egyptian Temple!" She darted up the wide aisle toward the temple.

"Emily Marie Allerton!" Mother's voice was sharp with anger but not loud enough for Emily to hear. Emily was already halfway to the temple.

Ted knew Aunt Marcia was too much of a lady to yell at Emily in public. It wasn't considered proper.

"I'll catch her, Aunt Marcia," he said, "and remind her not to run." He walked as fast as he could.

Emily was standing in the doorway, looking at the strange hieroglyphics that bordered the doorway. Of course, it wasn't a real temple, but it was interesting.

Ted liked the pillars inside the temple. They glowed with green light. The only other light came from the window displays.

Emily shivered. "Those lights make the room look strange—kind of. . .eerie."

Ted thought so, too, but he still liked them.

When the rest of their group joined them, Aunt Marcia and

Anna weren't nearly as impressed. "I think it's creepy," Anna said and walked away.

Her mother agreed. "I much prefer the cheerful displays."

"Are you ready to go upstairs?" asked Uncle Daniel.

Ted was filled with wonder at the things he saw upstairs. A door opened when he walked on a certain part of the floor. A person could write something down and the writing would be sent to another part of the country by a new machine called a tel-auto-graph. In a walnut shell sat the world's smallest steam engine, which they looked at through a magnifying glass.

"Whatever are these chickens doing here?" Aunt Marcia asked, looking into a sandy enclosure.

Ted and Emily hurried to her side. "Oh, they're so cute!" Emily said, looking at the fluffy yellow chicks.

A small house made of curtains stood in the middle of the sand. Ted read the banner stretched across the house. " 'Who needs Mother now!' "

"Well!" Aunt Marcia pretended to be insulted.

"What do chickens have to do with electricity?" Anna asked. "And why don't the chicks need a mother?"

A mustached young man attending the booth smiled at her. "If you'll step to the other side of the exhibit, you will see."

Ted and the Allertons did as he suggested. "This is called an incubator," the young man told them. "Electricity supplies the warmth needed to hatch the eggs and to keep the chicks warm. So as you can see, they don't need a mother."

Ted and the others stared through the side of the incubator. "Look! There's one hatching now!"

They watched, fascinated, while a little beak poked its way through a shell. In another part of the incubator, another chick broke free of the last of its shell.

"Poor thing," Emily exclaimed. "It looks cold and wet."

"It won't be for long," Ted said. "It's already headed for the lightbulb."

The damp chick stumbled and hopped to a lightbulb and leaned against it, gathering warmth.

"What do you do with the chicks?" Emily asked the man.

A smile beamed from beneath his mustache. "We give them away. Would you like one? I can put one in a box for you."

Emily swung around to her father. "May I? They are so sweet, and it would be such fun to watch one grow up."

Father laughed. "Where would you keep it while we visit the fair? It needs water and food and warmth."

"I could keep the box in our hotel room while we're at the fair," she suggested eagerly.

Richard shook his head. "I doubt the conductor of the Pullman car would let you keep the chick with you on the train. Besides, where would you keep a chicken at home?"

Emily turned to her mother.

Her mother lifted a finger. "Don't even ask, Emily Marie. I'll not have a chicken in my home or in my yard."

Ted flung an arm around his cousin's shoulders. "Don't worry. I'm sure there are lots of children in Chicago who will give the chicks homes."

"At least until the chicks grow big enough to eat," Richard said cheerfully.

"Murderer!" Emily gave him a dark look.

Emily seemed to forget about the chicks when they entered the model home where everything was done by electricity. They entered after ringing an electric doorbell. Aunt Marcia smiled. "How charming!"

The home was filled with electric wonders: a fire alarm, hot plates, an electric iron, an electric sewing machine, an electric fan, an electric stove, a carpet sweeper, and even a washing machine.

"I want a home like this when I grow up," Emily declared.

"I want a home like this *now,*" her mother added.

Uncle Daniel laughed and pulled her arm through his. "With all these inventions, there won't be anything left for a woman to do around the house."

"That suits me fine," Aunt Marcia declared.

"Me, too!" Emily and Anna chimed in.

Uncle Daniel's chuckle died away as he stood at the railing and looked down at the first floor. Ted stood beside him. Electrical wonders met his gaze everywhere he looked.

"This is a great time to be a child," his uncle said. "When I look at all these inventions, I get excited wondering what new things will be invented in your lifetimes."

"I wonder how many of these things were developed by Thomas Edison," Richard mused. "I read that it would take twenty-five acres just to display all the machines he's worked on."

"The things he's created have already changed the way people live," Uncle Daniel told them. "People say his creations will change the way people live in the twentieth century, too."

"He has a new invention here that I want to see," Richard said.

"His dynamo?" his father asked. "I understand he has one here. So do other inventors. Scientists say this kind of power will begin a new phase in history."

Richard shook his head. "What I want to see is much smaller than a dynamo."

His father swung out an arm. "Lead on."

As they were following Richard, Ted said, "I read in the newspaper that one hundred years from now, the person who is alive today who will be most remembered is Thomas Edison. Even more remembered than James Hill, the railroad king."

Emily grabbed Ted's sleeve so hard that she almost jerked him off balance. He heard her gasp.

"What is it?" he asked, tugging at his jacket sleeve.

She pointed toward three men in suits and bowler hats standing near the display they were passing. The men seemed to be in a friendly argument. They talked fast, laughed through their beards and mustaches, and waved their hands about as though trying to draw pictures in the air for each other.

"Isn't that. . .isn't it. . .Ed. . .Ed. . ."

"Edison. It's Thomas Edison," her father finished for her. His voice was low but filled with excitement.

Ted's heart seemed to jump to his throat and beat wildly.

Aunt Marcia laid her gloved hand on Uncle Daniel's forearm. "Are you sure it's Mr. Edison?"

"Oh, yes, I'm sure," he answered. "I've seen his picture in newspapers and magazines often enough."

"Me, too," Richard agreed. "I sure wish we had a camera!"

Emily looked up at her father. "Can we meet him, Father? We could introduce ourselves."

"I'm afraid not." Uncle Daniel shook his head, but Ted thought he looked like he wanted to say yes. "It wouldn't be polite. If he were meeting strangers, there would be others about him."

"But maybe those men he's talking to were strangers, too," Emily pressed.

Her mother smiled. "I doubt that. They appear to know each other well."

She laid a gentle hand on Richard's arm. "Let us move on to the exhibit you wanted to show us. It isn't polite to gawk at people, even if they are famous."

They moved on slowly. In spite of Aunt Marcia's words, Ted

couldn't help watching the great man. He noticed Emily was doing the same. She walked as close as she could to the three men as they passed. Ted stayed right beside her.

"I've heard that you believe in a personal God," one of the men was saying to Edison. "Is that true?"

"Certainly." The white-haired genius nodded. "The existence of a God can almost be proven by chemistry. Look at the atoms, at the orderly way the universe is put together. Could this have happened without a great, intelligent God?"

Ted and Emily smiled at each other. Once they were out of earshot, they kept on craning their necks to watch the famous man. Ted twisted his head about until his neck hurt. Suddenly he bumped into Emily.

Aunt Marcia cried out, falling against Uncle Daniel.

Ted saw in a flash that Emily had bumped into her mother before he had bumped into Emily.

Uncle Daniel caught Aunt Marcia before she could fall but not before her pride was hurt. Her cheeks flamed dark red. Ted groaned, and he saw Emily squeeze her eyes shut and wince.

"I'm sorry, Mother." Emily's apology rushed out. "I was watching. . .that is. . ."

Ted knew she'd remembered just in time that they weren't supposed to be gawking at Mr. Edison.

Aunt Marcia straightened her new hat. "You were ogling Mr. Edison, weren't you?"

For a minute Ted thought Emily was going to deny it. Then she clasped her hands behind her new green dress, looked at the floor, and nodded.

Aunt Marcia sighed deeply. "I can hardly blame you, though it was rude. It was also dangerous. What if I had been a stranger without a husband to catch me from falling? You could have hurt someone."

"Yes, ma'am," Emily murmured. "I'll try to be more careful, I promise."

Richard interrupted. "This is the exhibit I wanted to see. It's Edison's new kinetoscope."

"His what?" Ted asked.

"Kinetoscope," Richard answered. "You look into a box at picture film. There's a magnifying glass, and the film has an electric light behind it so you can see the picture."

"Like a stereoscope with a light?" Aunt Marcia asked.

"What is new about looking at pictures?" Emily demanded.

"Don't you read anything in the newspapers?" Richard asked. "These pictures move."

"*Moving* pictures?" Ted grinned. "You're pulling our legs."

Richard didn't smile. "Not only do the pictures move, but they talk."

Ted laughed again.

"You will see." Richard turned on his heel and entered the exhibit.

Ted and the others followed. Inside was a box about two feet square. It stood four feet high. Beside it stood a phonograph.

Richard climbed up on a stool. The man in charge of the booth handed him earphones. Then Richard looked down into the box. "Wow!"

Ted thought he sounded almost as excited as Uncle Daniel had when they saw Edison.

In less than a minute, Richard was removing the headphones and climbing down from the stool. A grin spread from ear to ear. His black eyes shone like new marbles. "That's fantastic!"

Ted waited impatiently to see what was so fantastic. All the Allertons climbed the stool and looked into the box first. Each one came away looking as excited as Richard had.

Emily was the last of the Allertons to view it. "You won't believe it, Ted!"

He climbed the stool eagerly and fitted the earphones over his head. He looked through a small slit on top of the box.

He saw a picture of a blacksmith. The blacksmith began moving! Ted gasped. The blacksmith used his sledgehammer and tongs, then laughed and looked like he was talking to friends in his blacksmith shop. The film stopped.

Ted was disappointed and excited at the same time. "That was great! I wish it would have lasted longer, though. Do you think Mr. Edison will sell his kinetoscopes for people to use in their homes with their phonographs, Uncle Daniel?"

His uncle grinned. "I expect they will be toys for rich people, like the automobiles we saw in the Transportation Building yesterday."

Ted spread his arms wide and laughed. "Well, I guess I'm just going to have to get rich one day! Now all I have to do is figure out how!"

When they left the booth, Ted glanced down the aisle, hoping for another glimpse of Mr. Edison. He was still there, but so was a small crowd. A man in a suit was angrily trying to grab a black box from one of the fair's policemen.

"What's happening?" Ted asked the guide who was standing outside the booth they'd just left.

The man nodded toward the disturbance. "A newspaper reporter tried to take a picture of Mr. Edison. The policeman took away his camera."

Ted felt like he'd swallowed a rock. The scene reminded him of the boy he and Emily had seen arrested the day before. He glanced at Emily. Her face looked as sad as he felt.

"Don't gawk," Anna reminded them.

Ted bit back an angry retort. Fourteen-year-old Anna sounded just like her mother.

Uncle Daniel cleared his throat. "Let's find a restaurant and have lunch. Then how about a ride on the Ferris wheel?"

Excitement sent a chill through Ted. Emily grabbed his arm and bounced up and down. They'd been able to see the Ferris wheel whenever they were outside. It was much taller than any of the buildings. Ted had never been up as high as it went. And in an hour or two, he'd be on it!

Chapter 9

Trouble on the Midway

As hungry as he'd been after spending all morning walking around Electricity Hall, Ted didn't think they'd ever get done eating and over to the Ferris wheel. Only Aunt Marcia's constant reminders kept him and Emily from running all the way from the restaurant to the wheel that towered over the fair.

Aunt Marcia raised her parasol to protect herself from the noonday sun. "I do wish we didn't have to go so far down the Midway to ride the Ferris wheel. I've heard the Midway is filled with inappropriate displays."

Ted opened his mouth to say something, then shut it tight. He'd heard the Midway was filled with fun exhibits, but Emily's mother often seemed to think fun was "inappropriate." Ted's mother said it was because Aunt Marcia was a proper lady and that more women should act like her.

Anna opened her parasol and leaned it against her shoulder. Ted smiled. She was always copying her mother. No wonder Aunt Marcia thought Anna was a perfect young lady.

Emily wrinkled her brow. "How is the Midway different from the rest of the fair?" she asked Richard.

"The Midway is more like a circus than like the White City."

The wide Midway was even more crowded than the walkways by the White City. Women with parasols and men in bowler hats or smart round straw hats peered in wonder at the buildings and exhibits that edged the street.

Roar!

Ted jumped. "What was that?"

Richard laughed. "A lion. Behind those walls on our left is a big animal show. Can't you read the signs?"

Ted grinned sheepishly. He'd been so intent on the huge wheel at the end of the street that he wasn't paying attention to what they were passing.

He looked to the other side of the street. He wasn't going to be caught daydreaming again! "That looks like a castle. The sign on it says Blarney Castle."

"It's a copy of a castle in Ireland," Richard explained. "Ireland sent over the Blarney Stone, and it's here in Blarney Castle. Legend says that if you kiss the Blarney Stone, you will have a wonderful way with words all your life."

Soft music filled the air. "That doesn't sound Irish," Emily said.

They all stopped and watched young Japanese women with gongs and tinkling bells. Ted thought the music seemed almost too sweet for the busy street.

A few steps later a stronger beat caught his attention. South Sea Islanders sat above the opening for their exhibit. The dark men wore only small cloths around their hips. They pounded out music on hollow logs.

Ted barely noticed the German and Turkish villages they passed next. He was too intent on the Ferris wheel, which seemed to grow larger as they neared it.

When they reached the ticket line, Ted and the others stared up, up at the revolving wheel.

"Oh, my," Aunt Marcia said in a little voice. One gloved hand slipped to her lace-covered neck. "It's so big and so high. Are you sure it is safe?"

"Absolutely," answered Richard, who had his trusty guidebook in hand. "Thousands, maybe millions, of people have ridden it since the fair started."

"I suppose," his mother said in that same tiny voice.

Ted followed her gaze back into the sky. The monstrous wheel did make a person feel small, but that didn't frighten him. He glanced at Emily. From the way her eyes sparkled, he knew she was as excited as he was.

Richard studied his book. "It says here that the wheel was designed by George Washington Gale Ferris—that's why it's called the Ferris wheel."

"Even I could have guessed that," Emily said, giving him a withering look.

Ted hid a grin. Sometimes Richard did sound like a know-it-all, but he had to admit he liked finding out what Richard knew about the things they saw.

"He built the Ferris wheel for the fair," Richard continued. "The fair planners wanted something that would be as spectacular as the Eiffel Tower that was built for the Paris fair."

Uncle Daniel paid for their tickets, and Ted swallowed a cry of surprise. Fifty cents each! That was as much as it cost to get into the entire fair. He remembered his father saying the cost was way too much for a working man.

The unhappiness of the country's money troubles swept over him. He pushed it away, angry that it had intruded on this wonderful day of fun.

The Ferris wheel came to a stop. The door of a large car was opened, and people poured out. They chatted eagerly with each other about the sights they'd seen from the wheel.

Ted and the Allertons filed into the glass and wood car and sat down in the plush swivel seats. Ted counted the seats while other passengers filed in. "Forty seats! And the sign near the ticket window said there are thirty-six cars on the Ferris wheel."

"Each car can hold twenty standing passengers besides," Richard said.

"That means the Ferris wheel can carry over two thousand people at once!" Emily's voice was filled with awe.

"Oh, dear," Aunt Marcia said in her small voice. "Are you *certain* it won't fall down?"

Uncle Daniel patted her gloved hand and smiled down at her. "I promise it won't fall down, my dear."

The door closed, and the car began to move.

Ted and Emily shared excited glances. Then Ted looked out the glass windows that went from ceiling to floor all about the car.

The car rose many feet then stopped. Ted looked down at the Midway. "The people look small from up here." Soon it started up once more.

When it stopped again, they were quite high above the buildings and could see a long way. The White City gleamed bright as ice cream in the sunshine. Its lagoons and basins were blue in the midst of the beautiful buildings.

"Oh, it's lovely!" Aunt Marcia leaned forward eagerly.

Ted and Emily grinned at each other. "Mother seems to have forgotten to be afraid," Emily whispered.

The next stop was at the very top of the Ferris wheel. "Wow! We're over 250 feet above the earth!" Richard said.

Ted's heart beat faster at the very thought. He almost expected Aunt Marcia to say "Oh, my" again, but she didn't. Instead, she pointed beyond the White City to a huge expanse of blue that seemed to meet the sky. "There's our hotel and Lake Michigan."

"The lake looks like it goes on forever," Emily said. "I know there's a shore on the other side, but it's hard to believe when you see the lake like this."

"Yes, it is," Ted agreed. "You'd think from this high, a person could almost see the other end of the earth."

"Or at least to Minneapolis," Emily teased.

As the wheel started down the opposite side, the people in the car turned their swivel seats and looked down the Midway. The shadow of the great wheel filled the street for a long way.

"There's the German Village and the Blarney Castle and the animal show," Ted said.

"And there's the elevated railroad we rode on the first day." Richard pointed out the track that ran a block behind the Midway.

Ted laughed. "The railroad seemed high when we rode on it. From up here it looks like a toy train."

When the car reached the bottom, Aunt Marcia stood up. "Well, I must say, I am almost sorry our ride is over."

"It's not, dear," Uncle Daniel told her. "We get to go around one more time."

When they finally left the car, Emily looked up at her father. "May we go again? Please?"

"Not today," he answered. "Perhaps later in the week."

Ted would have liked to go again, too. *But at fifty cents a person, I wouldn't dare ask,* he thought. If it weren't for his uncle, he wouldn't have seen the fair at all or ridden the Ferris wheel. "Thank you, Uncle Daniel. It was great!"

His uncle winked at him. "Glad you enjoyed it."

"I think I could use some refreshment," Aunt Marcia said, brushing the folds out of the skirt of her navy blue walking suit.

"Let's stop for something to drink and maybe a sweet."

"I'd rather visit some more exhibits, Mother," Richard said hesitantly.

"Me, too!" Emily chimed in.

"I'm not hungry yet, Mother," Anna added. "We did eat right before we went on the Ferris wheel."

"May we visit some of the exhibits while you and Father relax?" Richard asked.

Aunt Marcia frowned slightly and glanced at her husband. "I'm not sure that's a good idea."

"We'll be careful," Richard assured her.

"I'm sure they will be fine," Uncle Daniel told her. "Richard and Anna are responsible."

Aunt Marcia's frown still wrinkled her forehead. "Will you watch out for Ted and Emily?" she asked Richard and Anna.

They nodded.

Emily groaned. "We can watch out for ourselves. We are twelve years old."

Aunt Marcia looked firmly at Emily. "See that you mind Richard and Anna. And behave like a young lady."

Emily rolled her eyes but agreed.

"You'll need some money if you want to go inside some of the exhibits." Uncle Daniel handed Richard some money.

"Don't spend any of it on the inappropriate places," Aunt Marcia warned.

"No, Mother, we won't," Richard promised.

"Be back here in an hour," Aunt Marcia instructed.

"But that's hardly any time!" Emily cried.

"She's right, Mother," Richard said. "Can't we meet you back here at, say, five o'clock?"

The Allertons looked at each other. Ted held his breath, hoping they'd say yes.

They did, and the children hurried down the street.

"Watch out! Watch o–o–out!"

Ted leaped back. A boy who looked to be about ten led a swaying smelly camel past him. On top of the camel a young woman clutched a rope with one hand and her hat with the other. She rocked forward then jerked back at the camel's next step.

"Camel rides! That looks like fun," Ted called to Richard.

"Watch out!"

Ted looked to his left, expecting to see another camel. This time it was a donkey being led by a boy. The legs of the young man riding the donkey almost hit the ground.

"They're from the Street in Cairo exhibit," Richard said.

"Let's each ride one!" Emily suggested.

"You won't catch me on one of those smelly beasts," Anna declared. "I want to go where we can get out of the sun. Let's visit the Viennese buildings, Richard."

Ted looked longingly over his shoulder at Cairo Street but followed the others toward the entrance toward Old Vienna. "It costs twenty-five cents each to get in here." Ted pointed to the sign above the arched gateway. He hoped Richard would rather go back to Cairo Street than pay a dollar for all of them to visit Old Vienna. Richard only smiled and bought the tickets.

The street looked like a place in Old Vienna in 1750. Ted thought it was mildly interesting, but Richard and Anna thought it was wonderful.

Ted enjoyed the portraits of Egyptian mummy cases better. "Never know what you're going to see at the fair, do you?" he asked Emily.

"I wish Richard and Anna didn't take so long to see everything, though," she whispered.

Ted nodded.

Emily cleared her throat. "Richard, Ted and I are tired. We want to go out and find something to drink."

Anna frowned. "We aren't done looking here yet."

Emily ignored her. "We won't get into any trouble, Richard."

"Well." Richard hesitated. He glanced at Anna, then at Ted and Emily. "I suppose, if you're sure to meet us in front of here."

"We promise," Emily said over her shoulder as she and Ted hurried away.

Emily took a deep breath when they were back on the Midway. "I'm sure glad to be out of there! Let's try to find where we can ride the camels."

They hurried through the crowded street, dodging men's elbows, women's parasols, and an occasional tall-backed wheeled chair. "Anna and Mother should rent wheeled chairs," Emily told Ted. "They're always complaining their feet are hurting."

Ted stopped a boy leading a donkey with a laughing five-year-old girl on top of it. "Where are the camel rides?"

"On Cairo Street." The boy pointed toward the Ferris wheel.

"I wish adults didn't always walk so slow!" Emily grumbled. She darted around two men and a woman who were walking together.

Ted heard a crash and yells. A moment later he saw Emily in the middle of a tumble of people and a wheeled chair.

"Oh, no!"

The chair lay on its side. One large back wheel spun madly. An elderly lady in an expensive-looking purple dress was caught in the tipped-over chair beneath a sprawled Emily.

CHAPTER 10

The Mysterious Boy

"Why don't you watch where you're going?" The college-aged chair boy grabbed Emily by one arm and yanked her up.

"Ouch!" Emily clutched her shoulder. Running into the chair had knocked the breath out of her, but it hadn't hurt. The way the boy had pulled her up made her arm feel like it was on fire.

Ted rushed up to Emily. "Are you hurt?"

She shook her head and made herself quit holding her shoulder. "No."

The chair boy was already kneeling beside the woman. Emily knelt beside the chair, too. She put a hand on the woman's arm. "Are you hurt?"

"I. . .I don't think so," the woman said. "Do you always dart about in such an unladylike manner?"

Emily winced. "I'm afraid I do."

Emily tried to ignore the pain in her shoulder as she and the chair boy helped the woman to her feet. While the chair boy righted the large, heavy chair, she turned to look for the woman's hat and for her own.

"Oh, no!" she whispered when she saw them.

Her own little sailor hat with its broad navy blue satin ribbon was squashed flat where some passerby had stepped on it. She watched Ted pick it up and give her a pitying glance.

Worse was the lady's hat. A boy about Emily's age had sat on it! He was busy dusting the dirt from his frayed knickers, not paying any attention to the bonnet he'd ruined. The curly-haired boy looked familiar, but she was sure she didn't know him.

Emily picked up the bonnet. It had been a perfectly delightful little hat, she could tell. A deep purple ribbon sat over the point in front. White silk roses peeked from behind it. At the back was another glossy purple bow.

She turned back to the woman, whom the chair boy was helping back into the chair. Swallowing hard, she handed the hat to the woman. "I'm terribly sorry, ma'am; just terribly."

"Well, that doesn't restore my bonnet, does it?" The woman set her lips in a hard line.

"N. . .no, ma'am." Emily rubbed her suddenly sweaty hands down the sides of her skirt. "I. . .I guess I should offer to pay for it."

"That's the least you can do!" the chair boy agreed in a nasty tone.

Emily's gaze darted to his angry blue eyes and back to the woman. "I truly am sorry. I only have about twenty-five cents with me today. If you will tell me how much the bonnet cost and give me your address, I'll send you the money."

The hard lips relaxed a little. The woman waved a black-gloved hand. "Oh, never mind. I'm sure you didn't intend to run me down."

"I. . .thank you, ma'am," Emily whispered. "Are you sure you weren't hurt?"

"Only a couple bumps and bruises." She actually smiled. "This old body has known worse. I do remember being young and how it felt to run about on a summer's day. But you must be more careful."

"Yes, ma'am."

The chair boy scowled at Emily as he leaned into the back of the chair and started it again. The woman waved good-bye, and Emily lifted a hand in farewell. She wanted to stick her tongue out at the chair boy, but even she was too ladylike to do that!

"Is Mother ever going to be mad when she sees my hat," she said, turning back to Ted. "It seems I'm never able to hide my accidents from her."

"Ya mean yer like this all the time?" The boy who had sat on the lady's hat scowled from beneath curly blond hair. "Why don't ya watch where yer goin'? Think yer the only person in the street?"

Emily's cheeks grew hot at his angry words. "I didn't tip over the chair on purpose. And you're the one who sat on the lady's hat."

"Emily." Ted's voice held a warning tone. She looked at him. "When you knocked over the chair, you knocked him over, too. He was walking on the other side of it."

Emily stared at the boy's scowling face. "Oh." She cleared her throat. "I mean, I'm sorry."

"Ya should be sorry. Why don't ya act like a lady?" He hit his flat-topped hat against the side of his knickers before stuffing it over his curls.

Emily's green eyes blazed. "Why, you. . .you. . . How dare you say that to me?"

He held out a hand, palm up. "Ya can give me that twenty-five cents yer carryin', too."

"I'm not going to give—"

"Ya wrecked my doughnuts."

"Your doughnuts?"

"His doughnuts," Ted repeated.

She glanced at him. His arms were full of golden doughnuts.

"I think he was selling them," Ted said.

"That's right." The boy crossed his arms over his chest. A cloth bag hung from one shoulder. Emily could see it looked lumpy and decided that must be where he was carrying the rest of the doughnuts.

"I'm sorry I ruined your doughnuts," she said, "but surely they aren't worth twenty-five whole cents."

"A chap's gotta make a livin'." He held out his hand again.

Emily reached for her pocketbook and drew out her precious quarter. She'd been hoping to buy a camel ride with it. Reluctantly she placed it in his hand.

He dropped it into his knickers' pocket without a word.

"You haven't very good manners," she scolded. "You might at least have said thank you."

A sneer curled his lip. "Thank ya fer ruinin' my doughnuts, miss."

"Oh!" She curled her hands into fists at her side and stamped her foot. She knew she should be sorry for knocking him down and ruining his doughnuts, but he was such a nasty boy that she didn't feel sorry at all.

Something about him looked familiar. "Don't I know you?" She frowned. "Why, you're the boy who was arrested for taking pictures of the flour mill!"

"That's where I've seen you!" Ted cried out.

The boy's round chin jerked up. His blue eyes flashed. "What's it to ya?"

Emily could hardly believe she had felt sorry for this boy yesterday.

Ted must not have felt any of her frustration, for he said, "We thought it was terrible that you were arrested like that for taking pictures. Hadn't you heard that people aren't allowed to take pictures at the fair?"

"Yeah, I heard." Anger filled the boy's voice. "But a feller has ta make a livin'."

Emily remembered how this boy had reminded her of the newsboy, Erik, yesterday. Her anger began to go away. "Is. . .is your father dead?"

The round chin lifted even higher. Emily thought if he were any taller, he'd be looking down his wide nose at her. "No, Pa's not dead. He's just out of a job, like most of Chicago."

That's why he'd reminded her of Erik. Both their fathers were out of work, and both of them were filled with anger and sadness.

"I'm sorry," she said.

The boy's eyes flashed. "I don't need yer pity."

"We have a friend whose father is out of work," Ted said. "Our friend had to go to work, too." He held out his hand. "My name is Ted, and this is my cousin Emily. We're from Minneapolis."

The boy's blue eyes gazed at Ted warily for a few seconds. Finally, he shook Ted's hand. "I'm Frank Wells."

"Can I buy a good doughnut from you?" Ted asked. "I'm pretty hungry."

Frank dug into his bag and pulled out a golden brown doughnut. Emily's mouth watered. She wished she had some money left to buy one.

"They're a penny each," Frank said.

Ted dug a small leather pouch from his knickers' pocket and pulled out a penny. Breaking the doughnut in half, he handed part to Emily.

"These are really good," she told Frank after the first bite.

"My ma made them."

"How did you get back into the fair after being arrested yesterday?" Ted asked.

Frank shrugged, but he looked proud of himself. "It wasn't hard. There's lots of entrances to the fair. There's 2,500 fair police. Only a couple of them know I was caught with the camera."

"Did they put you in jail?" Emily asked. She'd never known anyone who had been arrested before.

"Naw. The judge said since I was a kid, he wouldn't make me pay the forty-dollar fine for bringing a camera into the fair, either."

"Did you get your camera back?" Ted asked.

"Yeah, but it belongs to a friend's pa, so I didn't think I better try smugglin' it in again." Frank shook his head. "Too bad, too. Make a lot more money sellin' pictures than sellin' doughnuts, even though the doughnuts sell pretty good. 'Course, doughnuts can get me thrown out of the fair, too."

Emily tilted her head to one side. "Why would anyone care if you sell doughnuts?"

"Ya can't sell anything at the fair unless ya buy a license. The license costs more money than I've got."

"Is it true most of the people in Chicago are unemployed like you said?" Emily asked Frank.

"Well, maybe it just seems like it," Frank admitted. "But the newspaper says about three hundred thousand men in Chicago don't have jobs."

Ted let out a low whistle.

Emily wished there were something she could do to help Frank and Erik and their fathers. She hated the helpless feeling that filled her when she thought of their troubles.

"We were going to ride the camels," Ted told Frank, "but we don't have enough money left. Since you know the fair so well, what do you think we should see?"

A mischievous gleam shone from Frank's eyes. "Follow me."

The look on Frank's face made Emily wonder if they should go with him. But he had already started down the hot, busy Midway with Ted on his worn heels. If she didn't start right away, she might lose them in the crowd.

Carrying her broken hat, she hurried after them.

Chapter 11

Caught!

From each side of the street, men and women called to people, inviting them to visit the exhibits. The invitations came in many languages, many accents, and sometimes in broken English. Ted and Emily had to watch out for camels and donkeys and wheeled chairs. Vendors offered all kinds of things for sale: jewelry, food, drinks, and official photographs.

Frank hurried past the places as though they were as familiar to him as Emily's home street was to her. She would have liked to linger at some of the shops and more unusual exhibits but didn't dare let the boys get too far ahead.

"Magic! Come see the Houdini Brothers escape from handcuffs!" A big man in a brown-checked suit called to the passersby.

Emily started to cross the street when she noticed Ted and Frank stopping at the door beside the large man with the booming voice.

She hurried over to them and jerked Ted's sleeve. "We can't go in there."

Frank gave her a smug look. "Scared?"

She was a little scared of anything with the word *magic* beside it, but she didn't want this tough boy to know it. She brushed her curls back from her shoulders and jerked her chin up in the air. “Of course not. It’s just not appropriate entertainment for a young lady.”

Ted bit his bottom lip. Then he said to Frank, “She’s right. Her mother would never let us see a magic show.”

Frank looked up at the sky. He took a deep breath that lifted his chest beneath his thin, mended cotton shirt. “It’s not *real* magic. It’s all about trickin’ people. Don’cha know anything? That’s the fun of it, tryin’ ta figure out how the guys do it.” He leaned closer to them.

“These guys are really good,” Frank said in a low voice, nodding as if to make sure they believed him.

“Well. . .” Ted looked at her with a question in his brown eyes. “It would be fun to see someone try to get out of handcuffs without a key.”

Emily nodded. “Mother and Father shouldn’t mind if it’s not truly magic.” She ignored the sliver of guilt that prickled at her conscience. Ted was right. It did sound like fun.

Ted had to pay ten cents for himself and Emily to go inside. Frank simply handed the ticket seller a doughnut. “Hiya, Jack. Can I go in and sell my doughnuts?”

“Sure, Frank,” the skinny, bald man said. “Just see ya don’t keep payin’ stooges from watchin’ the show, hear?”

Frank gave him a sharp nod and touched the brim of his flat-topped hat. “Sure, I hear ya. Thanks.”

Inside it seemed dark after the bright, sunlit street. Emily stumbled behind the boys until they found some empty wooden chairs.

Frank said, “I’ll be back. I’m goin’ ta try and sell some doughnuts before the show starts.” He walked up and down the aisles. “Doughnuts! Only a penny apiece!”

A couple minutes later a man came on the small stage and announced two young men: Harry and Dash Houdini.

Frank hurried back up the aisle. "That's them," he said in a loud whisper before sitting down beside Ted.

Two short men with wavy black hair walked onstage. They wore suits that Emily thought looked like the suits the waiters at the hotel restaurant wore.

"They don't look any older than Richard," she whispered to Ted, who nodded in agreement.

The older one flashed a big smile. "Ladies and gents, we're here to show youse a few experiments in de art of sleight o' hand."

The two performers made scarves appear and disappear. They did card tricks. They weren't very good. The older-looking brother dropped the cards. He shrugged his shoulders and gave the audience a big boyish grin. Most of the people laughed.

"That's Harry Houdini," Frank whispered. "He's not very good at this kind of thing, but wait until they do their escape tricks."

Emily wondered if they had wasted Ted's money.

Then the younger brother, Dash, pointed to someone standing between the stage and the audience at the edge of the room. "Youse there, come on up here an help us wid this experiment."

One of the fair policemen walked up onstage.

Emily gasped. "Aren't you afraid he'll catch you selling doughnuts, Frank?"

Frank waved a hand impatiently. "Naw. That's Al. He's a friend of mine. The Houdini brothers pay him to be part of their act when he's not on duty as a policeman."

Harry Houdini rolled up the sleeves of his short black jacket and his white shirt. He held out his arms toward the audience. "Youse can see I ain't got nothin' up my sleeves."

He held his hands toward Al, his wrists together. "Put on yer bracelets."

Al snapped the cuffs on. Then he held the key high for the

audience to see and stuffed it into his own pocket. Another volunteer was called up from the audience to make sure the handcuffs were tightly fastened.

Harry Houdini wiggled his hands about, trying to slip his wrists from the cuffs. His boyish face screwed into wrinkles as he struggled. Emily leaned forward in her seat, holding her breath.

Suddenly Houdini whipped the cuffs from his wrists and, grinning, held them above his head.

Emily and Ted pounded their hands together until they stung. The rest of the audience did the same. Frank stuck two fingers between his lips and whistled.

The curtain at the back of the stage opened, and a stagehand wheeled a large box forward. The box was taller than the Houdinis.

Dash Houdini swung an arm toward the box. "Ladies and gents, the Metamorphosis!"

It took Emily a minute to remember that the long word meant change.

The Houdini brothers opened the box, letting the audience see it was empty. Then they turned the box all the way around.

"As youse can see," Dash told them, "there's only one way outa this box." He held up a strip of braid, dangling it before the audience.

Harry Houdini held his hands behind his back, wrists together once more. Dash tied the braid around them. At Dash's request, Al the policeman checked the ropes to be sure they were tied tightly.

Then Harry Houdini walked inside the box. Dash closed the door and locked it.

Emily gasped. So did Ted and the rest of the audience.

Dash wrapped a long rope around the box, hesitated, then wrapped it around again and tied it. Once more, Al checked the rope and declared it was securely tied.

Emily inched forward on her seat. Her fingers clutched the top of the wooden chair in front of her. Her gaze was glued to the stage.

The stage curtains closed, hiding the box and Dash Houdini.

Dash's head appeared through the curtain. "One, two. . ." His head disappeared.

"Three!" Harry's face poked through the curtains where Dash's face had been a moment before.

Emily clapped a hand to her mouth. "Oh!"

Ted whooped.

The curtains parted. There stood the box, the door open. The rope lay on the floor. Inside stood Dash, his hands tied behind his back with the braid, just as Harry Houdini's had been.

The room thundered with applause and cheers. With huge smiles on their faces, the Houdinis bowed.

"That was great!" Ted said.

"Didn't I tell ya?" Frank gave him a smug smile.

"You said it's all a trick," Emily reminded him. "How did they do it? And so quickly?"

Frank looked at her in a way that made her feel sure he thought she was stupid. "They aren't likely ta be tellin' folks that. If they did, no one would pay to see them do their tricks."

"What else should we see?" Ted asked, as they blinked their way into the outdoors.

A smile slipped across Frank's round face. "Come on. I'll introduce you to a friend of mine."

"Watch out! Watch out!"

Emily stepped out of the way as a camel passed with its passenger. *If I'd been watching where I was going, I could be riding one of them,* she thought, disgusted with herself.

Frank stopped in front of an exhibit. "This is it."

Cheerful piano music came from the exhibit, the notes pushing aside the sounds of the street. Curious, Emily and Ted followed Frank inside.

A young black man was playing the piano. His hands flew across the white and black keys.

Emily leaned close to Ted so he could hear her. "He looks like he's having a good time." She bounced up and down to the music.

Applause filled the room when the man finished. He stood up and bowed. "More!" cried someone in the audience. The rest of the audience clapped harder and repeated the cry.

The young man shook his head, smiling. "Time to give these fingers a break. I'll be back before long, though. Thanks for coming." He walked behind a curtain.

"He was good," Emily told Frank. "I am glad you brought us here."

The crowd began filing out. Frank didn't follow. Instead, he headed toward the stage.

Emily and Ted looked at each other uncertainly.

Frank turned around and motioned for them to follow him. When he disappeared behind the curtain, Emily looked at Ted again. He shrugged and followed Frank, so Emily slipped behind the curtain, too.

Frank greeted a couple of the men who were working behind the stage. The black man who'd been playing the piano was standing at the back of the room drinking a glass of water.

Emily stared as Frank walked right up to him. "Hi, Mr. Joplin."

"Frank! Good to see you again. I could use one of your mother's doughnuts if you have any left. I'm famished."

Frank pulled one out of his bag and received a penny from Mr. Joplin.

"I brought some new friends by to hear your music," Frank told him.

Emily's heart swelled at the word *friends. I hope that means he's forgiven me for ruining so many doughnuts,* she thought.

"This is Ted and Emily," Frank told the man. His shoulders seemed to straighten a bit in pride. "And this is Mr. Scott Joplin. He's about the best piano player that's ever lived."

Mr. Joplin laughed. "Wish everyone felt like you do, Frank."

"I liked your music," Emily said. "I don't think I've ever heard anything like it, though."

Mr. Joplin smiled at her. "I call it Ragtime."

"Why don't you play popular music," Ted asked, "like the bands and orchestras back home?"

"The world always needs new kinds of music, don't you think? Ragtime is the kind of music I hear in my head. When I sit down at a piano, it just seems to come out the tips of my fingers and make these ivories dance."

Emily grinned. "I wish I could do that. It must be fun to have cheerful music in your head and fingers."

Mr. Joplin winked at her. "Little lady, I like the way you think."

Emily thought Mr. Joplin's break went by all too fast. She'd enjoyed talking with him. "Can we listen to more of his music before we leave?" she asked Frank.

"Sure." He took a doughnut from his bag and munched it while they waited for Mr. Joplin to be introduced.

Suddenly she heard Frank gasp. She swung her head toward him. A large hand was clamped onto one of Frank's shoulders. An angry face on top of a big man in a fair policeman's uniform glared down. "Caught up with you again, you little thief!"

Chapter 12

Frank's Escape

I'm no thief!" Frank twisted his shoulders, but he couldn't break the policeman's hold.

The big man snorted. "By selling your wares without a license, you're stealing money from honest food vendors. If that's not being a thief, I don't know what is."

People in the audience stared, wondering about the ruckus. Frank's cheeks glowed bright red.

Emily glared at the man. Her hands balled into fists at her side. "You don't have to be so rough."

"Don't meddle in police business, little lady." The man squinted his beady eyes at her. "Say, are you with this robber?"

Emily opened her mouth to say yes, but Ted answered first. "She and I came with my uncle. We have our tickets if you need to see them."

"I guess that won't be necessary," the man said. "You two look too well dressed to be friends with this hooligan. Besides, you're not toting any doughnuts."

He dragged Frank toward the door. Frank was still squirming and tugging, but the man acted like Frank was no more trouble than a kitten would be to a tiger.

"Ow! Why you. . .you. . . !"

The policeman grabbed his shin with one hand. Frank wrenched free and sped out the door, his bag of doughnuts banging against his side.

"Frank must have kicked him," Ted said.

"Good for him," Emily said in a low voice. "I suppose Frank shouldn't be breaking the law, but that policeman didn't have to treat him so rough."

"Do you want to stay and hear Mr. Joplin play some more?"

Emily shook her head. "I don't feel so cheerful anymore."

"Me, either."

When they were walking down the Midway once more, Emily looked at her ruined hat. "Maybe I should throw this away. I could tell Mother I lost it."

"You could," Ted agreed, "but that would be lying."

Emily sighed and nodded.

Ted stopped suddenly. Emily turned around. "What's wrong?" she asked. "You look like you've seen a ghost."

"I was having so much fun seeing the Midway with Frank that I forgot all about the time. Do you think Richard and Anna are still waiting for us?"

She groaned. "Oh, no! We'd better hurry."

They sped up the street. Emily tried to watch where she was going. She didn't want to run anyone else down!

Richard and Anna were nowhere to be seen near the entrance to Old Vienna, where they'd agreed to meet.

Emily's heart dropped to her shoes. This day was going from bad to worse.

"Come on." Ted's voice sounded grim. "We'd better see if we can find your parents. Maybe they're still at the restaurant."

Neither spoke as they rushed along. Emily wondered whether Ted was as nervous as she was about seeing her parents.

"They *are* waiting for us here," Emily said, relieved when the restaurant came into sight.

Her mother and Anna were seated on a bench outside the restaurant. Richard was standing beside the bench with his arms crossed and an impatient look on his face. Her father was pacing, hands in his pockets.

Emily and Ted glanced at each other, took deep breaths, and hurried across the street. "Hello!"

"There you are!" Emily's father glared at them. "We've been worried sick about you and had no idea where to look in the miles of fairgrounds."

Emily and Ted stood quietly while the older people scolded them for being late and not staying with Richard and Anna. They knew better than to try to make excuses for themselves.

"We're sorry," Emily said when there was a break in the scolding. "We know we were wrong to be so late."

"Everything was so exciting to see," Ted added. "We were having so much fun that we forgot we were to meet Richard and Anna."

"We forgot all about the time." Emily swung her arms wide.

Her mother stared at Emily's hand. "Whatever did you do to your new sailor hat?"

Emily gulped. She'd been hiding the hat behind her skirt when they came up to her parents. In explaining about the time, she'd forgotten she was holding it. "It, uh, it kind of got crushed."

"That is obvious," her mother said dryly. "How?"

Emily glanced at Ted. She didn't much like the pity she thought she saw in his almost-black eyes. "It, um, fell on the ground, and someone crushed it."

"How could it fall on the ground? Weren't you wearing hat pins to secure it to your hair?"

"Well, yes."

"Tell me the whole story, Emily Marie."

How does she always know when I'm not telling the complete truth? Emily wondered as she started the story of knocking over the wheeled chair.

"Was the woman hurt?" her father asked.

"No," Emily answered.

Mother shook her head. "When are you going to learn to act like a young lady?"

Emily bit her lip. *Why can't I just act like me?* she wanted to ask. She'd been told often enough that one of a mother's duties was to raise her children to act properly.

Father crossed his arms over his jacket and vest. "Unless you two prove to us that you can act more responsibly, you will not be allowed to visit any exhibits by yourself."

"Yes, sir," Emily muttered.

"Yes, sir," Ted said quietly.

Instead of going back to the hotel, they ate in a German restaurant on the fairgrounds. Bouncy tunes from a German band gave them something to listen to while they ate.

The cheerful music didn't lighten Emily's heart. She couldn't forget Frank. *It must be awful to be hunted by the fair police just because you're trying to make a living for your family,* she thought.

After dinner the family visited the Minnesota Building while waiting for darkness.

"When darkness falls," Father told them, "the main fair buildings are decorated with light, and there is a fireworks display."

Leaving the Minnesota Building, Emily overheard a well-dressed, middle-aged woman say to the woman beside her, "This fair seems a horrid waste of money. There are so many people out of work in the country. The money spent on the fair buildings would be better spent helping them."

The woman beside her agreed.

Guilt settled down on Emily's shoulders like a heavy cape. *Maybe I shouldn't be enjoying this trip to the fair when boys like Frank and Erik have to work,* she thought.

Later that evening, sitting in the dusk in the middle of the White City, Emily admitted the sight was beautiful. White lights chased each other along, outlining the buildings, framing them against the night sky. She'd never seen anything like it.

The water in the fountains sprayed up in many colors. "How do they do that?" she asked.

Richard knew, of course. "There are lights beneath the fountains. They shine up from beneath the water and make the water look like it's pink or green or blue."

Soon the fireworks were set off. They were beautiful against the night sky. But as beautiful as everything was, Emily couldn't seem to get excited about it.

Her father sat down beside her and slipped an arm around her shoulders. "Tired?"

She shrugged and leaned her head against her father's shoulder. "Maybe a little."

"Is something the matter?" he asked in a low voice. "You aren't your usual cheerful self."

She bit her bottom lip, wondering how she could tell him what was bothering her. She didn't want to get in trouble for going to exhibits with Frank.

"When I tipped over that wheeled chair this afternoon, I knocked over someone else, too. A boy. He was selling doughnuts."

"Was he hurt?" That always seemed to be her doctor father's first question.

"No," she answered. "But he was the same age as Ted and me. His father lost his job, so he had to quit school and go to work like Erik."

"That's happened to a lot of boys during these hard times," her father said quietly.

"I feel bad, playing and visiting the fair when Frank and Erik have to work."

He squeezed her shoulder. "I'm glad you have such a good heart."

His words made her feel loved, but she still felt guilty.

"Chicago's mayor is trying to help the unemployed men," Father explained. "He's started something he calls an unemployment bureau to help men like Frank's father find jobs."

"Tonight I heard a lady say that instead of spending money on the fair, the country should have given the money to the poor men who are out of work."

"Mmmm." Her father thought about her words for a minute. "I think the fair was good for the unemployed people. How many people do you think have jobs working at this fair?"

Emily looked at him in surprise. "Lots. Too many to count."

"When I see all the wonderful inventions at the fair," her father continued, "they remind me of the incredible things human beings are capable of doing, especially when they work together. One hundred years ago we couldn't have seen the lights that make the buildings so beautiful against the sky tonight."

"They weren't invented one hundred years ago."

"That's right. People wanted better light at night, so people worked and worked until they found a solution. The inventions at the fair give me hope that people will find an answer to our money problems, too. After all, we can see there are a lot of smart people in our world."

Emily looked up at the fireworks bursting in pops and roars

against the black sky. Her guilt eased and peace took its place.

Dear God, she prayed silently, *please help the smart people in our country find a way to help Frank and Erik's fathers and the other people who are out of work. In Jesus' name, Amen.*

When they left the fair, they walked along Lake Michigan back to the Beach Hotel. The breeze off the lake felt good. Emily liked the sound of the white-tipped waves that crashed against the boardwalk.

She glanced back over her shoulder. She could still see the lighted buildings of the White City. *The City of Hope,* she reminded herself.

"I wish there was something I could do so children didn't have to be hungry or live hard lives because their parents are out of work," she whispered to Ted.

"Me, too." His voice sounded sad.

But what can we do? she wondered. *We're only twelve.*

Chapter 13

The Falling Statue

Ted and the Allertons stayed away from the fair the next day. It was Sunday, so they went to church and then relaxed for the rest of the day.

There had been big arguments between the people who ran the fair and others over whether or not the fair should stay open on Sundays. The editor of the Minneapolis *Tribune* had even written a column about it. He believed no work should be done on Sundays unless it was necessary.

The fair planners said most people worked Mondays through Saturdays. That left only Sunday for people who lived in and near Chicago to visit the fair.

In spite of the many people against it, the fair stayed open on Sundays. Emily's father said the fair had won the battle but lost the war because not many people visited the fair on the Lord's Day.

The next time they visited the fair, they saw an old black man surrounded by people who were trying to speak with him and shake his hand.

"Excuse me." Father stopped a gentleman in the crowd near the Administration Building. "Is that Mr. Frederick Douglass?"

"Yes."

"I'd certainly like to meet him," Father said.

"I should like to, also." Mother's brows puckered. "It isn't polite to introduce yourself to someone, though."

"You didn't let us talk to Mr. Edison," Emily reminded them.

"I think this is different," Father said. "After all, Mr. Edison was in a discussion with two friends. Mr. Douglass appears to be welcoming the public."

"Who is he?" Ted asked. "Why do you want to meet him so badly?"

"Mr. Douglass is the ambassador to Haiti," Mother told him.

"He's done a great deal for black people," Father added. "He's a brave, intelligent, compassionate man."

"He was born a slave," Mother explained. "He taught himself to read and write. Most slaves weren't allowed to read and write. After the war, freed slaves needed someone who could do both well, like Mr. Douglass. Someone who could speak to the public and the lawmakers."

Father nodded. "Since the Civil War, Mr. Douglass had been fighting for the black people. When slavery was made illegal, blacks became free, but they weren't given all the privileges of white citizens. Mr. Douglass fought hard for the Fifteenth Amendment, which made black men citizens and gave them the right to vote."

"Today at the fair is set aside to honor black people," Mother reminded them. "Mr. Douglass will be speaking."

Finally, Emily's parents decided they would indeed join the crowd that was trying to meet Mr. Douglass. Richard and Anna were given permission to visit a nearby exhibit. Because of the troubles on Saturday, however, Ted and Emily were told to wait for their parents on the steps of a nearby building.

The cousins sat down on the broad steps, plunked their elbows on their knees, and watched the large group of people trying to reach the balding black man with the ring of bright white hair.

"This is going to take a lo–o–ong time," Ted said.

Emily nodded and felt a little guilty. It was her fault they had to sit here. If she hadn't knocked over the wheeled chair, they wouldn't have met Frank. If they hadn't met Frank, they wouldn't have been late meeting Richard and Anna and her parents. If they hadn't been late, they could be off seeing things, just as Richard and Anna were doing.

"Hiya!"

Emily and Ted whipped around at Frank's friendly greeting. The boy was just sitting down on a step above and behind them.

Ted laughed. "Back in the fair again. They can't keep you out. You're as slippery as Houdini."

Frank grinned. Emily thought he liked being compared to the young escape artist.

"Did the policeman catch you after you left Mr. Joplin's?" Emily asked.

"Naw. He's too out of shape ta keep up ta me when I'm runnin'."

"Are you selling doughnuts again today?" Ted asked.

"Nope. Candy," Frank answered. "Candy is easier ta hide than doughnuts. It doesn't take up as much room. And it's easy to sell. Say," he looked puzzled, "why are ya sittin' here? Your feet already tired? The day's just startin'!"

Emily smoothed the palms of her hands over the dark blue skirt that covered her knees. "We're waiting for my parents. They're hoping to meet that man."

"Which ones are yer folks?" Frank asked.

She told him and watched him study them a minute.

"Who's that black man?" he asked.

She told him about Mr. Douglass.

"Scott Joplin told me 'bout him." Frank's face shone with interest as he studied the man in the midst of the crowd. "He's almost a hero. He says blacks were freed from slaveholders, but they are still slaves to the white society."

"Mr. Douglass is speaking today because it's been set aside to honor black Americans," Emily said.

Frank snorted. "Honor black Americans, my eye!"

"What do you mean?" Ted asked. "Isn't this the day when there are special talks and events for black people?"

"Sure it is," Frank agreed, "but it's not what the black people wanted. Scott Joplin told me lots of blacks aren't comin' taday, 'cause they're mad at the fair planners."

"Why?" Emily asked. "Why would they be mad because there's a special day for them?"

Frank wrapped his arms around his knees and leaned forward. "They wanted their own exhibition building, see. They wanted ta show the world everythin' black people have done since the Civil War. The fair planners wouldn't let them do that."

"Why?" Ted wondered.

"They told the blacks ta ask their own states ta let them exhibit in the states' buildin's. None of the states let them."

"That doesn't sound fair," Emily said. "The fair planners let women have their own building."

"Yep." Frank nodded. "But that's not all. Mr. Joplin says blacks can't even work at good payin' jobs at the fair. Instead of being construction workers or clerical workers, they can only have low-payin' jobs like street sweepers."

Sadness began to fill Emily again. There were so many unfair, hard things in the world that she couldn't do anything about.

"At least the blacks have this special day," Ted said. "They can tell the world what their people have done."

"And what they want for their future," Emily said.

Emily's parents had made it to the great man's side now. She watched her father remove his hat and shake hands with Mr. Douglass, then introduce her mother to the wise old man.

"Guess I'd better be movin' on." Frank slipped his candy-filled bag over his arm.

Emily wondered if he knew that she and Ted were afraid of having her parents find him with them. Did Frank think they were embarrassed of him because he didn't dress or talk as well as they did? She hoped not, but she knew her parents wouldn't approve of their friendship, especially her mother.

Frank stood up. "I'm goin' over ta Wooded Island for a bit. At least there's some shade there. If ya get a chance, come on over and look me up."

The kids watched him walk jauntily down the steps and cross the wide bridge to the island. "I wonder if we'll ever see him again," Ted said.

After lunch, Father and the boys wanted to go to the Horticulture Building. Mother gently argued to visit the Woman's Building instead. Finally, it was agreed the men would go to the Horticulture Building and the women to the Woman's Building.

"I want to see the Woman's Building," Emily told her mother as they climbed the steps, "but I'd like to see the Horticulture Building, too."

"So would I," Mother admitted. "However, there isn't time to see everything before we leave. If the men aren't smart enough to want to visit the Woman's Building, we'll have to visit it ourselves."

They enjoyed the model kitchen, but Emily thought the model hospital was more interesting. "I've never even been in a *real* hospital," she told Anna.

The young woman guide in the model hospital told them of the history of women nurses and doctors. "There are almost 250 women doctors in Chicago now," she said proudly.

Anna gasped. "That many? There are women doctors in Minneapolis, too, but I didn't know so many women had become doctors."

The guide smiled. "Isn't it wonderful? Women have entered every area of work that men enter. There are women artists and writers, lawyers and merchants, journalists and editors, cotton planters and teachers, real estate agents and architects, and anything else of which you can think. All the art in this building is by women. A woman even *designed* this building. This is a marvelous time to be a woman!"

"Yes," Mother agreed, "and it will be a better time to be a woman once all women in the country have the right to vote."

Emily looked at her mother in surprise.

"Why, Mother, I didn't know you believed in suffrage for women," Anna said in a voice that sounded as surprised as Emily felt.

Mother looked at them serenely. "Of course I believe women should have the right to vote. We have the benefits of living in America. It is only right that we should have more of the responsibilities."

Anna stared at her. "But you've never gone to any women's suffrage meetings or marched in any of their parades or. . .or anything."

"I shouldn't think a woman needed to carry a poster down the street and holler unseemly things at men to prove to the world she has the intelligence to vote for the people she wants in the government."

Emily and Anna exchanged amused glances as they followed their mother down the hall to the next exhibit area. Emily had never heard her quiet, ladylike mother speak in such a manner. *What else does she think about a woman's place that she hasn't told us?* she wondered.

Emily stood in the middle of the building's Great Hall. She craned her neck to see everything beneath the two-story ceiling.

She stopped beside a small sculpture of a mother sitting beside a cradle with a tiny baby inside. She touched the mother's arm and smiled. *I wish I could make something as beautiful as this,* she thought.

"This is the best part of the whole building!" Emily told Anna as they stared at the seventy-foot murals on the walls.

One of the murals was called "Modern Woman." In it, women were dressed in up-to-date clothing chasing fame and working together picking the fruits of knowledge and science.

Emily leaned her head from one side to the other, studying the mural. "Isn't it beautiful, Anna? I wonder how the painter made it so bright."

"It's painted in the modern impressionist style," Anna told her. "Mary Cassatt is the artist."

Emily backed up, trying to get a better view of the huge picture.

Thud!

She came to a sudden halt when she backed into something solid.

"Emily!"

At the sound of Anna's strained voice, Emily whirled around. She'd backed into the base that held the sculpture of the mother and child. The base teetered. Emily and Anna grabbed for it at the same time. The beautiful sculpture slipped from its perch.

Chapter 14

One Accident Too Many

Emily's eyes slammed shut. The heavy wooden base thudded against the floor. She held her breath, waiting for the crash of the beautiful sculpture and her mother's "Emily Marie Allerton, how *could* you!"

Neither came.

Instead, she heard Anna's voice saying, "Thank you."

Emily opened her eyes. A tall young woman in a navy blue suit was on her knees, the sculpture in her arms. Her face beneath dark hair was almost as white as the marble sculpture.

"You caught it!" Emily clasped her hands together. "I am *so* glad. I thought there was no chance it could be saved, and it is so beautiful!"

The young woman smiled, still hugging the piece to her chest. "It is lovely, isn't it?"

Mother, who had been viewing a piece at the other end of the hall, hurried up. Her gloved hands lifted her skirt a couple inches above her ankles so she could walk faster. Her pretty face was filled with concern.

Emily bit back a groan and stood up. "I know, Mother, it's my fault. I should have been watching where I was going, but I was looking at the mural."

Her mother's worried glance found the sculpture in the young woman's arms. "It wasn't broken?"

The woman set the piece on the floor beside her and stood up. "No, ma'am."

Mother put a gloved hand over her heart, closed her eyes, and gave a sigh of relief. "Emily Marie, you shall be the death of me yet."

Emily's cheeks burned. It was embarrassing to have her mother speak to her that way in front of the smart-looking young woman who had saved the sculpture.

The woman smiled at her and gave her a quick wink. "The accident could have happened to anyone. Nothing was broken. No harm was done."

A little of Emily's guilt and most of her embarrassment were washed away by the woman's kind words.

"I am Miss Enid Yandell," the rescuer said.

Emily's mother introduced the three of them. Then together they righted the base. Miss Yandell set the sculpture carefully on top of it. "There! Everything is as good as new."

Emily frowned slightly. "Miss Enid Yandell. We were told that a Miss Yandell made some of the sculptures in the roof garden, but that can't be you. You're too young."

Miss Yandell laughed. "I'm twenty-two, and I did indeed make the garden sculptures. Have you seen them?"

When she found they hadn't been to the cafe in the garden on the building's roof, she invited them to join her there for coffee. Emily was thrilled when her mother agreed.

It was sunny and breezy on the roof. The garden was lovely. Mother and Anna walked about enjoying the plants and flowers. But Emily thought Miss Yandell's sculptures were lovelier than the flowers and told her so.

Miss Yandell pointed to some huge sculptures. "See the angels on the edge of the roof? They were sculpted by a girl of nineteen."

"Nineteen!" Emily looked at the huge winged sculptures in wonder. "How did you and this girl get to be so good so young?"

Miss Yandell smiled. "Remember the fair's motto?"

"Yes. It's 'I will.' "

"That's right. If you are willing to work hard for the things you want, you will be surprised at the doors that open for you."

Emily was glad for the oriental awnings that covered the cafe and shaded them from the bright sun when they sat down for coffee and desserts.

A group of well-dressed women stopped at their table to say hello to Miss Yandell. When the sculptress introduced the women to her, Emily was glad she'd worn one of Anna's hats today. Every one of the women was famous: Jane Addams, Susan B. Anthony, Frances Willard, and Anna Julia Cooper.

Jane Addams was known for her concern for the working people. "She's speaking at the World Labor Congress about the poor working conditions of women and children," Miss Yandell told them.

Frances Willard was known all over the country for her work with the Women's Christian Temperance Union, which tried to make the sale of liquor illegal.

Anna Julia Cooper was a black woman. She had an important position with the Colored Women's League. She spoke often to important groups, telling them that no one should be given or denied special favors because of their gender or race.

Susan B. Anthony impressed Emily the most. She was one of the main leaders of the women's suffrage movement. People either thought she was wonderful or awful.

Mother nodded politely to each woman as she and the girls were introduced to them. She spoke a sentence or two to each, thanking them for the work they were doing.

Emily turned to Mother. "Why are you only a mother and housewife when women can do so many things today?"

She was immediately sorry. She hadn't meant to embarrass her mother. She was relieved when her mother smiled. "Trying to keep you out of trouble keeps me far too busy to work outside the home, Emily."

The adults and Anna laughed. Emily managed a small smile.

A few minutes later, the women left Miss Yandell and the Allertons. Watching them depart, Mother said, "I'm a little surprised to see Anna Cooper here. I heard many blacks were angry because they don't have their own exhibit."

"It's true," Miss Yandell agreed, "that they weren't allowed to set up an exhibit that shows what contributions the black people have made to American history, and that's unfortunate. However, the work of black women artists is displayed in this building."

"Good," Mother said quietly.

Emily thought it was good, too.

"I am glad you believe women have a right to explore their interests, Mrs. Allerton," Miss Yandell said, "even when that means they cannot spend all their time at home." She took a sip of coffee from the delicate china cup. "Let me tell you a funny story.

"Mrs. Ulysses Grant, the widow of the former president and general, visited my sculpting studio one day. At first, I was flattered. Then she told me that a woman's place is in the home.

" 'So you don't approve of me?' I asked.

"Mrs. Grant scowled and said, 'Will you be a better housewife by your cutting marble?'

" 'Yes,' I answered. 'I am developing muscles in my arms to beat biscuit when I keep house.' "

Mother and the girls laughed. Then Mother asked, "Did she

change her mind, then, and decide she approved of your work after all?"

"She did not totally approve, but she felt my work had some good purpose."

Emily was sorry when the lovely coffee party was over and they had to leave their new friend to meet Father and the boys.

Her spirits lifted when her father said they were going for a gondola ride before dinner. Clapping her hands, she said, "Oh, I've wanted to ride in one ever since we came to the fair!"

They bought tickets for the gondola. Then they waited in front of the Agricultural Building on wide steps that led to the wooden boat landing at the water's edge, where it would be easier to board the long, narrow boat. On either side of the steps, statues of huge white bulls stared out over the water.

While they waited, Emily told her father and the boys about their afternoon.

"That's nothing." Ted dismissed her afternoon with a wave of his hand. "You should have been with us. We went in a cave! Not a real cave, of course. It was only a model of Mammoth Cave in South Dakota. But it was just like being in a real cave, with stalactites and stalagmites and everything!"

Emily had to admit she would have liked to see that. "But only if I could have my afternoon, too."

A gondola glided silently up to the steps, and Emily and Ted promptly forgot their exciting afternoon experiences.

"Oh, it's one of the prettiest gondolas," Emily cried in delight.

The bow of the gondola was shaped like the head, neck, and back of a swan, with wings raised as if it were about to leave the water. The back of the gondola was the swan's tail. Both the back and front rose taller than a man.

Richard sat on a narrow seat as close to the front of the gondola as he could get. Father took the seat in the back. Anna and Ted shared a seat, and Emily and her mother sat together near the middle of the low-sided wooden boat.

The oarsmen's outfits were brightly colored. Striped shirts matched wide, striped trousers. Colored vests covered the shirts and matched the men's hats. Even brighter sashes were tied about their waists.

The oarsmen—one in front and one in back—made the gondola move across the lagoon as smoothly and quietly as a real swan. They stood while they rowed. The oars were skinny and almost as long as the boat. Another oarsman stood high against the "swan's" tail, controlling the rudder.

The gondola went under a bridge, and they passed from the Great Basin to the lagoon. Ted pointed out white water birds that bobbed along the shore of Wooded Island. Other gondolas, canoes, and canopy-covered electric launches joined them on the water.

As they passed a statue of a warrior with his weapons, Ted asked Emily, "Remember that song we learned? The one about the ax?"

Emily grinned and nodded. Frank had taught them the song. He said all the children in Chicago were singing it.

Ted sang the first line. Then Emily joined in:

Lizzie Borden took an ax
and gave her mother forty whacks.
When she saw what she had done,
She gave her father forty-one.

They burst into giggles. Richard chuckled.

"Emily Marie!"

Emily looked in surprise at her mother, seated beside her. What had she done now?

"How could you sing such an awful song, let alone laugh at it? I'm ashamed of you. And you, too, Theodore."

Emily spread her hands. "But it's funny!"

Her mother's lips tightened into a thin line. "It most certainly is not funny to sing about a girl killing her parents! The Bible tells us to honor our parents."

"I must agree with your mother," Father said in his severest tone. "Don't let us hear either of you singing that tune again."

Emily and Ted exchanged disgusted looks.

The gondolier who was manning the rudder suddenly broke into song. His beautiful voice rolled out over the water. The music was pretty, but Emily couldn't understand the words. But she knew it wasn't the song about Lizzie Borden!

"What is he singing?" she asked her mother.

"It's from the opera *Faust.* It's in Italian."

As the gondolier finished his song, Emily saw her new friend walking across a bridge they were approaching.

"There's Miss Yandell, Ted. She's the woman I told you about." She lifted one arm as high as she could. "Miss Yandell! Miss Yandell!"

The woman didn't stop walking or look their way.

"Emily, do stop yelling."

Emily barely heard her mother. She jumped to her feet, waving both arms over her head. "Miss Yandell! Hello, Miss Yandell!"

The gondola started to rock. Emily waved her arms, trying to get her balance. She saw Ted stretch his arms toward her, but he was too far away to reach her. Everyone in her family was yelling at her to sit down. The oarsmen were yelling something in another language.

Her arms waved more wildly. "Help!"

Mother tried to steady her but couldn't. Finally, she jumped up and grabbed for Emily.

Too late. *Splash!* Emily held her breath as she hit the water.

Chapter 15

Fire!

Emily pushed herself to the surface, sputtering. Her hair clung like wet seaweed to her face. She brushed it out of her eyes with one hand and treaded water with the other.

"Grab the oar, Emily!"

At Ted's order, she looked around for the oar. One of the oarsmen was holding it out to her. She grabbed it and hung on for dear life. She didn't know how to swim, but she knew enough to kick her feet and keep her head above water.

"Help!" *Cough*! *Cough*! "Help!"

Emily whipped her head around to see who was calling so weakly. "Mother!"

Her mother was trying to wave her arms in the air instead of moving them in the water. Emily realized in a flash that her mother must have fallen in trying to keep her from falling. Her mother's head slipped beneath the water. Dread swept through Emily. Her mother didn't know how to swim, either!

A moment later, Mother's head popped back up. "Kick, Mother!" Emily called.

Out of the corner of her eye, Emily saw a large, dark shape flash by. *Splash*!

Relief swamped her when she saw that it was Father. He was helping Mother.

With Richard and Ted's help, Emily tried to climb into the gondola. It wasn't easy with her high-buttoned shoes full of water and her dress and petticoat soaking wet. She hadn't realized how heavy clothes were when they were wet!

The gondola rocked dangerously when Richard and Ted started to pull her into it. For a minute, Emily thought it was going to tip over. Anna and the gondoliers moved their weight to the other side of the boat. A moment later, Emily was safe on the bottom of the gondola.

"Thanks." She was panting so hard that she could hardly speak. She brushed her hair off her face again and looked to see if her parents were near the boat yet.

"Why, they aren't even coming to the boat!" she cried.

"I think when Father saw the trouble we were having getting you in the boat, he decided it would be easier to take her to shore," Richard said.

Father had one hand under Mother's chin. She was lying on her back, and he was pulling her along. Richard was right. In a couple minutes, their father reached a small landing and helped Mother up on the steps.

The gondoliers steered for the landing and reached it right after Mother and Father.

Ted and Richard helped Emily out of the gondola. She didn't want their help, but she couldn't manage by herself in the heavy wet dress. Her shoes made squishing sounds when she stepped out onto the paved step.

Fairgoers had seen the accident and surged to the landing to see if Emily and her mother were all right. *There must be hundreds of them,* Emily thought in despair. She turned her back and sank down on one of the bottom steps.

She glanced over at Mother, who was coughing. "Will she be all right?" Emily asked Father.

He nodded, a grim expression on his usually friendly face. "She just swallowed a lot of the lagoon."

Mother, who always took such care to look good in public and act like a lady, looked like something the dog had dragged in. She'd lost her hat. Half her hair had come unpinned and hung in a mass of wet dangles down her back. Her pretty white linen-and-lace gown had turned pale brown and was torn besides. She'd been embarrassed in front of hundreds of people.

Emily dropped her head into her hands. "Am I in trouble now!" she whispered.

A gentle hand touched her shoulder. "Are you all right, Emily?"

She looked up into a concerned face. Miss Yandell! She smiled weakly. "I'm fine, thank you."

I could sure use Houdini's trick box about now, she thought. *I'd like to disappear for good.*

Emily wasn't so fortunate. The next morning, seated on the train on the way back to Minneapolis, she looked from one face to another. No one had a friendly glance for her—not even her cousin Ted.

She'd known her parents would be furious with her. When they decided to cut the trip to the fair short, Ted and her brother and sister had turned against Emily, too. She couldn't blame them. She'd ruined their trip. They didn't get to go to Buffalo Bill's Wild West Show, which was right outside the fair.

Of course, her parents had given her yet another lecture with the old familiar chorus: Why can't you act like a young lady, like Anna?

I wish Mother and Father liked me as much as they do Anna, she thought.

Emily tried to curl deeper into the corner of the plush seat. She looked down at the book in her lap, *David Copperfield.* She pretended to read, but she didn't even see the words. The rhythmic clack of the wheels going around seemed to be saying, "Stupid girl! Stupid girl!"

You'd think I'd been punished enough for falling into the lagoon, she thought. After all, the new dress she'd loved had lost its beautiful dark green color. The lagoon water had washed it out and left it a streaked, unwearable mess. Her purse was somewhere at the bottom of the lagoon. Worst of all, wonderful Miss Yandell had seen the whole affair!

She glanced across at Ted and Anna, who were seated on the purple upholstered seat across from her. They both glared at her.

Emily drew her legs up under her skirt and pretended to read once more. It was going to be a long ride home!

The day after they got home, Emily was carrying a large crystal plate piled with cookies. She walked carefully down the hall from the kitchen toward the parlor. The house was filled with family. Uncle Enoch and Aunt Tina, Ted and his parents, and Ted's brother Walter and his Swedish wife, Lena, had all come to welcome the Allertons back and hear about the fair.

It's good to have people around who will smile and talk to me, Emily thought as she neared the open door to the parlor.

"*Tomma tunnor skramla mest!*" she heard Lena say, and smiled. Lena always had a Swedish proverb on the tip of her tongue.

"What does that mean?" Richard asked.

"Empty barrels make the most noise," Lena explained as Emily stepped into the room.

Everyone in the room began to laugh. "That does describe Emily to a *T,*" Richard said.

Emily stopped short. Pain stabbed her chest. Had they all been laughing at *her*? Had *she* been the empty barrel? Did sweet Lena truly believe that she had no brains?

The laughter in the room died. Emily realized everyone was staring at her. She could tell they knew she'd heard the unkind remarks.

"I'm sorry, Emily," Lena said in her soft, musical voice. "I spoke without thinking."

Tears blurred Emily's sight and made her eyes hot. She kept her eyes open wide to keep the tears from falling. Carefully she handed the crystal plate to Lena. Then she turned and left the room.

She wanted to run, but she wouldn't let herself. They laughed at her when she didn't act like a lady. So she made herself walk slowly into the hall and up the stairs. Only then, behind her closed door, did she let the tears come.

A week later, Ted was finally speaking to her again, though still he wasn't the friendly cousin he'd always been before.

On a Sunday in the middle of August, they went walking together along the Mississippi River after dinner. Near one of the bridges that spanned the wide water, they met Erik, the newsboy, talking with a young man about twenty-five years old.

Erik's grin spread wide with a welcome that warmed Emily's heart. Then she wondered whether he would still be friendly after Ted told him all the clumsy things she'd done at the fair.

"Haven't seen you two around in a while," Erik said.

"We've been to Chicago," Ted told him, "to the World's Fair."

Erik's eyes opened wide. "No kiddin'!"

"Who are your friends, Erik?" the young man with him asked, pushing his bowler hat toward the back of his curly black hair until Emily thought the hat surely must fall off.

Erik introduced them and then said, "And this is Mr. Thomas

Beck. He's a teacher at the Newsboys' Sunday School. He's a newspaper reporter for the Minneapolis *Tribune,* too."

Ted shook Mr. Beck's hand. "I've never met a reporter before."

Emily thought Mr. Beck looked like a reporter. He wore a fashionable brown-and-tan-checked suit with a matching vest. A pencil rested behind one ear. A notebook stuck out of one of his suit pockets.

"Mr. Beck is a good friend of mine," Erik said.

"Tell us about your trip to the World's Fair," Mr. Beck encouraged.

Ted and Emily told them about everything: the beautiful buildings in the White City, the Ferris wheel, the marvelous new inventions and new foods, the huge statues that had seemed to be everywhere in the White City, the famous people they'd seen, the copies of Columbus's ships, and even the Houdini brothers and their trick box. But when Ted started telling them about the electric launches and the gondolas, Emily cringed and grew quiet. Now Erik and nice Mr. Beck would find out what a silly thing she'd done. She stared at the tips of her new high-buttoned shoes—her old ones had been ruined in the lagoon—and waited.

Ted described the gondola and gondoliers. "We all went for a ride in one of the gondolas. One of the gondoliers even sang for us!"

He hesitated. Emily looked up, surprised to find him looking at her.

"And then," Ted started again, "and then we went back to the hotel. The gondola ride was the last thing we did at the fair."

Emily gave him a small smile. He shrugged, lifting the shoulders of his Sunday suit, but he didn't smile back. Sadness pinched her heart. It was going to take a long time for Ted and her family to completely forgive her.

A passerby bumped Emily's elbow. Mr. Beck looked up with a scowl. "Hey, mister, watch where you're going."

The man paid no attention. He was hurrying toward the bridge. Emily saw with surprise that *everyone* was hurrying in that direction or staring and pointing across the river. She and her friends turned to see what was so interesting.

"Fire!" Mr. Beck exclaimed.

Orange flames shot into the air along the opposite bank, where mostly sawmills and homes were built. The flames raced from building to building like a child at play. It seemed only moments before flame covered the riverbank for as far as Emily could see.

Mr. Beck grabbed his pad and pencil. He started across the bridge in a dash, his checkered coat flying out behind him as he ran through the crowd.

Without a second thought, Emily started after him. She could see from the corner of her eye that Ted and Erik were coming, too. Toward the other end of the bridge, she began to feel the heat of the huge blaze. Policemen were warning people to stay back for fear of their lives.

"I'm a *Tribune* reporter," she heard Mr. Beck tell one of the policemen. "I need to get through so I can report on this."

With a shake of his head and another warning to watch out for his safety, the policeman let him through.

Emily leaned against the bridge railing to get a better look at the burning bank. "Ouch!" She drew back, shaking her hands. "That railing is hot!" she told Ted and Erik.

The clanging of fire engine bells alerted the crowd, and the people pressed together to let the firemen by. The roar of the fire drowned out the rattle of the wheels carrying the engines and the hooves of the horses pulling them. The horses were covered with foam, already overheated from pulling the engines as fast as they could. Firemen hanging onto the fire wagons were covered to their chins in rubber coats. Sponges that would protect their mouths hung about their necks.

Wagons of every description began crossing the bridge from the burning side of the city, pulled by terrified horses. Household furnishings and frightened people filled the wagons. Men, women, and children clung to the wagons' sides. Their eyes were huge with fear.

At the sight of them, Emily's excitement died. She only wished she could do something to help them.

Clouds of gray and black smoke and columns of orange and red flames rose so high they almost met the sky. Emily and the boys watched small boats filled with more people move out of the smoke-covered bank.

"There's goin' to be a lot more people without jobs now," she heard Erik say, "and without homes, too."

Chapter 16

Emily's Prayer

Erik was right, Emily thought a few days later when she, Ted, Erik, and Mr. Beck again stood beside the river and looked across at the smoldering ashes that had once been over a mile of buildings. Even the part of the bridge they'd stood upon Sunday had been burned. Many sawmills had been completely destroyed. Over 160 houses had been burned, leaving more than two hundred families homeless.

"I can't imagine losing my home and everything I own," Ted said, shaking his head.

"At least the people have places to stay," Mr. Beck told them. "A church and two large halls have been opened for them. People and businesses have donated food, clothing, beds, and blankets."

"It must be awful to live that way," Emily said.

"It's not the same as having a home," Mr. Beck admitted, "but at least they won't have to live under the stars until the men find jobs and can afford to move their families into houses."

"The city is helping the men to find jobs, too." Erik's voice sounded bitter. "The city is even giving work to the men in return for their family's food and shelter."

Emily frowned. "Why does that make you so mad, Erik? It

sounds like a good thing."

"Why should the city make jobs for these men when they don't make jobs for men like my pa? He and thousands like him can't help being out of work any more than these people."

The anger and pain in Erik's eyes sliced through Emily's heart.

August slipped into September. Ted and Emily went back to school, where they spoke to their classes and wrote essays about their trip to the World's Fair.

Oklahoma Territory opened former Cherokee land to settlers. On September 16, one hundred thousand people raced over the land to claim their own acreage.

"The paper says a lot of the people are unemployed and came from other parts of the country," Emily told Ted. "I wonder if any of them are from Minneapolis."

Ted shrugged his shoulders. "Maybe, but we know Erik's father isn't one of them."

"Maybe Frank's father is," she said. Of course, they'd never know. It wasn't likely they'd ever again see the tough boy they'd met at the World's Fair.

Sadness slipped over her when she thought of Frank and Erik. She wished for the hundredth time that she could do something to help children whose fathers were out of work. She remembered the White City and her father's words about hope. Looking out the window at the gray, rainy fall day, she whispered, "It's hard to have hope sometimes."

Mayor Eustis opened an unemployment bureau like the Chicago mayor had done. Walter told Ted and Emily that the labor unions were pleased about that. Emily wondered if the unemployment bureau was a sliver of hope.

One day after school when she and Ted went to meet Erik and Mr. Beck, she brought a copy of the Minneapolis *Tribune* with her.

She opened it noisily to the article she wanted and pointed it out to Mr. Beck.

"Look at this! It says, 'The army of the unemployed is on the decrease. Nearly all who want work have found it.' " She glared at the reporter. "How can the newspaper print lies like that?"

Mr. Beck shoved his bowler toward the back of his black curls and spread his hands. "What makes you think it's a lie?"

Erik snorted. "Most anyone would know it. I know lots of men who need jobs."

Ted nodded. "My brother Walter says the labor unions are helping out a lot of their members' families."

"Walter's wife, Lena, is Swedish," Emily said. "The Scandinavians are trying to help their own people, like the labor unions are doing. Lena says there are many Swedish men here out of work. Many of the men send money back to relatives in Sweden. Now they can't send money back because they haven't got jobs. They can't even pay for their own food and rent."

Mr. Beck nibbled on the end of his pencil. "It's true there're very few people coming to America from other countries now. Since the panic began, for the first time in our country's history, more people are leaving the nation than entering it."

"You see?" Erik challenged. "Everyone but the city leaders knows how bad things are."

"If you want to be a newspaperman one day, Erik, you have to learn to deal with facts," Mr. Beck said. "The truth is, no one knows how many people are unemployed in the city. No one has counted the unemployed."

Erik lifted his chin and glared at Mr. Beck. "You always say newspapers make people aware of important things in the world. Why don't you write an article saying the city needs to count the unemployed men?"

Mr. Beck stared at Erik for a moment. "Maybe I'll do that." He pushed himself up from the wooden bench outside the soda fountain where they'd met. "I'd better get to work."

Emily crossed her arms and watched him walk down the street. The adults in the city weren't doing nearly enough about the jobless. It was so frustrating!

"I'm going to find a way to help jobless people," she declared in a low voice.

Erik and Ted whooped with laughter.

"You're only twelve!" Erik reminded her.

"What makes you think you can do more than adults?" Ted asked.

Her cheeks burned from their laughter. For a moment she was tempted to take her words back. Then she remembered the women artists at the World's Fair.

"Remember the motto of the World's Fair?" she asked the boys. "I will."

Erik chuckled. "A couple little words aren't goin' to help people get jobs and food and rent."

A trickle of doubt slid into her mind. She pushed it away. "The Bible says, 'I can do all things through Christ, who strengthens me.' If we ask God to show us something to do to help people, I'm sure He will. Will you two pray with me?"

Ted looked like he wasn't sure God would really answer them, but he agreed.

Erik just shook his head. "I think you're bein' foolish. God hasn't helped my family in all these months. Why should He help now?"

"You're wrong about God not helping your family," Emily said quietly. "He gave you a job as a newsboy to help your family, didn't He? I wish He would have given your father a job instead, but things would be worse if you didn't have a job, either."

Erik kicked at a brown leaf. "I still say you're foolish."

"I don't care." Emily lifted her chin. "I'm going to ask Him to show us a way to help anyway."

Chapter 17

The Plan

The logs in the parlor fireplace crackled and gave off a warm glow. Outside a late November snowstorm howled, whistling around corners and sending an occasional puff of wind down the chimney.

It's cozy here, Emily thought. She poked a needle through the gray wool school dress she was mending and glanced around the parlor.

Ted's mother and his sister-in-law, Lena, were spending the evening with Emily, Anna, and Mother. The women at church had collected used clothing. It had been sent home with the women to mend before being given to the poor.

"Isn't this lovely?" Lena held up a long black wool cape with a high collar trimmed in black velvet. "It barely needs any repair."

Mother smiled. "I'm glad so many people are giving things that haven't been worn to shreds. Every mother wants to be able to dress her family well."

"Have you girls bought your Christmas dresses yet?" Aunt Alison asked Emily and Anna.

Emily glanced at Anna and bit her bottom lip. "We. . .we don't need new dresses this year," she finally answered.

Aunt Alison raised her eyebrows in surprise. Her hand stopped with the needle above the brown trousers she was mending. "But both of you love pretty clothes!"

Anna bent over the child's red knit bonnet she was working on. "We decided to remake our dresses from last year instead."

"Oh." Aunt Alison and Lena gave the two girls funny looks but didn't ask any more questions.

Emily breathed a small sigh of relief. She was glad Anna hadn't said more. It would have sounded so proud. Last Sunday the pastor had spoken on giving to the poor. "If you find ways to save money," he'd said, "you will have money to give to those who need it more." She and Anna had decided to give away the money they saved by not buying new Christmas outfits. Their parents had agreed they could do so.

But I don't think that's the answer to my prayer, Emily thought.

She didn't think helping the church women was the answer, either, though she was glad to mend and sort clothes with them. *There must be something special God has that children can do together to help,* she thought.

At least Mr. Beck had written an article suggesting the city count the number of people without jobs. So far the city hadn't done anything about it.

"It's going to be cold walking to school tomorrow." Anna pretended to shiver.

"Can we put a pot of oatmeal on the back of the stove tonight so it will be ready to eat for breakfast?" Emily asked her mother. It always seemed easier to face a winter morning with warm oatmeal in her stomach.

She wondered how many of the jobless men's families would have warm breakfasts.

"Oh!"

Mother leaned forward. "Did you poke yourself with the needle?"

Emily shook her head. "No, I'm fine." She knew now what she wanted to do to help.

Emily searched out Ted first thing the next morning at school and told him her plan.

"I think that's a great idea," Ted said. "Let's ask Mr. Timms right away if we can do it."

Mr. Timms listened carefully then nodded so fast that his round cheeks bounced. "Wonderful! We've a few minutes before school starts. Let's go speak to the superintendent about your plan right away."

A nervous lump formed in Emily's throat as the three of them hurried toward the superintendent's office. She'd never actually talked to the head of the entire school before.

When they entered his office, the superintendent lifted his bald head. "What can I do for you?"

"The children have a wonderful plan, sir. I thought you should hear of it right away." Mr. Timms put a hand on Emily's back and urged her forward.

She gulped and wiped her sweaty palms down the sides of her dress. "My cousin Ted and I, we wanted to help the families of some of the jobless men. So we thought. . .that is. . ." She swallowed again.

"Go on," Mr. Timms urged.

"Could the students bring food to the school to give to their families?" The question came out in a rush. "I mean, if every student in the school brought just one thing, we'd have a lot of food to give."

The superintendent folded his hands on his desk and thought a moment. "Where would you collect the food?"

"We could put baskets in each classroom," Emily suggested.

"And how would you get the food to the jobless men's families?" the superintendent asked.

"I thought we could give it to the city's Associated Charities," she answered. "We could ask some of the students whose fathers' businesses have wagons to take the food we collect to the charities' offices."

A thin smile spread across the man's face. "It seems you've thought of everything, Mr. Timms. Please arrange for these two to speak in all the classrooms this afternoon. Now you'd best all get to your class. The morning bell will be rung any minute now."

A couple days each week, Emily and Ted had fallen into the habit of going home from school by way of a street on which Erik often sold newspapers. Today when they saw him, Mr. Beck was with him.

"We have something so exciting to tell you!" Emily told Erik almost before she finished saying hello.

Mr. Beck laughed. "If this is important, why don't we go inside the soda fountain across the street? I'll treat you all to hot cocoa while you tell us your news."

"What do you think?" Emily asked eagerly when she'd told them her plan.

Erik and Mr. Beck both thought the plan was great. "But you should get more of the schools involved," Erik said, lifting his mug of fragrant, warm cocoa.

"Someone should write a short article about the plan," Mr. Beck suggested. "The article could be distributed to the schools. Why don't you do that, Erik?"

Erik almost spit out the cocoa he'd just sipped. "Me?"

Mr. Beck nodded. "You want to be a writer, don't you?"

"But. . .but that's just a dream."

"If you write the article, I'll check it over and correct the mistakes," Mr. Beck assured him. "That is, if you make any mistakes. I'll ask the *Tribune* editor if he'll have his staff print copies of it."

Erik wrapped his hands around the warm mug. "Do you really think I can write it?"

Mr. Beck pushed his bowler back on his curls. "Wouldn't have suggested it if I didn't. Every writer has to start someplace."

Ted remembered what James Hill had told him and Erik last summer: *Believe in your dreams and a way will open.* Was this a way for Erik's dream to begin to be real? Would he take it or let it pass by?

"I'll try it," Erik said with a sharp nod.

Mr. Beck said Erik's article was well done. The reporter only changed a couple misspelled words. Later Mr. Beck told them, "When I showed it to the editor, he told me to do a follow-up article when the food has been collected and delivered. Why don't you try writing that one, too, Erik?"

Ted thought Erik couldn't look happier if he'd been handed a bag of gold coins.

The project went better than Ted and Emily ever imagined. The Minneapolis students collected enough food to feed 120 families!

Emily held up her best winter dress, looked it up and down, and sighed. "It's no use, Anna. There's nothing that can make this dress look new again for Christmas."

"Of course there is. You simply haven't given it enough thought. You are too impatient, Emily."

Emily laid the dress over the parlor couch. "I know, but I'm trying to change."

She picked up the sewing basket from beside the fireplace. "Maybe I can find something in here to help." She opened the basket and pulled out ribbons, lace, and buttons her mother had saved from different sewing projects over the years. She held up different pieces against the dress. "Nothing seems to work," she complained.

"Let me try." Anna went through the same process with no success.

"This seemed like such a good idea when Pastor Adams said to be thrifty," Emily told her. "Now it seems hard."

"I know! Do you still have that black velvet dress that you outgrew? We could cut it up and use the material to make a high collar and long cuffs. They'd look wonderful against this purple brocade."

Emily jumped up, excited. "Maybe a wide black velvet tie around the waist, too."

Half an hour later, they were busy cutting out the pieces from the old dress and talking happily about their Christmas plans when Ted and his brother Walter stopped by.

"Did you hear about the mayor's new plans to help jobless men?" Ted asked.

The girls hadn't.

"The cold weather has brought so many homeless men to the police station to stay at night," Walter told them, "that the mayor decided to go there and talk with them himself. He found out only two had had anything to eat."

Ted grinned. "So he decided to open a soup kitchen for the unemployed and homeless men who stay at the police station at night. The city leaders are planning to hire jobless men to remove snow from sidewalks and streets and help with road repairs."

"Which the labor unions and others have been asking the leaders to do for quite a while now," Walter added.

"Best of all," Ted said, "Mayor Eustis has ordered a count of the people in the city who are unemployed and in need."

"Do you think he did that because of Mr. Beck's article?" Emily asked.

"Maybe," Walter said, "but I think meeting and talking to the homeless men helped, too."

"The mayor is asking businesses to donate food so every family that hasn't a way to buy food can be given a Christmas basket," Ted told Emily and Anna.

Emily's heart seemed to grow with joy. "What a wonderful Christmas present for the people!"

Anna frowned slightly. "I think it's wonderful, too, but. . . won't the people be embarrassed to take charity from the city?"

"The mayor thought of that," Walter said. "Unemployed men will make the food deliveries to the families. That way the people getting the baskets won't feel as bad about others seeing them in hard times."

"I know the food baskets won't fix all the problems for the families of the jobless men," Emily told Ted, "but it's a start."

"At least no one will have to go hungry on Christmas," he agreed.

Chapter 18

Christmas Eve

Snow fell in large, fluffy flakes on the afternoon of Christmas Eve. The Allerton house was filled with smells of Christmas baking: sugar cookies and pies in the morning and now the turkey that was roasting for dinner.

In the parlor, Emily, Anna, and Richard were decorating their Christmas tree with colorful glass ornaments and white strings of popcorn. Ted was helping because he liked Christmas trees so much. His family had put their tree up the night before.

The tree stood in the parlor's bay window, where the children could watch the snow fall while they worked. Sleighs and runners on wagons made soft hissing sounds as they passed down the snow-covered streets. The horses' hooves could barely be heard for the snow.

"I like the bells so many people put on the horses this time of year," Emily said. "Their ringing is such a cheerful sound."

A large horse-drawn wagon on runners pulled along the curbstone in front of the Allerton home. "Johnson Brothers Market" was written in large letters on the side of the enclosed wagon. A driver and his partner men sat bundled against the winter weather.

Wool blankets kept the horses warm.

The children looked at the wagon curiously. "I didn't think Mother was expecting any more deliveries," Anna said.

One of the men jumped down and jogged toward the house with two flat packages in his hand.

"Why, that's Erik!" Ted hurried toward the front door to meet him with Emily right on his heels. They invited Erik to take off his things and join them in the parlor.

"Can't stay but a minute," he said, standing in the hallway by the front door. "My pa is waiting for me."

"He doesn't have to wait in the cold," Ted said. "Ask him to come inside."

"We have heated stones to keep our feet warm," Erik said, "and lap robes, too. We're delivering Christmas baskets, so we can't stay."

"Did the merchants make a lot of donations?" Emily asked eagerly.

Erik grinned. "The collection point was overflowing with food: flour from flour mills, beef and chicken from meat markets, thousands of pounds of butter from creameries, candy and bread from bakeries, oysters from packing houses, coffee, tea, fish, sugar, and rice from grocers. A town in North Dakota even sent a thousand jackrabbits for the baskets!"

Ted and Emily laughed. "I bet most of the people getting the baskets have never cooked a jackrabbit before," Emily said, "but they'll be glad for them just the same."

Erik sobered. "I heard at the collection point that when the city counted the jobless men, they found there were over eight hundred families who needed help. That's about six thousand people all together."

Ted let out a low whistle. "I knew things were bad, but I didn't know they were that bad."

"And that doesn't include the people who are being helped by unions and other groups," Erik added. "Mayor Eustis and the leaders were really surprised."

A shiver went through Emily, and she rubbed her hands over her arms. How awful to think of so many people without money to buy food!

Ted looked out the oval window in the door. "Why is your father driving Johnson Brothers' wagon?"

"Some of the large merchants donated wagons and teams to deliver the baskets." Erik's eyes were shining. "One of the Johnson brothers was helping put food in baskets and load the wagons. He thought Pa was such a good worker that he's offered him a job. He starts right after Christmas."

Emily bounced up and down in her excitement. "That's wonderful!"

"It doesn't pay nearly as well as the railroad work," Erik said quickly, "but at least he'll have pay comin' in regular."

"That's great," Ted said. "I know the Johnson brothers won't be sorry they hired him."

Erik gave him a grateful smile. "Oh, I almost forgot why I stopped!" He handed each of them a flat package wrapped in brown paper and tied with twine. "Go ahead, open them."

They made quick work of tearing off the paper. Inside were copies of the articles Erik had written about the students' food collection project. The articles were simply but neatly framed.

"They're perfect! Thank you," Emily said. It would be nice to have something to remember the project that had meant so much to all three of them.

"My pa helped me make the frames for them." Erik shifted from one foot to the other.

"We didn't get anything for you," Emily told him, feeling uncomfortable.

Erik stuffed his gloved hands into his jacket pockets. His cheeks grew redder than they'd been from the cold. "I guess you gave me your present early."

Emily and Ted frowned at him, puzzled.

He cleared his throat. "I mean when you came up with the idea for the students' food collection. I thought you were foolish, but you made it happen. And now my pa has a job, too. I guess you were right. Nothing is impossible with Jesus."

He opened the door and hurried out onto the porch before Emily or Ted could say anything. At the bottom of the steps, he turned around and waved. "Merry Christmas!"

That evening after Christmas Eve services, Ted's family and Uncle Enoch and his wife joined the Allertons for Christmas dinner. When Walter had discovered that Thomas Beck hadn't any family in town, he'd invited him to join them, too. Emily and Ted had introduced Walter and Mr. Beck when they were working on the students' food project. Now the two men were fast friends.

When dinner was over, they all visited in the parlor, where the tree ornaments sparkled in the light of the glass-shaded parlor lamps. The children sat on the floor by the tree so there would be enough seats for the adults. The smells of pine, burning logs, and cinnamon from mugs of cider filled the room.

"I must say, your Christmas dresses are lovely," Aunt Alison told Anna and Emily. "If you hadn't told me you were remaking old gowns, I wouldn't have known they weren't new."

Emily and Anna beamed at each other. Aunt Alison's compliment made Emily gladder than ever that they'd decided to follow the pastor's advice and be thrifty.

Uncle Enoch leaned back in his chair and took a sip from his mug of hot cider. "I must say I'm glad 1893 is almost over. I believe it's been one of the hardest years for the country moneywise in this century."

It seemed to Emily that Uncle Enoch, being a banker, always thought of everything in terms of money.

"Banks closing all over the country, people out of work, railroads going bankrupt." Uncle Enoch shook his head. "Yes, indeed, it's been a rough year."

"I'm glad the Great Northern Railroad didn't go bankrupt," Ted said. "For a long time, I was afraid it would. Then Father would have been out of work."

"Then *your* family might have received a Christmas basket." Richard gave him a friendly poke in the side with his elbow.

"It's no laughing matter," Ted's father said. "I had the same worries as Ted. But since everything worked out so well, I rather wish Alison and I had joined Ted and the Allertons at the World's Fair last summer!"

Father chuckled. "It was the experience of a lifetime," he admitted.

"Well, Congress has repealed the Sherman Silver Act," Uncle Enoch said. "That should get the country back in good shape, though it may take awhile."

Emily had no idea what the Sherman Act was, only that it had something to do with silver and paper money. Adults had argued about it a lot during the year. Still, she hoped Uncle Enoch was right about things getting better.

Walter leaned forward, his large hands wrapped around his mug of cider. "Even though this has been a hard year, it's a great time to be alive."

Ted nodded. "Uncle Daniel said something like that when we were at the World's Fair, because of all the wonderful inventions we saw."

"The machines people have made *are* wonderful," Walter agreed, "but I was thinking of a different kind of discovery. There seems to be a new spirit in the land today. People are becoming their brothers' keepers as never before."

"Because of the Christmas baskets?" Emily asked.

"Yes, partly. The city has usually let churches and charities take care of the poor. Now Minneapolis arranged to collect and deliver the Christmas baskets and fuel, too. Chicago, Minneapolis, and other cities have started unemployment bureaus to help jobless men find work. But there are new laws, too, to protect people."

"Like the railroad laws that make trains safer for passengers and brakemen like Erik's father?" Ted asked.

Walter nodded.

"There's another law that goes into effect January first," Mr. Beck reminded them. "Employers will only be allowed to let children under sixteen work between seven in the morning and six in the evening. No more sweatshops where children work themselves into early graves."

Emily remembered Frank and Erik and how hard they worked. She told Mr. Beck about Erik's gift and his father's new job.

Mr. Beck grinned. "It isn't only his father who has a new job. I told my editor that Erik had written those articles about the students' food project and that Erik hopes to be a reporter one day. I haven't had a chance to tell Erik yet, but my editor said Erik can have a job as errand boy at the newspaper if he wants."

"Hurrah!" Ted shouted.

Mr. Beck held up a hand. "He won't be writing any articles, but at least he can have a chance to be around the business and see if that's what he really wants to do. It pays better than being a newsboy, and he won't have to work out in the rain and snow anymore."

Ted and Emily exchanged grins.

"You two were some of the first in the city to help the unemployed men and their families," Mr. Beck reminded them. "I think your food collection project showed the city's leaders that the need in the city was greater than they thought. Maybe you started some of them thinking about other ways the city could help."

"That's right," Father said. "Our families are proud of both of you."

A few minutes later, Emily and her mother went into the kitchen. Together they piled crystal plates with Christmas cookies.

"Your father is right," Mother told her when they were done. "We're very proud of the young woman you've become this year. I used to worry over your impulsive nature. It was always getting you into trouble!"

Emily's spirits sank. Not another lecture! Not on Christmas Eve!

Mother folded her hands at the waist of her elegant Christmas gown and smiled. "Then one day I realized that it's that same energy that used to get you into trouble that you put into the students' food collection project. And I think that is a very good thing. I am very blessed to have such a wonderful daughter."

Emily carefully carried the delicate, cookie-covered plate up the hallway. Lena was playing the parlor piano, and everyone was singing Christmas hymns. But it was her mother's words that Emily was hearing in her heart.

American Rebirth: Bonus Educational Materials

Elise the Actress: Climax of the Civil War

Vocabulary Words

abolitionist—someone who thinks slavery should be done away with, or abolished
Before the war, he'd been an avid ***abolitionist****, aiding runaway slaves and defending them in court.*

acrid—having a strong, unpleasant smell or taste
As she approached the lake, she heard voices, and her throat burned from the ***acrid*** *smoke of a campfire.*

appease—to satisfy someone or something
That seemed to ***appease*** *him, and he continued walking Aleron around the paddock.*

atrocities—shockingly cruel acts
He spoke often of the unimaginable ***atrocities*** *of slavery.*

boycotted—refused to deal with, participate in, or purchase something
They ***boycotted*** *his shop.*

cantering—moving at a pace slower than a gallop but faster than a trot
Elise knew better than to run Dusty in the hot weather, but she alternated ***cantering*** *and walking as she hurried out of Walnut Hills and all the way into town to Papa's office.*

contrabands—enslaved people who escaped to, or were taken behind, Union lines during the Civil War
As she moved among the crowd, she heard her papa saying, "I never thought I'd live to see the day—Congress finally allowing the ***contrabands*** *to fight in their own war for freedom."*

convalescing—recovering from an illness or injury
By the time everyone had arrived, there were baskets of items for the ***convalescing*** *soldiers—everything from combs to stationery.*

cowcatcher—an inclined frame on the front of a locomotive, used for moving obstacles out of the path of the approaching train
Crepe-trimmed Union flags fluttered from the front ***cowcatcher****.*

daguerreotypes—early photographs
He showed Elise ***daguerreotypes*** *of his wife and son when their family was together and happy.*

dyspepsia—indigestion
"Only if it didn't give Berdeen a case of ***dyspepsia****."*

fraternizes—associates with
"And I wouldn't be caught dead playing with someone who ***fraternizes*** *with the enemy!"*

gallantry—bravery in a situation of great danger
It grieves me that their ***gallantry*** *is all for naught.*

gaunt—extremely thin and bony
He was pale and ***gaunt****.*

nib pen—a pen with a detachable metal tip; a fountain pen
She took up a ***nib pen*** *and copied two riddles onto a sheet of stationery.*

pallet—a makeshift bed, usually made from whatever materials were at hand
On a ***pallet*** *on the ground lay a handsome young man.*

peaked—sickly, thin, and pale
"You look a little ***peaked****."*

plait—to weave strands together, especially a length of hair
Elise hurried to pull on her day dress and to ***plait*** *her hair into two long braids.*

resolute—determined
The tone of his voice and the ***resolute*** *look in his eye told Elise he'd come to terms with the way things were—that he was powerless to change it.*

stoop—a small porch at the entrance to a house
A cast-off wagon wheel lay beside the rickety front ***stoop****.*

troupe—a group of performers
"It's time to gather our ***troupe*** *and go to the playroom," she said.*

wistfully—expressing a sad yearning for something lost or for something that might not be
Wistfully*, Verly said to Elise, "I wonder if I will ever see Alexander's wedding day."*

Salmon P. Chase

Salmon Chase was born in New Hampshire in 1808. After his father died in 1817, Salmon was put in the care of an uncle, who was the Episcopal Bishop of Ohio. Chase graduated from Dartmouth University and moved to Washington, D.C. in 1826, where he ran a school and studied law.

After being admitted to the bar in 1829, Chase returned to Ohio. There he practiced law, taking cases that challenged the social norm of the day. He was a very vocal opponent of slavery. Chase represented many slaves, arguing their cases before the United States Supreme Court. Between 1841 and 1849, he founded and led the Liberty and Free Soil Parties, two political parties opposed to the expansion of slavery.

Salmon Chase was twice elected to the Senate from Ohio, and in 1861, he became secretary of the treasury under Abraham Lincoln. The first U.S. federal currency was designed by Chase and printed in 1862, and Chase served as secretary until 1864 when Lincoln nominated him as chief justice of the Supreme Court. From 1864 until his death from a stroke in 1873, he served as chief justice, hearing cases concerning Reconstruction, state laws, and taxes. In 1868, Salmon Chase even presided over the treason trial of Confederate president Jefferson Davis and the first presidential impeachment trial, that of President Andrew Johnson.

The Gettysburg Address

It's only 258 words long, but those words, spoken by Abraham Lincoln on the battlefield at Gettysburg, Pennsylvania, on November 19, 1863, helped to change the mind-set of a nation.

Fourscore and seven years ago our fathers brought forth on this continent a new nation, conceived in liberty and dedicated to the proposition that all men are created equal.

Now we are engaged in a great civil war, testing whether that nation or any nation so conceived and so dedicated can long endure. We are met on a great battlefield of that war. We have come to dedicate a portion of it as a final resting place for those who died here that that nation might live. This we may, in all propriety do. But in a larger sense, we cannot dedicate, we cannot consecrate, we cannot hallow this ground. The brave men, living and dead, who struggled here have hallowed it far above our poor power to add or detract. The world will little note nor long remember what we say here, but it can never forget what they did here.

It is for us, the living, rather, to be dedicated here to the unfinished work which they who fought here have thus far so nobly advanced. It is rather for us to be here dedicated to the great task remaining before us—that from these honored dead we take increased devotion to that cause for which they gave the last full measure of devotion—that we here highly resolve that these dead shall not have died in vain, that this nation shall have a new birth of freedom, and that government of the people, by the people, for the people shall not perish from the earth.

Squirrel Hunters

In September 1862, Confederate soldiers captured Lexington, Kentucky, and set out to capture Cincinnati, Ohio, a town of 250,000 citizens. Union forces, under the command of Lewis Wallace, were sent to Cincinnati to prepare the city's defenses. When he arrived, Wallace declared military rule. Businesses were closed and civilians were told to report for military duty. Men in the regular army would fight on the battlefield while civilians prepared trenches and other defenses in anticipation of the attack.

Governor David Tod sent out a plea for men in other parts of Ohio to come and help defend Cincinnati. Reportedly, 15,766 civilians from sixty-five counties heard his call and came to Cincinnati's aid. (So many reported that, one day after he had asked for volunteers, Governor Tod had to ask the counties to send no more men.) These men became known as the Squirrel Hunters. Though many had no military training and possessed only outdated weapons, they rallied to defend Cincinnati from the Confederate troops. Confederate forces withdrew from Kentucky, and the Squirrel Hunters were given honorable discharges from military service. In 1908, the Ohio Legislature voted to pay each volunteer $13, a month's pay for a Union soldier.

History in Perspective Timeline

February 1, 1862—Julia Ward Howe's "Battle Hymn of the Republic" is published for the first time.

1863—Construction begins on the first transcontinental railroad in California.

January 1, 1863—President Abraham Lincoln delivers the Emancipation Proclamation.

February 10, 1863—Alanson Crane patents the fire extinguisher.

May 28, 1863—The first African American regiment, the 54th Massachusetts, leaves Boston to fight for the Union.

June 20, 1863—West Virginia is admitted as the thirty-fifth state after seceding from Virginia in April 1861. It is the only state to be formed as a direct result of the Civil War.

November 19, 1863—President Abraham Lincoln gives the Gettysburg Address.

August 22, 1864—The International Red Cross is founded in Geneva, Switzerland.

1865—The U.S. Secret Service is established.

April 9, 1865—Confederate General Robert E. Lee surrenders his army to Union General Ulysses S. Grant at Appomattox Court House in Virginia, bringing about the end of the Civil War. Other surrenders occur on April 26, June 2, and June 23.

April 14, 1865—President Lincoln is assassinated by John Wilkes Booth.

December 12, 1865—Several former Confederate soldiers form the Ku Klux Klan.

December 18, 1865—The thirteenth Constitutional Amendment is passed by the United States, abolishing slavery forever.

July 24, 1866—Tennessee becomes the first U.S. state to be readmitted to the Union following the Civil War.

July 28, 1866—Author Beatrix Potter (*The Tale of Peter Rabbit*) is born.

Janie's Freedom: African Americans in the Aftermath of the Civil War

Vocabulary Words

bondage—the condition of being a slave
But at least the ***bondage*** *was over, praise the Lord. She would never again be anyone's slave.*

chain gang—a group of slaves or prisoners who are chained together while they work
That day was a milestone in her life, like the day her father was sold to the ***chain gang****.*

Confederate—part of the Confederacy, the Southern states that declared themselves a new nation in the 1860s
They'd already been taken by ***Confederate*** *soldiers for the war effort.*

delirious—unable to think clearly, especially because of a fever or sickness
Blue eventually became ***delirious****, talking nonsense and even laughing in his feverish state.*

extricated—freed or removed from something, such as a trap or hard situation
Janie gently ***extricated*** *herself from the sleeping tangle of the Rubyhill Five.*

haunches—the upper part of a person's legs
Janie sank down on her ***haunches*** *and looked around, then up at the gaping hole in the roof.*

hospitality—kind and generous treatment of guests and visitors
Each plantation's slave quarters opened up to the couple and showed them the best ***hospitality***.

knoll—a small, rounded hill
Janie propped the straw broom against the log wall of the cabin and trotted up the ***knoll*** *toward seventeen-year-old Aleta.*

pewter—a heavy gray metal containing tin and lead
She placed the chain around her neck, and the ***pewter*** *cross dangled halfway down her chest.*

plantation—a large farm, especially in the Southern states in the 1800s, that used slaves to plant and harvest crops
He was from Bailey Meadows, a ***plantation*** *several miles away.*

preserves—sweet food made from fruit cooked in sugar, often kept in a glass jar
Janie thought she remembered where she had buried a jar of ***preserves,*** *and she set out with a large spoon for digging.*

ramrod—a straight metal bar used to push explosives down the barrel of old-fashioned guns
The driver, a white man, sat ***ramrod*** *straight, buggy whip in hand, eyes straight ahead.*

Rebel—describes people of the Southern states, who *rebelled* against the United States by forming the Confederacy
*"****Rebel*** *cash," remarked Blue. "Ain't worth a thing no more."*

saucers—small plates made to hold tea cups
Blue's gaunt face made his eyes look big as ***saucers***.

skirted—moved around the edges of something
The Rubyhill Five had ***skirted*** *Atlanta and now found themselves close to Tennessee on this rainy third day of travel.*

threadbare—shabby, thin, and in bad condition from being used too much
Everyone's clothing was looking ***threadbare***.

trundle bed—a low bed with rollers that can be slid under a higher bed when not in use
*Lucy lay in the **trundle bed** next to the high-poster bed.*

venturing—going somewhere new, unknown, and possibly dangerous
*The five young former slaves had waited only until the second day after the burial before **venturing** out.*

veranda—a long, open porch on a house or other building
*The door to the front **veranda** was tied shut with baling twine.*

water moccasin—a poisonous snake of the southern United States, also called a cottonmouth
*Once they had stumbled upon a **water moccasin** while drawing water at a river, but it swam away without incident.*

worrisome—upsetting, causing to worry
*There was one more **worrisome** thing, the most **worrisome** thing of all. Blue was coughing.*

Important People and Things around 1867

The Fourteenth Amendment

Adopted in July 1868, this addition to the United States Constitution (the "rule book" for our country) clarified that every American citizen—of whatever color—had to be treated equally under the laws of the nation and the states. The Fourteenth Amendment overruled a U.S. Supreme Court decision (*Dred Scott v. Sandford*) that said black people could not be citizens.

One of the "Reconstruction Amendments"—changes to the Constitution made in response to the Civil War—the Fourteenth Amendment did say that some people could be denied certain benefits of American citizenship: those who "have engaged in insurrection or rebellion. . .or given aid or comfort to the enemies" of the United States.

Andrew Johnson

The seventeenth president of the United States, Andrew Johnson took office in 1865, when Abraham Lincoln was shot and killed by John Wilkes Booth.

Johnson had been a senator from Tennessee when the Civil War began, but because he believed in the Union, he did not follow his state into the Confederacy. Known as a "War Democrat," Johnson supported the policies of the Republican Lincoln—and was chosen as the vice president candidate for Lincoln's 1864 re-election campaign.

As president, Johnson showed kindness toward the South in hopes of restoring the Union the Civil War had broken. But his policies angered many in Congress, who preferred to punish former Confederates. In 1868, the House of Representatives voted to impeach Johnson (that is, charging him with crimes against the country), but the U.S. Senate—by one vote—declared him not guilty.

Quakers
Many people recognize the name *Quaker* from a box of oatmeal—featuring a smiling, white-haired man in a black hat.

Quakers, also known as the Religious Society of Friends, are a Christian group that developed in the 1600s in England. They believe in the individual's personal experience with Jesus and have often led efforts to change society for the better. Quakers were very active in the abolition (the ending) of slavery in the United States.

Though the Quakers worked to end slavery during the U.S. Civil War, their pacifist beliefs prevented them from actually fighting in the war.

History in Perspective Timeline

July 1, 1862—The U.S. Congress creates the Internal Revenue Service, to raise taxes for fighting the Confederacy in the Civil War.

January 1, 1863—President Abraham Lincoln delivers the Emancipation Proclamation, declaring all slaves in rebellious states to be free.

February 17, 1864—The Confederate submarine *Hunley* becomes the first underwater craft to sink an enemy ship (the U.S.S. *Housatonic*). The *Hunley* sinks, as well.

April 9, 1865—Confederate General Robert E. Lee surrenders his troops to U.S. General Ulysses S. Grant, effectively ending the Civil War.

April 14, 1865—President Abraham Lincoln is shot by John Wilkes Booth at Ford's Theater in Washington D.C. Lincoln dies the next morning.

December 29, 1865—The abolitionist magazine *The Liberator* publishes its final issue.

July 24, 1866—Tennessee becomes the first state of the Confederacy to rejoin the Union after the Civil War.

February 7, 1867—Children's author Laura Ingalls Wilder is born in Wisconsin.

March 1, 1867—Nebraska becomes the thirty-seventh U.S. state.

March 30, 1867—The United States buys Alaska from Russia for $7.2 million.

July 1, 1867—Canada becomes a self-governing colony of Great Britain.

July 28, 1868—The Fourteenth Amendment becomes law, guaranteeing African Americans full citizenship and equal protection of U.S. law.

November 1, 1870—The U.S. Weather Bureau (later known as the National Weather Service) makes its first forecast, for high winds in Chicago and Milwaukee.

Rachel and the Riot: The Labor Movement Divides a Family

Vocabulary Words

arbitration—the hearing of a case and the deciding of a conflict by a third party who is not involved
*"He won't even come to the **arbitration** table."*

beeline—the shortest and straightest route
*But as soon as he was gone, Simon made a **beeline** for Sam.*

bullhorn—a cone-shaped device held to the mouth that makes the voice louder
*A man with a **bullhorn** leaned out the side of the car.*

chaos—a state of being unorganized or confused
*Sam and Rachel were not the only ones who had come to the hospital to escape the **chaos** of the streets.*

cloak—a loose outer garment resembling a cape
*She buttoned her new sapphire **cloak** under her neck.*

contorted—twisted into a strained shape
*His face was **contorted** and his cheeks puffed out as he tried not to spit out the bite of pie.*

droned—talked in a dull and boring tone
*Miss Martin **droned**, "We will begin our day with the mathematics assignment."*

exquisite—very fine and beautiful
*They were only a few inches tall, but they were painted with **exquisite** detail in bright colors and a glossy finish.*

fracas—a noisy quarrel
*In their rush to join the **fracas**, people were stepping on him or stepping over him.*

frock—a woman's or girl's dress
*"Perhaps you should take an old **frock** along to play in later."*

grimaced—made a facial expression of disgust
*Rachel **grimaced** at the picture Sam had created in her mind.*

gurney—a wheeled stretcher
*The man on the **gurney** before Papa began gasping for air.*

heckling—making fun of loudly, bothering by saying annoying things
*Even from down the block, Rachel could hear them **heckling** the driver.*

humane—characterized by feelings of compassion and sympathy for others
*"We are entering a more **humane** era."*

hypothesis—an assumption or good guess that's made for the sake of argument
*"I'll make a **hypothesis** about what I think will happen, then I'll try some ideas to see if the hypothesis is true."*

orderly—a hospital attendant who does routine jobs
*"Here comes the next one," the nurse responded, as an **orderly** wheeled in another patient.*

principle—a guideline, code of conduct
*"The strikers are standing on a **principle**, Ernest."*

propaganda—the spreading of ideas, information, or rumor for the purpose of helping or harming an organization, cause, or person
*"We don't need someone coming in here and spreading union **propaganda**."*

retorted—answered in a short, sharp manner
*"And their children are going hungry for the sake of that principle," **retorted** Uncle Ernest.*

simpleton—a person lacking common sense
*"I do not understand why you are behaving like such a **simpleton** on this matter."*

tension—stress, heightened feelings of anger or anxiety
*He could feel **tension** between his friends Jim Harrison and Simon Jones.*

unison—done at the same time
*"Yes, honey, happy birthday," Rachel's parents greeted her in **unison**.*

Jim Hill

James Jerome Hill was born in 1838. His dream was to establish a railroad extending across the United States, and in 1878, he bought a line in Minnesota called the St. Paul and Pacific Railroad. He immediately began to expand its route west, insisting that each leg of the railroad expansion be profitable and meet the highest standards. Hill's first goal was to reach the Canadian border. There he joined with the Canadian Pacific Railroad and continued west. In 1893 the railroad—now known as the Great Northern Railroad—reached Puget Sound in Everett, Washington. Along the way, Hill and the Great Northern Railroad encouraged immigrants to move west and settle along the railroad lines. This earned him the title of "Empire Builder." After he reached the west, he bought more railroads and developed a highly profitable trading partnership with Japan. He arranged the export of cotton from the South to Japan. Jim Hill died in 1916.

Thomas Lowry

Thomas Lowry was born February 27, 1843, in Logan County, Illinois. After passing the bar examination, he moved to Minneapolis where he practiced law and became involved in real estate. He also was president and primary owner of the Twin City Rapid Transit Company. In an attempt to break the employee union, he lowered the wages of the streetcar drivers and posted notices in the car barns prohibiting membership in the unions. Almost fifteen hundred employees stopped working. They were replaced by inexperienced drivers wearing cowboy suits—complete with guns. After the Easter riots, many of the regular drivers returned to work, effectively ending the strike. Lowry's transit company was the first of its kind in the Minneapolis–St. Paul area. Although it provided a needed service, it was not welcomed throughout the area. Noisy and dangerous streetcars ran through the neighborhoods. The extension of the routes drove up the price of real estate, making it difficult for working families to afford homes. The company went bankrupt in December of 1889. Thomas Lowry died February 4, 1909, in Minneapolis.

Charles Pillsbury

Charles Alfred Pillsbury was born on December 3, 1842, in Warner, New Hampshire. With money he received from his father, George A., and uncle John S. Pillsbury, Charles spent ten thousand dollars to receive a third ownership of a flour mill. The money was spent on machinery that allowed the mill to process the hard spring wheat of the area into fine white flour. The business was very prosperous, and Minnesota became the center of the flour milling industry. By 1886, the C. A. Pillsbury Company was doing approximately fifteen million dollars in business per year. In 1889, the company was sold to an English financial firm and became the Pillsbury–Washburn Flour Mills. Charles Pillsbury remained as managing director, before dying September 17, 1889.

History in Perspective Timeline

May 8, 1886—Coca-Cola is invented.

February 22, 1889—President Grover Cleveland signs a bill admitting North Dakota, South Dakota, Montana, and Washington into the United States. North and South Dakota are admitted on November 2, Montana on November 8, and Washington on November 11.

May 6, 1889—The Eiffel Tower opens in Paris, France.

November 14, 1889—Female journalist Nellie Bly (Elizabeth Cochrane) begins her attempt to travel around the world in less than eighty days. She will end her journey on January 25, 1890, seventy-two days, six hours, and eleven minutes later.

November 23, 1889—The first jukebox is unveiled at the Palais Royal restaurant in San Francisco, California. It costs a nickel.

1890—The cardboard box is invented by Robert Gair.

January 2, 1890—Alice Sanger becomes the first female staff member at the White House.

July 3, 1890—Idaho becomes a state.

July 10, 1890—Wyoming becomes a state.

January 9, 1903—Thomas Edison applies for a patent for an "electrical automobile."

Emily Makes a Difference: A Time of Progress and Problems

Vocabulary words

ambassador—a person sent to another country to represent his or her own country
*"Mr. Douglass is the **ambassador** to Haiti," Mother told him.*

bankrupt—financially ruined
*"The Northern Pacific Railroad has gone **bankrupt**."*

brocade—a rich, silky fabric with a raised silver and gold pattern
*"They'd look wonderful against this purple **brocade**."*

dynamo—a machine that converts mechanical energy into electrical energy
*"What I want to see is much smaller than a **dynamo**."*

famished—extremely hungry
*"I could use one of your mother's doughnuts if you have any left. I'm **famished**."*

gondola—a long, narrow, flat-bottomed boat famous for its use on canals in Venice, Italy
*Her spirits lifted when her father said they were going for a **gondola** ride before dinner.*

hieroglyphics—pictures that represent words, syllables, or sounds, as used in ancient Egyptian writing
*Emily was standing in the doorway, looking at the strange **hieroglyphics** that bordered the doorway.*

hooligan—a young hoodlum or troublemaker
*"I guess that won't be necessary," the man said. "You two look too well dressed to be friends with this **hooligan**."*

horticulture—the art of gardening
*"I want to see the Woman's Building," Emily told her mother as they climbed the steps, "but I'd like to see the **Horticulture** Building, too."*

impulsive—acting without thinking
*Her aunt never got as upset as her mother over the small scrapes Emily and Ted's **impulsive** acts got them into.*

jauntily—cheerfully
*The kids watched him walk **jauntily** down the steps and cross the wide bridge to the island.*

knickers—short, loose-fitting pants that are gathered at the knee
*Ted pushed his hands into the pockets of his brown **knickers**.*

lagoon—a shallow body of water usually connected to a larger body of water
*Its **lagoons** and basins were blue in the midst of the beautiful buildings.*

meddle—to interfere in someone else's business
*"Don't **meddle** in police business, little lady."*

parlor—a sitting room usually used for entertaining guests
*In the **parlor**, Emily, Anna, and Richard were decorating their Christmas tree with colorful glass ornaments and white strings of popcorn.*

pocketbook—a small purse for carrying money
*Emily reached for her **pocketbook** and drew out her precious quarter.*

porter—a person employed to carry luggage at a hotel
*His ears filled with the rumble of waiting trains, the calls of conductors hurrying passengers aboard, and the clattering of wheels as **porters** dashed about with luggage.*

ruckus—a commotion or disturbance
*People in the audience stared, wondering about the **ruckus**.*

suffrage—the right to vote
*She was one of the main leaders of the woman's **suffrage** movement.*

telegraph—a system or device for transmitting messages or signals
*She was glad to sit on the edge of the boardwalk with her feet in the street and lean against the bottom of a **telegraph** pole.*

Important People around 1893

Susan B. Anthony

Susan Brownell Anthony was one of the early leaders of the women's rights movement. She fought especially for woman's suffrage, or the right to vote. Born in Massachusetts on February 15, 1820, she grew up in New York and began teaching school at age fifteen. In time, Anthony took up social causes, opposing alcoholic beverages and desiring the immediate end of slavery; in 1863, during the Civil War, she founded the Women's Loyal League to fight for the freedom of slaves. Her work for women's rights began in 1851 when she teamed with Elizabeth Cady Stanton to fight laws that discriminated against women. From 1868 to 1870, she published a weekly journal called *The Revolution*, which demanded equal rights for women. In 1872, Anthony was arrested for illegally voting in the presidential election. Though she died on March 13, 1906, fourteen years before women earned the right to vote under the Nineteenth Amendment to the U.S. Constitution, Anthony is known today as the founder of the women's rights movement. In 1979, the United States Mint issued the Susan B. Anthony dollar coin in her honor.

Frederick Douglass

Frederick Douglass was an African American abolitionist, speaker, and writer. He was born a slave in Maryland on February 7, 1817, and at age eight was sent to Baltimore to work for one of his master's relatives. There he began to educate himself and found work in a shipyard. Douglass hated slavery, and in 1836 he tried unsuccessfully to escape from his master. He tried again in 1838, this time with success, and fled to New Bedford, Massachusetts. There he changed his name from Frederick Augustus Washington Bailey to Frederick Douglass to avoid capture. In

1841, he began his career as an abolitionist, fighting to end slavery and protesting racial discrimination. Six years later, he founded an antislavery newspaper called the *North Star*, and his home was part of the Underground Railroad that helped runaway slaves reach freedom in the North. During the Civil War, Douglass helped to recruit African Americans for the Union Army, and he even met and discussed the problems of slavery with President Abraham Lincoln several times. After the war, he fought for the Thirteenth, Fourteenth, and Fifteenth Amendments to the U.S. Constitution, while also serving in the District of Columbia and federal governments. Frederick Douglass died on February 20, 1895.

Thomas Edison
Thomas Alva Edison was one of the greatest inventors in history. He is most famous for his invention of the light bulb and phonograph, and for improvements to the telegraph, telephone, and motion pictures. Edison was born in Milan, Ohio, on February 11, 1847, the youngest of seven children. He attended public school for only three months and was mainly taught at home by his mother, a former schoolteacher. Edison was a fun and curious boy who liked to play jokes and ask questions. He also loved to read, experiment with chemicals, and build models. By the time he was fifteen, he was publishing and selling his own newspaper, called the *Weekly Herald*, and learning to operate a telegraph. When he was sixteen, Edison began working for the Western Union Telegraph Company and learned much about telegraphy, in part by experimenting with the company's equipment. Over the years, Edison invented many new devices and made improvements to existing ones. In 1877, he introduced his phonograph, and in 1879, he unveiled the light bulb. In 1888, he invented the kinetoscope, the first machine to produce motion pictures, and in 1913, he joined it with his phonograph to create the first *talking* motion pictures. In his lifetime, Edison obtained a total of 1,093 patents for his inventions, the most the U.S. patent office ever issued to one person. Thomas Edison died on October 18, 1931.

Harry Houdini
Harry Houdini was an American magician known throughout the world as an escape artist. He was born in Budapest, Hungary, but when he was young his parents moved to the United States and settled in Wisconsin. Houdini's given name was Ehrich Weiss, but he took a stage name from a French magician of the 1800s named Jean Eugene Robert-Houdin. In 1882, Houdini began his career as a trapeze artist. By 1900 he had developed an escape act, amazing people with his ability to free himself from any type of seemingly inescapable bonds—pairs of handcuffs, jail cells, nailed crates, even a tank filled with water. In one of his most famous stunts, Houdini was tied up and locked in a packing case bound with steel tape and then dropped into a harbor in New York City. In just fifty-nine seconds, he broke free and appeared on the surface of the water.

Scott Joplin

Scott Joplin was an American composer and musician, famous for developing a type of music called ragtime. Joplin, the son of a former slave, was born in Texas in 1868. He taught himself to play the piano and learned classical music from a German neighbor. When he was fourteen, he left home and played the piano in various saloons in the Mississippi Valley. In 1893, he played at the World's Fair in Chicago. The next year, he settled in Sedalia, Missouri, where he played at a saloon called the Maple Leaf Club. The owner of a music store in Sedalia helped make Joplin famous by publishing Joplin's "Maple Leaf Rag" and many more of his songs. All together, Joplin wrote more than sixty pieces of music including operas and his famous piece "The Entertainer."

History in Perspective Timeline

1868—The first professional baseball team in the United States, the Cincinnati Red Stockings, is founded.

October 8–10, 1871—The Great Chicago Fire destroys four square miles of central Chicago.

March 10, 1876—Alexander Graham Bell makes the first call on his invention, the telephone.

1885—The prototype for the first gas-powered automobile is introduced in a German factory owned by Karl Benz.

1888—The Kodak camera is invented by American George Eastman.

October 12, 1892—The Pledge of Allegiance is first used in public schools.

May–October 1893—The World's Colombian Exposition, also known as the World's Fair, is held in Chicago, Illinois.

December 17, 1903—Orville and Wilbur Wright make the first successful flight in an airplane.

1908—Henry Ford introduces the first Model T automobile.

1914–1918—The first world war, known at the time as the Great War, is fought.

Also available in the
Sisters in Time Series

American Dream

Including *Sarah's New World* (voyage of the Mayflower, 1620), *Rebekah in Danger* (Plymouth colony, 1621), *Maggie's Dare* (the Great Awakening, 1744), and *Lizzie and the Redcoat* (the American colonies, 1765)

American Challenge

Including *Lydia the Patriot* (the Boston Massacre, 1770), *Kate and the Spies* (the American Revolution, 1775), *Betsy's River Adventure* (westward expansion, 1808), and *Grace and the Bully* (frontier life, 1819)

American Struggle

Including *Emma's Secret* (the Cincinnati epidemic, 1832), *Nellie the Brave* (the Cherokee "Trail of Tears," 1838), *Meg Follows a Dream* (early civil rights efforts, 1844), and *Daria Solves a Mystery* (the Civil War, 1862)

Available wherever books are sold.